Three-times Golden Heart® finalist **Tina Beckett** learned to pack her suitcases almost before she learned to read. Born to a military family, she has lived in the United States, Puerto Rico, Portugal and Brazil. In addition to travelling, Tina loves to cuddle with her pug, Alex, spend time with her family, and hit the trails on her horse. Learn more about Tina from her website, or 'friend' her on Facebook.

Juliette Hyland began crafting heroes and heroines in high school. She lives in Ohio, USA, with her Prince Charming, who has patiently listened to many rants regarding characters failing to follow their outline. When not working on fun and flirty happily-ever-afters, Juliette can be found spending time with her beautiful daughters and giant dogs, or sewing uneven stitches with her sewing machine.

Also by Tina Beckett

Resisting the Brooding Heart Surgeon
A Daddy for the Midwife's Twins?
Tempting the Off-Limits Nurse

Buenos Aires Docs miniseries

ER Doc's Miracle Triplets

Also by Juliette Hyland

Mills & Boon Medical

Hope Hospital Surgeons miniseries

Dating His Irresistible Rival
Her Secret Baby Confession

Mills & Boon True Love

Royals in the Headlines miniseries

How to Win a Prince
How to Tame a King

REUNION WITH THE ER DOCTOR

TINA BECKETT

ONE-NIGHT BABY WITH HER BEST FRIEND

JULIETTE HYLAND

MILLS & BOON

First published in Great Britain 2024
by Mills & Boon, an imprint of HarperCollins*Publishers* Ltd,
1 London Bridge Street, London, SE1 9GF

www.harpercollins.co.uk

HarperCollins*Publishers* Macken House, 39/40 Mayor Street Upper,
Dublin 1, D01 C9W8, Ireland

ISBN: 978-0-263-32167-8

08/24

This book contains FSC™ certified paper
and other controlled sources to ensure responsible forest management.

For more information visit www.harpercollins.co.uk/green.

Printed and Bound in the UK using 100% Renewable Electricity
at CPI Group (UK) Ltd, Croydon, CR0 4YY

REUNION WITH THE ER DOCTOR

TINA BECKETT

MILLS & BOON

As always to my family. I love you!

PROLOGUE

HER GAZE FOLLOWED the bright pink piggy bank as it sailed through the air and then crashed to the ground with a shattering sound that seemed to go on forever. Something hit her hand, causing her to jerk in pain as she stared at all the silver coins and sharp pieces of glass that lay all around her. Then she started crying, unable to stop, even though she knew it would only make things worse.

"Georgia, do not move." Her mom's shaky voice reached her, even as her daddy stood over her, looking bigger and scarier than he ever had before.

Georgia, still in her nightgown—her feet bare, started to take a step back to get away from him, except her mother reached her first and scooted in front of her, staring up at the man in front of her.

"Get out. Get out now." The words were said with a soft hiss that made Georgia shiver, stopping her tears in an instant.

She had never heard her mom speak to her dad like that. Ever. Normally she was saying she was sorry to him over and over for things that Georgia didn't understand. But not today.

She leaned to peer around her mom in an effort to see her father's reaction, and it was strange. He no longer seemed mad. Instead he looked as if didn't understand something before he seemed to notice Georgia. His arm came forward, beckoning her over to him. Her mother smacked his hand away, pulling her phone out and pushing some buttons.

Evidently that meant something to her father because he backed up a step, the anger coming back to his face. "You'll be begging me to come back. You can't make it on your own."

There was a long silence, then her mom, phone still in her hand, seemed to grow taller right in front of Georgia's eyes. "You just watch me, Gavin."

Her dad threw his can of beer at the wall, and it made an ugly *thunk* as it fell, its contents spilling all over their only rug. Then he turned around and jerked the front door open and stomped out, not bothering to close it behind him. Snow began blowing into the room, turning it icy in an instant. Then he disappeared into the night.

Her mom rushed over and slammed the door shut, locking it and leaning against it for a second. Georgia wasn't the only one crying—her mom was too. "A-Are you okay, baby?"

She nodded. "But my new bank… Santa brought it for me."

"We'll get you another one. We'll…" She stopped, and her eyes went to a spot on the floor. "You're bleeding."

Georgia looked down and saw that something red

was dripping from her hand. Startled by the dark color, she held it up and stared at it. A scary feeling went through her. “Mama, I think I’m hurt.”

Her mom quickly grabbed a blanket from the nearby sofa and threw it over the floor in front of Georgia. As she walked across it, the pieces of the bank made a dull crunching sound under her feet. Then she picked up Georgia and carried her to a clean spot on the plank flooring. Looking at her hand, her mom’s eyes closed for a second. Then she went into action, grabbing some tissues and the tape that she’d used to wrap Christmas presents before covering the place on Georgia’s hand. It hurt. “Let me get your coat.”

“But my bank…”

“We’ll take care of that later. Right now we need to get your wrist looked at.”

Within minutes, they were both bundled in coats and boots and they were driving through the snow. Georgia wondered if her dad would be back when they got home.

She didn’t think so. For some reason she didn’t think he’d ever be home again.

CHAPTER ONE

GEORGIA SUMTER TOUCHED the scar on her left wrist as she walked through the doors of Anchorage Memorial Hospital. It looked exactly the same as it had when she'd left three years ago. It was funny how some things never changed, while other things changed forever.

Kind of like her childhood home, which was long gone. Her mom had been awarded the house in the divorce, but they hadn't stayed there. She'd sold it almost immediately, moving Georgia into a smaller one-bedroom home that, although cramped, had felt safe in a way that their other house hadn't. Only as she'd gotten older had she understood why that was.

Her pink piggy bank had been replaced with a big white rabbit bank. By the time she'd been eighteen, it had been stuffed to the gills with both coins and bills, although she'd never broken it open to get at the money, since the sound of anything shattering still had the ability to make her nerves take a giant leap, along with her heart rate.

She shook away the thoughts. The decision to return to Anchorage Memorial hadn't been an easy one. Not after all that had happened here. But taking a leave of absence from the hospital and running back to her hometown on Kodiak Island hadn't been the best idea either. She'd thought being near her mom would help her feel cocooned and allow healing to begin. And it had—in the beginning. But her mom's almost daily assurances that she'd done the right thing had eventually become like a funeral dirge, dark and repetitive and… unbearable. The cocoon had transformed into something claustrophobic. As had the small clinic where she'd opted to work once she'd made the decision to resign from Anchorage Memorial. There'd been no worries about seeing her dad. He no longer lived in the town. In fact, she had no idea where he was anymore, and she was okay with it staying that way.

A familiar face crossed the hallway, glancing her way before backtracking and then staring at her as if he thought he was seeing things. Finally his head cocked sideways. "Georgia?"

Her hair was about twelve inches shorter than it had been three years ago, now hanging just past her shoulders in choppy layers, and her bleached locks had been allowed to return to their natural dark brown waves. She could understand why he was taken aback. That plus the fact that she'd once told him she'd never return to the hospital that she'd loved so much.

"It's me. Just a little older and hopefully wiser than the last time you saw me."

William Harris turned and came toward her. "I had

no idea you were in town. Last I heard from you, you were still on Kodiak."

Her childhood friend, who'd been with her through thick and thin, had grown up on the same Alaskan island as she had, but he had left when he'd been eighteen. They'd kept in touch all these years, though, and had worked together at Anchorage Memorial until she'd made the agonizing decision to leave.

But she'd missed her life here. So very much. So much so that she was willing to risk seeing…

No. Don't think about that.

She reached into her pocket to find her charm and frowned when she realized she'd left her necklace in the car. She'd taken it off that morning to shower, and in her hurry to make it to the hospital on time, she'd tossed it into the glove compartment. Which was where it still was.

"I decided to come back. I missed the hospital—" she smiled at him "—and my friends. And enough time has passed that I think I'm up for it. Besides, Eli is married now, so it should be just—"

He frowned. "Hell, Georgia, why didn't you let me know you were thinking of coming back?"

His response stopped her flat. "I thought you'd be happy to see me."

He gripped her hand for a second and squeezed before letting go. "Of course I am. It's just that Eli isn't…"

Had her ex left the area? Even though that would be an even better scenario—letting her go back to life before she'd met him—something in her stomach sloshed at the thought of never seeing him again.

Isn't that what you'd hoped by leaving here three years ago?

Yes. She'd intended to put him in her past as firmly as she'd put her dad in the past. Except her reasons for doing so had been completely different. Eli had been nothing but supportive. He'd just wanted more than she could give.

"Did he move away?"

"No." William's voice came back, and he looked in her face. "But he's not married anymore either. He and Lainey got divorced a little over a year ago."

Her heart shot straight into her throat. Not married? "Why didn't you tell me?"

"I didn't think you were coming back and didn't figure you'd want to be kept up to date with everything Eli's been up to, considering how you guys left things. Besides, you kept saying that things on Kodiak were going great."

That's what she got for lying. Her hand went into her pocket again. She normally kept the butterfly with her as a reminder to always be free. She fiddled with it whenever she was stressed. And right now definitely fit that bill.

"I know. And of course I didn't want you to tell me everything. It's my fault for not saying anything about coming back. I just happened to see an ad for the ER position on a job board as I was looking for somewhere new to go. HR let me know almost immediately that they wanted me back, so I was busy trying to get things situated before leaving Kodiak General." She shrugged. "I thought I'd surprise you."

"Consider me surprised. In a good way." A smile accompanied the words. "I knew we were getting someone else. I just didn't bother to look to see if there was a name attached. I was just hoping it wasn't going to be another Dr. Mueller."

"Dr. Mueller?" That name didn't ring a bell.

William's brows went up. "Yep. Ronny Mueller. He actually took your place when your decision not to come back was finalized. And let's just say things haven't been the same since then. I wouldn't be surprised if he was part of the reason why Dr. Hawthorne left the ER."

"Oh! That's too bad. I really liked Becky."

Becky Hawthorne had been one of her good friends at Anchorage Memorial. Georgia had been looking forward to working with her again. In fact, Becky had tried to convince her not to leave…to give it some time. She didn't realize the open position had been the result of Becky leaving. She got an itchy feeling that her reasons for coming back were beginning to unravel.

"We all did. But she decided to go work at one of the smaller neighboring clinics. So she's still around." He shrugged. "Well, I'm glad you're back. More than you know. Are you working today?"

"No, I'm just going to HR to do some paperwork. I think I officially start tomorrow. I guess they'll tell me when I get there. Speaking of which, I'd better go before I'm late."

He smiled. "Would that really be something new?"

She swatted his arm. "I'm trying to turn over a new leaf."

"I'll believe it when I see it. Let's get together for lunch sometime, okay?"

She grinned back at him, trying not to think about Eli or what she was going to say to him when she eventually ran into him. "You've got it. And I promise I'll be on time."

He made a sound in the back of his throat. William was a hunk, and she was surprised he hadn't found someone by now.

But then again, neither had she. Nor did she want to. Her mom had spun enough cautionary tales to last a lifetime. Georgia had been willing to date, since getting out of those types of relationships were a lot less messy than a divorce. She'd proven that when she'd left Anchorage three years ago. But marriage? Her mom had had a heck of a time getting free of her husband. What Georgia hadn't known as a child was that her dad had actually fought for custody of her and had almost won, spinning tales of neglect and abuse. Which was so laughable, since it had been the other way around.

So yeah. Marriage and children? They didn't spell freedom in Georgia's book.

"Okay," William said. "Let me know when you get your schedule. I'd better get back to the floor too."

He retraced his steps and headed toward the emergency department, while Georgia made her way to the elevator.

God, Eli wasn't married anymore? That was one of the reasons she'd been tempted to take the job. She knew them both well enough to know that neither she nor Eli would ever cheat on someone, so she'd figured she'd be safe. They both would. The fact that Eli had married someone they'd both known from the hospital a little over a year after they'd parted had been soul wrenching, especially since Georgia had not so much as dated in all that time. But it also confirmed that she'd been right to walk away.

And now?

As soon as she got back to her car, she was going to dig that charm out of the glove box and put the talisman back around her neck. Then she'd make sure she had it with her wherever she went.

Eli stripped off his surgical gloves and tossed them into the bin before pushing through the double doors that led out of the operating room. The surgery to implant a biventricular pacemaker had been tricky, and he'd almost lost the patient twice before he'd even cracked open her chest. In the later stage of heart failure due to arrhythmias, her heart rate had been dangerously low. But the new pacemaker was geared to coordinate the rhythm between the chambers and would hopefully give the fifty-year-old a chance for a better quality of life. He'd combined it with an implantable defibrillator in case her heart decided to arrest again.

He still wasn't sure what the final outcome would be, but what he did know was that without surgery, his patient hadn't had a chance. She probably would have been dead in a matter of weeks, if not days. Right now, her heart was still weak, but it was at least beating in sync and at a better rate. Given time, the organ might even be able to regain some strength. Only time would tell.

He was due to have lunch with his good friend Steve Davis, who'd retired from his family practice several years ago. If not for Steve, Eli might not have been doing what he loved most in life. Eli's job had lasted longer than either of his romantic relationships, in fact. And he didn't see that changing anytime soon. Steve had been best man at his wedding, and although his friend had smiled and said all the right things, Eli had been able to tell he hadn't been sure about how well matched he and Lainey were. And he'd been right. Would he have had the same attitude if his bride had been Georgia?

No use even thinking along those lines, because Georgia had made it very clear that she didn't want that kind of relationship. He just wasn't sure why she'd waited so long to make that fact crystal clear. She could have saved them both a lot of heartache if she had. If he'd thought about it, though, the signs had all been there: Her quick, vague answers whenever he'd asked her about her childhood or her parents. The fact that she'd rarely talked about plans for the future, saying she preferred to live in the moment, because you never knew what life would throw at you. And he'd made a mistake by not gradually introducing the idea of marriage and feeling her out before just jumping in with a proposal. That had been an impulse decision, although he'd had the ring for months.

Lainey Grant had been right there to offer him a shoulder to cry on. He and Georgia had both worked with the hospital's pediatrician. But she'd listened and gone to the bar with him, being his designated driver when he'd gotten roaring drunk the night after Georgia had said the fateful words, *I'm so sorry, Eli. I just don't want to get married. Not to you. Not to anyone. It's not you. It's me.* And while Georgia hadn't officially broken things off, her message had been clear. As had her sudden decision to take a leave of absence.

And Lainey… Well, she'd seemed to be everything that Georgia was not. She'd been an open book when it came to her past. And she'd seemed to have the same interests and hopes for the future that he did. And eight months later, things had just kind of spiraled out of control when they'd slept together. Suddenly they'd been planning a wedding with a speed that had made his head spin. God, what a mess he'd made of that too. Maybe Georgia was right about marriage being a crock.

He took the elevator down to the ground floor, walking past a set of offices. His glance swung that way when he detected movement through the large glass panels next to the door. He stopped in his tracks, baffled…wondered if his earlier thoughts had suddenly summoned an apparition. An apparition he had no desire to see.

And it definitely wasn't Lainey.

His jaw hardened when he realized it was no apparition. The person was very real—a blast from the past. In the flesh.

What in the hell is she doing here?

His glance went back to the stenciled label on the door.

Human Resources.

There was no way. Life would not be that unkind. Would it?

The door opened with a swish, but her head was still cranked sideways, looking at someone inside the room. "Thanks. I'll stop in for my lanyard on my way in tomorrow, okay?"

"Lanyard?" He hadn't realized he'd growled the word aloud until she turned his way, suddenly white-knuckling the door as if she needed it for support.

"Eli."

Unlike him, there was no question mark behind the whispered word. She knew exactly who he was. The only question was, why was she back?

"Yes, it's me, Georgia. Surely you haven't forgotten?"

She let go of the door, and he watched as it swung silently back into place, but he could see Adrienne, the director of the department, staring at them with what looked like dismay.

Well, she wasn't the only one.

"No, well, um…" Her teeth came down on her lip

in a way that was all too familiar to him. She'd done it that last day they'd been together. Right after he'd asked her to marry him.

He decided to interrupt her before she said something he didn't want to hear. Although he couldn't think of anything he *did* want to hear. Not from her.

"Why are you here?" If the words sounded a little harsh, even to his own ears, he didn't try to backtrack or soften them. Realizing Adrienne was still looking at them, he motioned to the corridor across from them which contained nothing but janitorial closets and supplies. Once there he stopped again, making sure they were no longer in the line of sight of anyone from HR.

She glanced up at him, her chin jutting out. "I'm, um, taking Becky Hawthorne's place. She...er, left."

Did she even realize how that sounded? "That seems to be a common trait among ER doctors at Anchorage Memorial." His eyes speared hers. "Leaving, I mean."

She shook her head. "I know what you meant, and it wasn't very nice. I'm sure Becky had her reasons."

"I'm not a very nice guy. Not anymore. And I'm sure she did. It still doesn't completely answer my question. *Why* are you here?" This time he made sure to stress the first word in that phrase.

"Because I missed the hospital. Missed my friends here in Anchorage."

Missed the hospital and her friends, but not him. That omission was glaring. But then again, he hadn't expected her to declare her undying love for him.

"So you're headed back to our emergency room."

She took a step closer. "Is that so bad? We've both

moved on with our lives, Eli. Surely we can work in the same hospital, if not in the same department."

They could. But it didn't mean he had to be happy about it. "So if we were in the same department, you wouldn't have applied for the job?"

She looked at his face for a long time. "Probably not."

Then maybe he should've been sorry that she wasn't a heart doctor because this moment wouldn't have been happening if that were the case. "I'm sure we can avoid crossing each other's paths if we try hard enough."

Her teeth came down on that soft lower lip again before she released it, sending a spike to his gut.

"Just for the record, Eli, I'm sorry. I thought you were married, or I never would have—"

One of the nurses he recognized from the ER came skidding around the corner before stopping in front of them. "Adrienne told me she thought you went this way." The man threw a glance Eli's way before looking back at Georgia. "Sorry. Am I interrupting something?"

Oh, now he remembered who the nurse was. He was Georgia's childhood friend, William.

"It's fine." Georgia tilted her head. "Is something wrong?"

"I'm not sure. Can you come with me to talk to a patient? Dr. Mueller saw her, but there's just something…"

"Of course I can." The relief in her voice would have been comical, except there was nothing funny about Georgia suddenly showing up at the hospital. "I'll see you later, Eli."

Before he could say he hoped not, the pair turned and hurried away, William explaining something about whatever patient it was before they disappeared from sight.

Eli muttered a few choice words under his breath before giving up and heading toward his appointment with Steve.

Georgia was back. And he had no idea what to think about that, much less what his attitude was going to be. But he'd better figure it out and soon. Before they ran into each other again. Because despite his earlier words, he was sure it was bound to happen. And when it did, he wanted to be ready.

"Like I was saying, she complained of her heart suddenly racing without warning and Mueller completely blew her off. Offered to prescribe her antianxiety meds without running any testing other than the standard EKG."

"What makes you think it's something more?"

William shrugged. "Maybe because she didn't look relieved. If anything, it seemed like it was exactly what she'd expected him to say. Like she'd heard it before. Or maybe it's just because it's not the first time I've seen Mueller dismiss a patient's concerns, and one time it...well, it didn't end well for the patient."

"Okay. Which room is she in?"

"Three. Hopefully she's still there."

When they swung the door open, though, there was only a nurse in there wiping down the exam table. "Where's Molly Breckin?"

"Who?"

"The patient who was just in this room."

"She just left. Before Dr. Mueller could even come back with the paperwork."

"Damn."

The nurse looked closer at William before her face cleared. "You might still be able to catch her before she makes it to the parking lot. And by the way, I agree with you."

He didn't stop to ask what she meant, just glanced at Georgia. "Come on."

They hurried to the nearest exit, and William said, "There she is."

Georgia saw a slim young woman walking down the sidewalk, her head bowed and shoulders slumped—an air of defeat that was hard to miss. They pushed through the doors and called out to her.

"Ms. Breckin, could you wait for a minute?"

The slight form stiffened before turning toward them. "I've already tried antianxiety meds, and they did no good. Besides, it happens at times when I'm not stressed, like when I'm sitting down or reading. It's even woken me up from a sound sleep."

Georgia reached a hand toward her. "Why don't you come back inside, and we'll talk some more."

"Who are you?"

"I'm Dr. Sumter."

Molly sighed. "It won't do any good. The other doctor already did an EKG, just like the other doctors I've seen. And they never see anything because it's not happening when the machine is on."

"But…"

The other woman's head jerked from side to side. "No. I'm done with doctors. So far whatever it is hasn't killed me, so how dangerous can it be?"

Georgia's chest ached. It could be really dangerous, depending on what was causing the arrhythmia. She'd seen a seemingly healthy teenager drop dead from a cardiac problem that had gone undiagnosed. Most people never saw it coming. "Won't you reconsider? There might be—"

"No."

She looked at the woman for a minute, then took a piece of paper from a pad in her purse and wrote her name and cell-phone number on it. "If you change your mind, please give me a call. It doesn't matter when. If I happen to be with a patient, I'll call you back as soon as I'm done."

Molly's eyes widened, and she hesitated before reaching her hand out for the paper. "Okay." Then she gave a slight smile that made Georgia's heart ache even more. "You're the first doctor who's acted like they believed me. Thank you."

And before she or William could say anything else, the woman turned and continued down the sidewalk without looking back.

Georgia reached over and squeezed William's hand. "You did what you could."

"Then why doesn't it feel like enough?"

She couldn't answer that question because Georgia had asked herself that same thing over and over. There were those patients who you felt you'd failed. Like you could have given more to…done more for. And yet when you looked back, you were never quite sure what you could have done to make the conclusion any more satisfying.

Kind of like how things had ended with Eli. It had been anything but satisfying. And yet whenever she posed the question to herself, she couldn't think of anything she would have done differently. Because when it came down to it, she'd needed to leave. Not just for herself, but to save Eli a whole lot of heartache as well.

CHAPTER TWO

ELI WAS WORKING on paperwork the next evening when a knock came at his door. Without looking up, he said, "Come in."

He glanced up to see the one person he hadn't expected. At least not so quickly. And he certainly hadn't expected her to seek him out. "I thought we agreed to avoid each other."

"I know, and I'm sorry, but…" She didn't open the door all the way, instead simply asking, "Do you have a minute?"

Setting his pen down, he sighed. "You might as well come in."

It wasn't a very cordial invitation, but it was the only one he had right now. He still hadn't gotten over the shock of seeing her earlier.

Georgia came in and closed the door behind herself before perching in a chair in front of the desk. "I have kind of an odd question."

He couldn't imagine anything coming from her that wasn't "odd" at this point. "Okay."

"It's about a patient."

About a thousand muscles in his body relaxed. At

least she didn't want to talk about anything personal. Although why did that surprise him? Did he really expect her to come in and ask to take up where they'd left off? Or try to explain things from three years earlier?

According to the dream he'd had last night that was exactly what had transpired, and like an idiot, his dream self had wrapped her in his arms and kissed her before taking things much further. He'd woken up in a cold sweat, and even at the memory, his muscles were now bunching up all over again.

He shook off the thoughts and looked at her. "Which patient is that?" A thought came to him. "The one from yesterday, when William came to get you?"

She nodded. "She's not exactly my patient—she's Dr. Mueller's."

Eli gave an audible groan. "Dr. Mueller is pretty territorial about his patients. I've tangled with him a couple of times, and it's never been a whole lot of fun."

"And if a patient's life is on the line, would you tangle with him again?"

"Hell, Georgia, he's only here because of you."

She blinked, looking stricken all of a sudden. "What?"

He'd made it sound like she was at fault for that. And maybe part of it was that he blamed her for taking off the way she had three years ago. "I mean, he took your place."

"I had no control over that."

No. She hadn't. But she'd had control over what she'd done before that. When she'd decided to leave the hospital. And him. But it wouldn't help anyone to keep reliving what had happened back then. "I realize that. What's the problem? I can't guarantee I can help, though, unless Mueller brings me in on the case."

"Well..." This time her eyes wouldn't quite meet his. "She's not exactly at the hospital anymore."

Had the patient died? "Meaning what?"

"She left AMA."

Against medical advice. Doctors universally hated it when that happened. "I take it she was a cardiac patient?"

"No. At least not officially. Because he didn't believe her."

"Who didn't?"

She frowned at him as if he were dense. "Mueller didn't."

Eli had heard murmurs about Mueller—that he tended to coast along in the ER and avoided the more complex cases if he could help it. "Maybe you'd better explain exactly what is bothering you."

The fact that William had come to get her meant that it had bothered the nurse too. Enough to bypass the doctor assigned to the case, which was a very big deal at Anchorage Memorial. And since Georgia had come to see him, it meant she agreed with William.

"I didn't examine her, but I did read her file." She went on to tell him about a young female patient who'd come in complaining about periodic episodes of racing heartbeats. That in and of itself wasn't cause for alarm, especially given the age of the patient. Until he heard that she'd consulted several doctors and they'd all diagnosed her with anxiety.

That sent up an alarm, especially since, according to Georgia, the patient had tried the meds they'd offered and they hadn't helped.

"What tests were run?"

"At other hospitals? I have no idea. But here at ours, she got a fifteen-second EKG, which was declared unremarkable."

Her face showed her thoughts about that. But then again, she'd never been good at hiding her emotions, whether she was happy or sad or at the heights of ecstasy. And when she was at those heights…

Irritation spiked through him, and he forced his brain back to what she'd said about the patient.

EKGs certainly had their place, but for idiopathic arrhythmias they were close to useless since if the heart wasn't out of rhythm at that specific moment, it could be dismissed, much like Mueller had done with the patient. Eli certainly wouldn't have stopped at an "unremarkable" tracing. "Did she tell Mueller that she'd seen other doctors?"

Her nose squinched in a way he remembered all too well. It indicated frustration. Or embarrassment. "I'm not sure, but she told William and me that she had."

"If she left AMA, how did she tell you that?"

"William and I kind of chased her into the parking lot."

"You kind of chased her…" Hell, if that didn't sound like something Georgia would do. For some reason the picture of her and William running after some patient and then grilling her about her condition struck him as humorous, and he couldn't hold back a chuckle.

"What's so funny?"

"Oh, certainly not the patient's story. But the fact that you charged after her and…what? Tried to get her to come back inside? Have you even officially started your job yet?"

"Well…yes to the first question and no to the second. I start tomorrow."

"Then you know that she would have been bounced right back to Mueller."

"Not if I could have reached you before he found out about it."

Wow, so she would have asked *him* to bypass Mueller? That could have gone badly in so many ways. For both Georgia and himself. But he couldn't blame her. She was nothing if not a tireless advocate for her patients. So it shouldn't have surprised him that she would have risked the wrath of a colleague for a patient that wasn't even hers. It was one of the things he'd loved about her.

Loved. Past tense.

As if realizing the possible outcome, she shook her head. "I'm sorry. I shouldn't have even come here or said anything."

Yes, she should have. Because if she had succeeded in getting the patient back inside and had brought her up to the fourth floor, he would have undoubtedly taken a closer look at her. He'd already had it out with

Mueller about one patient. The other doctor had ultimately backed down when it had turned out that Eli had been right about the patient needing a heart cath. But if the patient hadn't even been referred to a cardiac doctor? He was pretty sure Mueller would have lodged a complaint against both Georgia and himself. He doubted the hospital would do anything to him, but they might rescind Georgia's job offer if she caused trouble so soon after being hired back again.

"Yes, you should have. But you need to tread carefully around Mueller. He's not someone to mess around with. He's lodged complaints against several other staff members."

"I don't give a damn who he is or how many complaints he's lodged. If I hear of him doing what he did yesterday again, I might lodge a complaint of my own."

Eli didn't laugh this time, but he did smile. "You might want to wait until your official start date before doing anything like that. You might just find yourself booted out on your rear."

She smiled back at him, and it was as if the last words she'd lobbed at him during the breakup hadn't held the sting he'd thought they'd had. "My rear's pretty tough, actually. And I don't normally stay down."

"Of that I'm sure."

Her smile slowly faded, and they sat there staring at each other for seconds that grew painfully awkward. At least on his side. And he probably shouldn't have said what he had, because the words had been pretty loaded and he had no doubt she'd read between the lines. Had he meant her to?

Probably.

"You didn't stay down for long either, evidently." Then she shook her head. "Sorry—that was uncalled for. I'll let you get back to what you were doing. I just wouldn't have felt right if I didn't at least try to get your opinion."

Her cryptic comment about him not staying down for long hit home. And she wasn't wrong, if she was referring to him and Lainey. But just like the patient, there was nothing he could do about that now. And as for his opinion on said patient, he realized he hadn't given her one. Because he couldn't. A suddenly racing heart could be caused by so many things. Some of them benign and some of them deadly. "I'll tell you what. If the patient comes back in and you're here, call me and I'll come down."

"I gave her my phone number. If she calls me, would you be willing to talk to her? Since you have a private practice in addition to your work at the hospital, I mean. You could do that, right—without it causing problems between you and Mueller?"

"Nowadays I normally need a referral, but yes, I would talk to her and offer to dig a little deeper into her symptoms. Does that help?"

"It does." She passed a slip of paper to him. When he opened it, he saw the name *Molly Breckin*. "That's the patient. And Eli…thank you. I mean it."

With that she got up and walked out of his office the

same way she'd walked in: with softly swaying hips and without any fanfare. But it dug into his composure just as much as when she'd first arrived. And long after she was gone, he sat staring at the name on the paper and wondering exactly what he was going to do.

Not about the patient, but about Georgia. About the way she affected him without even trying. With no answers in sight, he opened the top left drawer of his desk and dropped the slip of paper inside, but not before committing the woman's name to memory.

Why was Georgia so relieved that Eli had taken her seriously? Had she really expected him to throw her out of his office with a few harsh words? Maybe. And it could be that she deserved them. But why? She'd been true to her heart three years ago. How could anyone fault her for that? And if she'd known that Eli had been dead set on marriage when they'd first started dating she probably would have never gone out with him.

But how many men—or women, for that matter—expected to date someone indefinitely without any hope for the relationship to deepen and mature?

Evidently she'd been living in la-la land. But not anymore. If there'd been any doubts that he could accept anything less in a relationship than marriage, those should have been put to rest when Eli had ended up marrying someone else a year after their breakup. So to think he would have been satisfied with merely sharing a bed and some pretty words was a little ludicrous.

But that was exactly what she'd hoped. Oh, she'd

loved him, of that there was no doubt. She'd even said the words from time to time. But she hadn't wanted or needed a ring to go with that love. And when he'd acted like she had to have one for their relationship to continue? She'd checked out. Both physically and emotionally.

However, right now, it was time for her to go to her apartment and have a nice long bath and a glass of wine and try to forget about Molly Breckin and Eli Jacobsen. She wasn't sure it was possible, but she'd better try if she was going to have the courage to show up for work tomorrow. And the day after that. Otherwise, she might as well pack her bags and head back to Kodiak.

As soon as she got to the ER the next morning, she was met with a mess. There were several ambulances in the bay.

She caught up with William. "What happened?"

"A floatplane carrying a group of campers lost engine power on the way to Katmai National Park and made a hard water landing. The passengers and pilot had to ditch the plane. We're still waiting on three passengers, but the other four were picked up from the water and choppered in. Thank God the company followed the regulations for personal flotation devices."

"For sure. Serious injuries?"

"Actually yeah, a couple. You'd think that a crash involving water would be softer, but we've got a possible ruptured spleen. That patient has been transported to surgery. And we've got several broken bones. Also a pregnant lady is having abdominal pains. We're waiting on her."

"Okay, send me where you need me."

Just then a pair of EMTs pushed through the door with a woman holding her distended abdomen in a way that could only mean she was carrying a baby. That answered that question.

"I'll take her to a room," Georgia said. "Has Labor and Delivery been notified?"

"Yes. But there are two emergency deliveries going on up there, and they're swamped. If we can get her stabilized until they can send someone down, that's the preference. If it's dire, we'll take the gurney up there."

"Got it. Thanks."

She glanced at the big whiteboard to see if there were any exam areas open. "Okay, let's take her to room six."

Georgia hurried over to the woman. "I'm Dr. Sumter. We're going to get you into a room where I can take a look at you. Any trouble breathing?"

The young woman had to be in her early twenties. "No, but my stomach hurts and my baby..." Her eyes closed. "I can't feel her, and I'm so scared."

"I know you are. I know you're wet from being in the water, but can you feel any kind warm flow down there?"

"No."

Hopefully that meant there was no bleeding and the uterus hadn't been compromised. Intake wristbands were often color-coded during triage as an aid in the order patients were seen, but those scales weren't always reliable when it came to expectant women, so Georgia just took her straight to an exam room.

One of the EMTs handed her a chart. The woman's name was Lydia.

"Lydia, were you struck in the stomach by anything?"

"I—I don't think so. But everything happened so fast. We had our seat belts on when we hit the water."

"Was the belt low? Like down here?" She motioned to the area at the base of her abdomen.

"Yes."

"Okay, good. I'm going to help you out of your clothes and get you into a dry gown. Then we'll make sure the baby's heartbeat is still strong. How far along are you?"

The patient shuddered, probably from the chill of being in the water and in an ER that was kept cool on purpose. Most people complained of being cold while there. "Four months."

"Camping at Katmai is pretty rugged, isn't it?"

"Yes, but my doctor said it was still early enough to—"

Georgia laid her hand on the woman's arm. "I wasn't criticizing. I only meant that I've often thought about going to see the bears but haven't made it up there yet."

"This will be our third time going."

Her attention went on high alert. "Were you with someone? A relative?"

"My husband. They didn't have enough room for him on the first trip and he wasn't seriously injured, so he'll be here as soon as they can get another helicopter to pick him up."

Lauren Adams, one of the nurses who'd been here three years ago, came in and helped Georgia get their patient out of her wet clothing. "It's so good to see you back," she said.

"It's good to be back."

Lydia's undergarments showed no staining that looked like blood. Hopefully a good sign. "Any ETA on Obstetrics getting here?"

"They're both still tied up in surgeries."

"Got it. Let's go ahead and set up an ultrasound then, and if you can make sure the front desk is on the lookout for her husband..." She glanced at Lydia. "What's his name?"

"Mark. Mark Jones."

Georgia continued her instructions. "If we could get Mark in here as soon as he arrives, that would probably be helpful for all concerned parties."

"On it." Lauren popped out of the room.

She came back in a minute or two later, wheeling the ultrasound machine. "Where do you want this?"

"How about on the right?"

They got the machine set up, and Lauren typed in the patient's info while Georgia got a tube of lubricating jelly and squirted some on the transponder. She paused. "This is going to be a little cold, okay?"

Lydia nodded.

She squirted some onto the woman's abdomen, then glanced up at Lauren. "Are you ready for me?"

"Yep, go ahead."

She pushed the wand through the lubricant and used it to spread the gel around the area she wanted to scan. Then she pressed into the firm bulge and watched the screen, praying to hear a heartbeat that sounded normal and see structures that looked typical for this stage of pregnancy.

There was silence in the room, then Lydia winced when Georgia hit an area low on her belly.

"What is it?"

"I don't know. It's just really sore there." The area was right about where Lydia had indicated the seat belt would have sat.

"Okay, I'll try to be careful. Let me know if anything else hurts." Georgia prayed that was all the pain was from.

When she still couldn't find the heartbeat, she tensed. "Let me move to the other side."

"Is everything okay?" Lydia's voice was a little softer, her concern evident.

"I think the baby is just positioned differently." She tried to reassure the patient the best she knew how, but she was beginning to worry as well.

Standing over her, Georgia added more lubricant and then began a sweep of the new area. Still nothing.

Just as she was getting ready to move to a third area, she heard something and backed the transponder up.

There.

Lub-dub, lub-dub, lub-dub.

"Thank God." Lydia's whispered words threaded through the room. Georgia echoed them. And when she looked over at Lauren, she caught the nurse swiping at her eyes. She got it. She felt a little emotional as well. How would she feel if that was her on the exam table praying for everything to be okay with her baby?

Well, that wasn't a possibility, since she didn't think she would ever be a mother, since she didn't want a "forever" relationship. Not with a man, not with anyone.

Including having a child of her own?

She didn't know. She'd never really thought about it. Until now. But she really didn't think she had it in her to raise a baby on her own. She'd seen how hard her mom had had to work to provide for her after her dad had left. But despite that, Georgia had to admit her mom had seemed to come into herself. Becoming someone different than she had been. Happier. More confident.

She'd even led a support group, helping other women who were trapped in risky relationships. Georgia had gone to one of the meetings once to support her mom, and what she'd heard there had firmed up her belief that marriage was not for her.

"The baby's heart sounds good and strong. I'm just going to take a look at a few other things, if you're okay with it?"

"Oh, yes. I just need to know that everything's okay."

Now that the immediate crisis of knowing the baby was alive was over, Georgia took her time and pointed out various things on the screen. While they were looking, the baby seemed to turn its head to look toward them before its hand clumsily came up and stayed near its mouth. "I think he or she is sucking their thumb."

The miracle of carrying a baby had never ceased to fascinate her. So much so that she'd almost specialized in obstetrics, but something had stopped her—maybe her childhood trauma. Whatever it was, she felt like sticking with her original plan of being an ER doc was the right decision. She loved the variety of patients and the fast pace, not to mention heartwarming moments like this, when a quiet joy was all that was needed to make the rest of her day a good one.

"I think so too," said Lydia.

Just then the door opened and a man rushed in. "Lydia, are you okay?"

The woman burst into sobs, and the man's gaze shifted to Georgia, the panic in his eyes unmistakable.

"Everything's fine with the baby, as far as I can see," she was quick to reassure him.

He grabbed a chair and pulled it over to his wife and laid his cheek against hers. "It's okay, love. I'm here now."

"You must be Mark?"

When he looked up and nodded at her, Georgia smiled. "Are you okay? Were you injured?"

"No. Just my thumb, but it's fine." He held it up and showed her an ugly gash that went up the side.

"Hmm… I think that might need a stitch or two. And after being in the water, it also warrants a tetanus shot, just to be safe."

"Anything—as long as Lydia and the baby are okay."

"I still want the folks up in Obstetrics to check her out when they finish up with their emergencies, so you may be in for a little wait. Is that okay?"

"Absolutely."

"I'll get you stitched up while you're in the room, and I'm sure someone from the front desk will want to come and get some information from you, but you both were very lucky."

"I know we were."

Lydia wiped her eyes and pulled her husband down for a quick kiss before looking at Georgia again. "Thank you so much."

"You're very welcome." She wiped the transponder down with an alcohol wipe and handed it to Lauren, who took care of the rest. "We'll get you cleaned up and then patch your husband up, and once you're cleared by one of our obstetricians you can go on and enjoy your vacation."

Lydia gripped her husband's hand and looked at him. "Is it okay if we just go home and watch a documentary on bears instead?"

Everyone in the room laughed, breaking up what had been a nerve-racking half hour.

"Absolutely," Mark said. "And thanks again."

"Not a problem. Now, let's work on getting you cleaned up."

Forty-five minutes later, Mark had been stitched and given a tetanus shot and one of the OB-GYN docs had arrived to take over Lydia's case.

It left Georgia free to exit the room and see what was next on the plate. But it was eerily still all of a sudden. William was nowhere to be seen either.

She went up to the front desk. "Any other crash victims that need to be seen?"

"Nope—they've all been either discharged or moved to other areas of the hospital for further treatment."

"Okay." When she glanced at her watch, she was surprised to see it was one in the afternoon, and her stomach was grumbling. "Are you okay if I run to the cafeteria for a quick bite?"

"Yep, I think we're good."

"Okay, call me if you need me. I shouldn't be any longer than a half hour or so."

"Take your time and enjoy."

With that, she headed down the hallway that led away from the ER and into the rest of the hospital.

CHAPTER THREE

ELI WAS SITTING in the cafeteria nursing his second cup of coffee after finishing a ham-and-cheese sandwich. He was getting ready to get up to leave when Georgia came through the door.

Damn it. He should have just gotten his coffee to go and been done with it.

She hadn't seen him yet, moving with purpose toward the line and glancing at the offerings.

The ends of her dark hair curled around her face and neck and slid over her shoulders. The style was different from how she used to wear it, but it looked good on her. But so would just about anything.

Her black pants clung to the curve of her bottom and hips, and he could see a sliver of pale skin when she leaned over to reach for something in the refrigerated section of the counter. He swallowed, remembering all too well how that skin felt under his fingertips.

Get up and leave before she sees you.

He started to, but something held him back. Maybe he didn't want to look like a coward if she spotted him slinking away from the table.

But it was hard not to just flee. Like she had three

years ago? He thought he might know how she'd felt back then because he wasn't so sure he was up to staying in the same building as her. Lainey had stayed at the hospital for weeks after filing for divorce, and although he'd burned with anger over her betrayal, this was different somehow. Georgia hadn't betrayed him. She'd simply not thought he was worth sharing her future with.

Give it a rest, Eli. You've been over this way too many times.

She paid the woman at the counter and turned with her tray just as there was an explosion of sound, as if something had shattered somewhere in the back of the cafeteria. Probably a dropped plate or glass.

Georgia froze, dropping her tray back onto the counter, her eyes wide and unseeing. Her hand reached up and seemed to grab at something near her neck without finding it. She stood there for several seconds, even as another patron edged around her, glancing at her as he went by.

It was enough to make Eli leave his seat and head toward her. "Hey. Are you okay?"

As if some spell had suddenly been broken, she blinked several times, then turned to look at him. "Oh, I..." Then she shook her head. "I'm fine. It just startled me, that's all."

He didn't ask what had startled her. He knew exactly what it was. What he didn't know was why. His mind went back to a time in his apartment when she'd turned to say something to him and knocked a tumbler off the bar, sending it crashing to the ground, glass flying everywhere.

She'd frozen that time too and had seemed to not want to touch the shards. He'd cleaned it up, but when he'd asked her about it, Georgia had simply blown it off, saying what she'd just said, almost word for word. That it had simply startled her.

Ponto final.

"Here, let me carry your tray."

The fact that she didn't argue with him but simply let him lead her back to his table showed him how deeply she'd been shaken by what had happened.

He set her tray down and slid the chair across from his out and waited for her to sit down. Then he dropped back into his own chair. "Are you sure you're okay?"

"Absolutely. Don't you ever get startled by sudden sounds?"

Yes, but not like that. The way the other customer had edged around her said that that person hadn't thought it very normal either. "I guess it would depend on what it was from."

Her mouth twisted as if she wanted to say something else, but she didn't. Instead, she took a sip of her tea, the tea bag still in the cup, and sucked down a deep breath. "Thanks. I'm not sure why I reacted like that. Maybe my nerves were just stretched tight from what happened with a patient down in ER a little while ago."

"The floatplane accident? I'd heard we'd gotten some of those patients."

"We actually got all seven of them, if I heard right," Georgia said. "I treated a pregnant woman who, thank God, ended up being fine, but I'd heard there were a couple of seriously injured patients."

"There was a splenectomy done, and what else?"

"Some broken bones and I stitched up a thumb, but I thought for a few seconds that the pregnant patient might have lost her baby. I had a hard time finding the heartbeat the first time around."

"You said it ended up being okay, though?" he asked.

"Yes. The baby was just in a different position than I expected. But he or she was active, and there was no bleeding or contracting of the uterus. She had a sore spot on her lower abdomen, which I suspect was from the seat belt in the plane, but there were no other injuries that I could find. Then her husband arrived and was able to help reassure her."

"The way husbands and wives often do for each other."

She glanced at Eli quickly as if looking for something in his face, but he'd schooled the bitterness out of his features just in time. He hadn't even realized he still harbored those kinds of emotions.

Oh, who was he kidding? Of course he did. The same way he harbored some negative feelings toward Lainey for what she'd done. It was a natural part of failed relationships, right? Georgia probably harbored some ill will toward him as well. After all, she'd left the area, hadn't she? And now she was back. And he wasn't sure why. Not for him, obviously, since there was nothing left of what they used to have.

As if the silence had stretched too long for her comfort, she said, "So how has your day gone? Anything interesting?"

"It's still touch and go with one of my patients from yesterday. I put in a biventricular pacemaker and defibrillator."

"Sounds serious."

In the same way that he didn't know everything about emergency medicine, he shouldn't expect her to know everything about his specialty. "It is, and I'm still not sure she didn't come in too late to be saved. But I'm hopeful, even if I'm not very optimistic."

She smiled. "I remember you being one of the most optimistic people I'd ever met."

He had been. At least back then. He'd thought a kid who'd bounced around foster homes had a chance for a normal life and a normal family. His optimism had had known no bounds. Until reality had come in and dragged it through the mud. But at least being a realist brought with it less chance of disappointment.

"Maybe I'm just more judicious about who I use that optimism on."

"Meaning you won't waste any on me anymore?"

"I didn't say that." But he might have thought it. And she'd as much as caught him.

Georgia shrugged. "So your patient with the pacemaker—how long before you know if the surgery worked or not?"

"The surgery worked, but I'm just not sure her heart won't give out despite the surgery. The next twenty-four to forty-eight hours are critical. In reality, I don't know what kind of quality of life she'll have. And a lot of it will depend on how much she wants to live. I felt like she was resigned to her fate when her family asked her to try one more specialist."

"You?"

"Yep. I drew the short straw. Or maybe—if she lives—they'll see it as the right straw. It was the only hope I could offer her."

"Some hope is better than none, though."

Was it? Sometimes hope kept you hanging on to something that was dead and gone.

He decided to answer in terms of his patient rather than himself. "Her family sure hopes so."

"Well, I hope she makes it."

"So do I."

He glanced at her plate, realizing she'd eaten almost all of her lunch, although it had consisted of yogurt and granola that she'd mixed together to form a meal. And his coffee was now cold and bitter. He could think of nothing less appealing than that. So best to cut his lunch hour short.

"Well, I'd better head back upstairs. I have some phone calls to make and patient records to update." He paused as a thought came to him. "No word on your mystery patient from yesterday?"

"No, not a peep. If she decides to call or come back in, you'll be the first one I notify."

Eli stood. “Sounds good. I’ll see you later.”

“See you.” She got up as well, uncurling those long legs and standing, shaking her dark hair away from her face as she held her tray, her green eyes on his as if she couldn’t look away a second or two.

Then she turned and headed in the opposite direction, and he realized that was one thing that no one could contest about what she’d just said, despite his hopes for the contrary: They would indeed see each other later. Whether they wanted to or not.

There was no doubt about it, Eli had changed. She couldn’t say whether it was a good change or a bad one. He was just different from the man she’d once known. She hadn’t lied when she’d said he’d been the most optimistic person she’d known. But she couldn’t say that now. At least not from the little of him she’d seen over the last three days. Yesterday at the café that point had been driven home. His attitude about his patient had held almost a fatalistic air that she never would have equated with Eli Jacobsen. He’d said he was hopeful but not optimistic.

She’d woken up this morning still thinking about that. She hadn’t seen much hope in his attitude about his patient’s surgery. Maybe it was a reference to that particular patient rather than a complete shifting of Eli’s personality.

She hoped so. It made her sad to think of him as anything other than the guy who’d had a boyish charm that just wouldn’t quit. Who’d bowled her over almost from the very beginning, and he'd still bowled her over even as their relationship had been ending.

She still had a picture of him in her mind as he'd come over while she'd stood paralyzed by the crashing sound that had come from somewhere inside the café and asked if she was okay. Those deep blue eyes had been full of concern, and it had made her heart melt. She'd had to steel herself to keep from leaning against him like she might have done in times when they'd still been a couple. She'd never told him why that sound bothered her so much, even when they'd been together, although he'd seen her react more than once to the sound of breaking glass. Maybe because revealing that secret would have made her feel vulnerable in ways that she hated. In ways that reminded her of how her dad had relished making feel exposed and fearful.

She pulled the chain holding her butterfly charm from under her shirt and fingered it, her thumb tracing over the raised lines of the insect's wings. She might have bought it after her breakup with Eli, but she realized it was also symbolic of being free of her dad's abuse. A reminder that she didn't need to rely on anyone. She could fly all by herself.

That there might've been holes in that logic didn't matter. What did matter was that it made her feel powerful and self-sufficient.

Dropping the butterfly back to its hidden spot where it rested against her heart, she smiled and loaded her breakfast dishes into the dishwasher of her little rented studio apartment and went to get ready for work.

Ugh! The second Georgia put her purse in the locker area, she frowned. Had she missed this notice earlier? There was one of the hospital's mass meetings happening over the course of two days starting the day after tomorrow. If she remembered right, it was one of those things where they went over policy changes and so much other minutia that she often found herself nodding off. Eli would either send her a text or squeeze her hand to help keep it from being too noticeable. But she wouldn't have him to lean on this time.

You don't need to lean on anyone, remember?

Lauren came in, sticking her own purse in her locker. She caught Georgia's eye and must have seen something in her face. "You look like you're looking forward to that meeting about as much as I am. They're the worst. Do the people in charge not have advisors to…er, advise them?"

That made Georgia laugh. "It appears not because they've been doing it this way for ages. Including having to sign up for a spot." There were probably ten sheets of lined paper with days and times on it where they were supposed to put their names. "It must be how they make sure everyone has attended it. Can't they just put out a new policy manual with any changes highlighted or something?"

"Naw, that would be too easy, eh? Then they couldn't

have their hour at the microphone. I always feel like I'm being held hostage."

Georgia took a closer look at the list and saw that William was signed up for the first day at three o'clock. Rats, she was on shift until five that day, so they couldn't go together. She'd just take the 8:00-a.m. slot and get it over with. She scribbled her name. "When are you going?"

"I'm putting it off until the very last second. That way I can look forward to my day off even more."

"Probably a better strategy than mine."

"We can compare notes when we're done."

She smiled, handing the nurse the pen. "It's a deal."

Georgia had about a half hour to kill, so she went out to the courtyard. It was only useable for part of the year, so she'd always loved coming out here when everything was green and lush. She almost always came before her shift to enjoy it. Like a kind of meditation that prepared her for the frenetic pace that the emergency department sometimes had.

The hospital had planted flowers in huge urns that lined a stone walkway, which in turn led to a gazebo. Rocking chairs were set out in a circle inside its protected space. She couldn't remember how many times she'd come out here to read or eat a salad instead of eating in the cafeteria.

There was only one person in the gazebo, and she prepared to smile a greeting until blue eyes came up and speared hers. Oh, God, of course she would have to come when he was here. She didn't remember this being one of Eli's favorite spots. When he wasn't working, he'd wanted to be away from the hospital, not in it, even if the space was beautiful. She sighed. It was obvious they were going to run in to each other more than she'd hoped. Or maybe that was fate's way of laughing at her.

"Mind if I join you?" What else could she say? *Get the hell out?* That wouldn't stand out as unreasonable at all.

"Please."

It wasn't exactly an invitation, but his inflection hadn't oozed sarcasm, unless she'd missed it. She reminded herself that this Eli wasn't the same person she'd left three years ago.

So she sat down across from him rather than in the rocker beside his. "So are you just coming on duty or going off?"

"I actually got an early start, so I'm kind of between patients right now, and thought I'd come out to get a breath of fresh air."

"You used to just go to the coffee shop across the street."

"That's right. But I don't anymore."

That was a weird way to say it. It was as if something had turned him off the place. She and Eli had gone there occasionally, but it hadn't been "their place," so she didn't see that as being the reason.

Maybe it had to do with his ex-wife. Georgia realized she had no idea if the woman was still at the hospital or not. She and Lainey Grant had never been close friends, but they'd always been cordial to one another. And she'd liked the other woman. She couldn't imagine how Lainey and Eli had gotten together so quickly. But then again, people did strange things. She just wouldn't have expected it of Eli. Had marriage meant that much to him that he'd needed to jump right into it with the next available girl? Maybe the "who" hadn't been as important as the "what"? Maybe marriage had been the end goal…which he'd obviously achieved.

Was she being a little unfair? Probably. So she shifted back to the subject at hand.

"So you come out here now instead?"

"Sometimes."

Okay, so it didn't look like he was in the mood for conversation. Except she remembered something and suddenly had to know. "How is your patient doing? The biventricular-pacemaker one?"

This time he fixed her with a look that made her shiver. "Her kidneys are shutting down."

Those five words carried the weight of the world in them. "Oh, Eli, I'm so sorry. But maybe she'll pull through. Sometimes the shock of a big change like that upsets the balance of things in the body. It might just be trying to adapt to its new normal."

He didn't say anything right away, just looked off into the distance. When he did respond, he simply said, "And sometimes it can't."

Were they still talking about the patient? She couldn't tell. "Do you want to talk about it?"

"Not particularly."

"Okay."

She wasn't sure what to do other than to sit there in silence, wishing she had some magic quip that could make him feel better or would give him hope. But would that be doing him a favor or just making it harder if his patient did in fact…die?

A couple of minutes went by, then he shook his head. "Sorry. I know I'm not very good company right now."

She looked at him. His short hair looked like a million fingers had been dragged through it, making it stick up at odd angles. She remembered that from when they'd been together, from when he'd really been troubled about something. He was leaning forward, elbows on his knees, hands dangling in front of those. Strong hands. And yet they were hands that wrought work that was both delicate and amazing. Georgia knew she was good at what she did, but she couldn't reach inside someone and coax their heart to beat again. He'd once performed that miracle on her own heart, coaxing it to beat to its own rhythm rather than forcing it to match his own. Above all, he'd never once made her feel afraid.

So why had she left?

Because she'd needed to know that she was good on her own. She'd had a series of boyfriends through high school and beyond. Things had always been fun and easy until those guys had wanted a deeper commitment. And every time it had happened, something inside of her had churned, making her feel like agreeing to any of those things meant subjugating herself to someone else's will. After all, wasn't that what a proposal was? Asking someone to stay with them? Forever?

But it had never before been hard to end things. She'd always felt a freedom in doing that. A freedom that reiterated again and again that she had the power to say no. At least that was how it had always been. Until Eli. Leaving him had shocked her system, much like she'd talked about with his biventricular patient, and she wasn't sure her heart had ever really recovered. It was why she'd bought herself that butterfly charm. To remind herself why she'd left. To remind herself that her freedom was important, even when there was a terrible price to be paid for it. And maybe, on some level, Eli had paid the price for her need as well. And for that she was sorry. Truly sorry.

Something made her reach out and touch one of those strong hands. "Hey, it's fine. I'm not always the best company either."

He nodded, glancing up at her. "Did you hear from Dr. Mueller's patient?"

The question took her by surprise. "Dr. Mueller's… Oh, right—Molly Breckin, the heart-racing patient. No, unfortunately I haven't heard a peep. But I hope, even if I never hear from her, that she doesn't give up. That she keeps looking for answers until she finds them."

Like Georgia had done with her own quest for independence? She'd been so sure that she knew the answer to that. And yet, right now in this moment, like Dr. Mueller's patient, she wasn't so positive that the answer she'd found had been the right one.

Her eyes met Eli's, and something in her heart stirred. Swallowing, she let go of his hand and raised her arm to press the butterfly charm into the skin beneath her shirt, reminding herself again of why she'd done what she'd done.

Dropping her hand, she glanced at the watch on her wrist, catching sight of the scar just below the band. A half hour was up. Time to leave. "Well, I need to get back to work. I do hope your patient makes it, no matter how grim it looks right now."

"Thanks. I hope she does as well."

Georgia stood to her feet. "See you later." Then she turned and moved away from him, each step taking her farther and farther from him. As she did, she did her best to push the thought from her mind that this felt like another time—one in the past—when she'd walked away from him and never looked back.

CHAPTER FOUR

THE CONFERENCE ROOM was already filled with people, and Eli was glad he'd gotten there in enough time to choose a seat toward the back part of the U-shaped set of tables. These meetings were never fun, but the sooner they got started the sooner he could get back to work.

His biventricular patient had made it through the next two nights, surprising him. She'd even given him a wan smile when he'd visited her room on rounds this morning. Her urine output still wasn't great, and the decision would have to be made soon about dialysis.

Strumming his fingers on the table, he glanced at the clock on the wall. They were already running five minutes late. He was glad when the hospital administrator finally climbed to his feet and walked to the podium.

Just then the doors opened and Georgia entered the room. That made him smile. She was late as usual. She scanned the room, eyes lighting on his for a second and her own lips curving. Oh, hell, she thought he was smiling at her. He quickly schooled his face. Thankfully the chairs on either side of him were already occupied. He wished he would have remembered, though, that they both liked to get these meetings over with, unlike how him and Lainey were at opposite ends of the spectrum.

Looking back, Nicholas, who'd been one of his closest high school friends, had also liked to go to these meetings on the last day, which probably explained where their connection had formed. He'd introduced them, and of course, Nick had been at his wedding, but he'd never suspected anything would come of it.

Lainey had mentioned maybe commuting to work after they'd started dating. But their schedules had never quite meshed enough to do that. Probably foreshadowing what was to come. And looking back, Eli could now see the jump from friendship and sympathy to fiancée had happened far too quickly. He'd probably been trying to fill the void that Georgia's leaving had created.

And although Lainey had been all in, bringing up the subject of commitment before he'd really had a chance to think things through, he'd allowed himself to be swept along in the stream of her apparent happiness, justifying to himself that this was what he'd wanted with Georgia. He'd even convinced himself that maybe Georgia wasn't "the one," maybe Lainey was, since she'd seemed to want what he had: marriage and a family. He'd thought things would be okay, but of course they weren't, and it had soon become apparent that they were two different people with conflicting expectations. She'd needed constant reassurance that she was his all in all. And it had become harder and harder to give that to her as time had gone on.

But from all accounts she was happy now. She had stayed at the hospital after the divorce for a while before she and Nick had moved out to one of the Aleutian Islands, where they both worked at a small clinic.

Eli shook himself from his thoughts, glancing over again at Georgia. She sat in one of the only two seats left available, directly across from him on the other side of the U. Was that any better than her sitting next to him? Yes. Because he could remember a time during just such meetings when they'd sit side by side, their hands clasping beneath the table, his thumb unable to resist stroking across her warm palm. It was amazing how a simple touch could turn him on like it had. But then when it came to Georgia, just a look from her could make him hard and ready. No one else had gotten to him the way she had, not even Lainey. Looking back, he'd been lucky Georgia had left when she had because if she'd done what Lainey had done and found someone else, it would have destroyed him.

And her leaving hadn't?

Something he wasn't going to think about right now. He realized he was still staring at her when her glance swung from where the hospital's administrative director was talking about the latest fundraising campaign to him. Eli blinked back to awareness for a second time and turned his attention back to the speaker. These meetings were always the same. Talking about stuff that could have been done through their company email. There was a 5K walk/run planned for later in the summer, they were all encouraged to participate.

Running had never been one of Eli's passions, despite the fact that Georgia loved it. Eli's biggest passion had been his job. And later, his cabin. One that he'd built with his own two hands. He had bought some land forty-five minutes outside of Anchorage ten years ago, thinking when he eventually got married, he and his wife could put a house on it. But in the dark days after Georgia had left, the thought of doing something for himself on that land had consumed him.

So after getting drunk one night and needing Lainey to drive him home, he'd taken a two-month leave of absence and decided to build an off-grid cabin there instead of a family home. Cutting the timber and peeling the logs had been one of the ways he'd gotten through that time. It had been therapeutic in a way nothing else could have been. Lainey had appeared with food, coffee, and a listening ear whenever she'd had a day off. He'd come to look forward to her visits, since it had taken his mind off his own morbid thoughts.

Steve, his close friend and mentor, had also come periodically and helped him do some of the heavier work, like the loft and putting on the roof, and he'd given Eli some advice he'd never taken: to give Georgia a few months to think about things and then try to go talk to her.

It was only then that he realized he'd never actually met her mom. He knew she'd grown up in the city of Kodiak on Kodiak Island, but she'd never mentioned her dad, and when he'd asked one time she'd simply said he wasn't a part of her life.

He glanced at her again. Having parents that weren't part of your life anymore was something he'd become painfully conscious of after the automobile crash that had ripped his own from him in a slash that had taken a long time to get over. It was funny how few foster parents wanted to be saddled with a grieving teenager who acted out from time to time. So he'd bounced from one house to another until he'd finally landed at Steve Davis and his wife's home. Steve had just been starting his medical practice but had taken time away from it to spend with Eli, going with him to get therapy and letting him shadow him at work. It had been exactly what he'd needed, and it was a big part of the reason Eli was now a doctor.

The sight of hands going up all over the room made him realize that the man at the podium had asked about something. He wasn't sure if it was a vote or if it was just to get opinions on something. Georgia's hand had gone up, and when she glanced at him, her brows went up as if in surprise.

He asked his neighbor what he'd missed, and it was evidently a question about whether they would like to see more money put into the cardiac department. It was too late to put his hand up now, but he was pretty sure he was going to be asked about it later.

Time to really start paying attention before something else slipped by him. So for the remainder of the meeting he forced himself to keep his eyes on the front of the room and his mind off of the past—and more importantly—off of Georgia.

Then it was over, thank God, and people started getting up, including him. But just as his eyes met Georgia's again, the administrator called his name over the microphone. "Dr. Jacobsen… Eli…could I pick your brain about something for a minute?"

Oh, hell, busted. Still looking at Georgia, he saw her eyes sparkle, and her brows waggled in a way that said she wouldn't want to be him right now. Then she left the room.

She wasn't the only one who didn't want to be him, as he caught several sympathetic glances as people walked by him. Even Eli didn't want to be him right now.

Gathering his thoughts, he moved toward the podium. And met Marcus Adams, making sure they weren't near enough to that microphone that they could be overheard.

The administrator shook his hand. "I'm curious about something. Is there a reason you wouldn't want to see your department grow or have more money dedicated to it?"

Eli's brain whizzed through ideas and finally came up with something that sounded plausible enough. "I'd want to see what the ideas were before committing to them. I don't want to see growth that comes too fast and isn't sustainable."

Like his marriage to Lainey?

No. This really was about the hospital. He'd seen

that very thing happen from time to time, when they either couldn't hire enough staff to cover the rapid growth or there weren't enough patients to justify it. The latter wasn't something he saw happening, but good staffing wasn't always an easy thing to come by. And bad staffing… Ronny Mueller immediately came to mind.

"Okay, that's what I thought. I'll make sure to run our ideas by you before we make any hard and fast decisions. Does that ease your concerns?"

"It does. Thank you, Marcus."

"Thank you for running one of the best cardiac units in all of Alaska."

"There are a lot of people involved in running the department. I couldn't do any of it without them."

The man gave him a smile that Eli was pretty sure didn't mean anything. It was just that of a politician looking for votes so he could push his agenda through. Then he pulled himself up short. No, that wasn't really fair. The man was good at his job. This hospital had flourished because of some of the changes Marcus had made when he'd come aboard seven years ago.

"I'll send you some of my thoughts over the next couple of days," Marcus said. "When you have time, if you could get back to me on them, I'd appreciate it."

"I will. And thanks again."

"Not a problem. Thanks for coming to the meeting."

All Eli could do was smile, because it hadn't been an optional gathering. But at least he would get something in writing before the department was handed a big check without any concrete plans for what the money was supposed to go toward.

He headed for the door just as some of the next group made their way to their seats. One of his colleagues caught him before he made it out. "How was it?"

"About the same as it always is."

"That's what I was afraid of. Thanks."

Eli finally got out of the room and spied Georgia talking to William just across the corridor. The other man's eyes clipped his for a second before ending whatever conversation he'd been having with his friend and sliding through the door. But not without sending a nod in Eli's direction as he did.

Georgia came over. "Did you get in trouble?"

He couldn't stop a chuckle when she made it sound like they were still in school. "I didn't get detention, if that's what you mean."

"I thought he might make you sit through the meeting again." Thankfully she didn't ask him why he'd been staring at her through much of the hour.

"No, but he did ask why I wasn't in favor of growing my department."

"Oh, boy. I bet that was awkward."

He smiled again. "Only a little. Listen, do you want to get some coffee, or do you need to get back?"

"My break was supposed to happen after the meeting, so I have about a half hour. How about that coffee shop across the way?" Then she stopped short. "Or we could just go to the cafeteria."

Did she know why he avoided that coffee shop? No, how would she? He was pretty sure what had happened there had never made it through the hospital rumor mill.

The day that he'd walked into the shop and caught Lainey and Nick sitting at a table holding hands had been the day his marriage had ended. Lainey had tried to babble an explanation, only Eli hadn't been interested. He wasn't proud of his reaction. He'd simply unscrewed the wedding ring from his finger and walked over to the table and dropped it on the table in front of her. Then he'd walked out, moving his stuff out of their apartment before she'd gotten back. They'd never spoken again, except through their divorce lawyers, despite the fact that they'd both still been working at Anchorage Memorial.

The one thing he'd fought hard for had been his cabin, which she'd told her lawyer she'd wanted, even though once they'd been married she'd never expressed any interest in it again. Despite having visited the site during the building phase, she'd always acted like she was above staying in such a rugged place. Fortunately, she'd settled for money instead.

Realizing Georgia was waiting for his answer, Eli said, "The coffee shop is fine." He hoped to hell she wasn't going to start trying to be his friend because the time for that was long gone. And the last thing he thought he could manage was to get past everything that had happened and slip into an easy—and platonic—relationship with her. Because despite everything, the last thing he felt toward Georgia was anything approaching platonic. He'd proved that by the memories that had risen up during the staff meeting.

They walked across to the coffee shop, and when they pushed the door open a bell rang, announcing their arrival. He didn't remember that being there a couple of years ago. Had they put it up after he'd caught Lainey and Nick together to warn others who might be meeting in secret that someone was arriving?

Now, that was being paranoid.

The tables had been rearranged or replaced as well. The area where his ex and Nick had sat was now set up like a conversation area, with a circle of comfortable chairs and a few low-slung coffee tables. There were high café tables and barstools over on the left side of the shop. Despite the line of people waiting to place their orders, there were still plenty of spots left to sit, so most folks were probably taking their beverages with them.

The lighting in the place was low, with swagged lines of bare bulbs providing a casual but intimate ambience that made him slightly uncomfortable, although if it affected Georgia, he wasn't seeing it.

They got in line, and Eli was surprised when it moved quickly. "What are you getting?"

Her eyes were up on the menu. "And iced vanilla latte, I think."

He remembered she liked those cold caffeinated drinks. In fact, even when they'd been together she would sometimes make coffee and then take her time drinking it. Sometimes she'd even forgotten where she'd left her cup and once she'd found it would drink the rest of it cold, laughing when he'd made a face at her. He preferred his coffee hot.

He also preferred his coffee strong and black.

They placed their order, and the barista gave them a little plastic number to set up at whatever table they chose.

They went over to one of the high café tables, and Georgia climbed onto her stool. "I'm kind of afraid to ask, but did your patient make it?"

He didn't need to ask which patient she was talking about. "Yes. Her numbers are slightly better today, although there's still a possibility she'll need dialysis. But there's been a definite improvement."

"I told you that could happen."

"You did, but I've found it's best to be prepared in case things don't work out like you expect them to."

She looked down at the table for a few seconds before glancing back at him. "Are you talking about your patient? Or about something else?"

He nodded to acknowledge that she'd read the situation correctly. "It can apply to almost anything. Including my patient."

She didn't ask about his marriage, but she'd probably already deduced that it fit in that category as well.

"How about growing your department? Does that fit in there too?" This was said with a smile, and he let one side of his mouth kick up.

"Like I told the administrator, I don't want them going too fast and jumping ahead of themselves."

And just like that, he realized that's probably what he'd done with Georgia back when they'd been together. They'd been dating for three years when he'd realized he wanted to spend the rest of his life with her. His proposal had been impulsive, and he saw how she could have been shocked by it. They'd never really discussed the future outside of short-term plans. And they'd not even moved in together. It was no wonder she'd walked out on him. But surely it couldn't have come as a complete surprise that he'd want to get married at some point?

But then again, she'd never gotten married in the intervening time, unlike Eli, who probably appeared to have marriage as the end goal of every relationship. Looking at some of his colleagues, he'd discovered that not all of them chose to get married. Some lived together for long periods of time, having families and raising them together as partners rather than husband and wife. He didn't begrudge them that. He'd just always equated family to what he'd thought was the gold standard—a husband, a wife and a couple of kids.

But marriage didn't guarantee a couple would stay together. He'd known that in his head, but his heart had wanted it all. And yet that hadn't worked out either.

He could look back and see that he'd probably used Lainey as a substitute for Georgia. And it was something he wasn't proud of. Marriage had been his and Lainey's end goal when it probably shouldn't have been. And because he'd been so devastated when Georgia had left, he'd been less liberal about saying the niceties like *I love you* to Lainey—who seemed to have a deep need for those signs of affection. It was no wonder she'd found someone else to say those things to her instead. He wasn't even unhappy for her. Not anymore.

"Penny for your thoughts."

No way. "They're not even worth that much." He forced a smile and decided to change the subject. "So how are you liking being back at Anchorage Memorial?"

"I love it." She made a little face. "Well, most of it. Dr. Mueller still baffles me. He acts as if he doesn't even *like* his patients. And if I can see it, I'm sure they can too. Why does he even practice medicine? Surely it's not a good look for the hospital."

"Hundreds of thousands of dollars in student loans, maybe? I'll also admit that the hospital wants physicians who are not only good at what they do but who are fast. They feel they can skimp a little on bedside manner if they're excellent and fast, but if not..." Eli shrugged. "I'm not sure why he doesn't change specialties if emergency medicine ended up not being all he'd hoped it would be."

"Maybe he's good at what he does, but I sense from the nurses that he's too quick to let patients walk out of the hospital without a thorough workup. He probably saves the hospital a few bucks on those folks who don't have insurance, but if they have to come back in with the same complaint, then it causes a distrust of our profession. I saw that with Molly Breckin, who'd been dismissed by more than just our hospital."

"Sometimes when it's something that's more difficult to diagnose, things can fall through the cracks."

She gave him a frown. "Would *you* have sent her back out with only an EKG?"

Well, she had him there. "You know I wouldn't have."

"And that's exactly what I mean. Even if it turns out that it's something benign, knowledge is power, and the more information and reassurance a patient gets that tells them you don't think they're crazy, the more often they can settle into their body the way it is." Georgia paused for a minute. "My mom has a prolapsed mitral valve that has given her fits ever since she was a teenager. She was hyperaware of every skipped beat and every blip of irregularity in her heartbeat. But it was only after her divorce that she sought medical advice, and she said her doctor was great and took the time to not only diagnose her but to help her understand what was happening and give her the tools to deal with it. He put her on a beta blocker, and it was a game changer for her. It evened out her heart rate and let her feel like she had her life back."

This was more information than she'd ever given him about her family. It was on the tip of his tongue to ask about her father again, but if she hadn't been willing to share anything about him when they'd been together, it was unlikely she would confide in him now. And it was none of his business, even though Georgia knew pretty much everything about his life in foster care and about Steve being the person who—probably like her mom's beta blockers—had given him his life back.

So rather than going back through any of that, Eli simply said, "I'm glad for her. She still lives on Kodiak?"

"Yep. She probably always will. It's where her mom and grandmother were from, and she places a lot of value on that."

He wondered if her dad was still there as well, but again, he wasn't going to ask. "It makes sense that you went back there, then."

As soon as the words were out of his mouth, he realized he really had no business mentioning that. Once they'd stopped being a couple, she'd probably felt her life was her own again. Maybe leaving him had given her that. "I'm sorry if being with me made you feel any less than you are."

Her eyes widened, and she reached over to touch the hand that wasn't holding his coffee cup. "Oh, Eli, it didn't. I—I just...couldn't. Making that kind of commitment doesn't work for me."

How could she even know that without trying? And she'd never given him any alternatives that she *could* accept, although back then he'd been dead set on marriage and probably would have been unhappy with anything less than that. And now that he'd tried marriage and had it fall in ruins around his feet?

Disillusionment was too soft a word for how he felt about it now.

Despite that, commitment was still important to him. Important enough that he hadn't dated since his divorce because he wasn't sure he would fare any better the next time. So he'd decided that he would just stay single until he could untangle some of those threads.

"I think I get that now. Thank you for not just going along with it for the sake of keeping the peace." Something he'd done with Lainey? Ugh. He needed to stop comparing the two situations. They were miles apart. He glanced at his watch and saw that forty-five minutes had gone by in a flash. "You probably need to be back at work, don't you?"

She glanced at the wall where there was a big clock. "Oh, heavens, yes. I'm already late."

He gathered their trash and flashed her a smile. "Some things never do change, it seems."

"Maybe not. But I just keep trying." She hopped off her stool. "Thanks for the coffee, Eli. And the conversation."

Yeah, he was kind of glad they'd cleared the air about at least a few things from their past. Did it mean they could forge a new path from here and be colleagues who didn't actively avoid each other?

The jury was still out on that. But he hoped they could.

CHAPTER FIVE

"CALL AND SEE if Dr. Jacobsen can come." Georgia's words were not a request.

Dr. Mueller shook his head, a stubborn set to his jaw. "I think we can handle this."

Oh, no. He was not going to bulldoze her just because he thought he had some kind of seniority over her. Okay, well, he might technically have that, but he was wrong about the rest of it. And she was not about to let another patient be pushed aside by him.

"Can I speak with you outside for a minute?"

They had a sixty-two-year-old woman whose EKG was all over the place, sending flurries of PVCs across the tracings as well as two episodes of tachycardia within the space of a couple of minutes. Plus she had a history of heart failure and was having trouble catching her breath—the latter of which was what had brought her to the ER. These were not symptoms they could just ignore. Or at least Georgia couldn't.

Once they were in the hallway, Mueller tried again. "If we just up her dosage of losartan and furosemide, it may pop her back into sinus rhythm and reduce her water retention."

"I don't want to do that without having a cardiologist sign off on it. Her oxygen levels aren't the greatest. And reducing her heart rate even more could send her into bradycardia."

His frown grew stormy. "Look, we're wasting time here. I'm sure Jacobsen would follow the same protocol even if we called him in. She's not my first heart-failure patient."

Maybe not, but Georgia wasn't comfortable with either of the suggestions he'd offered. "Well, why don't we ask him, just to be sure?"

Lauren, who'd been in the room with them, popped her head outside the door and paused for a second as she glanced at their faces. "Is it okay if I go let her husband know she's being treated?" The nurse stared at her, as if looking for a sign, and catching her drift, Georgia gave a slight nod of her head.

"Yes. Go."

Mueller could report her if he wanted to, but if what she thought was happening truly was, then he probably wouldn't dare because it would expose just how little concern he seemed to have for his patients.

Lauren left the room without another word, and Georgia hoped to hell it was to go and ask Eli if he could come and take a look at the patient. She knew William would have gone and immediately checked, but she didn't know Lauren quite as well as she did her childhood friend.

She continued, "I want her to have an echo so we can get a really good look at what her valves are doing and where her heart function currently stands. You can't do that with a simple EKG." She realized her voice had gone up in volume when another nurse came down the hallway where they were standing and gave them a look.

When Mueller didn't answer her, she blew out a breath. "Well, I'm going back in there. Lauren is probably already on the phone with Dr. Jacobsen."

"Why would she call him? Neither of us asked her to. Or did you just..." He drew himself up to his full five foot eight and gave her a baleful look that sent a chill over her. But she didn't back down, matching him scowl for scowl. Finally he threw his hands up in obvious frustration. "Oh, I see how it is. Well, do whatever the hell you want, then. If you're having Jacobsen come down, then I'm not going to waste my time here. I'm going to go treat the next patient in line."

Thank God!

She didn't say the words out loud, but she was pretty sure he could read the relief on her face. In the week and a half she'd been back at the hospital, this was the first real run-in she'd had with Mueller, but he was everything William had told her and more. She couldn't believe the hospital let him go on like he did. But then again, she wasn't the head of the department and she could just about bet that doctor had heard a thing or two about Mueller. But he'd evidently never screwed up enough to be written up or censored. Although Georgia didn't know that for a fact.

She swiveled on her heel and went back through

the door to the exam room, leaving the other man standing outside. She hoped to hell he did go to see whatever patient was still out there, who, if Georgia remembered correctly, had hurt their wrist after slipping in the bathtub. She didn't trust Mueller with that any more than she trusted him with their current patient, but at least a wrist injury wasn't life or death.

Within three minutes, Eli strode into the room and took a look at her face and, like he always had, read her like a book. Or maybe Lauren had filled him in. "What have you got?"

"This is Edna Miller. She's short of breath and has a history of heart failure. I really wanted you take a look and maybe set her up for an echo." She handed him the tablet that contained Edna's chart. "Her husband is in the waiting room, hoping for some news."

And he'd thankfully not heard the tense exchange between the hospital's two ER doctors, although Georgia wasn't too sure how soundproof these rooms were. She'd never been in a situation before where she'd felt her blood pressure rise enough to lift her voice to the same level. But if calling in Eli hadn't been the right decision, she didn't know what was. She knew in her gut that upping a patient's meds without exploring things a little further was the wrong decision. She also knew from the huge sense of relief that had washed over her when Eli walked through the door that Edna needed to see the specialist.

She hadn't seen Eli since the coffee shop, and she, for sure, hadn't sought him out since then. Some of their topics of conversation that day had hit a little too close to home, like him saying he hoped he hadn't made her feel less than she was. Her eyes had burned, and she'd come dangerously close to telling him no, that the only person who had ever done that had been her father. But no one besides her mom, William and their neighbors in the city of Kodiak knew what had happened the day her dad had left for good.

Georgia wasn't sure why she hadn't told Eli when they'd been together other than that she'd learned at a young age to suppress her emotions and hide the details of their life in order to keep the peace with her dad.

Even though she no longer needed to do so, learned behaviors were hard to overcome, as she'd found out when Eli had proposed to her.

As if sensing her thoughts, he looked up from the tablet. But instead of saying anything of a personal nature, he simply said, "I agree with you."

At least she assumed his comment was in regard to their patient.

Their patient.

Well, since she'd called him in, it was true. And since Mueller had washed his hands of the case, at least he had no more say in what happened here.

While Eli went over to talk to Edna about the details of what the echocardiogram would be like, she tried to figure out why Ronny Mueller was the way he was. Was it genuinely that he didn't care, or had the idea that they needed to be as efficient as possible with their time to avoid long waits in the ER become so ingrained that it became automatic? Kind of like her behaviors from childhood. She bet if she looked at Mueller's time-per-patient ratio he would have the fastest times, hands down.

It might've been why he'd been so quick to nudge Molly Breckin to the exit, even though officially she'd been listed as AMA, since she hadn't waited for the discharge paperwork to be signed. That surely worked in Mueller's favor if things went south with her further on down the line.

"Thank you so much, Doctor." Edna's words were choppy and delivered between labored breaths. Even with the supplemented oxygen, she still didn't feel like she was getting enough air. Another reason why Georgia had doubted that simply upping her meds without trying to see exactly what was happening was the wrong choice.

"Do you want your husband here with you?"

"Could I?"

Georgia moved over to the patient's side. "Yes, of course you can. I'll go get him."

Again the sense of relief that Eli was going to do further testing was so strong that she wanted to hug him. Or kiss him.

No matter what, his calm demeanor never left him. Even when she'd broken up with him, he'd never expressed his disappointment in her—when he would have had every right to. They'd dated for a long time. And she'd never once mentioned that marriage was off the table. Mainly because she hadn't known that about herself until the moment he'd asked her to marry him. The horror that had gone through her had been like a tidal wave, and she'd had trouble not turning and running away without giving him an answer. Instead she'd somehow choked one out and then had left him standing there. Alone.

Her heart cramped.

Pulling herself back to the present, she gave him one last glance before leaving the room to get Edna's husband.

Eli had the bedside manner that other doctors only wished they had. He was gentle with his patients, never seeming rushed or hurried in the way he treated them. He'd been the same with her, never seeming to mind spending whatever time it had taken to keep them connected. Only in the end, it hadn't mattered how much time he'd taken, she wouldn't have changed her mind. Maybe she was a little more like Mueller than she liked to believe.

Pushing through the door, she walked down the corridor until she got to the waiting room. Thankfully she didn't run into Mueller on the way.

Edna's husband was the only one in the waiting room at the moment. "Mr. Miller? Would you like to come and be with your wife?"

"Thank you, yes." He got up from his chair, using a cane for extra support as he made his way toward the door. "How is she?"

"About the same. We're going to do a little more

testing so we'll know how to make her a little more comfortable." She hoped to hell they could. "But I thought you being there would make her feel better."

"The other doctor didn't seem to want me anywhere near her."

She was careful about how she worded it. Taking away a patient's trust in the medical team could harm the hospital and the doctors who did try to do their best for their patients. And maybe Mueller really had thought upping her medication would help, although something in her soul said otherwise. "We all have our own ideas about what's best for our patients."

He seemed to accept that without question, instead asking, "Do you have any idea why this is happening? Her heart failure seemed to be under control."

"Not yet. But we have a cardiac specialist in there with her at the moment. He'll tell you a little more about our game plan."

"Good. We're actually here on vacation, so her cardiologist is thousands of miles away."

"Really? Where are you from?"

"Florida."

She blinked. "And you came to Alaska?"

"Edna has always wanted to do an Alaskan cruise. And she's loved every minute of it…up until yesterday. The ship's doctor saw her and sent us here to the emergency room."

And Mueller wanted to just up her dose of medications without knowing if it would work while she was thousands of miles away from home? At least with an echo, they would have a better idea of how good or bad her heart function was right now. If the news wasn't good, the couple might have to forgo the rest of their cruise and have Edna admitted for observation. At least until she was stable enough to make the trip back home. Right now, she wasn't. And if they discharged her, she might very well die on the cruise ship.

"He did the right thing," Georgia said. "I'm hoping for the best."

They got to the room, and she pushed the door open to let him go in. Eli was standing next to the bed talking to the patient, who seemed calmer than she had when Mueller had been in charge.

Eli glanced over at Mr. Miller as if including him in the conversation. "I was telling your wife that we have two options for an echocardiogram—which will give us a better visual of how her heart is working. We could start with a handheld unit that I have in my pocket, but my preference would be to do a standard echocardiogram that will give me more information and is displayed on a larger screen."

Mr. Miller went over to Edna and grasped her hand, and they seemed to exchange a look. "We'll go with whatever you think is best."

Edna nodded. "Can Artie stay with me through it?"

"Absolutely," Eli said. "We'll need to move you upstairs to the cardiology unit. I already know I'd like to admit you at least overnight for observation and see if we can get your oxygen levels up."

"But the cruise..." Her eyes watered as she looked up at her husband, who stroked her head.

"There will be other cruises, hon. How can you enjoy this one when it's so hard to breathe?"

"I know."

He leaned over and kissed her cheek. "Let's just get you better, and then we'll talk about the other stuff."

"Okay."

Lauren, who'd come back in the room and overheard the last part of the conversation, said, "I'll go let them know so they can get the paperwork started."

Georgia was pretty sure Dr. Mueller was going to be incensed when he heard, but that was fine by her.

Edna glanced at her. "Can you go with us?"

"I'll need to stay here in the ER in case there are more patients, but I'll try to come up and see how you're doing when I get off work in a couple of hours, okay?" Hopefully Eli would be okay with that, although she was sure she'd hear about it later if she had overstepped her boundaries.

When she looked over at him, there was no expression on his face. No approval or disapproval, so she was going to take that to mean he wasn't vehemently opposed to her entering his domain.

She'd done it before when she'd been at the hospital. It was how she and Eli had gotten to know each other. In fact, when they'd finally started dating, she would go up there under the pretext of checking on a patient when really she'd wanted to see him.

That wasn't the case now, but she cared about her

patients. In fact, if Edna couldn't be helped, Georgia was going to feel terrible. She genuinely liked the couple. And they'd been high school sweethearts and had been married for decades.

An orderly came into the room, saying he was here to transport the patient. Georgia went over to the couple and laid a hand on Edna's shoulder. "Dr. Jacobsen is an excellent doctor. There's none better here in Anchorage. If anyone can help you, he can."

When she glanced over at him, she saw he was frowning, although he had given the orderly the okay to take Edna. "I'll be up in a few minutes. I'm just going to call and have them ready to meet you when you get upstairs."

With that, the gurney was wheeled out of the room, with Artie following them, his cane tapping on the floor as he made his way down the hall.

She was pretty sure Eli had something he wanted to say to her, so she hurried to cut him off. "Are you okay with me going to check on her?"

His frown was still there. "Yes, I just wanted to ask if you wanted to be updated on her condition."

She blinked. "Could you do that?" It was something they'd regularly used to do when a patient had been transferred from her department to his, but part of that was because they'd been a couple and she'd been genuinely interested in her patients. Not every specialist wanted to be pestered by an ER doc who was being nosy and wanting to know how someone was doing.

"I could."

"Thank you," she said. "I would really appreciate that. Mueller gave me hell about wanting to call you in. He basically washed his hands of her once he realized Lauren and I were going to override him."

"Lauren?"

"The nurse who called you."

"Ah, that makes sense now." He shook his head. "And don't worry about Mueller. He gets a bug up his butt every time anyone calls for a specialist."

"But why?"

"I have no idea. Delusions of grandeur, maybe?"

"He wanted to just up the doses of her medication."

Eli nodded. "I think I heard he was going on vacation soon, so he'll be out of your hair for a couple of weeks anyway."

"Is it bad that I hope he looks for another hospital while he's gone?"

Eli sighed. "It's getting harder and harder to fire staff, so the administration tries to save that card for serious infractions."

"I would probably argue what constitutes serious."

"Yeah, me too. It's probably why I don't get to make those kinds of decisions. There's a shortage of doctors right now in Alaska, so it's not always an easy task to replace someone."

Was that a jab about her leaving and basically forcing the hospital to hire someone like Ronny Mueller?

And maybe she should feel guilty. She might have made a different decision if she'd known what the consequences would be. Oh, not about turning Eli's proposal down, but about leaving before the hospital had found a suitable replacement. The ER was most hospitals' bread and butter. To be short-staffed in that department was a disaster in the making.

"I get it. I just feel like I have to look over his shoulder now. It's the second time I've heard of or seen him try to get a patient discharged as fast as possible."

"Your young patient?" he asked.

"Yes, Molly Breckin. Although she wasn't my patient. If she had been, she wouldn't have walked out of the hospital without at least talking to a cardiologist."

"Hopefully she'll be back or try another hospital."

"But she shouldn't have had to do either of those two things," she said.

He nodded. "I know, but there's nothing to be done about it now. We have to take care of the folks who are here now. Speaking of which, I'd better be on my way."

"Okay, sounds good. Thanks for coming down."

"I'll see you a little later, if you come up." He walked toward the door.

"Are you sure you don't mind?"

"I think Edna will be disappointed if you don't come."

No hint of whether he'd be disappointed or not. But then again, why should he feel one way or the other? They weren't together anymore.

"Okay, I'll be up when I get off in a few hours. If you know something before then, you'll call?"

"Yes. I'll call."

He went through the door, and Georgia breathed a

sigh of relief. It wasn't as awkward working with him as she'd feared it might be when she'd first thought about coming back to Anchorage Memorial. And while the fact that he wasn't married anymore had filled her with dread when William had first told her, even that hadn't been the catastrophe she'd imagined after she'd heard.

But unless she remained on her guard, it might become one. Especially if that little nudging voice inside of her didn't let up. It was basically telling her they were both single and so why not let her defenses down a little?

She couldn't. Because if she did, she could very easily fall back into old patterns. And now that she knew where those patterns could lead, she knew she couldn't let herself do that. Because she didn't want what she'd done to him three years ago to ever happen again.

Myocarditis. Both the echo and cardiac MRI showed inflammation of the lower sections of the heart, and Edna had said she'd been pretty sick a few weeks before the cruise. It explained all of her new symptoms like shortness of breath and arrhythmias. A blood test had confirmed she had antibodies for Covid. Myocarditis could be self-limiting and go away on its own, but with Edna's history of mild heart failure, the inflammation could put a strain on the already overworked organ. Thank God Georgia had pushed for the echo. Simply upping her medications wouldn't have helped, and it might have made things even worse.

Eli sat down and came up with a treatment plan, taking into account Edna's existing heart failure, which could complicate treatment. He decided that a round of steroids might knock down the inflammation and allow that portion of the heart to heal. When he was done researching current models, he was fairly confident that his approach was the most likely to succeed. Unfortunately it meant the couple would have to forgo the rest of their cruise so that he could monitor her for a week or so. The only other alternative was to fly her back to the lower forty-nine and wait to start treatment until she got there. But with her shortness of breath, that meant a pretty uncomfortable trip.

He got up from his desk and went to Edna's room in Cardiac Intensive Care, where she had been placed. Once he got there, he found his patient asleep, her husband sitting at her bedside.

The man stood. "Do you know what's causing her symptoms?" His voice was quiet, so as not to wake up his wife, but his face showed how worried he was.

"I have a pretty good idea. The testing we did indicates cardiomyopathy, an inflammation of an area of Edna's heart." Eli pulled out his phone, where there was an anatomical picture of the heart, and waited as Artie put his glasses on. Then he pointed to the area of the heart affected. "We think it was caused by the body's response to when she was sick a few weeks ago."

"You mean her heart has an infection?"

"Not exactly. But her heart reacted to the virus and became inflamed."

"Can it be treated?"

"Yes and no. There's no direct treatment, and antibiotics don't work because it's not an actual infection. What we can do is try to knock down the inflammation with a steroid and give the heart a chance to heal."

"Will the cardio…whatever it is make her heart failure worse?"

"Our goal is for that not to happen. I can't make any hard and fast promises, but the treatment I'm proposing has a pretty good track record as far as that goes. There's one caveat." He paused. "I'd like Edna to stay here while we begin treatment and until she's stable, which means—"

"We can't finish the cruise."

"Unfortunately. That's not to say that you can't go on another one at a later date, but it won't be right away. She'll need three to six months of solid rest so her heart can heal, which means she'll have to limit most of her activities."

"Do you know my wife?"

He shook his head. "No, but I know myocarditis. And while it can go away, strenuous activity runs the danger of putting so much strain on the heart that it causes sudden death."

Artie seemed to blanch. "Sudden death?"

"I'm not saying that would happen, but I want her to have the best possible outcome. I talked to her cardiologist in Florida, and he agrees with me on the treatment protocol and on the time frame."

"Then that's good enough for me. She's been going to him for a long time. Her heart failure had been getting better, which is why her suddenly having these symptoms was so scary."

"Myocarditis, like any inflammation, can come on suddenly. But our goal is for it to cause as little damage as possible," Eli said. "When she wakes up we can go over everything together."

"Is Dr. Sumter able to come up?"

He glanced at his watch. He'd called Georgia about a half hour ago, and she'd said she was just finishing up some last-minute things and then would come up to see the couple. He wasn't sure how he felt about her doing that. It was a throwback to the days when they'd freely shared cases and allowed their personal lives to bleed over into their professional lives. Just like when she'd come to his office last week with the question about Molly Breckin. The more they allowed their lives to overlap now that she was back, the harder it might be for both of them to keep things on a professional level. And one thing he did know was that he wasn't willing for things to move beyond that. Not after the way their relationship had ended.

He was pretty sure that if he allowed them to get involved again—like last time—he couldn't see himself being happy with just dating her for twenty years or longer. And after his and Lainey's divorce, he was pretty sure he wasn't going to want to get married again anytime soon, if ever.

He was pretty happy with his life the way it was right now. It was uncomplicated and easy going back and forth between his apartment and his cabin in the Mat-Su, where he liked to spend most of his days off.

"She should actually be here pretty soon."

"Good. I know Edna will want to see her. If not for her, I don't know what would have happened. We might be back on that cruise ship out on open water. If something had gone wrong... If something had happened to Edna, I just don't know what I would have done."

"Georgia takes a lot of interest in her patients, so I doubt she'll let you get out of here without visiting at least once or twice."

As if on cue, the door opened and the ER doc walked in. Her glance skipped from him to Artie, who was still on his feet, his cane left beside the bed. "Everything okay?"

Eli nodded. "It's fine. We were just going over treatment options, and I was telling Artie that I want to keep Edna while she's on the steroids, just to monitor how she does on them."

"I think that's a great idea. I'm sorry you won't be able to finish your cruise, though."

Eli had already talked to Georgia about how he'd hoped to proceed as far as the steroids and rest were concerned.

"Edna will be devastated," Artie said, "but I'm willing to do whatever will get her through this."

"It also means I'll be able to come up and see you guys more times." Georgia sent the man a smile.

Eli tensed. He'd expected once or twice…was she actually saying she'd come more than that? He should have realized it, though. He hadn't been lying when he'd said she always took a lot of interest in her patients, probably more than a lot of doctors. She used to have pictures of herself with some of them taped to her locker in the doctors' lounge. Eli had no idea which locker she'd been given this go round, and he purposely had tried to avoid looking for it. He didn't want anything to interfere with his need to keep things with her on a professional basis. And going to look for her locker definitely seemed beyond the purview of doing that.

Edna's voice broke through. "Am I hearing you wrong? I'm going to have to stay in the hospital? And we can't finish the cruise?"

Her voice still sounded breathy and weak, but hopefully a couple of days on the steroids would help with that.

Artie went to her side. "The doctor thinks it's best. And even after we get home, you're going to have to rest for a couple of months."

"Months? But what about our garden?"

"I'll take care of that. You can just give the orders, and I'll carry them out."

Eli couldn't stop a smile of his own. This was what a partnership was supposed to be, with one person supporting the other when they were at their weakest. A love like this was what he'd hoped to find ever since he'd been a teenager, when he'd felt like a castoff so many times—a burden that nobody had wanted.

Edna grabbed her husband's hand. "Well, ordering you around might not be such a bad thing after all." She took a breath and let it out on a half cough. "I'll be glad when I feel better, though."

"And you will feel better. But it's just going to take some time. I know patience has never been one of your strong suits."

"No, it is not."

That was as emphatic a statement as he'd heard his patient make, and Eli couldn't prevent a smile.

Georgia moved closer to the bed. "It sounds like you're feeling a little better than you were when you came to the ER."

"I am. Because I have answers, thanks to you. I might not even have a treatment plan if you hadn't fought for me."

"Eli was the one who had the game plan. I just knew that you shouldn't go back to the cruise ship in the condition you were in."

Artie sat in the chair beside his wife. "Our son is flying up today and will stay until we're ready to head back to Florida."

"I'm glad you'll have someone to help you get back," Eli said. "And I think we should leave you two alone for a while to plan your garden. That chair you're sitting in pulls out into a bed. We can have sheets and blankets brought in if you want to stay with her."

"I wouldn't want to be anywhere else. Thank you again—for everything."

"My pleasure."

He nodded for Georgia to follow him out. The couple was right. If she hadn't fought for them...if Mueller had been left to his own devices, Edna very well could have died. And Artie would be without his wife and their children would be left without a mom. And while no one at the hospital would ever know it, since she wasn't a local, it still would have been a tragedy that needn't have happened.

This was the Georgia he remembered: Tenacious, fearless, unafraid of standing up to anyone. Even him.

Once they were out of the room, he glanced at her. "Are you off duty?"

"I am." She looked at him for a minute before reaching over to squeeze his hand, much like Artie had done with his wife. "It's moments like the one with that couple that I remember why I wanted to go into medicine."

Her fingers were warm on his skin, and the memory of being able to just hold his hand out and know that she would take it washed over him. Eli suddenly didn't want this moment to end. "Do you want to go for a walk?"

She smiled. "That would be nice. It's been quite a day, and going home to a peanut-butter-and-jelly sandwich doesn't hold a lot of appeal."

They made it out to the street, and five minutes later they were at a local park. This time of year, the greenery was in full swing, and Eli took a deep breath, knowing in a few months this would all be covered in snow. But knowing that didn't make him want to move to a warmer climate—it just made him appreciate Alaska's summer all the more. Just like he could enjoy these few moments with Georgia, knowing they wouldn't last.

"I'm so glad Edna is going to be okay," she said.

"I am too," he said, "and I'm hopeful that by trying to knock down the inflammation so quickly the myocarditis won't cause any lasting damage to her heart muscle."

There was no need to adjust his pace for her—Georgia had a long stride and had always moved with grace and speed. And he had to admit it felt good just to walk alongside her again. There would have been no doing this when she'd first arrived back at Anchorage Memorial. He'd even doubted they could work at the hospital together. All that had changed. And it seemed that maybe they could as well, although the jury was still out on that.

"How soon will you know?"

He stiffened before realizing she was referring to Edna and not his thoughts. "We should see a change in a couple of days if things go the way I hope they will."

They entered a curved stand of evergreens, where several benches were laid out. Georgia dropped onto the nearest one and breathed deeply. "I missed this place. I used to come here all the time after work. On days I was alone, I'd run. It was freeing."

He sat down beside her. He remembered coming here with her more times than he cared to remember. They'd often stopped at this very same place to talk. About work. About the weather. And about them.

"And I remember skiing in this park in the winter on our days off," he said.

Knicker Park had groomed trails in an area of woods for all levels of skiers. Or flat areas where you could cross-country ski. They had often come here just to burn off some of the stress of the day.

"That was fun," Georgia said. "So was meeting up with that moose when we were headed to the chalet for Hot Chocolate Night when the hospital hosted their annual Christmas party there."

He chuckled. "I was busy judging the distance between it and us and wondering if I should just scoop you up and run for the chalet."

She turned toward him with a laugh. "I didn't know that. Thankfully it decided we weren't very interesting and turned and went the other way."

The mirth on her face drew him in. They'd had a lot of good times together. He'd never quite understood where it all had gone wrong. One day they'd been fine and the next, she'd been gone.

It had always been hard to resist her. And right now, as the breeze made strands of dark hair sift across her face, it was no different. He lifted a hand to touch her cheek, easing away some dark tresses that dared to blow into her eyes. She was still smiling, lips parted slightly. She was so beautiful. And when she looked at him like this, it made a dark heat generate in his gut.

This time was no different. Her head tilted slightly as if judging the angle of his, and before he realized what was happening, he leaned over and touched his mouth to hers.

CHAPTER SIX

HER WHOLE BEING IGNITED.

It was as if Georgia had been waiting for this moment ever since she'd come back to Anchorage. Eli's mouth was just as firm and warm as she remembered. Just as sexy. And it sent a bolt of electricity through her body that morphed into some equally dangerous reactions. All of which were addictive.

And she wanted more.

Her hands went behind his neck and tangled in his hair as if afraid he might try to pull away before she'd gotten her fill of him. Not that she'd ever been able to do that. No matter how many times they'd kissed, no matter how many times they'd made love, she still craved him.

Despite the three years she'd spent away on Kodiak, that was one thing that evidently hadn't changed.

She pulled him closer, relishing the feel of his tongue pressing for entrance—an entrance she granted far too quickly. And yet it wasn't quick enough, judging from the way her senses were lighting torches. Torches that paved the way for an ecstasy she could only remember.

His tongue filled her mouth, and she couldn't stop the quiet moan at how good it felt for him to do this. And when the crook of his elbow went around her waist and hauled her against him with a bump, her arms twined around his neck. How utterly heady it was to be wanted by a man like this. A man who was so different from the others she'd dated during her younger years. A man so different from her father. She was never afraid when she was with him. Not even when he'd proposed.

The scar on her left wrist seemed to burn for a second, and it startled her, making her break free. She sucked down a quick breath, unsure of what had just happened. Or why.

Eli's low voice came through. "Are you okay?"

"Yes." But she wasn't sure. She untwined her arms and slid a few inches away. Far enough that she could feel her thoughts coming back to taunt her, telling her they knew she couldn't resist letting things go further than they should. Telling her she never should have come here.

"I'm sorry, Georgia. I'm not sure why I did that."

She shook her head and gripped his hand between hers for a few seconds before letting go. Her emotions were still scattered, and she wasn't sure she was going to get them back under control. "It wasn't just you. It's this place. It's always been this place. There's something magical about it. Almost as if it traps you in a fairytale the moment you come through the gates."

"I know." He shut his eyes. "But fairytales aren't real. And they don't always come true."

A slice of pain went through her. He was right—she knew he was. Things had not changed on her end, and unless he'd changed drastically in the last three years, they'd not changed on his end either, especially since he'd gotten married while she'd been gone. It might not have lasted, but that didn't mean that he wasn't still after the same things in life that he'd been after back then: marriage and a family. And who could blame him?

"Maybe I shouldn't ask, but just in case I run into her, is your ex still at the hospital?" She hadn't seen her or even heard anyone talk about her, but that didn't mean Georgia wouldn't ever have a child come through the ER and find it necessary to call in a pediatrician. And she and Lainey had had a pretty drama-free relationship, although there'd been a moment or two when Georgia had thought she'd caught the other woman looking at Eli in a way that had made her pause. Had the woman had a crush on him even while Georgia and the cardiologist had been dating?

"How did you know…" Eli pulled in a visible breath. "Of course. William."

"He didn't tell me everything you did, but he also didn't want it to come as a huge shock if I found out you'd gotten married a year after I left."

Eli seemed to stiffen. "It was hard after you left, and Lainey…well, she was there for me."

"I bet she was."

"What's that supposed to mean?"

God, she was making an even bigger mess out of this than she had that kiss that they'd just shared.

She touched his hand again. "I'm sorry. It doesn't mean anything. I'm sorry it didn't work out. I—I wanted you to be happy."

"Thanks. It just wasn't meant to work out, evidently. And to answer your question, no, she's not at the hospital anymore. She's in the Aleutians with her current husband."

Her current husband. Poor Eli. That had to have been hard. And he didn't deserve it. Just like he hadn't deserved what she'd done to him by turning down his proposal and leaving town.

She suddenly realized how her abrupt change of attitude had probably hurt him back then. But she hadn't been able to find the words to explain how utterly terrifying the thought of being chained to someone in marriage was. It was irrational, like a phobia that wasn't based on real experience. Except hers was. It was based on how her mom's entire identity had been subsumed by her dad, her existence only important insofar as it had served his wants and needs. It had taken her mom years to be able to think for herself. And once she had, there'd been no going back. Her mom wasn't risking her independence again. For anyone.

And as much as Georgia might've wanted to deny it, some of that had rubbed off on her. That fear of being engulfed by a partner. Eli's earlier choice of words about not wanting to make her feel less than had hit the nail on the head. While he hadn't made her feel that, there was a fear of that happening…with anyone, not just Eli.

"So what do we do about what just happened? Chalk it up to the park—our history here?" he asked.

"I think that's exactly what happened. And I think we were both happy that Edna's case didn't look as hopeless as it might have," she said. "So maybe this time we should just cut ourselves some slack and agree that it can't happen again."

"Cut ourselves some slack, eh? That concept is a little foreign to me, but I'll try."

She couldn't stop the spurt of laughter because he was right. She'd always had to remind him to do that, to not be so hard on himself, and it seemed that was something else that hadn't changed. "You can do it. I have faith in you."

And she did. Despite everything that had happened between them, Eli was one of the good ones. She'd never seen him do anything out of spite or even anger. So if she hadn't been able to allow herself to deepen her relationship with him, it didn't bode well for any other relationship she might have in the future. She would never meet another Eli. Not in this lifetime, and probably not in the next either.

He stood to his feet and held out his hand. She shook her head, softening it with a smile, and stood under her own power. Not because his offer was insulting, but because she was afraid if he touched her, she might pull him down for another kiss…or three or four. And that wouldn't be good. At all.

"So I'll see you at work tomorrow? I think I'm going to walk a little more," she said.

"I'll see you there. Be careful." He didn't offer to go with her, but then again, she had not asked him to, hoping he'd get the hint and not try to walk with her back to the hospital.

"I will. I'm not going far, and I doubt I'll see a moose this close to the park's entrance."

Georgia started off, giving him a little wave as she moved in the opposite direction of the exit. As soon as he was out of sight she would turn around and head back. She just needed some time to clear her head and try to figure out exactly what had happened here.

And to figure out how to avoid it ever happening again. Step one: never visit this park again with him. Step two: she had no idea. But hopefully she would come up with a game plan that made sure she was invulnerable to his charms. Or anything else the universe might throw at her. What was it they said? The best defense was a good offense. Which meant she needed to be proactive when it came to Eli Jacobsen. Proactive as hell about making sure she didn't find herself in a situation where she might be tempted to do or say anything that might lead to more kissing. Or worse.

Eli spent the next few days trying to figure out exactly what had happened at the park. Had he initiated that kiss, or had she? He still didn't know. And while it had been shocking to have her ask about Lainey, it had brought home the fact that he'd had two failed relationships and didn't want to risk a third. So that kiss could not happen again.

He actually hadn't seen Georgia since then. She'd been up to see Edna—the woman had gushed about how much she loved the ER doc and had made her into almost a superhero who had single handedly saved her life. He had to admit, she wasn't wrong. Georgia had put her butt on the line and risked having a complaint lodged by Ronny Mueller. Although, at this point, Eli couldn't see that happening, since it was obvious that the other doctor had made the wrong choice when recommending Edna be discharged with a change of meds.

Speaking of Mueller, Eli hadn't seen him either, even when he'd been called down to the ER by one of the other doctors who worked there. Unfortunately none of those patients had been the one that Georgia had told him about when she'd first come back to Anchorage Memorial, and he'd been actively looking for that name to come up. It hadn't. He could only hope that her symptoms had either died down or she'd sought the advice of another doctor.

Maybe Mueller had left for his vacation a week earlier than planned. That wouldn't be such a bad thing.

Shaking off those thoughts, he headed on his morning rounds, his first visit being Edna. The steroids seemed to be working. Edna's breathing had eased, and while she still needed oxygen, an MRI this morning showed less inflammation in the myocardium than the previous scan.

Knocking on the door, he entered and smiled when he saw that Edna was actually sitting in the recliner while Artie lounged on the bed.

"I just couldn't stay lying down any longer," she said. "My butt hurt."

"Hurt how?" Pressure sores were always a worry when patients were in one spot for too long, but according to her chart, Edna had been shifted every two hours just like protocol dictated, and when he glanced at it again, there was no mention of anything that would indicate the beginnings of a bed sore.

"It's nothing. I was just tired of lying down."

"But there's no deep pain anywhere?"

Edna laughed. "You mean like my son? He's been hovering over me ever since he got here. He went for a coffee, so he's out of my hair for a while. He didn't want me to move from the bed to the chair, even though the nurses gave the okay yesterday."

Eli smiled but tracked back to what she'd said about pain. "I just want to make sure you're not getting a pressure sore."

"Oh." Her face cleared. "No. I had one of those ages ago when I had pneumonia. It was not fun. No, this pain is nothing like when that started. The weird thing was when that sore was at its worst, it no longer hurt."

That was because pressure sores destroyed the nerves as they worsened, so patients often had no idea how bad things were until someone actually looked at the area.

"You're still getting bed baths?"

"Yes. Because no one will clear me for an actual shower."

He walked over and laid a hand on her shoulder. "Remember what I said about needing to rest? This is part of the not-so-fun part of that. But you really do need to take it easy in order to let your heart muscle heal." When a look of horror came across her face, he was quick to add, "That doesn't mean it'll be months before you can shower. We just want to take it slow and easy."

He made a note in her chart to have the nurse look for signs of a pressure wound when Edna was bathed next. Just in case.

"Okay."

"Did Dr. Sumter come by today?"

Artie hopped off the bed.

"Yes, she just left a few minutes ago," Edna said. "She was actually the one who suggested Weston go for coffee. She could see how worried he was and how frustrated I was getting. She made sure I made it from the bed to the chair without a problem."

Of course she had. But he was glad that someone had been there for that first solo transfer. "And your breathing was okay with the exertion?"

"I'm still on this tube stuff, but yes, it was okay. How much longer will I need oxygen?"

"Until your levels are within normal limits without the supplemental oxygen. They're getting closer. We've already weaned you down from one hundred percent oxygen to seventy-five."

Artie spoke up. "I'm only asking because Edna has been pestering me to—any idea when we can fly home?"

"I'm hoping by the end of the week, when we finish the steroids. I've been keeping your cardiologist apprised of your progress, and once we set up a discharge date, he's offered to clear a spot in his appointments so that you can go straight from the airport to his office just to make sure the flight wasn't too much of a strain on you. You can't walk through the terminal, though—you'll need to be wheeled to the gate."

He had to admit he was going to miss having her as a patient. She was funny, and yet she didn't dismiss his suggestions, even when she might not like them.

Her husband smiled. "Edna's already talking about coming back to visit. She likes what she can see of Anchorage from the window of her hospital room."

"Yes. I want to see a moose."

Eli's brows went up. "They're not quite as romantic as they might seem." He thought back to that day in the park with Georgia and how it had brought back memories of their times there. That moose encounter had been one of several. Fortunately none of them had resulted in an animal charging them.

One of the nurses popped her head in. "We have an air ambulance with two patients touching down from

Dutch Harbor. ETA for the squad to get here is about ten minutes."

Dutch Harbor was part of Unalaska in the Aleutians, and air ambulances—when weather conditions permitted—carried patients to an airstrip near Anchorage Memorial. "Cardiac involvement?"

Eli had treated fishermen from the island from time to time who complained of chest pain or who were actively having a heart attack, but it wasn't an everyday occurrence. Usually the ER staff met the patient at the door and did the preliminary triage before calling in a specialist.

"From what I understand a young adult tried to jump from a rooftop onto a trampoline and missed, hitting his head on the side," the nurse said. "He's been unconscious since it happened. And when his father arrived on the scene and saw what had happened, he started having severe chest pains. They asked if you could meet the ER doctor out there since they're short-staffed today. Mueller is out sick."

Ah, so the man hadn't left for vacation early after all. "Okay, I'll head down there."

He made sure Edna was comfortable before he left, asking her to have one of the nurses there when she decided to get back on the bed. Artie was staying in the room with his wife. He wasn't sure where the son was staying, but probably in one of the local hotels. Despite what Edna had said, it sounded like their son was a caring individual and would make sure the couple got any help they needed once they arrived back in Florida.

Eli took the elevator down to the ground floor and headed to the ER, which was busy. Not good if they were short-staffed.

Georgia met him in the hallway. "Thanks for coming. There are just two doctors in, and we're backed up already this morning. The medevac team evidently had a hairy ride to Anchorage, since the winds on the island weren't cooperating."

He heard the sound of a siren, and she visibly tensed. "I hope to hell that's the EMT transport from the airstrip rather than another emergency on top of everything."

Two minutes later the truck pulled up and the driver jumped out. "We've got Ted Parker, the possible heart-attack victim here. The medevac team said he passed out in transit despite the treatment and his EKG is all over the place."

Georgia frowned. "And the other patient?"

"They should be here any minute. They're having to be careful. Suspected spinal involvement in addition to the head injury."

"Got it," she said.

They unloaded the first patient, and Eli noted the bluish tint to the man's lips and nails. Something was definitely going on. His heart wasn't getting enough oxygenated blood to his body. "Let's get him inside."

"Good luck," Georgia said. "I'll wait here for the head-injury patient."

"Sounds good." Eli could only hope things were better than they sounded.

They got the patient into an exam room first so he could at least get a handle on what was happening. "How long's he been like this?" he asked the EMT.

"About five hours. The air-ambulance team said he got progressively worse in the three hours the team was in the air. They were having to work on both the patients at once."

Not the best-case scenario, but sometimes it was unavoidable.

"Okay—thanks."

Thankfully the ER was ready for them, and they got the patient shifted from the EMT's gurney to the one in the room, and Lauren and another nurse came in to hook up leads for an EKG. As soon as he saw the tracing he knew they were going to have to act fast if they hoped to save the man. "I want to get him up to Imaging. Can you call ahead and let them know I have a patient who needs a CT coronary angiogram?"

"I'll call." Lauren left the room, and he helped the other nurse take off the leads so they could move him.

An orderly came in, and he and Eli rushed the patient to the elevator. The sooner they got him upstairs the better.

The patient was still unconscious, and so they got him into the imaging department, where they were just finishing up with another patient. But it didn't take long, and soon they had the dye injected and Ted put into the CT machine.

Eli went into the control room, where a tech sat, to watch as the images appeared on the screen, and within five minutes, he saw the issue. There was a major blockage in two of the arteries that supplied the heart. Almost completely shut. Damn.

"Too big for catheterization?" the tech asked.

"It's right on the border. I want to try that first, though, before jumping to bypass surgery. Let's get him out."

While he waited for them to finish up, he called to see if there was a surgical suite available, wondering how Georgia's patient was faring. But there was no time to call and ask.

Fortunately there was a room available. If the stent didn't work, they were going to have to crack his chest and do a bypass. He called up to the cardiac unit and asked them to send some of the team in for the catheterization and to call for the rest to be on standby in case a more invasive procedure was needed.

Within twenty minutes, Ted was in the operating room and Eli had made the cut in the groin that would give him access to the vessel needed. Watching the screen, he slowly advanced the catheter, making his way to the arteries that supplied the heart. When he got to the first blockage, his jaw tightened. It was going to be tricky. But it was worth a try.

If all went well, they would put the stent in place and then use a balloon to expand it, pushing the blockage against the walls of the artery.

The hard part was getting the stent through the

blockage. Calculating the best placement, he worked the catheter through, got it into place and then put the stent where it needed to be.

"Okay, inflating the balloon now." He watched the monitor until the stent was fully expanded. As soon as it was in place, he saw an immediate increase in blood flow through the vessel to the heart. A sense of relief filled him. He'd done the hardest vessel first because if Ted was going to need a bypass, he'd rather know now than wait until the second stent was ready to go and realize it wasn't going to work.

"We got it," he said. "Now let's go on to the second one."

It took less time to place a stent into the second blocked vessel, and that one was also a success. He withdrew the catheter, noting the cyanosis was already markedly improved.

"Let's call that a success. Thanks, everyone." He talked to one of the surgical nurses. "Liz, can you call and let them know I won't need the bypass team right now? Thanks." He handed the catheter to one of the other nurses. "I'm going to close the entry site, and then we'll get him up to Cardiac ICU for observation."

Hopefully during that time Ted would wake up. Seeing his child seriously injured had certainly precipitated the cardiac crisis, but it had also probably saved his life. If he hadn't been treated now, in a few short months he might have had a full-blown heart attack and not made it to Anchorage in time to survive.

Eli hoped the son was faring well too, although he didn't know the state of the young man's injuries.

By the time Ted was settled into a room in the cardiac-intensive-care area, he was beginning to come to. An ultrasound had shown that blood flow had been returned to the heart, although they still weren't certain how much tissue damage there'd been. A blood test had shown elevated enzymes that indicated some damage. Whether that damage was temporary or permanent was still to be seen.

Eli leaned over the bed. "Ted, can you hear me?"

The man nodded, his eyes coming up to meet Eli's. Grizzled cheeks spoke of a life lived outside in the elements, and he thought he remembered hearing that the man was a fisherman. That occupation in Alaska was not without dangers of its own, and he could see how the stress of a dangerous job might have contributed to Ted's heart condition. And he might have to make some major life changes in the future.

"M-My son?" The words were weak, but Eli understood what he was asking.

"I haven't heard anything yet, but he's getting the best care possible."

"Substance..." The rest of the words were too low to hear, but a flicker of alarm went through him.

"Does he have a substance-abuse history?"

The man nodded. "Heroin. In treatment."

Eli wasn't sure if the medevac team had this information or not, but it was important. "Okay, I'll make sure his doctors know that. Hang tight here while I make a phone call."

He bypassed the desk and took a chance that Georgia's cell-phone number was the same as it had been three years ago. He frowned at the fact that the number was still saved in his own phone, but it was more due to neglect of keeping up with those types of things than due to any hope of reconciling with her.

She answered on the second ring. "Hello?"

"Are you still treating the medevac patient?"

"He's getting an MRI right now. It doesn't look good, though. Possible brain bleed, and there's no pain response in any of his limbs."

"Fractured cervical vertebrae?"

"Yes. C3."

"Damn."

"That's what I said when I saw it."

He sighed. "I hate to add to your worries, but his father just woke up and says the son is in treatment for a heroin addiction."

"Oh, no. Is he off it?"

"Not sure. The dad is still too weak to communicate clearly. Can you call Dutch Harbor and see if you can find out any information? It might make a difference if he's going to go through withdrawals. And jumping off a roof… It could be either a stupid stunt, or he could have been high at the time. I'm guessing he wasn't in a residential treatment center, or it's doubtful he would have been home."

"Agreed," Georgia said. "I'll see if I can find out. I'm not even sure if the kid's mom is in the picture."

"Yeah, I didn't get any information on that either. I'm going to guess not, since we haven't heard from any relatives," he said.

"Okay, I'll let you know."

Georgia sounded exhausted. If the busy ER was any indication, she was probably run off her feet, and although a neuro team had likely taken over the son's case, Eli knew her well enough to know that she would follow the young man's progress as much as she could.

"Hey," he said, trying to catch her before she hung up.

"Yes?"

"Are you okay?"

"I think so. He's just so damn young. Just nineteen. There's no guarantee he'll even pull through, and if he does and if his cord has been severed or compromised, he may be paralyzed for the rest of his life. How's his father doing?"

"I just got done placing two stents. He's stable, but the jury is still out on how much permanent damage his heart has sustained."

"Okay. Keep me updated."

"I will. You too on the son."

"Will do. Bye, Eli."

She disconnected, and he stood there for a few minutes holding the phone, realizing how ridiculous it was to have thought they could work in the same hospital without ever interacting with each other. If she'd been in another department, say Oncology, it would've probably worked. But the ER was the heart of the hospital—it pulled patients through its doors and then pumped them out to whichever department was necessary to continue treatment. So of course he was going to see or hear from her on a regular basis.

But they'd just communicated without any problem. That was a good sign, right? They'd been professional, and there hadn't been any hint of anything happening under the surface. At least on her end. On his, however, the second he'd heard her voice his nerves had taken a hit and his heart rate had sped up. He'd been in no hurry to end the call. She'd done it instead. Not good. But if they remained at this level, he could handle it. As long as she didn't show any romantic interest in him.

You mean like that kiss?

That has been an anomaly. Nothing like that had happened since then. And it probably never would again. If Lainey suddenly came back to the hospital, there'd be no chance of them getting back together. So if Eli just treated Georgia like he would Lainey there would be no problems.

Except she wasn't Lainey, and from what he'd seen, she hadn't left him for another man. She'd left because she didn't want to commit to marriage or to him for the long term. And while that should have provided him with some level of comfort, it never really had.

Well, it was doing no good to stand here trying to figure out how things were going to go between them in the future. He needed to get back to his patients—Ted and the rest of them, including Edna. But it looked like Ted was going to make it anyway. That was something worth celebrating. Then he would hope that Ted's son would do better than expected with his injuries. And that his mind could stop dwelling on Georgia every time they interacted. Because down that path lay nothing good.

CHAPTER SEVEN

BRANDON TEETERED ON a precipice. His condition was so precarious that no one talked in terms of the future. Everything right now was measured in minute-by-minute increments. Twenty-four hours after being admitted, his team had still been dealing with multiple concerns. The most troubling was bleeding on the brain. If it continued, they'd have to make a hard decision about whether to remove a section of his skull to relieve the pressure and hope that it would soon let up. Because the bleed was deep in the brain and surgery was not looking promising.

Another complication was that the fractured vertebra was pressing on the spinal cord. If it had been severed, survival would have been less likely as breathing would have been compromised. But even without being completely severed, if they couldn't knock down the swelling and inflammation, he was still in danger of paralysis below the neck, and if it got bad enough, he might need to remain on a ventilator for the rest of his life.

As for his heroin addiction, they were trying to balance his meds so that he didn't go into full-blown relapse. And right now, he was in a medically induced coma to try to manage all of that. The question was whether or not he would ever wake up or regain normal brain function after such a traumatic injury.

Time would tell. But it was hard knowing that if Brandon died, his dad would be alone in the world. Ted's wife had died of cancer when his son had been just entering his teens. It had evidently played a part in his drug addiction.

Georgia couldn't imagine the heartache of Ted losing both his wife and his only child. It was incomprehensible.

Her shift had already ended for the day, but for some reason she found herself hanging around, just in case they needed her.

For what? What could she do that the best specialists in Alaska couldn't do?

She took out her butterfly charm and twirled it between her fingers as if it held some kind of healing power. But in reality it didn't. It was just a reminder of something that didn't seem to matter at the moment.

How much more heartache would it be for Ted if his son's brain function was severely damaged? He might not simply be confined to a wheelchair but unable to feed himself or communicate. What if Ted had to care for him for the rest of his life? And having a heart condition himself, she could imagine him worrying about what would happen to Brandon if he had a heart attack and died.

She hadn't heard from Eli since yesterday's phone

call, and it bothered her that she kind of hoped he would call her today as well, if only to give her an update on Ted or Edna.

But she'd seen Edna earlier today, and she was doing well. In fact they were getting ready to fly out of Alaska the day after tomorrow. Ted had made it through his surgery, and Eli had said he expected the man to make a full recovery. So what would he even be calling her about? Just to say hi? To say he missed her?

Gah! The one thing she did not want to do was start hoping for that. Doing so would put her back on a road that had dead-ended three years ago. She already knew what was at the end of it, so why was she still hoping to talk to him?

She had no idea. It had to be the good memories of the past that were leaving her so unsettled. If she could focus on how their relationship had ended, it would be better for both of them. But how did you do that when your emotions were craving just the opposite? She had played that kiss in Knicker Park over and over in her head, trying to remember every nuance and sensation, fearful that it would just disappear if she didn't. Especially since she didn't think it would ever happen again. She was pretty sure Eli was a whole lot stronger than she was in that area and wouldn't be caught off guard a second time.

Georgia could only hope that she could do the same. Because she'd come to the conclusion that *she'd* initiated that kiss. She remembered staring at his mouth and tilting her head to an angle that…that what? Would give her the most satisfaction?

Yes.

And if she did it once, wasn't she more likely to do it again? Or at least want to?

Because she did want to, even now. No matter how high the price. How pitiful did that make her?

It had to be her libido. She hadn't been in a relationship for the last three years, so her body was craving something that her mind said she shouldn't have. At least not with this man. So was she planning on being celibate the rest of her life?

No. But as hard as it was to have sex without the relationship part, surely there were ways around that. If she knew that Eli wouldn't expect more down the line, it could even be with him. After all, Georgia knew they were compatible in that area. More than compatible. In fact she'd never had better.

In her heart of hearts, though, she knew it wouldn't be fair. Knew that he would want the deeper emotional intimacy that went along with the physical part. And she couldn't give that to him.

Her cell phone chirped, and her whole body went tight with anticipation. She dropped the butterfly back into her shirt before looking at her phone. Then she frowned. It wasn't Eli. It was one of the hospital's internal numbers.

Probably just calling to give her an update on Brandon.

"Hello?"

"Hi. Dr. Sumter? This is Terri Kinsley. I'm one of the nurses in the neuro ward."

Ah, so it was an update. "How's our guy doing?"

There was a pause. A heavy one, and she suddenly knew what was going to be at the end of that pause. Her heart went still for a moment.

"I'm sorry, but Brandon passed away a few minutes ago. Despite decompression surgery, we weren't able to get the bleeding in his brain to abate. Between that and the continued swelling…" There was another pause. "And his spinal cord was severely compromised. It was doubtful he would ever have regained use of his body below his shoulders, and—"

"I get it. He's gone. Thank you for letting me know." She ended the call knowing she'd been abrupt, but the sudden rush of tears made her fearful she'd start sobbing over the phone, something that was neither professional nor helpful to anyone. It wouldn't change the outcome. Nothing would.

Sitting on a bench in the hospital courtyard, she swiped at the moisture on her face, irritated at herself while mourning the news Ted would soon be hearing. It wasn't fair. Neither was life, though. Her mom had not deserved what her husband had put her through. Neither had Georgia. And yet it had happened.

She bowed her head, cupping her hands on either side of her temples to hide her sudden emotional meltdown from anyone passing by. She'd hoped he would make it. Had hoped Ted, at least, would get a happy ending. At nineteen, Brandon had had his whole life ahead of him. He could have beaten his addiction, had a wife, kids, provided hope for his dad, who'd already lived through one loss. Now Ted had another to contend with.

She squeezed her eyes shut, trying to get control of herself. But another tear plopped onto the ground, despite doing her best to hold them in.

A hand laid on her shoulder, and she stiffened. God. She didn't want someone she didn't know asking her what was wrong.

"Georgia..."

She recognized that deep voice, could picture the face that went along with it.

Glancing up, knowing her chin was wobbling and her eyes were not only wet but probably red as well. "He died, Eli. Brandon died."

"I know. I just got the call and came to find you." He dropped down onto the bench beside her. "I hoped he'd make it too." He tipped her face up and used his thumb to dry the area under one of her eyes.

"I—I just can't believe it. I knew it was a long shot, knew in my heart he probably wouldn't make it." She shook her head. "But I wanted it for him. So much. Isn't that crazy? I didn't even know him. Never talked to him. I don't even know what color his eyes were."

"Not crazy at all." He looked at her face, and there was a long pause. "Are you working tomorrow?"

"No. I have the day off." She sucked down a breath. "God. I am such a mess, and I'm not sure why."

"Listen, I have a cabin about forty-five minutes outside of Anchorage. Do you want to go there just to get your mind off of things for a while? I can give you the keys, and you can—"

"I don't think I can go there alone. Not when all I'll be able to think about is—"

"How about if I go with you? If you think that would help. Or do you just want to go home?"

She didn't. It was probably one of the reasons she'd hung around the hospital. She did her best to remain objective when she did her job, but every once in a while a patient came along and got under her skin. Both Edna and Brandon had done that.

"No, I don't want to go home either. The cabin sounds nice, if you can spare the time away." She wasn't even sure why she was agreeing to him going with her. But she really didn't want to be alone.

"I don't have anything pressing right now. Ted is out of danger, although he hasn't been told about his son yet. That can happen later tomorrow, when he's stronger."

Tears welled up all over again. "That poor man. First his wife and now his son."

"I know. But all we can do is be there for him. Or call someone who can."

"Yes." She glanced at him. "Are you sure about the cabin?"

"I am. We can leave right from here if you want."

Her shoulders relaxed. "Thank you. I have a change of clothes in my locker. Let me just grab them, then I'll be ready."

Eli stood and held out his hand, and unlike in the park, this time she accepted his offer. "I'll let the staff in my unit know where I'll be and meet you in the parking lot. If you get there before me, it's a white SUV."

As opposed to the sleek black sports car he'd had back when she'd known him? A heavier vehicle made a lot more sense for Alaska anyway, although she'd liked the other vehicle. Especially the time they'd parked on a plot of land he owned and…

No. Don't think about that.

Trying not to dwell on Brandon, or things in the past that she couldn't change, Georgia headed toward the staff lounge and pulled out the tote from her locker that held an extra set of clothes. She was feeling shaky and slightly sick with the turmoil of emotions she'd been dealing with after hearing the news of Brandon's passing. Maybe the cabin would give her a chance to reset and push away the deep sense of melancholy that was cloaking her like one of those weighted blankets. Except those blankets were meant to instill the user with a sense of security and warmth, and this felt nothing like that. This felt suffocating, like she couldn't draw a deep breath. So she'd let Eli take her to the cabin, where her mind could dwell on things other than death. Or loss. Or things that nothing could change.

Eli waited beside his car. He wasn't sure why he'd offered to let Georgia go to his cabin. Or worse, why he'd offered to go there with her. He had no explanation other than the fact that she seemed so broken over the fact that Ted's son had died. Eli was sad too, but at least his patient had made it, and that helped balance any sorrow he might have felt. Taking her to the Valley with him probably wasn't his smartest move, but what else could he do? It wasn't like they were going there for some kind of liaison that would end with them in bed.

It was just a neutral place where Georgia could decompress a little bit and try to get her emotions back under control. Everyone who worked in a hospital setting found themselves needing that from time to time. Not everyone owned a cabin, but almost everyone had a place they could go to to pull themselves together—even if that place was a just a spot in their own home.

Eli could at least give Georgia a spot like that. He knew how much she hated to lose control in a public place. She liked to be fully in command of her emotions at all times. But sometimes that just wasn't possible. It wasn't that Eli lost his cool in public, but he had his office, where he could go when he needed privacy at work. Like when Georgia had left him holding that little ring box. The ring had been as much an impulse buy as the proposal that went with it had been.

He hadn't saved the ring. Hadn't wanted anything that reminded him of what had happened, so he'd talked to Steve, who had offered to find a couple in need who were getting married. He had and had gifted the ring to them. This couple was in the Big Brothers Big Sisters program, something Steve had gotten involved with after he and his wife had been ready to retire from their foster parent duties—which had been pretty soon after Eli had graduated from college. He'd often joked with his mentor that fostering him had made Steve realize how tough that gig was. But Steve had been kind, just as he'd always been, and said that he'd wanted to go out on a high note.

Georgia came out of the building carrying some kind of flowery canvas bag. It must've contained the change of clothes she'd talked about. Seeing her made him wonder again what the hell he thought he was doing. Going to a cabin where it was just going to be the two of them? That seemed like behavior of a crazy man.

But he had to remember this was to help Georgia. And because she hadn't wanted to go alone. He hadn't had the heart to sit there in silence, especially after seeing how hard Brandon's death had been on her.

He opened the back door for her and let her put her things in. "Do you mind if we stop by the grocery store for supplies? The cabin is off-grid, so I don't keep the refrigerator running when I'm not there." Fortunately, they'd had several days of sunlight, so his solar panels should have charged his batteries fully.

"It's fine."

"Anything in particular you want?"

"Coffee?"

"You got it." While he was there he could pick up a couple of steaks and some things for breakfast in the morning. He didn't imagine they'd spend more than just a day there, and he had an extra cooler up there that he could use to transport any leftovers back to his place.

Eli pulled into the big local grocery store. “I’ll just be a minute…unless you want to come in.”

She glanced at him through the big sunglasses she’d put on. He wasn’t sure if they were because she was still weepy or because of the sun. But whatever it was, he couldn’t read her expression and found that he didn’t like that. “Do you mind if I just wait in the car?”

“Not at all. See you in a few minutes.”

Getting out of the car, he headed up to the store.

Fifteen minutes later, he had everything, including some hot chocolate. Even though it was warm outside, the nights could be cool, and she might want to sit out by the fire pit once it was dark enough—not that they had many hours when the sun wasn’t in the sky this time of year. But Georgia had always loved hot chocolate the few times they’d gone camping.

After he got back into his vehicle, they headed down the road.

“Where is your cabin?” she asked. Her head was tilted back against the headrest, and she looked exhausted. Or lost. Or maybe a little bit of both.

Something in his heart shifted. A protective instinct that he had always had with her, for some reason. She was a perfectly capable, strong human being, but every once in a while he’d spotted a fragility in her that he hadn’t quite understood. Kind of like one he’d spotted today. The one that had made him offer her the use of his cabin.

"It's actually in Mat-Su Valley. You were there once. The land didn't have anything built on it at the time."

Her head jerked toward him. "You mean…?"

"I'm afraid so. Do you still want to go?" He remembered every second of making love to her there when he'd still had his other car. It was part of the reason he'd gotten rid of the thing.

"There's a cabin there now, right?"

He wasn't sure what that had to do with anything. "Yes. Steve helped build it."

"You guys built it? On your own?" That seemed to shift her away from what had happened there.

He nodded. "We got some help setting up the solar array, but other than that, yeah." He smiled. "It's not very fancy, so don't get your hopes up. It has a well, so there's running water, but it's powered by solar panels." It only had one bedroom, but he did have a couch that converted into a bed, so he'd figured he'd sleep there.

"It sounds wonderful. That land was beautiful, from what I remember of it." She paused and then continued. "How is Steve anyway?"

Georgia already knew his whole life story, so she knew that he'd been raised in foster homes and that Steve and his wife had been his saving grace.

"He's doing good. Still doing the Big Brothers Big Sisters stuff."

Eli wanted to ask how Georgia's mom was, but she'd

always been a pretty private person, which he hadn't found odd when they'd been dating for some reason. He knew where she'd grown up and that her mom was basically her only living relative, but as far as how her life had been as a child, he'd been pretty much in the dark, other than the fact that her mother had raised her single-handedly.

"That's wonderful. Does he ever go and stay in the cabin?"

"Every once in a while. But he's more of a homebody, so he'd rather just stay at home with his wife, unless it's their anniversary or something."

"But you evidently go there?"

"Whenever I can. I love it out there. It's peaceful and quiet and on ten acres, so there aren't other cabins right on top of mine."

"It sounds like heaven."

It hadn't been right after Georgia had left him, and the memory of them making love out there had almost spoiled the property for him. But he'd decided to build the cabin anyway, thinking he could sell it if he still felt the same way in a year or two. Surprisingly, the building process had somehow numbed the pain. Brandon had turned to drugs, while Eli had turned to sweat and hard work. Two months later, his cabin had been born. A place where he could go lick his wounds in private, and hell if he hadn't needed that during the six months that had followed his breakup. He'd only surfaced to go to work and do what needed to get done. Sometimes he still did that: escaped whatever hard case he'd been working on, using the cabin as a place of solace and time to recharge his emotional batteries. It worked, and he doubted he would ever get rid of the place now.

"I like it. It gives me time to be alone."

As soon as he said the words he regretted them, hoping that Georgia didn't take them to mean that he was sorry he'd offered the place to her.

Instead she nodded. "I completely get that. It's why I've always liked Knicker Park. I used to jog there. I may start up again. I saw that the hospital has a 5K coming up. That might give me a goal to look forward to."

The last summer she'd been here, they'd run that race together, even though running had never really been his thing. It had been a lot of fun, though, when she'd been there with him. And afterward at his place… He closed his mind off to thoughts about what had come after, knowing it wasn't a smart idea to reminisce about things like making love when that was not what they were headed there to do. It would only make the stay awkward and difficult, especially if she guessed the reasons behind his discomfort.

He didn't want to make her feel uncomfortable. Besides, this wasn't about him. It was about Georgia, and he'd do well to keep his mind on that fact and not let it retrace avenues that were best left in the past.

"The park is the perfect place to do that." Eli hoped she wouldn't ask him to join her in training for the race. Because he couldn't do it. Not anymore.

Even the thought of spending time with her at the cabin, when there wasn't any work to keep his mind occupied, was seeming more and more like the worst choice ever. But there was no going back and undoing it. Trying to get out of it at this point in time would mean driving all the way back to the hospital and letting her drive herself to the cabin. At this point he doubted she would even go, and from the look of her, she needed this time. And he wasn't going to do anything to take that away from her. Even if it meant he was going to have to deal with a little discomfort.

CHAPTER EIGHT

GEORGIA GOT OUT of the car, a sense of amazement coming to her. When they'd traversed the track leading to the cabin, she hadn't been able to see much besides a rutted path that made her wonder if they would even make it. And there was absolutely nowhere to turn around. They'd have to back up, and with the brush scrubbing the sides of the vehicle, she didn't quite think that was going to happen. What happened if the conditions were so bad that he got halfway and got stuck?

No wonder he'd traded his sports car in for an SUV. And honestly, this vehicle seemed to suit him much better.

When she glanced at Eli, he was staring at her. Was her hair sticking up at an odd angle or something? "What?"

"Just waiting for you to say something. You held on to that armrest with a death grip the whole way down the driveway."

"It didn't make you nervous?"

"What? My driving?"

She laughed. "No, of course not. There's just not

much room for error down that driveway. What if we'd gotten stuck?"

"There hasn't been much rain and the vehicle has four-wheel drive, so that wasn't likely. But I agree that I need to do a little work clearing it back again. I just haven't had time this year. Sorry you came?"

She looked again at the cabin, and some of the horror and sorrow of today seemed to melt away. "Oh, no. Not at all. This is beautiful."

When he'd said it was a cabin, she'd pictured some kind of stick-built structure with siding. Kind of like a smaller version of a house…or more of a shed-type building. But this was nothing like that. The outside walls were made of hewn logs that interlocked on the corners, kind of like those building blocks she'd had as a kid. In contrast to the cabin, the door was painted a sleek turquoise color that made it stand out from the natural color of the logs, something she couldn't imagine Eli choosing for himself.

She glanced at him. "I like your door color. It's so…you."

He grinned, the sideways tilt making him look boyish and carefree, like the man she'd once known. Her heart swelled. She was glad he had someplace like this he could run to in hard times.

"The color was actually Julia's—Steve's wife's—idea. It used to be brown, but she said in the dark it was hard to find the entrance and asked if I'd mind if they painted it. The next time I came up, it was that bluish-green color. It's not something that I would have chosen, but I actually do like it now that I'm used to it. And the door is definitely easier to find in the dark."

"It fits the place perfectly. It looks like something out of a magazine, actually."

Nestled in a little clearing, there were still big pine trees around the cabin, but the spot wasn't crammed full of brush and other plants. It looked like the place had been here for hundreds of years. She vaguely remembered the land itself from the time he'd brought her here, and it had been wild and beautiful, even then. But now? It was something most people only dreamed of having.

"You said you built this place?" she said.

This time when he looked at her, there was a darker air to his face, his smile fading away. "Yes. A couple of years ago."

A couple. As in two? Or…three? Had he built this in the aftermath of their breakup? Somehow the thought of that made her incredibly sad. But then again, at least he'd put whatever emotions he'd had about what had happened into something he'd be able to use over and over again. And what had she done? Bought a silly butterfly charm.

The piece of jewelry seemed to burn against her skin, and she put her hand there for a second. It hadn't seemed silly at the time, though, and it had served as a reminder of why she'd done what she had. And Eli had gotten married again a year later, so he hadn't been that torn up, evidently. He'd moved on and been happy again. At least for a while.

Georgia was beginning to wonder if she ever had. Because right now, it seemed as if she were stuck in some kind of twilight that was neither night nor day. A kind of limbo where the days seemed to run together. Kind of like the deep summer of Alaska, when the dividing line between days wasn't always clear. People talked about the difference between night and day, but sometimes the contrast wasn't as stark as that. Sometimes it was just a kind of gray that had little to delineate it from what came before or after.

Like a brown door on a brown cabin? Where one element seemed to merge with whatever was around it? Was that what her life had become?

She realized Eli was waiting for some kind of response. So she blurted out the first thing she could think of. "I bet Lainey loved this cabin."

Oh, God. What a thing for her to have said. Especially since Eli and his wife were no longer together.

"She actually wasn't the biggest fan of the place."

Her eyes widened. "What? Why?"

He shrugged, face hardening. "I'm sure she had her reasons."

Georgia couldn't imagine anyone not falling in love with a place like this. "Okay, tell the truth. Did she decide she wasn't a fan before the turquoise door or after?" She wasn't sure if her attempt to lighten the moment was in the best taste, so she added, "I'm sorry, Eli. I shouldn't have brought her up."

"It's okay. Our relationship has been over for a while. I'm surprised William told you about it at all, actually."

"He didn't tell me much. Only that you'd gotten married and to whom." And Georgia could remember that moment like it had been branded onto her heart. Lainey. The woman who'd seemed to lick her lips whenever she'd looked at Eli. That was probably an exaggeration, but still…

A little part of her had imagined that he'd go on like she had, with no significant other anywhere in the picture. The fact that he'd fallen in love again—and with Lainey of all people—had been a cut that had never quite healed. She kept telling herself that she wanted him to be happy, but…had she really? Or had she wanted him to suffer after the breakup like she'd suffered. Except she'd been the cause of all that angst, not him.

"I see." He opened the rear passenger door of the car and got her tote bag out as well as the few bags of groceries he'd purchased. "Are you ready to go in?"

"I am." Anything to derail her thoughts and to change the topic of conversation. Which, of course, she'd been the one to initiate. Again.

She spotted a fire ring a short distance from the cabin along with a covered three-sided building that housed an impressive supply of firewood. "Do you think we could have a fire? Or is this not the right time of year?"

"It should be fine," he said. "While it's dried up some, we did have some rain a couple of weeks ago. Plus I have the firepit set up with a large area of sand around it, so there's not much chance of the fire spreading. We can even cook our dinner over it if that sounds good to you."

"It sounds amazing. Thank you for bringing me here," she said. "I think I really needed this. I'm not sure why Brandon's death hit me so hard—maybe it was just because of all the loss that Ted has been through. I hope he's going to be okay."

"Me too. I hope he'll be able to channel his grief into something that will help him in the future."

Like this cabin? Was that what Eli had done—channeled his grief over their breakup into something that would help him in the future? He'd confirmed that he hadn't built it after his marriage had broken up, because he'd said his ex-wife hadn't been a fan of the cabin. So it meant he'd built it sometime between his and Georgia's breakup and his marriage to Lainey. But whenever it was, she was glad he had it, hoped he would keep this place for the rest of his life. She knew if she had something similar, she would use it as often as she could. And it sounded like he did.

"I hope he will too. Even if Brandon had survived he probably wouldn't have been the same," she said.

"No. He probably wouldn't have been the same."

Something about the way Eli said that made her glance over at him, but he'd already started walking toward the door, leaving her no choice but to follow him.

If she thought the outside of the cabin was beautiful, it was no match for the inside. Most of the walls that she could see had drywall covering them, except for the one where a wood stove sat. That one showcased the cabin's natural logs. And it fit, looking rustic and homey. There weren't a lot of windows in the main living area, but the ones the cabin did have boasted spectacular views. In the middle of the space was a worn leather couch, its overstuffed cushions looking inviting and comfortable.

"Do you come here in the winter?" she asked.

"When the roads are passable, I do," he said. "I've started taking my vacations in the winter and just holing up in the cabin for a couple of weeks. It's peaceful. And as you know the hospital can have a frenetic pace that wears you down to the bone."

"It does, but the opposite is true as well. When the pace lags too much, it can be just as hard to deal with."

The facility she'd worked at on Kodiak had been smaller, and there'd been times when she'd sat around for hours at a time with nothing to do but help straighten up the waiting room. But then she hadn't had a lot of people like Brandon come through the doors either. Oh, there'd still been drugs there, just like in most places on the planet, but smaller populations still meant fewer people came through the doors of the ER—other than with minor complaints like runny noses or sore throats. It was one of the reasons she'd come back to Anchorage.

"The hospital you worked at wasn't busy?" Eli asked.

"It could be. But we weren't the largest clinic on the island, so the most serious cases were automatically sent to main hospital."

"That makes sense."

He set the groceries on a wooden counter in the kitchen on the far side of the room, which, despite its small size, had a full-sized fridge. That made sense if, like he said, he came here for weeks at a time. It looked like the cabin was one large room. Which made her wonder what the sleeping arrangements were going to be. A tingle went through her that she tried to stop in its tracks. He hadn't brought her here for that. Besides, she'd noticed two doors. Surely one of those led to an actual bedroom. Or maybe there were two.

"What's behind those doors?" she asked.

"I'll show you." Crossing the space and leaving her to follow him, he opened the first door.

Ah, yes, so there was a bedroom. And what a bedroom it was. The bed had massive posts on each of its corners, much like the logs that made up the walls of the rooms. "Did you make that bed?"

"I did. I had some leftover wood and needed something to do with them, so…"

The headboard that connected the logs was a live-edged plank, the irregular border along the top giving it a sense of movement that no straight board could replicate. "I love it." She glanced at the walls, which were devoid of pictures or artwork, but there was a large rug covering much of the plank flooring. "Hmm…no moose antlers anywhere? I thought that was a requirement of every cabin in the woods."

"I've never been much of a hunter, although I do enjoy the moose or elk jerky I can buy at the local mom-and-pop grocery," he said. "We'll look at the trail camera and see what kind of visitors we've had, if you want."

"I'd love that." Her mind put to ease about the sleeping arrangements, since she assumed she would bunk on the couch, she asked about the other door.

"It's a bathroom," he said.

"So no outhouse?"

He laughed. "Actually, there is one. I tend to use it during the winter, when I can get to it."

"What? Why on earth would you do that?" The idea of tramping out to another building in the snow didn't sound like very much fun.

"It's actually not that bad. Remember I told you the cabin is off-grid? That means I'm not hooked up to the city's sewage system, and getting the land surveyed for a septic tank seemed like a lot of trouble. So the toilet in the cabin is a composting one."

"Interesting." She wasn't sure if she was telling the truth or not about that, but she was game to try it. And the cabin didn't smell like anything except for the warm scent of wood, so it must've worked pretty well.

He opened the door to the bathroom, and it was actually surprising. The countertop was polished wood, like in the kitchen, but there were faucets and a pretty blue bowl that served as a vessel sink. There was also a shower made up of shiny corrugated metal walls and ceiling. A rainfall shower head hung in the middle of it.

"I thought you didn't have plumbing," she said.

"I have plumbing, just not a septic tank. I have a

well and an on-demand water heater that runs off a propane tank—that tank also supplies the gas stovetop and oven. The water used for showering or washing dishes goes to a gray water–holding area that I use to water the plants, if and when needed."

Even the toilet looked clean and modern. Not a simple bench with a hole cut in it, like she'd been expecting. "You'll have to explain how to use that."

"It's not very hard, and it's a pretty efficient setup."

"I'll take your word on that," she said.

Maybe that was what his ex hadn't liked about the cabin, because everything else was perfect. More perfect than Georgia could have pictured, actually. And to get to spend time here? With this man? She couldn't imagine anything that sounded more like paradise than that.

She swallowed. Yes, it did sound like paradise. But it was a paradise that she'd been banished from due to her own neuroses. So she had no right to expect to be able to reenter it. Ever. Because when it came down to it, nothing had changed. She was still terrified of being tied down to another human being. Her fingers started to go up to her charm before she realized he was looking at her expectantly. Maybe he thought she'd be disgusted or hate the cabin like his ex-wife evidently had.

She moved toward him and touched his arm. "I love this place. It's beautiful. And peaceful. I can't imagine anything more perfect."

Except to maybe share that bed in the other room with him. Or that inviting-looking shower.

Neither of those things were an option.

"Thanks. I'm glad you like it." They left the bathroom. "Are you hungry?"

She tried to remember the last time she'd eaten. Lunch? Definitely not dinner. She glanced at her watch. Seven o'clock. Way past the time she normally ate. "I am, actually."

"Good. Let me get a fire started outside, and we'll cook our steaks out there. I have potatoes too that we can fry or wrap in foil and throw in the fire to bake."

Her mouth watered. "Baked sounds delicious and a lot less work."

"I like the way you think."

Did he? He might have at one time, but he definitely hadn't liked it on the day he'd proposed to her. She never wanted to go through anything like that again.

"Can I help with something?" she asked.

"No, I need to chop a little bit of wood, but that shouldn't take long," he said. "There are some books in those shelves over there, if you want to sit and relax for a while."

She was still feeling pretty antsy, so the thought of sitting on the couch stewing in her thoughts didn't sound like a whole lot of fun. "Do you mind if I look around outside instead?"

"Not at all—help yourself. There are a few trails if you want to explore a bit. As long as you come back the way you go, you should be fine."

She didn't really want to go on a hike by herself, so she opted to walk around the clearing area while he gathered an armful of wood from his neatly stacked pile. A few minutes later, she settled in one of the rocking chairs on the wide porch and tucked her feet underneath her and let her eyes close.

A sharp sound made them pop back open just in time to see Eli wield an axe and bring it down on a piece of wood, splitting it on the first try. He was still wearing the red polo shirt that he'd had on at the hospital, and the sleeves showed off his biceps to perfection as he chopped another log into pieces. There was something mouthwateringly attractive about a man chopping firewood. Or maybe it was just because it was Eli, but she couldn't take her eyes off him. He was gorgeous and talented and strong. And he'd once been hers.

How stupid had she been?

Pretty damned stupid. But better to end things when they had than to get married and find out that she couldn't bear having to report her comings and goings to someone or tell him how she spent her money. To let someone control her the way her dad had controlled her mom.

Eli would not have tried to control you.

She knew that. But no matter how many times she tried to convince herself that he was nothing like her father, the fear remained. A shadowy phantom that never really showed its face. At least not in a way that she could fight it. It was just a wisp of gray that materialized and then drifted away, just like the smoke from the campfire that Eli would soon be building. And she hated it. Hated that she'd allowed that fear to destroy the best thing that had ever happened to her. But better that than to destroy Eli by forcing him to live in a nightmare of her own making. And she wouldn't do that, no matter how tempted she might be to give them another chance.

A few minutes later he had the fire going and had the potatoes bundled into aluminum-foil jackets. He then seasoned the steaks and put them into a wire basket that he set on a grate over the fire. The scents were out of this world. She wandered closer and dropped into one of the Adirondack chairs that sat near the fire. "That smells so good."

"Hungry?" he asked, sending her a smile from where he knelt by the firepit.

"Yes." The one word came out, and she realized it encompassed so many things. Things that had nothing to do with the food he was cooking. She'd been hungry for the sight of him for the last three years. Hungry to have him look at her with something other than the shock and anger that she remembered from their last night together. Hungry for his touch, for his mouth on hers. To feel him deep inside of her.

She swallowed as the sense of melancholy threatened to wash away the peace she'd felt when she'd walked around the cabin. She'd messed up so many things. And there was nothing she could—or would—

do about them. It was better just to let them go and try to find a way to be friends with Eli. Surely that would be enough.

Except she wasn't sure it would be. Because leaving had never erased the feelings she had for him. It was why she'd never gone back to casual dating after their split.

She loved the man. With all of her heart. She just couldn't trust herself to be with him. Or with anyone. She closed her eyes and tried to process the emotions that had risen from the dead after being buried deep in her subconscious for the last three years.

"Are you okay?"

His words made her glance over at him again. "Yes. Just enjoying the outdoors."

A lie. Just like so many she'd told him over the years when her fears would rear their ugly head.

This time when he looked at her, there was a dark look on his face that said he didn't believe her. "What's wrong, Georgia? Is it Brandon?"

"No." She stared at him for several seconds before simply saying, "I've missed you."

There was no sound other than the sizzling of the steaks for what seemed like an eternity.

"Don't." His voice was low and gruff and filled with something she didn't understand. But it told her he didn't mean what he'd just said.

She went over and knelt down next to him. "I'm sorry. But you wanted the truth."

* * *

Did he? Eli didn't remember using those words. But now they were lodged like a spike in his gut. A spike he didn't dare pull out without risking a lot more damage.

She missed him? Somehow he'd pictured her as moving back to Kodiak, feeling a relief similar to the one he'd felt when his divorce from Lainey had been finalized. He'd pictured her going about her life with a sense of laissez-faire, while he'd been up here splitting logs and trying to forget that Georgia Sumter had ever darkened his doorway.

But he wasn't quite sure he'd ever succeeded, no matter how much sweat and backbreaking work he'd poured into this place.

Eli hesitated for a second, trying to figure out whether to brush off her words or to dive headfirst into them.

He picked up his silicone mitts and took the wire basket containing the steaks out of the fire and stood.

"W-What are you doing?"

"Come on. We're going inside."

Georgia rose to her feet. "But the potatoes..."

"Do you really want to worry about potatoes right now?"

"No." There was a breathiness to her voice that said she'd just realized exactly what he was saying. Knew exactly what was in his thoughts.

Madness. That was what was in them. Pure and

utter madness. But he couldn't get her words out of his head. They were playing over and over again.

I missed you.

Hell, he'd missed her too. Only he'd thought he'd finally gotten rid of all of that when he'd gotten together with Lainey. But maybe it had still been there. Maybe Lainey had sensed it and had been driven into his best friend's arms because of it. He knew he'd withheld part of himself from her. At the time he'd told himself that he wasn't, that he'd given Lainey all he had left to give, but looking back, it wasn't true.

He set the wire basket on a table outside the door, dropping the mitts beside it, uncaring that the juices from the meat might puddle all over everything. Right now he didn't care anything about the food, despite the fact that a half hour earlier they had both claimed to be hungry.

Pushing the front door open with his back he held out both hands to her and willed her to take them. This was the moment of truth. Either she'd backtrack and say he'd misunderstood her meaning or she'd take his hands and let him pull her inside the cabin.

The second her fingers slid across his palms, a deep shudder went through him. He tugged her against his chest, backed with her into the living room.

"Shut the door, Georgia."

When she went to pull free to do so, though, he tightened his grip, afraid if he let go she'd somehow slip from his grasp.

Maybe she sensed that because she mimicked what

he'd just done a few seconds earlier. She put her back against the door, walking him with her until the barrier shut with an audible click.

He moved in, crowding her against the wooden surface. But she didn't complain when he let go of her and pressed his palms on either side of her, bracketing her with his arms.

She leaned her head against the wood behind her and looked up at him, lips parting. God. Just like when he'd kissed her less than a week ago. That now seemed like forever.

Too long.

His head lowered, and his mouth met hers with a hard groan that spoke of how much he had missed her too. He lost himself in the sensations that came roaring back to greet him.

Home.

It was as if he'd come home after a long, long absence. And it felt so good. So damned good to be able to touch her without feeling guilty. She'd asked him to do this. It was in the way she returned his kiss, her lips moving beneath his. It was in the way her arms twined around his neck and she raised up on tiptoe to get closer to him.

Eli couldn't resist her. He never could. His body was already strung so tight, he didn't think he was going to be able to make it to the finish line. But he would give it his best shot. Reaching down, he hauled her up against that tightness, relishing the way her legs wrapped around his hips…the way her body seemed to cradle his against her.

He pressed into her, wishing their clothes were gone, wishing he could take her right against the door she'd admired when they'd first arrived.

Had that been only an hour ago? Surely not.

But right now, he didn't want to leave this place. Wanted to stay here with her for weeks, making love to her on every available surface until they were both spent. But they didn't have weeks. They only had a matter of hours.

Don't think about that. She's here. That's enough. At least for right now.

So he kissed her again before spinning her away from the door and carrying her toward the bedroom. How crazy was it that a few hours ago he'd been thinking about sleeping conditions?

He was thinking about them again, but in a completely different way. In a way that had anticipation singing through his veins. Normally his body waited until after it had gotten its satisfaction before wondering when it would happen again. But it was greedy and was already planning scenarios in every available spot on the planet. Including his office. Including his apartment. Including his heart.

No. Not that.

Taking those words off the table, he went through the bedroom door and dropped her onto the mattress. She gave a laughing screech and bounced a time or two. He gave himself a few seconds to stop and look at her, hardly able to believe Georgia was at his cabin and that he would soon be making love to her in it.

This place had been built *because* of her, not *for* her, and yet here she was. And unlike his ex, she seemed to love everything about the place.

Even him?

It was a question he didn't dare ask. Didn't want to ask because he wasn't sure it would make any difference. He'd been broken when she'd walked away from him, and it had taken a long time for him to put himself back together. But he had. And he vowed he would never give anyone that kind of power over him ever again.

Stop thinking, Eli. Start doing...

He was going to live in the moment and not worry about tomorrow or any other day.

Leaning over Georgia, he kissed her thoroughly, taking his time before reluctantly pulling away so he could undress her.

And God in heaven, how he wanted to undress her.

He tugged her up so that she was sitting, and then he pulled her gauzy white blouse over her head, noting a smudge of dirt from the fire on her left sleeve. She didn't seem too worried about dirt. She had a necklace with a butterfly that dangled almost to her breasts. He'd never noticed it before, but then again, she probably kept it out of sight when working since it could get hung up on equipment and the hospital wasn't a big fan of wearing jewelry while on the job anyway.

He kissed her again as he reached behind her to

undo the clasp on her bra, then eased it away. It was amazing how he still had every line and curve of her body memorized as if it hadn't been years since he'd seen it. Right down to the freckle she had on the side of her right breast. It was still there. Unable to stop himself, he bent over to lick it. Georgia's response was immediate. She arched up to meet his touch, and he couldn't stop himself from wrapping his arms under her back to keep her in place, moving his attention to her nipple and suckling deeply. She moaned, and it sent him into the stratosphere.

Suddenly, he couldn't get her clothes off fast enough, even though she kicked her shoes off and then lifted her hips to help him get her pants off. Then her panties, which he peeled down in slow motion, relishing the final reveal and what it meant.

For a second he stood over her, staring down. A brief moment of disbelief made him wonder if he was sleeping and this was all a dream. But then her eyes opened and she looked at him with those gorgeous green eyes, and he knew this was real. Very, very real.

She was here. In the flesh.

Still sitting, she tugged his shirt free from his pants and pushed it up his torso, the slide of her fingers along his skin making his flesh come alive. He ached. Needed more. So much more.

He yanked the shirt the rest of the way off and tossed it to the side, where it landed on top of hers. Just like the way he would soon land on top of Georgia.

His pants and briefs were soon discarded as well,

and she held her arms out to him, wordlessly asking him to come down and meet her. But he had something he needed to do first, even though it was the last thing he wanted to think about right now.

He went over to the nightstand next to the bed and retrieved a packet from the drawer and ripped it open with his teeth. She looked at him, and her eyes widened. Had she totally forgotten about it? Or did she not want him to use it?

He had to. Couldn't take the chance that whatever was happening between them could fall apart all over again. So he sheathed himself and then walked over to the bed. He nudged her knees apart and slid his palms up her thighs.

She squirmed at his touch. "Eli…"

"Shh, I just want to enjoy you." When he got to the juncture of her thighs, he covered her with the heel of his hand, pressing it against the spot that he knew was the most sensitive.

Georgia made a noise deep in her throat as he released the pressure and then repeated the act in a rhythmic motion that mimicked what he wanted to do to her. Her hips lifted to meet his every touch, and the sight of it was sexy in a way that his brain couldn't put into words. But she was his. At least for tonight.

Then she was swiping his hand away. "Eli, I need you. Please…"

Her meaning was clear, and he was more than ready to oblige her. He lowered himself onto her as her fingers found him…encircled his length. The light pressure was almost his undoing. Then she was guiding him to her, and the second he was in position, he plunged deep, the moist heat at the heart of her making him see white for a second or two. Then he was kissing her, moving over her. The scrape of his skin against hers was something erotic…was something he'd almost forgotten but not quite. It was stored in his muscle memory, along with everything she liked. Everything that drove her wild. Everything that made her want him all the more.

And that made him want *her* all the more.

She was incredible…the way she fit against him… the way her hands slid over him.

He couldn't stop himself. He moved faster, his fingers going to her hips and gripping them to bring her along with him. The momentum built like a piece of music that was scaling up for something big. Something that would drive it over the top.

Suddenly Georgia's feet were on the bed and she was pushing her hips into him with a force that drove him deeper…deeper. And then he felt it. Her body went off, the crazy motions ending in the deep rhythmic pulses that demanded something of him with every contraction—every time it gripped and released him. Until he couldn't resist the lure of it any longer.

He fell over the edge into insanity. He thrust into her over and over again, pouring himself into her until there was nothing left. But he didn't want it to stop. Not yet. So he kept moving, kept trying to preserve this moment for all time.

Then the frantic movements slowed, easing him back to Earth as he pressed his lips to her neck and breathed her scent, letting it waft into his very cells.

Her arms went up his back, hugging him close. It made him feel wanted in a way he hadn't felt in a very long time. He pressed his cheek to hers as he caught his breath and just let himself be held.

Three words swirled around in his head before landing on his tongue. He had to grit his teeth together to keep them from spilling out over them both. Now was not the time. And it had to be just sentimental notions from their past that had somehow melded with the present.

So he would hold on to the words. Until he was sure. Until he knew that it was about today and not about what they'd once had together. Until he was sure that the words were reciprocated. Because one thing he didn't want was for that last awful event of their relationship to happen all over again.

CHAPTER NINE

THE NEXT MORNING brought new wonders as Georgia sat astride him, loving the feel of him with each pump of her hips. She'd woken up before him and had rained tiny kisses over his neck. What she'd thought had been a dream had turned out to be very, very real. The slight ache of her body that had greeted her along with the light flooding through the windows had said last night had really happened.

His arm had anchored her to him, her body molding to his nakedness. Waking up next to him had been a study in decadence. And she loved it. Loved him.

"God, Georgia..."

His husky words made her smile. She couldn't remember the last time she'd felt so fulfilled. So content to just...be.

There was no rush. No hurry.

He palmed her hips, not pushing her toward an invisible finish line but letting her continue her leisurely pace. Last night had been kind of a blur of need and want, and she was having trouble remembering exactly what had happened or how it had even started.

This time she wanted to commit every second of her time with him to memory.

Her fingers slid up his firm abs, seeking out his flat nipples, and she strummed her thumbs over them, loving the way his breath huffed out as she did so. He cupped her nape, drawing her down to his mouth. Kissing her deeply, his tongue and teeth echoed what she was doing to him. But again, it wasn't rushed. It was slow and methodical, as if he, too, were relishing every second of their time together, as if he wanted it to go on forever.

So did she. And she wasn't quite sure how to make that happen.

But right now, she didn't want to ponder the future.

She just wanted to be with him.

She sat up again and touched a finger to his lips, outlining the firm curve, her eyes taking it in with a new sense of wonder.

The man was perfect. In every way. And he did it for her. He always had. Fast or slow. Hard or gentle. She'd always wanted whatever he'd been in the mood for back when they'd been a couple. But this time it was different. It wasn't that he'd always called the shots before. But this time it was as if he were deliberately letting her take the lead. And it gave her a newfound sense of power. And she found she loved it.

"What do you want, Georgia?"

She smiled down at him, seating herself fully onto him and then rising up again in slow increments that made her sigh with pleasure. "When I know I'll tell you."

Her words weren't just about sex, although she knew that was what he'd meant by his question. But she didn't know what she wanted. Not really. Not outside of these few precious hours that they'd spent together.

His hand reached up, and she felt a slight tug of something around her neck. She glanced down and saw he'd captured her butterfly charm and had it trapped between his fingers, gripping it tight.

Something about the sight made her blood run cold, and her movements faltered.

"This is pretty."

His words were low and rumbly. He was still holding it, and it was as if he were imprisoning more than just her charm. It was as if he was holding her too, although she knew that wasn't his intent. Still, a sense of claustrophobia began building in her chest. Within seconds it threatened to overwhelm her. The longer he held that charm, the more panicked she felt.

She couldn't stop herself from trying to yank it from his hand, but when she did the chain broke and the butterfly tumbled to the bed beside them and lay as still as death.

No one said anything for the next few beats. The only sound was of their breathing.

"Georgia?" He tried to touch her cheek, but she jerked away, climbing off of him and kneeling on the mattress. She stared at the butterfly, the broken gold chain still gripped in her palm.

"Georgia?" he said again. "What's going on?"

"I don't know. I—I just can't. I need to go home."

He sat up, still trying to look at her face. "I'll take you."

Oh, God, the thought of being trapped with him in the car for the next forty-five minutes was unbearable. Her face burned in humiliation over her reaction to him making a simple comment about her necklace. What would happen if a much bigger subject ever came up?

Coming here had been such a big mistake. "No, I can call someone to—"

"Take my car. Steve has been wanting to spend time at the cabin. I'll just have him come over, and he can take me back to the hospital. Just leave the car there."

"I don't know the way." She gathered the sheet around her naked form. In reality her words were about a lot more than just how to get back to Anchorage.

"Just take the track back to the road. Your GPS will get you back to the hospital from there. My keys are on the table in the kitchen." He paused, face inscrutable. "Call if you have any trouble."

A wild sense of hope came over her. He was giving her a way out—without making her feel crazy or ridiculous.

"A-Are you sure?" She did her best to ignore the fact that he was still lying naked on the bed. She'd taken the sheet for herself and the duvet was on the floor, so there was nothing left for him. Something about that seemed prophetic.

"I've never been more sure of anything in my life."

Georgia swallowed. Prophetic indeed. This was the end. She could hear it in his measured tones. In the calm, cool blue of his eyes. There wasn't a wave or a ripple of emotion within them. No, he hadn't made her feel crazy, but he was letting her know that there was no coming back from this. Not for them as a couple anyway.

It was for the best, right? It was what she was asking for.

She scrambled off the bed and gathered her clothes, taking them with her into the bathroom. She didn't bother showering—she could do that once she got home. Instead she pulled her clothing on piece by piece, glancing into the mirror as she zipped up her jeans. Her face stopped her short. Her hair was a hideous tangled mess and her mascara smudged from sleeping in it, but that wasn't what caught her attention. It was the pale unhappiness that she saw in her reflection. The raw pain that came with knowing she was about to leave the only man she'd ever dared to love. And he was done. Done with this trip. Done with spending time together.

Done with her.

She should've been relieved that this hadn't been messier. That he'd let her off the hook basically unscathed.

Unscathed? No. She might not show it on the outside, but she was cut and bleeding on the inside, from wounds of her own making. Her fingers went to the rippled flesh on her wrist and rubbed it until it ached.

This scar might have been caused by her father, but the rest of them? Those were on her. And Georgia had no idea what to do about any of it. For right now, though, all she could do was run away from the situation. And she was so tired of running. So damn tired. So this was the last time for her as well. And she meant that with all of her heart.

She grabbed the keys off of the table and got into Eli's vehicle, pulling the seat forward so she could reach the pedals. Then she started the SUV and carefully made her way down the overgrown track, wincing as branches caught at the large vehicle, but it never hesitated. Not once. It was as if it knew what she needed.

When she got to the road, she stopped, laying her head on the steering wheel and allowing herself to cry in the silence for several minutes. Then she sat up and scrubbed the heels of her palms over her eyes and told herself to suck it up. She'd made her choice, and now she was going to have to live with it. Then, setting her GPS, she turned right like it told her to do and took the road that would lead her back to Anchorage. Back to a life she was no longer sure she wanted.

The drive seemed to take forever, but finally the hospital was in sight. Carefully pulling the big vehicle into the employee parking area, she saw her car. Someone was leaning against it. Her heart stopped for a second before she realized there was no way it could be Eli. She got closer and saw the person was William. She frowned. God! Had something happened to her mother? To Ted or Edna or one of her other patients?

There wasn't a spot right next to her car, so she had to park Eli's car a few spots over. Then she got out, grabbed her tote bag that she somehow remembered to get before leaving and left his keys under the floor mat like she told him she'd do. Then she hurried toward her friend.

She didn't waste time on pleasantries. "What's wrong?"

William's brows went up, and he pushed away from the car. "I could ask you the same question."

That puzzled her. There was no way he could know what had happened, other than the fact that she was driving Eli's vehicle. "What are you doing out here?"

He shook his head and came over and gave her a hug. "Eli called me and asked me to make sure you arrived safely."

"He told you?" Horror washed over her.

"He didn't say much other than telling me that you'd had to return to Anchorage and were driving his vehicle. Is everything okay with your mom?"

"Yes. It's..." She licked her lips as tears again rose to the surface and threatened to spill over, just like they had as she'd left the cabin. "Can I call you later? I—I just need to get home and do some thinking."

Draping an arm around her shoulders, he looked into her face. "Think long and hard, Georgia. Because I have a feeling that whatever decision you come to in the next several days, it will be one you're going to have to live with. Now, I have to get back to work. Call me."

"I will. Promise." She looked at her friend. "And William, thanks."

She watched him walk toward the entrance, then leaned her back against the car and shut her eyes. Yes, he was right. This decision was one she was going to have to live with. What William didn't know, though, was that it had already been made.

She reached up for her necklace and realized she'd left her charm on Eli's bed. The events of the last hour played through her mind like one of those video clips from a social media site. And that was all that was left. Her memories.

Because she had nothing else to show for it. Not even the butterfly charm that had brought her world crashing down around her.

Eli fingered the butterfly, turning it over and over with his fingers as Steve sat on the couch in his cabin. Something about this little charm had wrecked what had been happening between him and Georgia on that bed. In reality, he had only commented on it as a way to take his mind off what she was doing to him, kind of like that old joke that all men thought about baseball as a way to slow down their rush to sexual release.

"Do you want to talk about it?" Steve asked.

The question jerked him from his thoughts. "No."

His friend already knew the basics. That he'd come

here with Georgia and that she'd had to leave unexpectedly, so she'd taken his car. His friend hadn't asked why Eli hadn't driven her back himself, but he was sure Steve had worked some of it out for himself. William had been the same way. He hadn't asked why Georgia was driving his vehicle back to Anchorage alone. But the nurse had texted to say that she'd made it. And that was it. No insight into what had precipitated her suddenly needing to leave.

Except Eli knew what it was. He just didn't know what it meant. The charm that had caused such panic in her seemed to burn his fingers. And that was what it had been. Some kind of full-blown panic attack. She'd been fine. Until he'd touched her necklace and commented on it. Then it had been as if a switch had turned on in her face, and she hadn't been able to get away from him fast enough.

Had the butterfly been given to her by another man, and she felt guilty for being at the cabin with Eli? No, Georgia wouldn't cheat on someone. Besides, if there was someone else, then she'd left him behind. Just like she'd done with Eli three years ago. On Kodiak, more than likely.

But he didn't think that was it either. Her reaction mirrored what had happened when he'd proposed to her three years ago. Her eyes had widened, and then the same frantic expression had crossed her face. It had ended in her taking off and then finally moving away from Anchorage less than a week later. His attempts to call or contact her had been met with silence. There'd never been any explanation other than the fact that she couldn't marry him.

Would she leave Anchorage again? If so, he didn't want to be there when that happened. He preferred to wait here in his cabin, where there was no chance of having to say any kind of goodbye. He'd already called and checked on Ted and Edna. Edna was actually leaving to catch her flight back to Florida today. He'd spoken with her on the phone. And although Ted was grieving the loss of his son, the stents had done the trick and he was recovering. A colleague of Eli's who was semiretired but who rotated through the hospital on days that he couldn't be there had agreed to work his shifts this week. It would give him time to think. And time for Georgia to leave the hospital—if history was going to repeat itself.

"Well, if you don't want to talk, let's go do something besides mope around the cabin."

"I'm not moping." But he was. He was sitting here feeling damned sorry for himself, and it was solving nothing. Whatever was going to happen was going to happen.

"Whatever you say. But I'm going to take one of your fishing poles and I'm going to head for the lake," Steve said. "We're eventually going to need something to eat."

Eli had thrown the partially cooked steak from the previous night far into the woods when he'd taken a walk to clear his head. He was lucky a bear hadn't come along and torn up his porch trying to get the meat out of the wire basket. He'd been stupid to leave it out.

Actually he'd been stupid about a lot of things.

But what was done was done.

"I'll come with you. And you're right." He gave his friend a smile that was devoid of mirth. "You always could tell when I was bullshitting you. But I really don't want to talk about what happened with her, okay? Not now. Maybe not ever."

"You don't have to talk about anything but the weather if that's what you want." Steve got up and slapped Eli on the back. "Besides, too much talking'll scare the fish away, eh?"

Eli hadn't come back to the hospital. Two days had passed, and there'd been no sign of him. Edna, who'd been discharged yesterday afternoon, had said that the surgeon had called her to wish her well on her trip.

Georgia hadn't gone up to his floor for fear of seeing him. In fact, she'd been hoping not to run into him anywhere at the hospital. But after talking to Edna, she finally did go up to check on Ted, and he seemed to be well on his way toward a physical recovery, even though he'd been shattered to hear that his son had died without regaining consciousness.

Georgia had thought through her options. She could run back to Kodiak like she'd done before, or she could stay and try to work through her problems. That didn't include getting back together with Eli. But could she work here at the hospital with him after what had happened? She wasn't sure. What she did know was that she was going to start training for the hospital's 5K race as if she were going to be here for it. It was just a couple of weeks away, so there wasn't a whole lot of time. But it would keep her mind off of things and hopefully help with the lethargy that had stolen over her ever since she'd walked out on Eli.

With her shift for the day done, she went to her locker and pulled out her running clothes. She'd go to the park and train a little before going home. To her empty studio apartment. Something that seemed sad and lonely all of a sudden.

It had touched her heart that despite the way she'd left Eli's cabin he had been concerned enough to contact William and ask him to check on her. Her friend had texted her a couple of times asking if she wanted to grab lunch together some time, even cornering her as she'd come out of an exam room yesterday. But she'd kept putting him off. She wanted to talk to William about all that had happened but needed a little time and space so that she wouldn't be a complete and utter wreck when she did decide to tell him.

Georgia got changed and scraped her hair back into a ponytail, shaking her head at the strands that wouldn't stay in place. She really should let it grow back out some. But when she'd left Anchorage three years ago, she'd wanted a new start, and chopping her hair off had been part of that transition. Only she'd stopped jogging and so hadn't needed to pull her hair back any longer. Until now. But she wasn't about to change her appearance again because doing that had made no difference the last time, and it would make no difference now. She'd missed Eli like crazy three years ago.

And she missed him now. She couldn't believe she'd voiced that truth to him as they'd sat by the fire. But it had seemed like the right thing to do. At least at the time. In reality, that was what had precipitated them making love in the first place.

Heading out to the park, she ran hard, a stitch forming in her side almost immediately...the result of her body not being prepared to deal with the sudden return to training.

Actually her body hadn't been ready for any of the other changes she'd thrown at it in the last couple of weeks either—like finding out Eli wasn't married any longer, sleeping with him and then leaving him behind all over again.

She kept running, and the cramp in her side grew despite her efforts to just run through it. She finally stopped and leaned over to catch her breath, bracing her hands on her knees until the pain lost some of its fire. She had no doubt that part of it was caused by stress. But that wasn't something she could control, although keeping everything bottled up inside wasn't helping her deal with the emotional devastation that littered her heart and mind. She was pretty sure that psychological pain was now manifesting itself in physical ways. Like the pain in her side.

Gripping the cramped area, she made her way over

to a nearby bench and dropped onto it and waited for the sensation to leave. So much for training and hoping it would take her mind off things. It hadn't. It had just brought everything into sharp focus.

Twenty minutes later she could finally take a deep breath without it feeling like something was going to rip apart inside of her. That was funny because she was pretty sure something already had when she'd left Eli's cabin two days ago. What if he never came back? His SUV was still parked in the lot. Her eyes had automatically been drawn toward it whenever she'd arrived at the hospital and then again when she'd left.

Surely he wouldn't leave it there indefinitely? Maybe his friend Steve hadn't been able to come and he was stuck at the cabin with no transportation.

He had a cell phone. He could call her—or someone else—if he needed help or needed a ride back to Anchorage. He obviously had reception on his phone, since he'd been able to call William a few days ago.

But she felt guilty about even the thought of him having to call for a ride. She had no idea what to do. About any of it.

Georgia really wanted her charm back. But how could she look Eli in the face and ask for it? Maybe she could tell him to leave it at the information desk on the ground floor of the hospital. Or maybe William would have an idea.

She finally did what she had put off doing. She pulled her cell phone out of her back pocket and dialed William's number. When he answered, she took a deep breath and said, "I'm ready to talk. You tell me when and where you can meet me, and I'll be there."

"How about right now at the Bear Claw?"

"I'm out jogging right now at the park, but I'll head back to the hospital. I can shower there and be at the Bear Claw in, say, forty-five minutes?"

"Forty-five minutes it is. See you there."

Steve and Eli sat in camp chairs on the shore of the good-sized lake, their fishing lines in the water, poles propped up next to where they sat. So far, neither had said anything outside of talking about the latest sports figures. Eli had put the butterfly charm on a table in the dining area of the cabin. He would have to get it back to her somehow. If worse came to worst and she disappeared again, he could always give it to William, who could probably get it back to her.

"The girl you were here with was the one you used to date before Lainey?" Evidently Steve was done beating around the bush because he opened up the subject with a point-blank question.

"Yes, she was."

"You still care about her?"

He shrugged, shifting in his chair. "Does it matter?"

Steve fixed him with a look. "Maybe. Maybe not. But what you do from here might dictate what happens over the next several weeks."

Several weeks. He couldn't even fathom that much time passing without being able to see her.

"I still care. But she…" He dragged his hand through

his hair. "I have no idea what she feels. But this is the second time that she's suddenly run out on me."

"Since she's been back in Anchorage?"

"No," he said. "The first time was when I proposed three years ago. And the second time was two days ago when I made a comment about a piece of jewelry she had on. She suddenly said she couldn't and that she needed to go home. I have no idea what even happened."

"So we'll go back to my previous question. You still care about her. I'll add something to that. Do you care enough to go ask her how she feels about you?"

"She'll just run again."

"Maybe," Steve said. "But maybe, like you, she's mulling things over in her head. Something spooked her, and I know you well enough to know you didn't hurt her or try to scare her. That butterfly you were fiddling with back in cabin might have triggered some kind of fear, though. What do you know about her past?"

"Nothing, really. I know her mom is still alive and divorced, although I've never met her. I know her dad is no longer in the picture, according to her."

"As in she's estranged from him?" Steve asked.

"I think so. I tried to ask about him one time, and she was pretty quick to cut me off."

Steve reeled his line in, checked his lure and then sent it sailing back out over the water where it landed with a small splash. "Did you ever stop to think that maybe she's reacting to something in her past—

whether it's from her family or someone she dated? After all, you went through some hard times when you were a teenager."

What was his friend talking about? His parents' deaths? Or about the questionable foster homes he'd been in?

"Yes? And…?"

"Did any of that stuff color the way you perceive the world?"

Eli raised his brows. "You saw how I was when I first came to your house."

"I did. So that would be a yes." Steve shrugged. "Don't you think that this girl could be struggling with some junk from her past too? We all come with baggage, Eli. Even me. And it took you quite a while before you were willing to talk about any of it."

"What if she refuses to talk? Or if she somehow can't get past whatever it is?"

"Did Julia and I give up on you?"

"No, but I don't know why you didn't sometimes." Eli really didn't. He'd put them through the wringer for almost a year.

"Because you were worth fighting for." Steve picked up his fishing pole and began reeling in his line again. "I remember meeting Georgia back when you were dating the first time. She seemed like a pretty special girl. Not the kind who likes to play games with people's emotions."

"I didn't think she liked to either," Eli said. "And yet she walked away. Not once but twice now."

"But you don't know why. And until you do, you'll never know if her reasons for walking away are something you can work through together or not."

Maybe Steve was right. He'd tried to call Georgia the first time she'd left, but he hadn't been very persistent. In the end, he'd given up. Whether he should have gone to Kodiak and confronted her was something he'd never know. And yet she'd told him she'd missed him by the fire not three nights ago, and the deep longing in her voice had made him think they might have a second chance. She hadn't left after they'd made love that first time. And he was more and more positive she wouldn't have after the second time either if he hadn't noticed that charm.

"So you think I should go and ask her."

"I think you should go and ask her." Steve stood to his feet and set his pole on the ground.

"Where are you going?"

Steve smiled and looked at his watch. "Julia should be here in about five minutes."

"What? You called her?" he asked.

"No. But I told her if she didn't hear from me by noon, she should just plan on picking me up at one."

"What if it doesn't work out between me and Georgia?"

"Then call me. But only after you try your best to talk to her and come to some consensus about your future," Steve said. "If it doesn't go well, I'll bring a six pack and some food, and we can eat and drink until nothing matters anymore."

The sound of tires crunching on the track to his cabin sounded, and Steve grinned. "Sounds like she's a few minutes early, so I'll head up there."

When Eli picked up his own pole to go back up to the cabin with his friend, Steve stopped him. "Why don't you sit out here for a while and enjoy the quiet? I'll tell Julia you send your love. And I'll leave the keys to my car on the table. Just in case."

"Thanks, Steve. For the company and the talk. And you're right—she's worth it."

Steve clapped him on the back. "So are you, Eli. Don't you ever forget that."

With that his friend was gone, whistling a tune as he walked back toward the cabin, which was barely visible between the trees he had cleared last year. Steve had left his chair and his pole right where they were, which made Eli smile. It was okay, though—it would give him time to think through a game plan. He could either drive back to Anchorage this afternoon and try to see if Georgia was still in town or he could wait until tomorrow. Because this time he wasn't going to just try to call her. He was going to go see her, whether she was still at the hospital or had moved back to Kodiak. If things were going to end this time, he wanted them to end face-to-face. And he wanted to know why.

He couldn't force her to tell him. But he could ask. Something he hadn't done last time. Until then, he was going to sit here for a while and enjoy the lake.

He picked up Steve's pole and cast the line back into the water and sat back in his chair, pulling his ball cap down over his eyes.

CHAPTER TEN

SHE WAS BEING FOLLOWED.

As soon as Georgia turned down the road that led to Eli's cabin a small white car had turned its signal on as well and crept up the track behind her. A shiver went through her. Was this a mistake? Maybe Eli had already left and gone back to Anchorage.

But his car had still been in the parking lot. Once she'd talked things through with William, she'd decided she'd been a bigger fool this time about Eli than she had been the last time. She owed it to him to tell him why she'd acted the way she had. Both this time and when she'd left for Kodiak three years ago.

He might laugh in her face or tell her to get lost, and she wouldn't blame him. She was still feeling shaky about coming out here and telling Eli about any of this. And yet from the moment she'd met William at the Bear Claw, she knew she had to come and at least try. Her friend hadn't even needed to say a word because all of it had just come pouring out of Georgia's mouth in a stream of consciousness monologue that had left her breathless and aghast at the time she'd wasted.

Why had she never told Eli about her dad? It wasn't

as if she'd expected him to look down on her for something she'd had no control over. But she hadn't felt strong enough back then. Was she any stronger now? She didn't know, but she at least owed him an explanation.

And if he was willing to let her back into his heart?

Oh, God, she didn't even dare hope that he would understand. That he would be willing to help her figure out a way to be together in a way that was acceptable to both of them.

But right now she was worried about being out in the middle of nowhere with a car staying right on her tail. Maybe it was Eli.

No. As far as she knew, he only had the SUV.

The cabin came into sight, and she saw a second car in the parking lot. She swallowed. Maybe he was having some kind of party. One she hadn't been invited to.

Could she blame him?

Maybe he was glad to have her out of his life.

He hadn't seemed glad three days ago. In fact, he'd seemed pretty stunned by her sudden change in attitude. Well, party or not, she was going to see if she could pull him aside and talk to him.

She stopped in front of the cabin, just as a man—who was definitely not Eli—came out onto the porch. This man looked vaguely familiar with his gray hair and slight build. She glanced to the side as the white car pulled up beside her. In the vehicle was a woman, who waved at her with a smile.

Julia! This time she had no problem identifying the

occupant. And when she glanced back at the porch, she saw it was Steve, Eli's foster parent from his younger years. She'd had dinner a couple of times over at their house when she and Eli had been dating.

Another thought came to her. One that made her leap out of the car. Why would they both be here? Unless…

Not wasting time on pleasantries, she leaped from the car. "Is Eli okay? Has something happened?"

Steve came down the porch and met her. "He's okay. But he was pretty devastated when I got here."

Georgia closed her eyes. "That was my fault. I was stupid and took off without telling him what was wrong."

Julia grabbed her close in a hug. "I'm hoping that means you're here to do just that and not just to return his car."

"Yes, but…" She glanced at the door, which was still closed. No sign of anyone inside that cabin. "Where is he?"

Steve dropped a kiss onto his wife's cheek. "He's over at the lake fishing. I was going to leave my car here for him to get back to town with, but…"

"I'm hoping after I tell him what I came here to say that he'll be willing to spend the forty-five minutes trip back to Anchorage with me."

Steve laid a hand on her shoulder. "I rather think he'll be willing." He glanced at Julia. "That means I'll have to follow you back home. Or I could leave my car here to pick up later."

She gave her husband a slow smile. "Why don't you leave it here? I missed you and could use the company on the drive back."

"That works for me." He went back to the porch and picked up a small duffel bag and threw it into the back seat of Julia's car. "Like I said, he's down by the lake." He pointed through a stand of trees. "You can't miss it."

She pulled in a deep breath. "Do you think he'll be willing to talk to me?"

"I'm pretty sure he's not going to let you walk out of here *without* that talk."

Julia gave her another hug. "Go to him. We look forward to hearing something good from your visit."

Promising she would do her best, she left her stuff in Eli's car and headed in the direction Steve had pointed, hoping she didn't run into a moose or bear on the way. Eli never had had a chance to show her that trail cam he'd set up on the property.

She'd never been so aware of the sounds of twigs crunching underfoot, of the sounds of leaves rustling in the breeze or the way the sun cast dappled patterns on the ground. Less than two minutes later, she saw two camp chairs and a man sitting in one of them.

Eli. At the sight of him, her eyes began to burn and her heart thumped a hundred miles an hour. What if Steve was wrong? What if Eli had washed his hands of her? She couldn't blame him. But God, she hoped he would at least listen to what she had to say.

She quietly walked in front of him to catch his attention, only to find he had a cap pulled down over his face.

Was he asleep?

Going over to the second chair, she slowly lowered herself into it, trying to make as little sound as possible. If he was asleep, she couldn't think of anything she wanted more than time to just sit here and study him. Sit here and imagine that they were here as a couple and that he would wake up and smile at her. That he would walk her back to the cabin and make love to her without fearing she would walk out on him again.

Maybe that was what true freedom was. Being with someone without being afraid of what might happen. Of being secure enough in a relationship that you didn't have to walk on eggshells every time that person was around. She'd found that person. She hadn't realized it three years ago. But she realized it now. If only he would give her another chance.

"Forget something?" Eli popped his hat back onto his head and turned toward her. The smile that was on his face disappeared in an instant when he saw who it was. A cold shiver went over her. Maybe Steve was wrong. Because he sure didn't look happy to see her.

He sat there for a minute or two before reaching over to twirl a strand of her hair, looking into her face. "Did Steve call you?"

"No. Why would he have?"

Eli shook his head as if confused before letting go of her hair and leaning back in his chair. "Why are you here, then?"

She tried to find some eloquent way to explain herself and failed. She finally settled for something that was simple but true. "I wanted to explain why I left so abruptly the other day."

He nodded. "I was planning on heading back to Anchorage today to ask you that very question."

Again the thought that Steve had misjudged Eli wound through her head like the smoke from the fire the last time she was here, making everything cloudy and uncertain.

"You were?"

"I was. I was going to try to find you and ask what you're so afraid of." He touched her cheek, his touch warm and gentle, inviting her to tell him the truth.

She reached up and took his hand, twining her fingers through his. To her relief, he didn't pull away, just allowed her to keep his hand in her lap.

"It was my butterfly charm."

"I somehow worked out that much." He squeezed her fingers. "I just didn't understand what it meant. I still don't."

"I know. And if I hadn't been in such a blind panic, if I had stopped to take a breath or two, I might have realized that I wanted you to know."

"I'm listening now."

This time she didn't try to put the words together, she just started talking, hoping he could somehow untangle the jumbled thoughts and phrases.

"I bought that charm three years ago, right after we broke up. When you asked me to marry you, I panicked. Just like I did the other day. The butterfly was supposed to remind me that I could only be free to fly if I was on my own. Anything that tried to hold me down was immediately brushed aside, and I would take flight." She shrugged. "The funny thing was I never really felt free, even then."

"Does this have something to do with your childhood?"

She turned their hands over, exposing the scar on her wrist. "You're very astute. My dad was a controlling and jealous man. My mom couldn't do anything without telling him. She couldn't work. Couldn't have friends. Couldn't spend money without accounting for every penny that left her purse."

Eli lifted her hand to his lips and kissed the scar. "Did *he* do that to you?"

The graveled tones and the look in his eyes was enough to make her hurry to explain. "Not directly. But he got mad at me one day and threw my piggy bank on the ground, smashing it to pieces. One of the shards flew up and cut me. My mom kicked him out, but as I grew up, I saw my friends in relationships along with the petty fights and jealousies that happened in those relationships. I decided that I would not be controlled by anyone ever again. Not my dad. Not my boyfriends. Not even someone I cared for more than anything."

She hoped he would understand she was talking about him.

"Why didn't you tell me?"

"I'm not sure. I guess I thought it wouldn't change the way I felt. That it wouldn't change my mind about relationships preventing me from being free."

"Do you still think that?"

She sighed. "I have to admit, I'm still scared. But I think I'm coming to realize that true freedom only comes when you can be vulnerable around someone without fear of being hurt or ridiculed and ignored."

"Oh, honey, I am so sorry that *anyone* made you feel that way," Eli said. "If I knew where he lived…"

"No. He's not worth it. I don't know where he is, and I don't want to know. The most horrible thing is realizing I've let what he did back then control me for the last thirty years. I still gave him power over me. But no more."

"I'm glad." He pulled free of her grip and cupped her chin, turning her face toward him. "So what does that mean for you from here on out?"

"I'm hoping you can be patient with me and give me another chance. I'm hoping you still feel something for me because I still love you," she said. "I never stopped. And if there's a chance for us, I'm hoping that someday you'll ask me to marry you again. It doesn't have to be right now. It doesn't have to be within the next year. Or even ten years. I just want to know we'll be together. With or without the piece of paper. If you still want that."

He leaned in and kissed her. A kiss that was bright and beautiful and full of hope. "Georgia, I've never stopped loving you either." He paused. "But ten years really doesn't work for me."

A sense of fear went through her. Was he saying he loved her but didn't want to be with her again? She couldn't blame him for not trusting her after what she'd put him through. When she thought of the time she'd wasted, she didn't think she could—

He smiled at her, and the crooked tilt of his lips erased every trace of fear. "If I get down on one knee, are you going to run?"

Did he mean, like, right now? She waited for the sense of panic to set in, but there was only a sense of peace. Of fulfillment. Of love.

"No, I'm not going to run. Not this time." The words came out in a whisper. She was so afraid that she was dreaming. That she would wake up and find nothing had changed. That Eli was still at the cabin and that she was in her little studio apartment, feeling for her butterfly charm every time something made her nervous.

"In that case…" He slid from his chair and knelt in front of her in on the pebbly ground. "I don't have a ring, but we can fix that later. Georgia Ann Sumter, will you marry me? I love you, and I promise never to hurt or ridicule or ignore you. I promise never to make you feel afraid. For all of our days."

He was using her words from earlier and promising never to make her feel the way her dad had. And she loved him for it. And most of all, she believed him.

Believed he would let her fly high and that he would be right there soaring right along with her.

"I will, Eli. I will marry you. I love you."

With that he pulled her out of her chair and down beside him, rolling her on top of him and holding her tight against him. And there was no claustrophobia, no sense of being trapped. They were together and in love. And there was no greater freedom than that.

Suddenly there was a splashing sound, and a sense of movement caught her eye. Eli sat up and laughed, hugging her tight. "Can we press pause for a minute? I think I have a bite."

She glanced beyond him and saw that one of the fishing poles was indeed being dragged toward the lake. She leaped off of him and let him grab it, watching as he reeled it in.

"I hope whatever it is is big enough for dinner because all of a sudden I'm starved."

He motioned her over, and she put her arm around his waist as he continued to reel in the line. Just then the other line twitched, the pole it was attached to bent almost in half. "Can you get that?" he said. "I'm a little busy here."

"Gladly." The next several minutes were spent getting their catches closer to shore. They were two beautiful bass. More than enough for the both of them for dinner. But when he started to land his, she reached out a hand to stop him. "Eli, let's let them go."

He tilted his head and must have read something in her eyes because he nodded and waded in to pull the hook from first his fish and then repeated the process with hers, watching as they both swam away. "Here's to freedom."

Tears blurred her vision as she realized he'd understood exactly what she'd meant. "Yes. Here's to freedom. And to forevers."

With that, both poles were abandoned on the ground as they took up where they left off, both promising the other that today was the first of many days. And Georgia knew in her heart that it was true.

EPILOGUE

THE HOSPITAL'S YEARLY 5K run in Knicker Park was today. And both Eli and Georgia had signed up to be in it. But they didn't run. Instead, they walked hand in hand, talking about the future and what their hopes and dreams were.

Eli had taken her necklace in to have it repaired, and the butterfly charm was once again around her neck. And she'd told him that while it still meant freedom to her, that freedom no longer meant she had to be alone. He was her companion on this journey, and there was nowhere he would rather be.

She'd also bought him an engagement present. A narrow black braided wristband with a silver bead, also engraved with a butterfly. He loved it. Wore it whenever he was not doing surgery.

Edna had texted him from Florida saying that she was doing great and following her doctor's orders to take it easy. She was getting stronger every day. They'd already booked an Alaskan cruise for next summer, and she'd promised she and Artie would stop in to see them.

They'd attended Brandon's memorial service two

weeks ago, and while it had been a time of sadness, Ted had asked Eli about the Big Brothers program after seeing a flyer on the wall of his office. His heart function was still doing well and the stents were doing their job, and he was looking to the future. He talked about seeing what Dutch Harbor had in the way of mentorship programs to try to help at-risk youths like Brandon. Eli had no doubt that Ted would do a great job and that it would also help fill the void left by the passing of his son.

The last couple of weeks had been filled with activity, both in their professional lives and in their private lives. Georgia had given up the lease on her studio apartment and had moved in with Eli. She said she wanted to get married as soon as possible, so their days were filled with lying in bed with brochures and making love. Her mom had flown up from Kodiak to help Georgia shop for wedding dresses. They'd found one the very first day they'd gone out shopping, and while his fiancée was happy with her choice, she told him he would have to wait until their wedding day to see it.

And that was okay with him. At least this time there was going to be a wedding day. And he knew that theirs would be for keeps. They'd met Steve and Julia at the cabin, and they'd celebrated their engagement with steaks cooked over the fire and a lot of laughter.

Eli was happier than he could ever imagine he'd be. Squeezing Georgia's hand, he let it go so that he could wrap an arm around her waist. "I think the finish line is just up ahead."

She smiled, pulling his head down for a kiss. "Do you think we're the last ones to arrive?"

"Does it matter?"

"No. It doesn't matter at all."

They got to the line that had been taped to indicate the end of the race and stood on it and kissed some more. The place was almost deserted, but they didn't care. What was someone else's finish line was their starting line. Their lives together were just taking off.

And who knew how high they would soar?

* * * * *

Look out for the next story in the
Alaska Emergency Docs duet
One-Night Baby with Her Best Friend
by Juliette Hyland

And if you enjoyed this story,
check out these other great reads
from Tina Beckett

ER Doc's Miracle Triplets
Tempting the Off-Limits Nurse
A Daddy for the Midwife's Twins?

All available now!

ONE-NIGHT BABY WITH HER BEST FRIEND

JULIETTE HYLAND

MILLS & BOON

For Tina Beckett—

Writing a duet with you was a dream come true
for me (and my sister).

PROLOGUE

FIERY PERFECTION.

William had always beaten away the question of how Jessie kissed. For years, any time his brain awkwardly wandered into thoughts about craving the woman, and best friend, he never wanted to lose, he'd force them away. Tie them into a solid knot and dump them in the back of his mind with the hope they'd finally stay where he'd put them—but they never did.

Now he knew. For the rest of his life, he'd know that Jessie's kisses were fiery perfection.

"William."

The breathy way she said his name made him hard. Again. A feat that should not be possible this soon.

Her fingernails gently circled his belly button, not dipping down to his manhood. Was she going to bring up how they'd gotten here?

She was an ER doctor and he was a trauma nurse. They'd picked up dinner to share after losing a minor to suicide and a young woman who'd had a fight with her boyfriend, gotten drunk, driven home and impacted against a tree.

The ER shift from hell. But this wasn't their first trip to Hades.

Yes, the second case was a painful reminder of his past, but that still didn't explain how they'd landed tangled in Jessie's light blue sheets.

He ran a finger down her back, enjoying the tiny whimper she let out.

"You are so beautiful." William turned on his side, pulling her leg over his so he could stroke her core.

"You keep saying that." Jessie's lips brushed his, once, twice, and on the third pass she deepened the kiss.

The urgency of their first coupling was over. The fear that she'd dart out of bed, say this was a mistake and order him from her townhome was dissipating. He wasn't sure how long the dream was going to last so he was going to enjoy every minute of it.

His hand brushed over her hip, pausing on the tiny row of scars. "Jessie?"

"That's BA." Jessie grabbed his hand, directing it to exactly where she wanted it.

Before Anchorage. BA. Their code words for *off limits*.

It was the foundation of their friendship. She'd arrived at Anchorage Memorial fresh off her residency in Colorado. He'd shifted the conversation away from the "where'd you come from, tell us how you got here" talk on her first shift. Made a joke about his customary question to ask a new person was their favorite fish.

To his surprise she'd immediately said guppy, started talking about her love of hiking. He enjoyed it too and boom, a friendship was born.

But Jessie didn't talk about her past.

And he got that.

He'd run to Anchorage after his engagement had fallen apart. Until his childhood friend Georgia had shown up as the new doc at the hospital a few weeks ago, no one had even known the name of his hometown.

He and Jessie knew nearly everything about each other's present. Favorite food. Favorite color. Hiking shoe size. The fact that she hated coffee but faked liking it because that was easier than explaining that the cliché exhausted doctor with a hug mug of coffee was a television stereotype, not the truth.

Now he knew she made the softest little noises just before he brought her to completion. As he ran his hand over her hip, his thumb again traced the cluster of tiny scars.

Jessie tensed, then put her hands on either side of his face and kissed him. She rolled, pinning him to the bed; her red hair draped across his chest as she trailed kisses down his cheeks, his jaw, his stomach, ever lower.

The scars were BA. She didn't want him asking but the questions bubbled in his brain.

Until she took him in her mouth. As her soft lips closed on his manhood, he could think of only one thing.

Jessie and her fiery, perfect kisses.

CHAPTER ONE

EACH OF THE ER rooms was full and the clock hadn't struck five yet. That did not bode well for the next shift, coming on in an hour. Dr. Jessie Davis had spent her shift bouncing between rooms. She hadn't sat once since her shift started ten hours ago. So far, she'd casted two broken arms, ordered fluids for a grandmother dehydrated from a stomach bug, stitched up multiple hikers who hadn't taken the trail warnings seriously, handled a car accident and one cardiac arrest.

In other words a little bit of everything. Which was why Jessie liked the ER. Sure, her feet were achy, exhaustion pulled at her and she sometimes saw the worst, but the ER felt like home in a weird way.

"You're looking a little green." Nurse William Harris, the best nurse at Anchorage Memorial, her best friend and the man she'd fallen into bed with six weeks ago, pressed a granola bar into her hand. "Eat this."

"Thanks." Jessie smiled, ripped it open and tried to pretend that the press of William's fingers against her palm didn't make her want to ask him to come home with her.

Six weeks had passed since that horrid shift. The young man, who'd looked so much like her brother, Bran, had had too much stress put on him by his family, and had made a choice the ER hadn't been able to reverse. Hopefully, Bran had comforted him on the other side of the mortal coil.

Grief, the past, the heat of William's body next to her in the car, the feel of his fingers as they reached for the pho dinner they'd ordered to try to forget the shift…they had all collided.

She'd leaned across the car console and kissed him. That had thrown their years of friendship—a friendship she cherished—into chaos just because she'd lost control of the not-so-tiny crush she'd developed on her best friend.

As her cheeks warmed, she grabbed a tablet, trying to pretend like she wasn't still craving William's touch as she gobbled the granola bar.

William was her safe harbor, the person she couldn't lose. She knew that but it didn't stop the feelings she hadn't found a way to push away. There was no way to pretend the lump in her throat was from the granola bar. It was memories and achy need.

Until six weeks ago, she hadn't known he kissed like a god, hadn't known that he got turned on by turning his partner on so the foreplay had been simply divine.

One night. A spontaneous flash point she'd hold in her memory forever. They'd spent the night wrapped in each other's arms after that awful day, moving as though they knew what each wanted. They were connected in a way she'd never felt with another lover.

In the morning they'd agreed it was a mistake. Their friendship was too important to leave to hormones and chance.

It didn't matter that she still woke to memories of his kisses trailing her body. It didn't matter that the crush she'd barely kept under control refused to return to the carefully maintained mental box she'd fashioned for it years ago.

William was the one person she'd truly gotten close to. When she'd arrived in Anchorage, Jessie was cut off from the world. He'd saved her that first shift when everyone was playing the get-to-know-you game. When he brought up a silly question about fish, he probably hadn't expected her to answer, but she knew a lot about fish.

Her brother, Bran, had loved fish. They'd read books and planned fish tanks he never got to create. She didn't talk about Bran. About anything before Anchorage—BA, as William called it.

She'd crafted a new life here. If they tried a relationship and failed… Jessie wasn't willing to risk that. And William agreed. Though part of her wished he'd fought at least a little when she'd suggested ignoring the night they'd lain in each other's arms.

Nope.

William hadn't flinched. Hadn't said…*but maybe.* She'd listened to him parrot back the same talking points she'd just used. All the right words, even if she hadn't wanted to hear them.

"The granola bar helping?" William's voice brought her back to the present, and an uncomfortable warmth spread through her body.

Ignore it, Jessie. Ignore it.

"It's fine. Very granola-y…"

"That was a terrible joke." William looked at her, but it was with his nurse's gaze now. No heat. No desire. The patient-assessment expression.

She was fine. Mostly. She bit her lip, trying to ignore the rise of bile in her stomach. Jessie needed more than a granola bar in a ten-hour shift, but in the last few days everything she'd put in her stomach seemed to turn to lead.

Maybe she was coming down with the stomach bug that seemed to be going around. Germs floated through a hospital no matter the season. Doctors and nurses were far from immune.

William leaned over, his broad shoulders nearly touching hers.

Damn, keeping desire in a box was harder than she'd expected.

"If you are feeling ill, you can go home."

He always saw too much.

"I'm fine. I should have eaten more throughout the day." The words were said with such ease. The reality was, most ER professionals raced through their shifts, rarely consuming more than a granola bar and some nuts. They ran on caffeine and adrenaline.

William raised an eyebrow but didn't say anything.

"Hey, I've got a seventeen-year-old in room 4 complaining of abdominal pain. I can't get her to talk to me." Dr. Georgia Sumter blew out a breath as she strolled to the nurses' station and leaned next to William.

"You think she's pregnant?" William looked down the hall toward the room with the teenager, then back at Georgia.

"I don't know." Georgia's gaze landed on Jessie. "But there is something off with the guy who brought her in. He says he's her brother. But…"

Jessie tilted her head, waiting for Georgia to continue. "But?"

"I don't know. Like I said, something is off. But I want another read on the situation before I make any move. Maybe I'm jumping to conclusions at the end of a long shift. I am tired—I could be oversensitive."

Or something is wrong.

The unstated words hung with worry.

"Would you try?" she asked as she ran a finger over the scar on her left wrist—a reminder of her father's abuse.

Georgia was one of Jessie's favorite colleagues to run shifts with. Georgia and William had grown up together in Kodiak and she'd brought a wave of fresh energy when she'd returned to Anchorage Memorial a few months ago. The woman was fun and professional and had top-notch instincts. If the independent dark-haired doctor thought something was off, then Jessie suspected something was. And the patient was a minor too.

"Any idea what is going on?" William was looking at his tablet, clearly going through the patient's chart.

"No." Georgia crossed her arms, a line appearing in her the middle of her forehead. "Usually, I feel pretty confident when something is up and can suss out the reason. But—" she looked toward the room and sighed "—I feel like a broken record. Something is just off. They can tell I'm suspicious, and they've clammed up."

"All right," Jessie said. "I will go and see if I can't figure anything else out." Though if the patient hadn't been willing to talk to Georgia, Jessie wasn't sure she'd fare any better.

"I'm coming too." William stepped around the desk. "I've been told I'm easy to talk to."

And no one should be alone in there if we aren't positive everything is safe.

William didn't have to say it. He was protective of the staff—and very protective of her. It was a weird and comforting feeling.

Her parents had protected her growing up. Protected her too much. She'd practically lived in a bubble. In fact, if that had been an option her parents would have elected to take it.

But none of their concern had been for her. She was kept well for their son, the firstborn, the only boy. He was the golden child they loved more than anything in the world. And if Jessie got sick, she might not be able to provide Bran with parts.

The sad truth she'd realized before she could write her own name was that Bran mattered. She was on this planet because Bran mattered. And she'd failed in her universal mission to protect him.

Jessie and William walked to the room, knocked on the door

and entered quickly. If something was off, they didn't want to give the couple time to get nervous.

"Why the new faces?" The man, though he couldn't be much older than the girl in the bed, gripped the teen's hand. He squeezed it three times and she squeezed back twice.

A secret code? She and Bran had had one. Though theirs was for silly stuff. One squeeze meant Mom was in a bad mood. Two meant Dad was on the warpath. Three meant ice cream was needed stat. Four meant *I love you, sis.*

"Dr. Sumter thought you might have gotten off on the wrong foot. So she sent me and Dr. Davis in. Mostly me, because I am very smooth." William winked, a bright smile on his face, but Jessie knew it was an act.

He'd seen the possibly secret communication too.

"We just need something to help her stomach. Something to make the pain go away. We are traveling. We need to be on our way soon."

Two hand squeezes from the girl and the man stopped talking. So they were communicating with their hands.

Jessie began, "I want to get you something for your stomach but we have to run some tests. I have to make sure it is the right treatment. Otherwise, it won't help for long." Pain was difficult—she understood that—but it was a symptom not a diagnosis.

The woman looked at Jessie, her teeth biting into her lower lip. At least she wasn't looking away from her. Small steps.

"Let's start with names. Easy enough. I am Jessie, Dr. Davis, and this is my nurse, William."

She looked at the girl in the bed and stepped closer. "I know you are scared. I don't know what of, and right now, I don't need to. But you are safe here."

The teen looked at her partner and took a breath. "Katie. This is my brother, Ian."

"Brother, not boyfriend?" William's question was a good

one. Unfortunately some claimed a family relation when there was none in order to stay with a patient they were coercing.

"Ew…"

Katie's reaction was intense, unscripted and brought a smile to her brother's face.

"I feel the same, sis."

Jealousy pinched at Jessie's side as she stared at the brother-sister pair. She and Bran had had a close relationship. He'd been her only confidant for so long.

Then he was just gone. And she'd been left alone with her parents' angry grief and the knowledge that she'd failed the one person who'd loved her. For weeks after he'd passed, her parents hadn't even spoken to her. It was like she'd vanished with Bran.

"Okay, what is going on with your stomach?" Jessie stepped closer to the bed.

"I'm not pregnant." Katie closed her eyes tightly, a tear leaking down her cheek. "I know that is what everyone thinks when I say that my stomach hurts. But I am not pregnant."

"Everyone?" William was standing on the other side of the bed. "Did Dr. Sumter ask about pregnancy?"

"Not directly." Katie shrugged. "But she immediately asked about my last cycle, and when I said they are irregular…" She bit her lip again and looked at her brother.

"She wanted more information about the cycles. And Katie…" Ian looked at his sister. "Katie clammed up."

So her brother had too. Jessie understood that. Maybe it wasn't the best reaction, but she and Bran would have done the same.

"It's what everyone starts with. My mom said I put on weight and then when the stomach pain started, she assumed and…" Katie let out a sob and buried her face in her hands.

"And our stepfather used a belt to express his disappointment." Ian took a deep breath, color rising in cheeks and his eyes flickering with a barely controlled rage.

"I see." Jessie made a few notes in her chart. There was no way to work in an ER and not see situations of abuse. But no matter how many times she saw them, she never got used to them. She hoped she never did.

She also couldn't fault Georgia for asking about menstrual cycles. It was important to rule out pregnancy. But if Katie was already sensitive to the questions, it was a recipe for misunderstanding.

"When did the stomach pain start?" Jessie continued to take notes.

"Six weeks ago. It wasn't bad at first. Just like cramps. I used a heating pad and some pain meds but none of it really helps for long." She shifted, cringed, and the color dropped out of her face.

William looked at Jessie and she nodded. Katie was in significantly more pain than she was letting on.

"Is it on one side or both sides?"

"My left side. I know the appendix is on the right. So…"

"So you've been researching it yourself?"

Self-diagnosis was common and Jessie didn't mind. It sometimes gave her a head start when patients had suspicions. Of course, some physicians disagreed. Dr. Mueller, the resident grump, regularly complained that patients thought they knew more than him. Luckily, he'd taken a vacation so Katie wouldn't have the "pleasure" of running into him.

"Katie, I want to feel your abdomen. Palpate the area and see if I can feel anything. Can I check it?"

Jessie needed to do this, but patient consent was important. Katie was a minor, but at seventeen, she was old enough to understand and to make some decisions about her treatment.

Katie nodded and lifted her shirt. If the girl had put on weight, she must have been a skeleton before because there was very little muscle or fat on her stomach. The good news was that meant feeling the organs in her abdomen would be easier.

Jessie started on the right side. Katie's belly was soft. A good sign, but then she moved her hands to the left side.

Katie stiffened before Jessie applied any pressure.

"I can't promise this won't hurt, Katie. But I will do my best to be quick."

William held out his hand. "You can squeeze this as hard as you like, if you need to."

Her brother offered his hand too.

Katie accepted both hands, took a shaky breath and nodded to Jessie. "Ready."

The word was wobbly, but Jessie didn't dare wait.

Her scream filled the room as Jessie's fingers pushed against the ovary on the left side. The giant ovary was at least three times as large as the one on the right.

"Find me an OB now. Tell them we need a transvaginal ultrasound, stat." It wasn't how she normally liked to order things, but if she was right her patient needed to be in the operating room as soon as possible.

William moved to the door; she heard his footsteps race down the hallway.

"No. I am not pregnant. I'm not. I'm not. I'm not. I'm not." Katie choked on her sobs as she starred at the ceiling. "I'm not. I'm not."

Ian had tears in his eyes as he looked at Jessie. "If she says she's not, I believe her. Katie doesn't lie."

"I don't think you're pregnant. I technically can't rule it out without a blood test, but I am not calling OB for a pregnancy check. I think you have an ovarian torsion. That means that your ovary and maybe the fallopian tubes have twisted on the tissues supporting them. It is incredibly painful."

"What would the treatment be?" Ian looked at his sister,

then at Jessie. Concern was clear in his eyes but he was trying to be brave.

"Surgery. Immediately. And we need to contact your parents."

"No!"

"No!"

The siblings' echoes were loud enough the nurses' station must have heard them. She likely had seconds before security was at the door.

"I understand you don't want them here, but as a minor—"

"We ran away." Katie was shaking, "I guess, Ian is an adult but I… I… I ran away." Katie bit her lip so hard she had to be tasting blood. "I can't go back. I can't."

"Please."

This was the *something off* Georgia had noticed. They were terrified, and Jessie doubted the belt punishment was the first one Katie ever received.

That didn't change the law unfortunately. Katie was a minor, so the hospital had to alert the parents.

"They won't grant consent." Ian kicked the air under the hospital bed. "They hate hospitals and doctors and…well, most people."

Jessie nodded to security when they walked in. "We're fine. I'm fine. Thank you for checking." Then she turned her attention back to her patient. "Katie, you are under eighteen, so I am required by law to let your parents know that we must treat you. However, if I am right, this is an emergency. In an emergency I do not require their consent."

"She'll get treatment?" The relief on Katie's brother's face brought a little to Jessie too.

"Yes."

"I have the ultrasound." Dr. Padma Lohar, one of the hospital's OBs, stepped into the room, an ultrasound tech following close behind. William stood holding the door for them both.

Padma looked to Jessie, and she started her recitation of symptoms and concerns.

"If it is an ovarian torsion, we need to diagnose now and start prepping you for surgery. The best way to diagnose is a transvaginal ultrasound. Do you want your brother to stay?" Padma's face was grim as she explained the procedure.

Jessie suspected she was already mentally planning the surgery.

"No." Katie looked at him and nodded. "I guess give Mom a heads-up before the hospital calls."

Ian stepped out and William closed the door to give them some privacy.

Padma wasted no time conducting the ultrasound. "Torsion on the left ovary," she confirmed. "It's been twisted for a while. You are a very brave young woman to have lasted with this much pain. You need surgery. Now."

Dr. Lohar nodded to Jessie. "Can you walk her through it?" She didn't wait for Jessie's agreement before hustling out. Padma needed to prep for the emergency surgery. In cases like this, minutes counted.

"You are about to meet a lot of people." Jessie pointed toward the doors. "This bed will be wheeled to the OR, where they are going to put you under. The surgical team will go in laparoscopically. That means they won't cut you all the way open. They will untwist the ovary and do their best to save it."

That was always the goal, but given how large the ovary was, the degree and the length of time Katie indicated she'd been in pain, Jessie suspected they may have to remove it.

"However, if they can't save it, they will remove it. You still have another ovary, so you will still be able to have children."

"I don't want children." Katie leaned her head against the pillow. "I know I'm young. But I don't."

"Okay." Jessie had friends that had said they never wanted children when they were Katie's age. They were still child-free.

Jessie had wanted kids. Still wanted them. She'd played with a baby doll in the hospital playrooms for hours as a child. But life? Well, life didn't always grant you your wishes.

She'd spent all her karma on Bran. Every good deed was for him, as if she could will the universe to give him all her karma points. Force it to keep him safe and healthy. Nothing was left for her and in the end, the universe had taken her brother anyway. He was the reason she existed, and she'd failed him.

That was a karmic debt Jessie doubted there was a way to rectify in this life.

"Let's roll!" A surgical nurse breezed in. "It is very nice to meet you, Katie. My job is to get you up to the OR as quickly as I can. My current record is one minute six seconds. But I think we can beat that."

The nurse released the brakes on the bed and they were off.

"You can head home—I'll stay," William offered. "Katie won't be out of recovery for at least another hour. Ian is aware that they had to remove the ovary. She was damn close to sepsis."

He slid onto the sofa next to Jessie. She looked exhausted. Not that she would admit it. Just like she never admitted to being hungry or thirsty or anything else. The woman would raise hell for her patients. Go into battle with insurance companies or HR staff that didn't prioritize patient health to her satisfaction. For them she was a fiery goddess.

But she never acknowledged what she needed.

Almost everyone in the medical profession tended to let others' needs take priority until their bodies forced them to put themselves first. If Jessie's body ever gave that warning, she ignored it.

The woman never put herself first. He wasn't sure she even knew how. It was why William kept a never-ending supply of granola bars, nuts and dried fruit in his locker that he never ate. A Jessie Reserve, he called it.

"It's fine. I'm good." Jessie yawned and rolled her shoulders. "If her parents show up..." The edge on the word *parents* told him she was planning to protect Katie and her brother.

"They aren't coming." He was torn. Part of him wished the parents would show their faces. Most of the nursing staff wanted a word. A private word. Just a brief conversation... before the police took control.

The other part, the rational one, knew it was likely better for Katie and Ian if the parents didn't arrive. Life would be hard for them on their own, but hard was something the siblings were used to. The siblings had had an unfortunate head start on understanding the world. They'd be okay.

His early life had been a dream. The false sense of security had left him unprepared for the reality when he'd discovered that it was all fabricated. He'd fallen flat several times before finding his place.

"I spoke to her brother a few minutes ago. Their parents said she ran, so it's up to her to figure her life out." They were blaming Katie, but William suspected the real reason they refused to show was because the hospital was a mandatory reporter of abuse.

The authorities would deal with them eventually. But by not showing up, they had time to figure out their story. If they arrived now... There were still bruises on Katie's backside from the belt, and child protective services had already taken temporary custody.

She'd be eighteen in six months. Her brother, only twenty-one himself, had tried to gain custody for almost a year. Now with the emergency placement, he'd get it until she aged out of the system on her eighteenth birthday.

"You need to rest." William put his arm on the back of the couch they were sitting on. If they were at his place or hers, she'd slide over and put her head on his shoulder. Probably fall asleep too.

Or she would have. Until he'd kissed her forty-five days ago. Technically he'd kissed her back, but technicalities didn't really matter.

His dating history was littered with broken hearts…one had broken permanently. Harris men weren't good at love, and there was no way he was risking Jessie. She was too important.

They'd clicked. Theirs was a friendship built on hiking and movies and living in the present. It was a gift he didn't deserve.

So, he swore to himself each morning that this would be the day he stopped counting the days since those kisses. This would be the day he'd drop the feelings into the well they'd bubbled up from and just be her friend again.

And each morning the next number appeared in his brain and the feelings refused to accept their banishment into the basement of his soul.

"You aren't getting enough sleep, and don't get me started on your inability to understand the basics of relaxation. You aren't eating well." It was a well-worn speech, one he gave at least every other week.

"William." Jessie patted his knee, the gentle touch sending sparks directly to his heart. Memories of her fingers touching him in other ways forced their way into his brain.

He wasn't good enough for Jessie. He wasn't good enough for anyone, but particularly for her. He shouldn't have to keep reminding himself of that. The patriarchal line of the Harris family was trash with relationships.

His grandfather had abandoned his grandmother for a younger woman the moment she hit forty. His father played the family man perfectly. Mostly. There were missed ball games here and there. But generally his family seemed fine. He certainly hadn't seen anything that had made him question it. Looking back, however, it was clear.

Other families didn't have weeks where the adults refused

to look at each other or talk. But there was no yelling. Everything looked fine—at least on the surface.

His father's entire facade was exposed when he was sixteen. That was when his half brother, also called William, reached out via social media. William!

His father had shrugged it off and dropped any pretense that he cared about anyone but himself. His mother had stopped pretending too. She didn't leave his father—no that would make tongues wag even more—but she made sure William understood what trash the men in his family were.

Once William had thought he was different. Once. He'd gotten engaged. Planned a wedding, a life…and cost his ex-fiancée the dream she'd wanted.

The line of wicked karma that destroyed the women unlucky enough to love Harris men stopped now.

"Jessie…" He squeezed her tightly—a friendly check-in on a friend who looked under the weather. She'd spent more days than he cared to think of looking ill this last week.

"I'm fine, William. I've just been busy."

She was always busy. At the hospital. The woman worked all the legal hours she could. And volunteered in the children's ward when she wasn't on call, when she would read stories to the kids. She included all the kids: the ones in for treatment *and* their siblings, who were often overlooked by others.

That was another reason he wasn't cut out to be more than her friend. Jessie would be a great mother. She was nurturing and attentive, even to the most mundane stories the little ones told. She deserved a partner without the baggage he'd always carry.

Padma stepped into the staff room and threw her scrub hat into the dirty hamper with extreme force before she leaned against the wall and let out a sob.

Jessie was on her feet before William could blink.

"You did a great job." Jessie was rubbing Padma's back.

"She is going to make a full recovery. You did everything you could. Everything."

Those were all words the ob-gyn knew, words others in the surgical suite had probably said too. But success didn't always make you feel better.

"That girl should have been in the hospital weeks ago. She should have been cared for. I deliver babies for a living and I hate that some people..." Padma let out a tired sigh. "I could have saved the ovary two days ago. Hell, maybe even twelve hours ago. But no, her parents assumed she was pregnant. Like that is the worst thing that could happen. Please!"

"And even if she was, she should have seen a doctor. Been told her options." Jessie said what he'd been thinking.

There was no excuse for what had happened to Katie. But at least she had someone in her life who cared about her.

"I swear people mistake the early symptoms of pregnancy for flu or a stomach bug far more often than they do appendicitis or severe abdominal pain. Don't feel like eating for a week? Can't seem to get up in the morning? Then I suggest you pee on a stick."

Padma let out a ragged breath. "Have pain that makes you feel like your abdomen might explode? Get to the ER. How hard is that?"

Padma walked over to the wall of lockers, opened hers and grabbed her backpack. "I'm changing, going home to shower and then screaming into my pillow. Thanks for letting me vent on this one."

"Anytime." Jessie walked over to the lockers too, then nodded to William. "We aren't doing any good here. Her brother is with her. That is who she will want when she wakes. I'll check in on her tomorrow. We should all get some rest."

The words were music to his ears. Jessie needed to get out of here and sleep. Maybe tomorrow the bags under her eyes wouldn't be there—or at least wouldn't be so dark.

William grabbed his own bag and followed her to the elevator. He hit the button for the parking garage and leaned against the wall.

He took the chance to look at his friend, really look. Jessie had been different since they'd spent the night together. He understood that. One did not spend an evening of bliss with one's best friend without everything changing. Even if you both thought it best to go back to the way it was.

"You okay?" The question slipped out and he hated the roll of her eyes. A few weeks ago she'd have laughed at the question, offered a playful retort that he worried too much. Their easy friendship had vanished when he'd returned her kiss. He wanted it back.

No. He wanted something he couldn't have. But if a lifetime with Jessie wasn't an option, having her as his best friend was the next best thing. And it felt like each day they were drifting a little further apart. He wasn't sure how to pull them back together.

"Come on, Jessie. I am checking on you. You seem tired and you aren't eating. You complained about nausea. I mean you fit all the criteria Padma mentioned for pregnancy."

The joke fell flat. What a stupid thing to say. They were trying to move past the night they'd agreed to ignore.

Besides, there was almost no way she was pregnant. They'd used protection. William always used protection. No children would ever call him Daddy.

The memory of holding her morphed into a flash of desire to pull her close and kiss away the awkwardness that he'd just thrown into the room.

Like a kiss would fix anything.

"Sorry. Bad joke." He pushed his hand through his hair. "It's not as easy to just pretend nothing happened."

"I know." Jessie looked at him. Her cheeks weren't flushed with color. In fact she was paler than he'd ever seen her.

"Jessie—"

Before he could say any more, the elevator doors opened and two other nurses waved at them as they switched places with him and Jessie.

"Have a good shift." Jessie waved back and started moving toward her car.

"Jessie, wait." William was desperate for just a few more minutes.

Her hand landed on his chest as she turned from her car to him. Heat rippled up his body but ice traveled down his spine. There was a chasm threatening to open before them. What if she pulled away, said it was too much, that they'd ruined what they had?

He took a deep breath. "You're my best friend." Those four little words held so much truth.

"You're mine too." Jessie let out a sigh as she looked to her feet. "I can't lose you, William."

She didn't want to lose him either. They could weather this. They *would* weather this. "You won't." He wrapped his arms around her, grateful that she let him hold her. "You and me, Jessie. We are peas in a pod. One little hiccup. But all friendships have hiccups."

Most of those hiccups were disagreements over food choices, holidays, meet-and-greet times, a romantic partner the other didn't like. Not falling into bed and holding each other with such passion you thought the world would stand still just to sing praises of two people finding each other.

Then the morning hits and you remember that you come from a long line of shitty men who cheat on everyone. Every girlfriend you've ever had has complained that you have commitment issues, which is a truth you can't even deny.

All of that was enough to make sure you didn't tarnish your best friend's love live. But you ruined the dreams of the woman you once planned to spend the rest of your life with.

No one deserved him.

"You can't lose me, Jessie. You're my best friend." She was his person. They'd clicked the first day she'd walked into Anchorage Memorial, a brand-new doctor so closed off to the world that no one knew where she came from. She'd panicked when people had asked about her past. He'd stepped in and talked about hobbies. The next thing he knew they were making plans to hike and before long, they were always together. Anything they didn't want to discuss, was before Anchorage, BA. And they respected that boundary.

Others pretty much only knew about details you could find on her résumé. Med school: University of Colorado School of Medicine. Residency: Indiana Health University.

But William knew she had a sweet tooth that rivaled any he'd ever seen. Knew she cried in movies that weren't sad. Knew she had a green thumb that made her house look like a tiny jungle with plants she babied like others might care for a pet. Those were the important details of Jessie's life.

Besides, his entire existence before the age of eighteen was BA. So, he got it. Jessie was his best friend. Pure and simple.

"Movie night at my place, day after tomorrow?" It was their standard Sunday-night activity when they were both off. The standard hadn't felt so standard lately.

"You feel like laughing or crying?" He winked and grinned as she put her finger on her chin. That was a typical Jessie move—maybe the chasm he feared wasn't on the verge of appearing.

"Hmm. I guess let's see how tomorrow's shift goes. If it's another day like today, then I say crying. I heard the new kids' movie is a real tearjerker."

"Only for you, Jessie. I think everyone else thinks the emotions are cute and funny in cartoon format."

He leaned against her car and instantly regretted the motion as the scent of her strawberry shampoo invaded his nose.

They'd worked a twelve-hour shift, racing from room to room, and she still smelled like strawberry shampoo.

Best friends did not care about the berry scent wafting from the messy bun on the top of their friend's head. Didn't think of how their friend tasted or how they felt when they slept on their chest…naked.

"You've drifted away." Jessie's hand was on his chest again and his heart screamed that he should bend his head just a little, see if she lifted hers to kiss him like she had that night.

But that wasn't what they'd agreed to.

"Long day." It wasn't a lie. He needed to go home, take a hot shower and remind himself why he was no good for others. Particularly Jessie.

She deserved the best—and he was no prize.

Her fingers tapped on his chest, then she pulled away. "It was a long day. See you tomorrow."

She got in the car. He stepped back, lifted a hand and forced himself to walk away. He was simply a best friend who walked his tired colleague to the car.

He did not stay to watch her drive off, wishing he was in the seat next to her.

CHAPTER TWO

TWO PINK LINES. *Two pink lines.* One plus sign. And one read-out that simply said Pregnant.

Five tests. Four too many.

And that was on top of the two she'd taken last night. Both had shown Pregnant then too, even though it was the end of the day, and the instructions recommended waiting until first thing in the morning.

The only difference between last night and this morning was the tests this morning had turned positive faster. She looked at the collection of them on the counter, like somehow anything would change.

Jessie ran her hand over her as-yet-unchanged abdomen. She knew exactly how far along she was. There was only one possible time in the last year.

She texted Padma, asking her to meet her in the hospital coffee area before her shift. Padma sent back a question mark, which was understandable. Jessie had started over in Anchorage. No one knew her past. She'd never been allowed to make friends growing up. They might have had germs and she couldn't risk giving them to Bran. A standard cold could cause her brother to spend a week, or more, in the hospital since the chemo had destroyed his immune response.

As a result she sucked at making friends. The only reason she and William were so close was because he'd done all the early work. She'd asked him once why, guessing that it was pity for the girl from the lower forty-eight who'd frozen at simple get-to-know-you questions on her first day of work.

William only said she'd seemed like she needed a friend. He'd been right. She hadn't known how much she'd craved companionship, how much she'd needed someone in her life, until he'd forced his way in.

And because he was her friend, she knew how he'd respond to this pregnancy. Not well. Not well at all.

She'd met so many of his girlfriends over the years. Lately, a tiny bead of jealousy would form when he'd announce a date with someone new. Which was ridiculous, because he was her friend…and because he didn't want what she wanted. Deep down, Jessie wanted a partner and kids.

She wasn't sure why he refused to settle down, but he was clear; no one was meeting him at the altar and no little ones with his eyes were in his future. His line ended with him. "Time to put the genes to rest," he'd said once.

Sure, each woman he dated seemed to think she'd be the one to tame the hot nurse. But he never strung them along.

She'd asked why once and he'd shrugged and said, "BA."

That was enough. Besides, Jessie had given that same shrug many times in her life.

Why do you have scars on your arms and hips?

A shrug was easier than saying she'd been poked with so many needles as a kid she was surprised she didn't have more than just a few. That response, or anything like it, brought on questions.

Why were you homeschooled?

Again, a shrug was better than explaining her parents hadn't wanted her to miss days when they needed her at the hospital, undergoing tests to make sure whatever part Bran needed was in good working order.

What is a savior sibling?

That was a question she'd answered exactly once. The horrified look in the resident's eyes confirmed what she already knew about her childhood. It was a horror story. Maybe it wouldn't have been if Bran had lived, or maybe the horror would have come later.

As Jessie looked at her phone, she tried to think of the right way to reply to Padma. She'd never contacted the OB outside of hospital hours, but she didn't want to wait.

I need to ask you some questions. About pregnancy.

She looked at the text then hit Send. Might as well be direct. She needed to know her options. All of them.

Padma sent back a thumbs-up and a coffee cup.

Great.

"Never expected you to be someone who responded to texts with emojis." Jessie stepped behind Padma in line at the coffee shop. "This one is on me. I appreciate you agreeing to meet before shift."

Padma looked back. "Don't worry about it, I'll get my own. This isn't a hardship, Jessie. I like that you asked me to coffee. We should do it, even when you don't need something."

Padma grinned and continued. "And the emojis are easiest. They convey the message quickly." Padma ordered, then stepped out of the way.

"A peppermint tea, please. Large." Jessie looked toward Padma but she wasn't paying any attention to the order. Peppermint was the only thing that calmed her stomach at the moment.

She grabbed her order and headed to a table in the corner. There wasn't much privacy here but it worked. Most people took their drinks to the rooms where their loved ones were, or drank them fast on their way to start rounds. No one was sticking around to see what Jessie and Padma were doing.

"How far along are you?" Padma asked as she slid into the chair across from Jessie. Her voice low, her eyes looking over Jessie in the clinical way she recognized.

Jessie knew what her colleague would see. Someone tired, achy and already having issues with morning sickness. For most people it didn't start this early. When it did, it usually meant that the sickness might lead to hyperemesis gravidarum—a severe form of morning sickness that often resulted in hospitalization for dehydration.

"Because of your little vent last night, I went to the pharmacy and bought one of each test on their wall. One of each, Padma." The woman behind the counter had told her she only needed one. Maybe two, if she wanted to be really sure, but Jessie had just thanked her and purchased the lot.

"Jessie?"

"Six weeks and four days." At least it was easy to know the exact date of conception. They'd used protection. Each time. But prophylactics were never a hundred percent. "I missed my period a week and a half ago but I was so busy at the ER that I didn't notice."

Until Padma had made her comment in the staff room last night.

She'd opened the calendar on her phone where she tracked her cycles even though she knew immediately she was late. That was when it had all fallen into place: her achy breasts, the exhaustion and the nausea. The test just confirmed it for her still-disbelieving brain.

Hell, even William had joked about it last night. A joke. So flippant. So pointed without knowing. She fit all the criteria Padma listed.

"Does William know yet?"

"No. And I didn't say who the father was." Jessie blinked,

glad she'd set the peppermint tea down. She might have dropped the hot liquid right into her lap on hearing that accurate statement.

"Please." Padma raised an eyebrow. "Hospital gossip is one thing. But you two have been off for weeks. One-night stand?"

Jessie's mouth was open. Her brain had left the building. Padma was direct. It was one of the things Jessie liked about her. But wow.

Maybe they weren't as discreet as they'd thought.

"I need to know my options." Jessie tapped the plastic top of her tea mug.

"You know them." Padma looked at her. "You did a turn in OB for residency."

"What are the laws in Alaska?" Jessie took a deep breath. Her residency was in the lower forty-eight. She knew what she told her patients in the ER, but now that it was her in the situation, she wanted to hear it from someone else.

"In Alaska, you can terminate for any reason until twenty weeks. So you have time."

"Twenty weeks." Jessie nodded. "Can you keep this between us?"

"Of course. But right now I want to talk about taking care of you, Jessie. The ER is stressful on the best days, and most days in the ER are *not* best days."

"I'm fine." Jessie reached for the tea but Padma grabbed her hand.

"I am not going to listen to BS right now. You are less than eight weeks along. Most people don't even notice symptoms this early."

Jessie shrugged. "I've always been in tune with my body." That was true. Bran's cancer came back when she was three. The stem cells she'd donated as a baby had given him a few nice years. She'd been too little to remember the good days.

All her memories started with the hospital. Nurses in fancy

scrubs, smiling…and frowning physicians. Her mother's tears…her father's quiet stare.

The procedures, another bone marrow transplant, blood transfusions and chemo had given Bran almost ten more years. Though the last year he'd been so miserable. He'd barely made it to his sixteenth birthday. And he hadn't looked forward to any of the milestones.

Bran had known he'd never get a driver's license. Or his own car. No staying out past curfew or sneaking out with friends.

Padma tipped her coffee cup, draining it. "Even if you know your body super well, symptoms this early are not a good sign. If you decide you are going through with the pregnancy, you need to get enough sleep. You need to scale back at the hospital."

"What do you think?" The question was out but she didn't have a mother, or a fun aunt, or even a best friend that wasn't also the father of this child, to ask.

Padma reached for her hand again; she squeezed it. "I think you should know *your* decision when you talk to William. His support is important but it is your body. Your decision."

Jessie's hand went to her stomach. She'd always wanted to be a mother. In the hospital, when she was free to walk around between Bran's appointments, she'd pushed a little stroller with her doll she'd named Baby. So on brand for a little kid.

The nurses used to treat Baby while she was getting poked. The baby doll had worn bandages matching hers. It was her comfort item. And she'd laid it next to Bran in his coffin. The one last thing she could pass to him.

Her eyes filled at the memory, at the need grabbing on to her soul. She wanted this baby. This was her child. Hers.

There was no decision to make. Not for Jessie.

But how was she supposed to tell William?

Time seemed to slow, then speed up, then pause as the world moved around her.

"Good morning." Georgia held up her cup of coffee and slid into the chair next to Padma.

"Morning." Jessie smiled, trying to place all her thoughts in a box so she could function today. Not that it seemed to be working.

Work. Focus on work. "Katie is doing better." Jessie had checked in on her before coming down to meet Padma.

"Thanks to you two and William." Georgia took a sip of her coffee. "How are you gals this morning?"

"I'm having a baby." Jessie opened her mouth then closed it. That was not what was supposed to come out. She was supposed to tell William first. Or second, since Padma now knew. Now he'd be third. Just saying it out loud made it somehow more real. "I'm *having* a baby."

Her nerves and joy were blending into a slushy of emotions that was threatening to overload her system.

Georgia blinked, her head bopping between Jessie and Padma. Her mouth was as open as possible. "Um…"

"Regretting popping into that seat now?" Jessie asked. "My emotions are all over the place. Literally bouncing everywhere and my brain just popped that out. It's probably too early to blame hormones. Guess it's the shock."

Georgia laughed, but the noise was more nerves than chuckle. "I thought we were just having a girls' coffee. I forced my way in. I can leave."

"No. Stay." Jessie sipped her tea. "But you can't tell William. Not yet."

"Right." Georgia pressed her palm to her forehead. "Right."

"And we should do girls' coffee. At a coffee place that isn't also our work location. Or dinner. Or dessert and drinks," Padma added, then turned her attention to Jessie. "But no alcohol for you—you need to take care of yourself."

"Right." Jessie nodded. So many thoughts were racing for attention in her mind.

"Now that you are having his baby, want to hear any stories about before Anchorage?" Georgia threw finger quotes around the *before Anchorage* term. She'd been trying to give out some ideas about William's childhood since she'd arrived. And she could not believe that Jessie wouldn't ask.

Jessie shook her head. If there was something William wanted to tell her, he would.

"Fine." Georgia gave a playful wink.

"Since you're in on this now, Georgia, I expect you to keep an eye on her." Padma pointed to Jessie. "Seriously. She will overdo it. You know that."

Georgia gave Padma a salute. "On it." Then she directed her attention to Jessie. "I have my orders, and I will follow them. She is scarier than you. By a lot!"

"True." Padma grinned, looked at her watch on her free hand, then squeezed Jessie's hand one final time. "You have any more questions, you text or call."

"Will you answer with emojis?" Jessie leaned into the joke; she was happy. So happy. Worried, confused, more than a little terrified. But happy.

"Absolutely! One of the best things about my field is I can use the cat emoji for all its meanings." Padma made a silly meow noise.

"No fair. If I'd thought of that, I might have gone into OB." Georgia giggled. "We don't have any fun emojis for ER work." Georgia playfully pouted. "Though maybe a light bulb and a peach when the patients 'fall' on something and have an item stuck. Flared base, people."

An ER nurse had made a handout for those that came in with foreign objects inserted in their nether regions. The handout explained the importance of flared bases for that kind of fun. It had cut down on the number of repeat patients, but it was always going to be an issue the ER dealt with.

"See." Padma nodded. "You can use emojis in the ER. Creativity, ladies!"

Jessie couldn't control the bark of laughter as Padma waved goodbye.

"You sound happy."

Jessie's hand went automatically to her belly as she turned to see William.

"Good morning. I see you two already have your morning beverages." William leaned toward her, like he was going to kiss her, before pulling himself back.

Things were already weird enough between them. After she told him about the baby…*weird* wouldn't come close to describing it. Assuming he stuck around at all. That was an issue for another day. Or later today.

"I need to…to…go." Georgia scooted back and was off in a flash.

Subtle it was not.

"She's in a mood," William commented as he looked after the friend he'd grown up with in Kodiak, Alaska. "Enjoying your English breakfast tea?"

"Actually, it's peppermint. I felt like mint." That was kind of the truth. She stood. "Are you getting more coffee?"

"More?" William put his hand over his heart as he grinned.

"We both know you start your day with at least three cups, and that is not counting the car coffee." One of the pros of a best friend was knowing their quirks. It also meant she knew he definitely didn't want kids. Even though he was so good with them.

He'd told her once that he'd considered going into pediatrics, but wanted the thrill of the ER. He loved kids; he just didn't want any of his own. It wasn't a crime. The world would be a happier place if people didn't bring children into the world they didn't care about. Of course, if her parents had followed that mantra, she wouldn't be here.

"The car coffee is the reason I am so peppy for my shift." William winked, looked at the counter and shook his head. "No. My heart will probably be happier if I wait until hour six to get another caffeine hit."

"Padma doing better?" He followed Jessie as they started down the hallway to the staff locker room.

She hadn't asked. Oh, my—she hadn't asked! What was wrong with her? "I… I don't know."

William raised a brow. "Oh." He shook his head as he opened his locker. "Just a morning caffeine meetup then. Nice."

"No." *Jessie!* How easy would a simple yes be? Georgia sitting down helped the fib. And it was a nice meetup. One they'd need to do again. But her brain had refused to offer the quick response. And it was too early to blame that on pregnancy brain.

What the hell?

"Jessie?"

"I'm pregnant." She let out a sigh. "We can talk about it later. I just needed to know some things from Padma… We'll talk later. Sorry." She grabbed her stethoscope and bolted for the door.

That was a disaster. Pure and simple, a disaster.

William was needed on the floor; he knew this. His feet just refused to move.

Pregnant. Jessie was pregnant. Pregnant.

His mind had lost the ability to focus on anything else.

"William. William. William!" Dr. Georgia Sumter pushed on his shoulder. "Are you there?"

"Yes." He cleared his throat. He couldn't focus on this right now.

Georgia raised a brow but didn't call him a liar. Though her bright eyes said it for her.

They'd grown up together, so she knew his past. Some of it at least. No one knew what happened behind others' closed doors, but she did know he hadn't been home since he was eighteen.

"I just wanted to thank you for Katie yesterday. I don't know why they wouldn't open up to me. No, I do. I thought he was her boyfriend or worse." Georgia blew out a breath. "I had worse a week ago, and I feared I was seeing it again."

"I get it. We see…a lot." William rolled his head, though there was no way to release the tension in his body.

Georgia handed him a tablet chart. "Are you all right? I know you and Jessie are a little out of sorts right now."

"We didn't fight. We don't fight." They occasionally disagreed on what movie to watch. And silly choices about dinner. He hadn't liked her last boyfriend; the man had been a walking red flag.

And if he was honest with himself, he'd been jealous. Jessie wasn't his girlfriend; she wanted the life his ex-fiancée had wanted. And William couldn't give that to anyone.

"I never said the word *fight*. Though everyone fights, William." Georgia rolled her eyes.

"Even you and Eli?" William stuck his tongue out. It was the definition of immature, but he seemed outside his body right now.

Georgia and Dr. Eli Jacobsen had reconnected when she'd returned to Anchorage Memorial a few months ago. They were basically inseparable now.

He was happy for her, and hated the tiny pit of jealousy that settled in his stomach anytime he saw them together. They were perfection and even knowing he couldn't have it didn't stop all the wanting.

Georgia raised both her eyebrows. "Yes. Even Eli and I have

arguments. Love doesn't mean perfection. But you are ignoring my questions. Are you all right?"

He didn't know Jessie was pregnant with his baby. A child he'd never planned to have, with a woman who was too important to lose.

"I don't know."

"Honesty. I like it." Georgia bit her lip, then continued, "But I need Nurse William right now. I've got a twenty-year-old male in room 7. Jumped off a 'small ledge' while hiking." Georgia made air quotes around *small ledge*.

"Impaled his foot on a stick." William made a face as he looked at the notes in the chart. It took a lot to make an ER nurse grimace, but the image his mind created did it.

"Yep. So you and me, time to see if we can pull it out. The X-rays say we can, but..."

"But surgery is standing by?" Even if the X-ray indicated it was possible, there were times when it didn't work.

"Yep." Georgia shrugged. "I know guys claim to have superhigh pain tolerances and I will numb it up best as I can but..."

She left off the rest. He'd worked in the ER for almost two decades now. Scientific studies were finally starting to back up what most professionals could tell you. Women had high pain tolerances. Scarily high sometimes.

Men talked a good game, but when it came down to it, the reality was they didn't come close to carrying the pain load women did.

This was good. It would give him something to focus on besides the woman carrying his baby who'd clearly blurted it out unintentionally then bolted.

Georgia led the way, thankfully not making any small talk. There was no way he could carry a conversation today.

They entered room 7 and William knew his eyes widened as he took in the stick protruding from the young man's heel.

"Hi, River." William smiled, trying to exude calmness as the young man on the bed squirmed.

"I need you to stay still. I know it's hard," Georgia moved to the sink and washed her hands before putting on a pair of gloves, while William pulled the X-rays up on-screen. "The last thing we want is for the stick to shift and cause more damage."

River let out a groan, pinching his eyes closed.

"It's okay to cry. Or even let out grunts." William looked over his shoulders as he washed his hands. "Screams can lead to security rushing in, but if you need to let one out, do it."

"No." River pushed air out, his face pale. "You taking it out?"

Georgia pointed to the X-rays. The branch was in about two inches. It had missed the heel bone. But pulling it out without leaving splinters or causing it to break more was going to make this time consuming.

"I am going to try." She looked at William before giving River her whole focus. "I need you to stay as still as possible while I numb your foot. William is going to hold your ankle down. The numbing may burn."

"I was trying to impress Peyton." River balled his fists, pressing them against his eyes. "And she still went home with Asher."

William sat on the bed by River's foot, holding it still while Georgia got the lidocaine shot ready. "It happens." William had spent his teen years and early twenties trying to impress girls. He'd been good at it too. Just like his father.

When he was a teen, his mother had pointed that resemblance out each time he broke up with a girl. She reminded him of their tears, projecting onto William the pain his father had placed on her. It was a tale as old as time.

"We've hooked up a few times, not that she tells any of her friends. Nope, she likes to kiss me, but going out with me…"

"This will pinch." Georgia inserted the needle.

River flinched and let out a groan. "Damn, that stings."

She'd warned him, but until the burn was coursing through your system it was hard to imagine it might be worse than the pain you were already feeling.

"I'm an idiot. Maybe I should just bounce from girl to girl. Might be happier that way. Pining over one certainly isn't working."

"Not sure that will make you happy either." William gripped River's ankle as Georgia sat down to try to pull the stick out.

"Yeah. You married and happy? Don't see a ring."

River was in physical pain and the girl he liked was leading him on. That was tough. But it didn't justify being an idiot.

"Breathe and focus on staying still." William kept his voice low but authoritative.

"No answer? Right, because marriage and happiness don't go hand in hand. Because commitment is for suckers. I should just sleep around and not care about the consequences."

Georgia blew out a breath but didn't add any commentary. A shame, because the independent woman, holding what looked like tweezers on steroids, could give the best tongue-lashings.

"Want to scream into a pillow? Even numb, you're going to feel some tugging that will be uncomfortable."

"Whatever." River gripped the side of the bed but stayed mostly still while Georgia finished working.

"It's out. I've packed the wound and I will prescribe you antibiotics for the next two weeks. It's a puncture wound so it will be sore and you will be on crutches. I recommend you follow up with your primary care doctor." Georgia stood. "Any questions?"

"Nope." River looked exhausted, heartsick, in pain, and not mature enough to handle it all. It was a rough combination.

Georgia and William took off their gloves, then left the room.

"That was something." Georgia blew out a breath. "Awful young to be so jaded."

William nodded. River was handling it poorly, but commitment wasn't for everyone. If his father had just admitted he had no intention of remaining faithful, there were several women who might have had a chance at finding a loyal partner.

His mother included. Instead of changing, accepting a new reality, she'd become bitter, resentful and more content to be unhappy than to chase something that made her feel alive.

"Hopefully, he grows and doesn't take that resentment out on future partners." William saw Jessie walk into a patient room and felt his heart jump.

They still had eleven hours left on their shift. Eleven hours before he could ask the mother of his child basic questions.

"Can I get some extra blankets in room 3?"

The page went over the loudspeaker, and he was moving even as Georgia grabbed his arm. A call for extra blankets over the page system was the code for security needed. Now. Jessie! She'd made the page within moments of stepping into the room.

It was against protocol to enter the room before security, but if something was wrong…

There was no point in finishing that statement. His decision was already made. He'd pay whatever price HR wanted to discuss later.

"You stupid bitch!"

The hateful words were directed at a young woman who couldn't be more than twenty-five.

"I need everyone to take a deep breath." Jessie's words were soft but authoritative. Her eyes widened as William stepped into the room but she didn't verbally acknowledge his presence.

"Why don't you wait outside, sir?" William wasn't sure

what the issue between the couple was, but separating them was the top priority.

"No. She's carrying my baby."

"Which you don't want." The young woman coughed through the sob, burying her face in her raised knees.

"Of course I don't want it. What will my wife think!"

"Sir, my priority is treating Bethany and the baby right now. Her heart rate is elevated, she has shortness of breath and—"

"And she's four months pregnant and didn't think I needed to know." The man's face was close to purple as he shook his fist at the woman on the bed. Luckily her head was still buried in her knees.

Where the hell was security?

"Do you know how this feels?" The man pointed a finger at William. "Finding out you have a baby on the way you don't want?"

"Yes." He held up his hands and took a step toward the man. Often agreeing with someone who was upset was a good way to deescalate the situation, even when the answer was abhorrent. "It's scary and out of your control. I get it. I really do."

William wanted the man in the hall. Away from Bethany and Jessie.

And their baby.

The man took a deep breath, his glare still focused on Bethany. "You're messing up my *life.* You trying to trap me?"

William needed this brute out of the room. Now. "I had a plan too. No kids. No marriage. Nothing. It feels like a trick of some kind when those things change." He hated these words but he needed to make the man believe he was on his side.

"Life happens and suddenly you're like, this sucks and I hate it. Right?" William took a small step forward, maneuvering so he was between the man and Bethany and Jessie. If he lunged, it would be William he'd encounter.

"Exactly." The man glared at Bethany, ignoring the sobs

coming from the woman he'd no doubt claimed to love not long ago.

"Why don't we go outside and we can chat a bit more."

Just come outside. Leave the room. Get away from Jessie... and our baby.

Fear trickled down his back at that thought. The man was threatening Jessie, Bethany...and his child, no bigger than a fingernail at the moment.

The man shook his fist at the woman one more time, then stepped toward the door. William followed him.

Hopefully, Jessie would make sure Bethany found the support she needed and recommend she stay at a friend's house or hotel. Somewhere her loser boyfriend didn't know about.

"Can you believe this shi—" The man didn't finish that curse as security flanked both sides of him as soon as the door closed.

"You need to come with us, sir." The security officer didn't touch him but the words were not a request.

"Wait—"

William stepped back. He had a lot of things he wanted to say to the man as security led him away. But none of them would change the brute's mind. William rolled his shoulders, trying to calm the anger the exchange brought on.

He headed back to the room with Bethany, but another nurse was already in with Jessie and the pregnant woman. He tried to catch Jessie's eye but she was focused on her patient, which made sense.

Still there was a pinch of worry. Was she intentionally avoiding making eye contact, worried about their upcoming conversation regarding the baby?

The baby... The world seemed to rush at him. He had no idea what they were going to do. But he was certain of one thing: he wasn't good enough to be anyone's father.

CHAPTER THREE

"IT'S STABLE ANGINA," Jessie said to Dr. Eli Jacobsen, trying to keep all her focus on Bethany's diagnosis even though she felt numb inside.

"She's had multiple attacks over the last four days. Shortness of breath, chest tightness, nausea. Each lasts about twenty minutes and happens when she moves too fast." Jessie recited the issues Bethany had listed, watching Eli nod at each one.

The cardiothoracic surgeon always took in as much information as possible during consults. Normally, Jessie appreciated it. Too many doctors rushed consults in the ER. Right now, though, she wanted to finish this quickly and find somewhere to hide for a few minutes.

Her mind was racing. Her heart felt like it was bleeding, and her stomach was more nauseous than ever. No small goal considering she hadn't had a full meal in days.

Sure, she'd unintentionally sprung the pregnancy news on William. But for him to tell Bethany's partner that he understood—to agree with that awful man on anything…?

Her soul had cracked. If they hadn't been dealing with a crisis, she might have hit the floor.

She'd known William didn't want children. She knew he never planned to marry or have a family. And she was carrying their baby. A baby that messed up all his plans.

That was a problem for after her shift. Right now her patients needed her focused.

"Bethany came in today because she thought she was having a heart attack. Triage thought she might be having a panic attack. She is seventeen weeks pregnant."

"Pregnancy can cause heart complications." Eli tilted his head. "But stress and anemia can also worsen them. Any history of that?"

"No history of anemia. However, did you hear about the altercation here?" Hospitals were basically small towns. Everyone worked long hours together and it was a gossip hub. Though maybe most workplaces were like that.

Eli shook his head. "No. I was in surgery. What happened?"

Jessie gave a brief rundown. Even explaining how William got him out of the room.

By telling the truth. His truth.

She blinked away tears as she looked down at Bethany's chart. She knew everything it said. She just needed a moment to regroup.

Pregnancy hormones played havoc with your body. But this wasn't hormones. It was the pain of knowing the thing she'd wanted most for so long was the thing her baby's father wanted least.

Karma was a tricky fellow. It had given her a gift while likely taking away the thing she'd needed most when she moved to Alaska. Her safe space.

They'd drifted apart after their night together. But she'd figured that was normal awkwardness as they tried to regroup. In a few months, maybe a year, everything would be normal again. That dream was forever out of reach now.

"So definitely ongoing stress for Bethany. Good thing William was there. Distracting him. Quick thinking on his part."

"Right." Jessie nodded. It had gotten the job done. She had to give William that. "I've recommended Bethany see a cardiologist as soon as possible. They are admitting her to maternity shortly and a cardiologist will see her there when available. They are going to monitor her and the baby."

Jessie took a breath. She'd called Eli over for a purpose, not just to ramble on. "I saw you talking to Georgia and thought you might stop in too. I know our shifts are over but she's scared."

And alone.

Bethany's family and friends hadn't approved of the relationship. She couldn't technically blame them. Dating an abusive married man was not something anyone should want for their child or friend.

Tough love could work in some situations but when abuse was involved, it just destroyed some of the escape routes people like Bethany needed.

Jessie understood being alone, understood how scary, and sometimes liberating, it was. But loneliness was your constant partner when you were cut off from family and friends. And Bethany had just started her loneliness journey. She'd had no time to find any new place to land.

Jessie had been alone for so long once upon a time. She'd tried dating in college, but her one long-term relationship ended when he no longer needed a "hyperfocused" study buddy. He'd used her…like her parents had.

The few men she'd gone out with once in a while all said she had trust issues. How could she not?

Only William had ever slipped past all her barriers. Their connection might be forever severed by the baby their one night of bliss had created.

"Of course she is scared. About a lot of things, I suspect. I'll stop in. Georgia won't mind waiting a few minutes." Eli continued, "The good news is that she likely won't need to see me for more than just reassurance this time around. Usually it can be treated with nitroglycerin and will resolve once her pregnancy concludes."

"Let's hope so." Jessie let out a breath, grateful that her shift was over. She could get her stuff, go home, shower, have a good cry and figure out all her next steps.

She put the tablet chart back on the charger and headed for the locker room.

"There you are." William was waiting by her locker, looking so casual. Like he didn't have a care in the world after a little over twelve hours ago she'd blurted out that she was pregnant to him feet from where they were standing now.

"I was finishing up with Bethany. Eli is going to chat with her, hopefully give her a bit of reassurance since the cardio consult is taking forever." Her tone was professional. That was how she'd get through the next few minutes. This wasn't the time or place for the discussion they need to have.

He shifted and she saw the pain flicker through his eyes. Not that he'd ever react as Bethany's now-ex-boyfriend had, but he'd always been clear that he never planned to have children.

"Does she have a place to stay tonight?"

"Here." Jessie moved toward her locker and grabbed her bag. Exhaustion was nipping at every facet of her being. She owed William a conversation but she didn't have the strength to have it right now.

"I admitted her. She is heading up to OB for monitoring and a twenty-four-hour heart check. They've been notified of everything that happened so she is considered locked down. He won't be able to get back in."

"I doubt he's coming back." William said it with such finality.

Was that what he wished he could do? Technically he still could if that was what he wanted. She could handle everything.

Others weren't so privileged. Some needed the child support to keep afloat. Bethany was owed that.

"They are having a baby together, whether he, *or his wife*, is happy about that or not. Doesn't change the facts." Jessie didn't know why she'd argued the point.

"Doesn't mean he has to be involved. The courts can force the issue on a monetary level. But if a father wants to walk away, it's pretty easy. Hell, even if he is present, he doesn't have to really be present."

He was right, of course. However, he was saying the words to the woman who was carrying his child. His best friend. Or was she now his former best friend? Was William already planning to just send a monthly check?

Pain ripped through her. She placed a hand over her belly; whatever came she'd make it through. But that didn't mean she wouldn't spend days…years…mourning the loss of her best friend.

William pulled a hand across his face. "His barely controlled violence was worrying."

William's mouth continued to move. She knew words were coming out, all focused on Bethany, but she couldn't unhear his casual observation that the father didn't have to be involved.

"So, we should probably talk, right?" William's hand was warm on her shoulder.

She looked at the hand, so gentle compared to what Bethany had endured. But she couldn't stop replaying his words of agreement with Bethany's boyfriend.

Yes, agreeing was a de-escalation technique. But they were words she'd heard him say before. Not as harshly. But, whenever a woman he was dating mentioned wanting a family, he ended things quickly. Hell, the nursing staff had stopped setting him up on any dates because he went on one or two dates, then let the women down easy.

"Right?" William squeezed her shoulder as he repeated the word.

She took a deep breath and stepped away. "You don't want children. You've said it for years. *My line ends with me.*"

She'd known him long enough that she could parrot his words back to him.

William's chestnut eyes met hers. Even knowing it would be a lie, she wanted him to deny it.

Her entire life she'd buried her needs, her wants, her desires. She was the savior child. The girl born to save her brother's life. And she'd failed at that.

Bran had held her hand as he passed. Her mother had sobbed over his body and in a moment of grief told Jessie she was a failure, that if life was fair, she'd have never been born. But she wanted this baby. Wanted the family. Wanted something William would never want.

"Jessie—" Whatever words he'd planned to say fell into the silence hanging between them. William rocked on his feet and looked at the floor.

"It's fine, William. I get it. I really do. But I am keeping the baby." She grabbed her bag and threw it over her shoulder. "I don't expect anything from you. I know this isn't what you wanted. I get that."

Before he could say anything else, she bolted for the door.

Wow, twice in one day she'd dropped life-changing information on the father of her baby and then run. That was not the most mature way to handle this.

Horns blasted behind him and William wondered how long he'd sat at the green light before the cars behind him started their symphony. He raised a hand and proceeded to pull through the light and into the shopping center. William's stomach had rumbled on for a while, so he may as well grab some sort of sustenance.

He'd driven around for almost an hour attempting to decide if he should go home and work out the rambling feelings blasting through him or head to Jessie's and try…

And try?

His brain refused to take any further action when he traveled that route. What should he do?

Food might help resolve the conundrum. Or at least it wouldn't hurt.

Opening the door, he got out and started walking toward the front. What did one buy the day your best friend told you she'd gotten knocked up from the one-night stand you both agreed wasn't happening again? Pasta? Alcohol?

Alcohol was how his father and mother had drowned their problems. The bottle was the companion his ex-fiancée had spent her spent her final hours with. William had no plans to follow that route.

"Nate! Nate! Nate!" A man around William's age, with a walking cast on his left foot, hollered at a toddler as he dashed toward the store's front door.

William opened his arms and the toddler raced right into them, laughing and squealing. He wasn't sure what the boy's game was, but he knew toddlers tended to either avoid all strangers or not know any.

In this situation, it was good the little one was in the latter category. The boy's small arms wrapped around his shoulders as William lifted him up and carried him back to his father.

"Thank you." The man was exhausted but smiled as he reached for his son. "Nate, I can't chase you right now and running is dangerous in public. You can race all around our backyard, but here you could get hurt or hurt someone else."

The little boy went to his father, love shining between the pair. After seeing Katie and her brother and Bethany's boyfriend on shift the last two days, it was nice to see a parent who cared about their child.

"His mother is nine months pregnant with his sister. I am trying to give her some rest, but this little guy is a lot faster than you'd think."

William grinned and waved back at Nate as the little boy waved at him. "I get it. The little legs are deceptive. It might not be my place, but the backpack harnesses can provide you with more security for toddlers that—" he looked at the little munchkin "—have a habit of darting off."

"You mean leash him." The man sighed. "His mother suggested it. I worried people might judge us."

William had seen too much in the ER not to think the harnesses were a good idea. Little ones did not have the capacity to understand the dangers around them. It wasn't Nate's fault, but the consequences could range from a bump on the knee to a life-changing disaster. "It's a safety device at the end of the day. And if people judge you for keeping them safe, then they aren't people you need in your life."

"True." The father looked at his son. "Want to go pick out a harness?"

The boy grinned, not understanding but happy and secure with his father. That was a feeling that William hadn't known in so long.

William's father wouldn't have won any father-of-the-year prizes. But when he was younger, he'd idolized his father. He'd worked hard—or that was the story his father told for the many unexplained absences. He brought home fancy jewelry for his mother and anything William asked for.

But stuff wasn't love. And as he'd grown older, he'd realized the best gifts arrived after his father had let him down: missing basketball games, or the state final debate contest where he'd taken second place. Those were memories that couldn't be recaptured.

It wasn't until he was a teen that he'd figured out the "work trips" were code for visiting mistresses and his other families.

William had at least two siblings that he knew about: a half sister who lived in Massachusetts, and who had never met her father, and his half brother.

For reasons he'd never understand, the man kept up the role of "family" man with his younger brother. He'd even named the boy William Henry Harris so he didn't forget and call his two boys by the wrong name.

From what William understood, his half brother went by Will. They looked a lot alike too—or they had before William covered his body in ink.

When he'd gotten angry and asked why his mother stayed with such a loser, his mother had shrugged. She said his father came from solid money and said that she'd known what she was getting into. If you didn't expect the Harris men to be more than trash, then you weren't disappointed—a direct quote when she'd learned of the other William.

The Harris men did not settle down.

That was his mother's excuse for accepting it. After all, she'd gotten the ring, and as his wife she got most of the financial benefits. She refused to change paths, to seek better for herself.

Once William thought he might change that sad patriarchal line and at least be loyal to the woman he loved. He and Tess had met in college, fallen hard and fast.

Then…then…he'd killed her. Not directly but his family's demons had sealed her future. And his.

No baby deserved the karmic lineage his ancestors had left.

Now Jessie was pregnant with his son or daughter. A warmth slid through his system. Pregnant. She was having his child. Would the baby look like her with red hair and green eyes? Or would it look like him? Maybe it would be a mixture of both.

The image of Jessie holding their son or daughter forced its way forward. His best friend, holding a little one with red hair, smiling. Jessie was going to be the mother every child deserved. Could he be alongside them? Would Jessie even want that if she knew his past?

There was so much BA. He'd respected her boundaries but he'd loved having a close friend who never asked about his past. He'd craved it. But what would she do if she knew everything? It was Jessie; she might be fine with it.

William didn't want to let himself hope. Didn't want to contemplate his role in the baby's life.

Wandering over to the bakery, he looked at the sweets. The iced cookies were Jessie's favorite. In the summertime they were shaped like flip-flops, flowers and ice cream cones. He bit his lip as he looked at them.

This was the crossroads. His father would walk away or ask his partner to terminate the pregnancy. He would think only of himself, of what he wanted.

Jessie wanted to be a mother. He'd known that about her. She always said the timing hadn't worked out or hinted that maybe the universe didn't think she'd be a good mother.

Such BS. Jessie was going to be a great parent. It was himself he was worried about. But walking away and acting like his father was the last thing he'd ever choose.

So, he grabbed two flip-flop and three ice cream cone cookies. Then he headed down each aisle, grabbing the few things he needed and some stuff for Jessie too.

Exhaustion had plagued her all week, and he doubted there was much food at her place. So, he'd grab some stuff she liked and make sure she had something besides granola bars in her stomach.

Finally, he swung down the baby aisle. His knees didn't buckle, and his body didn't ignite. The universe wasn't smiting him…at least not yet.

Anytime they saw a newly pregnant person in the ER, the nurses always recommended buying a pack of diapers each time you went grocery shopping. That way you had a stockpile for when the baby arrived.

He looked at the colorful packaging. All featured babies smiling and playing. He understood the sizes, but what was the difference in the brands, besides a few bucks—or more—in the price tag?

Two claimed to be "mommy's first choice." One said it was "pediatrician recommended." How did that even work?

"I get these for nighttime—they hold more, in my experience—while my son is sleeping and then the store brand for daytime." A mother with a baby strapped to her front smiled as she grabbed a box.

"You can't mess up diapers. Promise." She kissed her baby's head and wandered out of the aisle before he could offer his thanks.

He grabbed a box of newborn size and pushed the cart out of the aisle as fast as possible. He wasn't concerned about messing up diapers. He was concerned about messing up his child.

William had the box of diapers under one arm, and the groceries he'd purchased under the other as he made his way up to Jessie's townhome. She'd decorated the place in earth tones, and during the summer the front walk was covered in plants that later invaded her home when the first frost threatened.

He didn't know what he was going to say, didn't know what the next steps were. But he was showing up for Jessie. He was not going to be his father, was not running from this responsibility.

Hammering echoed as he pounded on the front door, but he wasn't sure she'd heard his knocks. Usually, he'd knock once and just walk in. Hell, he'd had a key for at least two years now. But he'd stopped just walking in after they'd spent the night together—another little shift in their friendship that felt so huge.

William took a deep breath and raised his hand again, careful to keep the cookies level in the bag as he knocked for a third time.

A few seconds later he heard, "You might as well just come in, William," yelled from the other side of the door.

He looked at the doorbell, still not a camera one, even though he'd suggested it. Jessie said she had everything shipped to her postal box, so package theft wasn't something she was concerned with.

"How'd you know it was me?" His voice was raspy. Everything in their relationship had shifted when they'd slept together. And the resulting jumble had been turned topsy-turvy by the pregnancy announcement.

"You're the only one who comes over, William."

She was kneeling beside the stairs that led to the basement, adding spindles to the light green painted handrail that had separated the room from the stairs heading down.

"What are you doing?" William sat the stuff down and walked over. The black spindles didn't exactly match what he playfully called her "witchy-cottage-trapped-in-a-townhome look."

"I've nearly tripped on this staircase for the last time. It should have a railing and I needed something to do. I need to paint it a fun color, but it will do its job. What are you doing you here?" She didn't look up from her job. Just screwed in the top bolt, scooted over and started securing the next section.

"I came to talk. To see how you were. To bring you cookies. To apologize."

Jessie bit her lip, then turned. "You don't have anything to apologize for. I should be the one apologizing. I know there isn't a script for what happened, but no one will use how I handled this to write one."

"I brought you cookies. And diapers." William pointed to

up his haul. "And you don't owe me an apology either. I am sure this is more than a bit of a shock."

"Cookies?" Jessie was on her feet as he reached for the bag.

"The iced ones." At least she was smiling. Step one was to get through the door and feed her—which he'd done. Though she needed more than sugar. Step two was to talk.

"The best ones." Jessie winked, pulled out a flip-flop and bit into it. "Man, I love these. I might use this whole pregnancy as an excuse to have a cookie a day."

Her eyes fell to the diapers. "That was nice of you. But I meant some of what I said. I know you never wanted to be a dad."

"I didn't but..."

"No." She held up a hand. "I've been thinking while hammering out my frustrations. You could always be the fun uncle."

"Fun uncle?" The words tasted weird in his mouth. "Meaning...?"

"Meaning no pressure." Jessie shrugged. "We don't have to tell my little peanut that they share your DNA. At least not until they are older. You can still be my best friend. And in the baby's life with no pressure. None."

No pressure. None. Words that should soothe the aching in his chest. Words a man who'd declared children off limits should want to hear. This was the perfect solution.

So why did each syllable make him want to weep?

"Is that what you want?"

Was it what he wanted?

It would make his life easier. Maybe if his son or daughter didn't know that they came from a screwed-up line until they were older, it would save them from the karma that seemed to doom everyone else.

Jessie laid a hand over her belly. There was no sign that their child was growing there. No hint that in a little less than eight months this townhome would have a tiny new resident. She'd be a great mother.

"You never wanted children. Right?" Her gaze held no glint of hope. She knew the answer.

Denying it wouldn't change what she'd known for most of their friendship. Hell, his ex-fiancée, Tess, had thought he'd change his mind. And when he'd heard her say it to her maid of honor two weeks before their wedding, he'd called everything off.

It hadn't been fair to lead Tess on, to let her think they had a chance at a life he never planned to have. He'd hated himself that he'd led her to believe they had that kind of a future. Sure, she'd known he hadn't wanted children. And he thought she was okay with that.

She hadn't taken it well. She'd spent all afternoon in a bar, then gotten behind the wheel of a car… No. He wasn't thinking of Tess now. Not in this moment.

"I've never thought I'd make a good father." The truth so easily spoken, but the past that came with it? That he wasn't going to get into. Those demons were just for him.

Jessie's eyes widened. "I think you'd make an excellent father, William. Whenever a pediatric patient comes in, all the doctors want you on the case. You are great with kids." She covered her mouth. "Sorry, that is neither here nor there. I know being good with kids is not the same as wanting children."

She took a deep breath, her gaze meeting his, "I am going to raise this baby. I'd like you to stay in my life."

"I'm your best friend, Jessie. I'm here for good. Period. I will help with the baby, be the fun uncle."

"All right. Great. If that is what you want." Jessie eyed the rest of the cookies. "I'm eating a few more of these and we are going to say it is because I am eating for two."

She smiled as she grabbed the bag and headed for her

kitchen. And he tried to pretend that there wasn't a pit in the bottom of his stomach telling him to take the risk.

He was desperate to tell her he wanted to claim the child. Scream from the mountaintops that they were having a baby. Jump at this new and unknown path. Ask if she wanted to give them a chance at a life together as more than friends.

Maybe, if he hadn't met Tess and lost her… Maybe if he were younger and dumber… Maybe then he might throw all caution to the wind.

The problem was the risk wasn't his. Not really. No. It all fell to Jessie and their unborn child. If it was only his burden to carry…

"You coming? I might let you have one of these, but only if you don't hang out in my foyer. You have five seconds to carry that other bag up the stairs and into my kitchen or all these cookies are mine. This is not an idle threat!" Jessie's laughter carried through the townhome.

"Don't I know it." He wandered into the kitchen, letting her mood lighten his.

CHAPTER FOUR

WILLIAM WALKED UP to Jessie's place. Movie night was their routine, something she'd insisted last night that they continue. Yes, there was an awkwardness between them. But it would go away eventually. Right?

He knocked, then walked in just like he normally did. It felt right and off, a weird mix.

Tonight was movie night with his best friend. Whose kisses were fiery perfection. Who fit perfectly against him. Who was carrying his child.

Jessie was in cutoff shorts and a dark blue tank top that hugged her breasts and accentuated her hips. Her hair was pulled into a loose braid with flyaway hairs around her face. She was looking relaxed and pretty as hell.

Gorgeous. She'd been gorgeous every moment that he'd known her. And it wasn't the only sexy thing about her. There was her brain, her smile, her caring personality, the way she cried at sad and happy movies.

He forced down the need creeping up his spine. This was not the purpose of tonight. He was here for movies. Laughter. *Friendship.*

Best friend. Fun uncle. Those were his roles in her life. They'd have to be enough.

"Hey." She held up the plastic bowl that always contained two popped bags of popcorn. One was never enough, but with two they always had leftovers. It was a "price" Jessie joked she was willing to pay.

"Hey." He walked over, gave her a hug, doing his best to ignore the strawberry smell clinging to her hair. He also ignored the tiny voice in the back of his head screaming to ask to kiss her. It would pass. It would. It had to.

"Think you need something to make you cry tonight?"

"Nope! I am looking for a laugh. But first—" she held up her tablet and the pen she used for her notes app "—family history time. I have an OB appointment scheduled. They will ask for known issues. I know all the things that run in my family."

"Right, do you worry the baby will have an issue like you did?" She had scars like he saw on some of the pediatric patients who'd had chronic issues and needed multiple IVs and such. William had felt the scars along her hip the night they'd spent together. They suggested a bone marrow issue. She'd flinched when he touched the cluster of scars, and he'd wanted nothing more than to please her. So he'd traced his hand along her side. Down her neck. Over the top of her tight buttocks. All places that made her moan with pleasure. He'd avoided the spot that made her freeze.

But those were not helpful thoughts right now. He'd not asked about the scars, since it would be a reminder of the night that they weren't speaking of.

"My brother had leukemia." Jessie sat on the couch, crossing her perfect legs, holding the tablet pencil and looking at him with her big green eyes like he hadn't felt the scar on her back. "I guess we have to get into some of the BA stuff now."

"You donated bone marrow. I felt the scar on your hip when…" His mouth dried out and his tongue couldn't finish the words.

"That was for Bran. My brother." She took a deep breath.

Her trembling lip nearly brought him to his knees. He sat on the couch, took the tablet from her hand and sat it on the coffee table. Taking her hands, he stroked his thumb across her wrists. "Bran?"

"Yes. My brother, Bran. He developed leukemia when he was three. No donor matched so my parents used IVF to have me."

Damn. There were tons of reasons to have a child. Creating one specifically to save another had significant ethical concerns.

"The good news is that because I was tested in the lab as an embryo, I know just about everything I need to know about my medical history. So that helps the baby."

She'd mentioned her parents a handful of times, mostly when holidays and birthdays came with no family. But this was the first time he'd heard of a brother.

"Where is Bran now?"

Jessie pinched her eyes closed, and tears leaked out the side. He knew the answer and it broke his heart.

"I couldn't save him. I failed. Failed my family."

Wow. He hadn't thought it possible to hate people you hadn't met, but those were words placed on her or not removed from her. Any parent that would let the child they'd had to save another think they were a failure because medical technology hadn't been enough was trash.

He pulled her into his arms, stroking her back. "You did not fail. You didn't. You work in medicine—you know that sometimes we can't beat the fates. It wasn't your fault."

She hiccupped and laid her head on his shoulder. Her crossed legs made the position uncomfortable for him but William didn't care.

"I had one job. It is the entire reason I was born, William. And Bran… Bran died. Nothing I did changed anything. I held his hand as he took his last breath, knowing, knowing, my parents wished it was me."

She let out a sob, an aching feral hurt. Jessie uncrossed her legs and moved into his lap. "It wasn't fair. It wasn't fair."

He rocked her as she let out anger he wasn't sure she'd ever acknowledged. Life wasn't fair. It was a truth doctors and nurses were taught early. You couldn't save everyone.

To survive in the medical world, you had to compartmentalize. But that knowledge didn't matter when it was family.

William didn't know how long he held her. He did know that it wasn't long enough when she pulled back and wiped her eyes.

"Sorry. Can I blame this on pregnancy hormones?"

"You don't need to blame it on anything." William reached for her hand, but she moved to grab the tablet. His hand hung in in midair for a moment, unattached to the anchor that was simply Jessie.

His life felt like it was tipping and whatever control he'd had seven weeks ago was snapped in half.

She took a deep breath, held her pen and offered a watery smile. "We *were* supposed to be talking about you. Anything I should know for the doctor's visit?"

"Not sure. My family wasn't big on talking about anything. Luckily for us, toxic masculinity is learned, not acquired genetically."

She leaned over, placing a far too platonic kiss on his cheek. "You want to talk about your family? Heaven knows I just unleashed a torrent of BA material."

She'd needed to get that before-Anchorage material off her chest. He didn't have anything he wanted to share. The men in his family were trash.

Sure, he was better than they were. But starting from negative one-fifty and hitting negative fifty wasn't anything to brag about.

Perhaps if he'd done a better job of being honest with Tess

she would still be here. Living the life she'd wanted, with a man who could give her everything she'd dreamed of.

"I think it's movie time." He squeezed her hand and grabbed the remote. "And we are watching the funniest thing we can find!"

They'd earned the laughter.

William let out a groan as he shifted the pack on his shoulders. Normally they shared the load on their hikes, but today he'd insisted on taking most of the stuff in her pack.

"I can take some stuff, if it's too much for you." They'd climbed Rabbit Lake Trail dozens of times in the course of their friendship. It was a long hike, four-plus hours. But at the end of it was a crystal-clear lake that she could never get enough of.

She'd could sit there for hours, just basking in it. And when she camped up here, that was often what she did. When she needed to escape on her own for solitude and contemplation, this was her happy place.

"Nah. I got it." Those were the same words he'd said when he'd taken most of the stuff from her backpack this morning and repacked his own.

Hers now only had the first aid kit, her windbreaker, extra socks and her headlamp. Though right now Alaska got about nineteen hours of daylight so the odds of needing the headlamp were next to none. Still, she'd seen far too many disasters in the ER related to unprepared hikers to not carry enough for being out for at least forty-eight hours if needed.

"You know they say pregnant women can continue to do all the activities they did before. In fact, it is recommended." Her first prenatal appointment at eight weeks had gone easily enough. There wasn't much that happened at the first appointment anyway.

Her doctor did a basic health check, family history and

blood work. And sent her home with a ton of pamphlets. Most of it was information she knew as a doctor, but it was nice to have anyways.

And a prescription for antinausea meds was making a small difference. At least she could keep some things down now. Though it would be a while before she had any more cookies. That indulgence had cost her dearly.

At least William had left before that round of illness kicked off. Right now she was surviving on broth, granola bars and peppermint tea.

"I have heard that." William adjusted the pack again—and let out another grunt.

For someone who claimed he didn't want to be anything more to this baby than the "fun uncle," he was certainly overprotective of her and their little peanut.

It would be so easy to let herself believe she might get the fairy tale: the loving home she could create for herself and the picture-perfect image of two parents who loved each other and the little life they'd created.

That was the dream of the little girl who'd sat in so many hospital waiting rooms and played in hospital playrooms while watching other parents care for their children.

Her parents loved each other. She couldn't fault them on that. So many marriages ended in divorce during medical struggles, either for a spouse or a child. Her parents' devotion to each other had never wavered.

It was only she who didn't get to bask in love's radiant glow. She was the afterthought. Her brother's savior, brought into the world to give him a second chance and a failure.

When Bran died her parents lost all need to pay attention to her. The good news was that she finally got to go to public high school when any germs she might pick up no longer mattered. She'd graduated top of the class, gotten a scholarship and gotten out.

She'd daydreamed of the happily-ever-after. The life she could lead when she got to choose. The life that had never been within reach for her.

Jessie's hand fell to her belly, the growing life that was there. This child would never doubt they were loved. They would never know that their conception was an accident. Maybe they weren't planned but Jessie would love her little one. Protect them. Make sure they knew when the world got tough, they always had a safe place to land with her.

William let out another soft groan and she'd had enough. "Put it down. I am taking some stuff back and if you don't agree then I will start marching down this trail to the car right now. And I will leave your stubborn butt if I get there first."

She put her hands on her hips, ignoring the looks of the hikers around them. The trail was always busy this time of year, so waiting until they were alone was not an option.

William looked up the trail, not making any move to take the pack off.

"I'm not bluffing, William."

"Trust me. I know that." He pointed up the trail, "But there is a rest place about three hundred yards up. Why don't we stop there? We can adjust my pack and take a water break."

Part of her wanted to argue on principle. His shoulders had to ache, and his back was probably screaming. They were in good shape. Hell, William was in great shape, but the extra weight still took its toll. However, three hundred yards wasn't that much to travel.

"Fine."

"I know you want to argue." William winked as he started up the trail again.

"I do." She stuck her tongue out at his back.

"I saw that." He chuckled.

"No, you didn't."

"Did so." He looked over his shoulder, confidence radiating

off him. For a moment it was like they were back to the William and Jessie they'd been before their night together. Friends giving each other a hard time. A playfulness she missed so much. Maybe they were finally finding their way on the new path they'd unintentionally carved for themselves.

"Then tell me what I did." The climb was a little rocky here so she couldn't put her hands on her hips like she wanted to.

"Stuck your tongue out and rolled your eyes."

He knew her well—too well. But he'd technically gotten it wrong. "I did not roll my eyes."

"But you *did* stick out your tongue." He stepped off the trail at the rest point. He took a deep breath and dropped his pack, not quite letting it fall to the ground, but it was close.

"Sit." She pointed to the bench and William dropped onto it immediately. Stepping behind him, she took her elbow and dug it into the pressure point by his left shoulder blade.

"Yes. God, yes, that feels good."

Luckily, he was looking away as heat traveled to her cheeks. He'd made that same guttural noise of pleasure the night they'd spent together. Several times.

"The good thing about taking years of anatomy and physiology is that I know all the pressure points in the back."

"Why the clinical tone?" He rolled his head to the left side as she pressed her elbow into the crevice between his neck and shoulder.

Once more, he knew her so well. There was no reason to use her "clinical tone." Except that was easier than the low tone she wanted to use.

If they were dating, she'd lean into him, whisper in his ear that that was the exact way he'd groaned when she took him in her mouth. The exact sound he made when he joined their bodies. The noise he made just before climax took him over the edge.

Then she'd trail a line of kisses down the back of his neck

and make promises to rub out all the tension in his body when they got home.

She blew out a breath and forced herself to step back. As a physician she knew that pregnancy hormones increased your libido toward the end of the first trimester and the start of the second. Could she blame the heat blasting through her body on those?

"Better?" She needed to stop touching him. Focus on something, anything else.

William rubbed his right shoulder with his left hand. "Can't complain." His dark eyes glittered, and her eyes fell to the tattoos poking out from under the long-sleeved moisture-wicking shirt that hugged him in the best way possible.

Ugh. They were friends. Friends did not think of each other that way. That thinking was what had led to the little one growing inside her.

Her hand fell to her belly and his eyes followed. He looked at her in such a way it was easy to wish for the fairy tale she knew she wasn't getting.

"Ready to take a few things?" William stood, the magic of the moment broken.

Probably because it was in her head the whole time.

"Right. Yeah. Yeah." She opened her pack, taking a few things from his and packing them without even looking at them.

"Try that out." He waited while she pulled the pack on and tightened the strap around her belly to help balance the weight.

Stepping around her, he slid fingers under the back. His finger ran along her shoulder. "The weight okay?"

It was such a simple touch. A friendly gesture to check on her. It was her turning it into something more. Something it would never be.

Yes, she'd asked to be just friends after they'd spent the night together. But if he'd pushed back, if he'd whispered any of the things he'd said to her while they'd lain skin to skin, if William had shown any interest in continuing…she'd have jumped into his arms, damn the consequences.

Maybe she'd even wanted that.

"It's fine. You still have half my stuff. Let's go." She needed to be moving, needed to force her brain to focus on the trail instead of the man who made her feel…feel…

Tears clouded her eyes. He made her feel whole. In a different time and place, a different universal story, this was a hike between lovers.

And the fact that she wished for that was something she needed to focus on.

Alone.

Jessie was always gorgeous, but staring out at the lake, the sun kissing her red hair and freckles, she was stunning. Here he could soak her in. Even though he had no right to.

She'd practically jumped away from him when he was checking her pack. He swallowed and pushed his hands into his pockets. Jessie had been hiking since college. The woman knew when her pack was too heavy. He was just being overprotective. Which she didn't want or need.

And he had no right anyway. The "fun uncle" did not lust after the mother of his child. Not when they'd planned to stay friends.

Jessie tilted her head, her ponytail shifting as she looked out at the water. This was her special place. She'd found it on a hiking trail app she used and hiked it the first weekend she'd moved to Anchorage.

She'd brought him a year later when it was safe to hike after the winter melt. They made this pilgrimage several times every summer.

Would they come next summer?

She was due the end of February. There were hiking packs

that let you strap a baby to you. Would her son or daughter love the trails as much as their mother?

Jessie was still staring out at the lake, her eyes lost to another world. Was she wondering about next summer? Or the summers after? Imagining a little one running along the banks of the lake? Learning to pitch a tent and start a fire?

It was so easy to imagine.

And what if another joined them, a man who loved her and their child? She would be so easy to love. She deserved that.

His heart ached knowing the faceless man wouldn't be him. Jessie deserved better.

"What are you thinking about?" He picked up a pebble and skipped it along the surface of the water. He needed to talk rather than let his brain wander to a happily-ever-after that did not belong to him.

"If the multiverse is a real thing."

There were a million things he would have guessed before that. No. There were infinite possibilities because that would never have crossed his mind.

"What?"

"The multiverse. It's a scientific hypothesis that there are multiple universes, comprising all the possibilities." Jessie sighed as she picked up a pebble. But she didn't skip it. Instead she dropped into the lake, staring at the rings.

"I am aware of the premise. It's a pretty big theme in superhero movies."

"Right. Yeah. More than a few of my young patients have talked about it. Some of the older patients too. But I was thinking of the possibilities." She grabbed another rock, dropped it into the lake, staring at the rings again.

Was she wondering about a universe where that happily-ever-after included them? If such a thing was possible, that William was the luckiest being across all of the universes.

"If the theory is true, my brother is alive in one or more

of them. Celebrating becoming an uncle. Begging me not to name the baby after him, while secretly hoping that maybe I do. Bran would have loved being an uncle. He'd have spoiled this little one so much."

She sucked in a breath and dropped another rock. "In that universe I save him."

"Maybe in some universes he never got sick." William stepped toward her. He'd been dreaming of them, and she was thinking of her brother. As she should.

"If the theory is accurate, then yes. But in those he never gets to become an uncle, because in those universes I don't exist. If he doesn't get sick, my parents don't need me."

She picked up one more rock. "In that universe I am not even a thought. They get their happy family."

"They're wrong." William squeezed her tightly. "Seriously. Anyone that doesn't want you is an ass."

"You don't."

The words were so quiet, they were not even technically a whisper. Yet they burrowed into the hole in his heart. And he knew she hadn't meant to speak them.

She froze, clearly waiting to see if he reacted to her tiny whispers. He didn't move. There was no way to respond. And she was right—sort of.

It wasn't that he didn't want her; he wanted more for her.

Tess had wanted what Jessie wanted and he'd stolen it from her. Not intentionally and not directly. But if he'd never proposed, if he'd broken up with her when she'd spoken of maybe wanting children just before he proposed, she'd have been heartbroken but alive. If he'd hurt her then, he'd have avoided destroying her.

William looked at the fading ripples. He hoped the multiverse theory was true. That Tess was happy and healthy in some. That she had a husband, kids and a few pups, as well as the happily-ever-after his selfishness had stolen from her.

Jessie stepped out of his hands, picked up another rock, skipping this one. “Mine went farther than yours.”

He wasn’t sure that was true, but the challenge was issued. He’d rather argue over whose rock traveled the farthest than contemplate what she’d said.

CHAPTER FIVE

WILLIAM WALKED AHEAD of Jessie in the ER hallway, his head bent over a tablet chart. He stepped into the triage room to assume the hospital role he'd occupied the last three shifts.

Jessie knew that triage was William's least favorite job. It was exhausting, you didn't get to see patient results because you were just passing them back to the ER for care and people with minor injuries and issues often complained. The misguided belief that the squeaky wheel got the attention was at odds with the truth that, in the ER, it was simply about who needed care now.

William preferred to be in the ER running codes, staying busy in a different way. Which was why she wondered how long he'd continue to volunteer for triage. Clearly he was avoiding her.

Their hike this weekend had been a disaster. Feelings she couldn't help had bubbled to the surface. Her plan to slip back into friendship looked painfully silly after that hike.

And Jessie had already planned to pull away a little. She needed to give herself space to collect her thoughts, box up her needs and put them on a mental shelf so she could offer William the "fun uncle" experience she'd promised.

But he'd beaten her to it. Funny how much that hurt even though she'd planned to do the same. It wasn't a competition, but she wished she'd made the first move.

"I've got a female patient coming back. Complaining of back pain. Needs to be seen right away." William's voice sounded over the system they used to relay critical patient updates.

"For back pain?" Dr. Ronny Mueller, her least favorite colleague to work with, rolled his eyes as he asked the question through the walkie-talkie-like device. The man had recently taken a few weeks' vacation and none of the staff had missed him.

"Yes. I am taking her to room 8. Please have a doctor see her immediately." There was something in his tone, a concern that made a tingle run down her spine. And not the kind of tingle William's voice had caused so often since their night together.

"I'm not dealing with back pain." Ronny didn't bother to hide the heavy sigh as he moved away.

"I'll do it." Jessie grabbed a tablet chart. If William was that concerned over back pain, then there was something else going on. Something he didn't want to say in front of the patient.

As she stepped into room 8, the patient was just setting her things in the chair usually reserved for friends or family visitors. William had vacated quickly.

The patient turned and Jessie swallowed.

Her face and arms were covered in bruises and her belly was swollen. To the uneducated eye she looked to be about six months pregnant. But there was no baby, and according to her chart the woman was over seventy and well past menopause.

No. This was ascites, a fluid buildup in the abdomen typically caused by liver failure.

"I'm Dr. Davis." Jessie nodded as the older woman slid onto the bed and let out a sigh.

"Elaine Mathews. I'd like to say it's nice to meet you but..." She gestured to the room, then closed her eyes and took a deep breath.

Extreme exhaustion.

"Don't worry about that. I get it a lot. Never great to meet someone in the ER. William, our triage nurse, said you were here for back pain." Surely that wasn't the symptom that had sent her into the ER.

"Yeah. I mean, it feels like my back is burning. I think there is a rash or something back there. Not sure, but it probably isn't pretty."

"What makes you say that?" Jessie walked to the sink, washed her hands and put on gloves while Elaine took another deep breath.

"The nurse flinched when I lifted my shirt. I know my body has seen better days, but it's never a good thing when the triage nurse flinches, then tells ya that ya don't gotta wait." She laughed, then coughed, a deep hacking rattle that sounded like it was calling for death.

Jessie heard several footsteps slow outside, no doubt worried for the patient within.

When Elaine finally got her voice back, Jessie asked, "How long has the cough been going on?"

"A year or so?"

A year or so.

Jessie forced her features into a neutral state as she asked, "Have you seen anyone?"

Elaine gave a look that answered that question flat.

"Good afternoon." Dr. Eli Jacobsen stepped in, his eyes taking in Elaine's stomach as he walked immediately to the sink. "I'm a cardiothoracic surgeon here at Anchorage Memorial."

"A surgeon. I do not need a heart surgeon. Please." She let out a laugh that brought on another round of barking coughs.

Eli looked at Jessie and she saw the worry in his gaze. This was bad. Very bad.

"We don't know anything yet." Jessie knew the words weren't reassuring but this case was far more than back pain. "Can I have a look at your back, please?"

Elaine huffed a little, then sat up and pulled her shirt up. There was a line of bruises on her back but it was the row of shingles crossing from her lower back to the bottom of her shoulder that was causing the burning sensations.

"You have shingles." Jessie looked at Eli and saw him taking note of her swollen fingers and ankles. Shingles was painful. And if it was on the face, it could be life-threatening.

But on the back, it was the least of their concerns.

"Great. Can you give me a shot? Then I'll be on my way."

"There is no shot for shingles once you have it. Just a round of antivirals." Eli smiled as he held up his stethoscope. "Can I please listen to your heart?"

Elaine shrugged as she looked over to Jessie. "I saw a commercial for a shingles shot. This guy not know what he's doing?"

"The commercial is for the vaccine. Dr. Jacobsen is correct—right now we will treat the shingles with a round of antivirals. But we are concerned about the other symptoms you have. The cough. The swelling."

"The irregular heartbeat," Eli added to the end of the list. "I am afraid that William's concerns were likely correct. I believe you have congestive heart failure."

"Yeah. Probably." Elaine winked and looked over to Jessie. "I might not have seen a doctor but I could tell something was wrong." She gestured to her swollen belly and shrugged.

Jessie wasn't quite sure what response Elaine wanted. Patients reacted to poor news in as many ways as it was possible to count. And just because they seemed to take it okay to begin with did not mean they'd continue to in the next minute. The human brain's capacity to wall away bad information never ceased to amaze her.

"I think it would be best if we admit you, Elaine. Get you up to the..."

"Nope." She shook her head. "I came in for back pain. We

know what that is now—shingles. I am seventy-two. I know that isn't *that* old. But it ain't that young either. I've made peace with the time coming." She looked at Eli and reached out a hand to him. "It's okay to not fix everything."

Eli took a deep breath, placing his hand over hers. "That is true."

In the ER, Jessie saw patients well into their nineties whose families begged the staff to do everything possible to save their loved one. She understood the desire; if there'd been any way to save Bran, she'd have done it.

But at some point, medical intervention became more painful than the final result. Refusing to acknowledge that reality was why Bran had spent the last year of his life in such pain.

"It was nice to meet you." Eli squeezed Elaine's hand, then released her.

She turned her attention to Jessie. "I won't turn down those antivirals and maybe some pain meds."

"Fair." Jessie pulled her gloves off. "I will prescribe those, but would you mind speaking to our hospice intake nurse before you are discharged? They can provide support at home to keep you comfortable until the end."

"I'm already here. Provided they don't want to cut me open." She waved to Eli as he exited the room.

"No. I often joke that they are the funnest medical staff you ever meet. They don't care about dietary restrictions, alcohol intake or smoking. Their goal is to let you live the way you want till the end."

"Sound like angels."

"They are." Jessie put the order in for the hospice staff to pay Elaine a visit, then said her own goodbyes.

"So she doesn't want any care for the heart failure?" William crossed his arms as Eli leaned against the door of the tiny triage suite he'd occupied for the last three shifts.

He'd already volunteered for tomorrow but after that he'd find a way to be around Jessie again, find a way to suppress every feeling that overwhelmed him the second he saw her.

He'd wanted her to say… Well, it didn't matter what he'd wanted her to say on the hike. He had no business wanting anything, let alone wishing she'd been thinking of him with pond ripples.

She was thinking of the brother she'd loved and lost. And he'd been selfishly hoping she was wondering about him. Then she'd said he didn't want her and he'd kept his mouth shut. He deserved a few shifts in triage for that blunder alone.

"No. She says she is content to just keep living as she is—without the shingles." Eli moved and Jessie took his place as he stepped to the other side of the doorframe.

"I've had the hospice team speak with her. They will help make her comfortable. And I promised her they wouldn't monitor her diet." Jessie winked then turned her attention to Eli.

"Thanks for coming so quickly. William must have requested your services at exactly the right moment."

"He got Georgia to get me. She said he spent the points he'd earned helping her out a few weeks ago." Eli winked. "Not exactly sure what advice you gave her, but seeing how happy we are now, I should probably offer you my thanks."

"Ah." Jessie crossed her arms, "So I shouldn't expect cardio to race to a bedside consult each time."

"Probably not." His beeper went off and Eli held up a hand as a goodbye as he headed to the next patient needing his expertise.

Jessie didn't follow him.

"And you." Jessie smiled at William, and the world seemed to hold its breath.

She was perfection. When the mother of his child smiled, he wanted to risk everything to pull her into his arms.

But hurting her, letting her down…he couldn't risk that.

"I went to put in a note that we didn't need a hepatology consult for the liver but found that you didn't get that far." Technically nurses didn't put in consults at all, but the long-timers were known to give doctors a heads-up that they needed to see a patient.

Most of the time patients showing with ascites were in acute liver failure. But congestive heart failure could mimic the same symptom.

"She wasn't yellow." William looked out to the waiting room, but no new patients had arrived. No distractions were available.

"Looking for a way to get rid of me already?" Jessie's smile broke as she bit her lip. "No worries. I can take a hint. But… um…good catch."

She turned and walked away without saying anything else.

Damn it. William had promised to be the best friend he'd been before they'd shifted everything. He was failing hard. And once more it was someone else taking all the hurt.

"Thanks, young man." Elaine waved as she slowly moved toward the entrance.

Her feet were swollen and she was breathing heavily. The woman was not long for this world, but she didn't seem bothered by it.

William left the triage suite and stepped beside her, offering his hand. He caught Lauren, one of the newest ER nurses, and motioned toward the triage room.

Technically, it was her shifts in triage that he'd taken over the past several days. She held up a thumb. If a patient needed something in the next ten minutes or so, she'd take it.

"You don't have to walk me out, young man. I will get there." Elaine's words were soft, each one taking up more air than her lungs wanted to produce while walking.

"I needed a break anyway. Besides, if you fall and break

something, you will have to come see us again. And Jessie, Dr. Davis, says you don't want to be here."

"Dr. Davis is a good one. She didn't push. Didn't tell me I should try more things. My partner's been gone three years. She was my whole world. Whatever is next, I'm fine. I've had a good life."

"That's good. I wish I heard it more." Working in the ER, he saw far too many lives cut short. On the other hand, there were also those who'd lived long lives but were facing the end with loads of regrets and no time to fix them. "I hear a lot of regrets."

It was a job hazard nursing school didn't truly prepare you for.

"No life is lived without regrets. It's just figuring out which ones you can live with, and which ones you can't." She pointed to a beat-up red pickup. "This is me. Thank you."

He waited until she was driving away before heading back into the ER. He had a ton of regrets. Living with them was his only option.

"Stop, Dad. Stop! Stop!" A young woman was trying to hold an older man's hands, but he pulled away. Agitation was clear on his face.

"Agnes. Agnes! *Agnes!*" The older man's cries filled the mostly empty waiting area. "Agnes!" Tears streamed down his face as he pushed against his daughter.

"What is going on?" William ran up next to Lauren, whose eyes were huge as she took in the situation.

"Mr. James Parsons. Early-onset Alzheimer's disease. He's dehydrated, and his daughter swears she can calm him down. I don't want to involve security."

Jessie stepped into the waiting room just as the man pushed his daughter to the ground. Lauren's intuition to not involve security was a good one, but they might need to.

"Agnes is taking a rest." Jessie held up her hands. "I'm Dr.

Davis and she sent me to tell you that she wants you to take care of yourself too."

The man's daughter let out a sob as she looked at Jessie. "Agnes liked…likes to sing." The daughter's words confirmed what he feared. Agnes wasn't here and the man who loved her didn't remember that.

"Why don't we sing while we let the doctor take a look at you?" James's daughter started humming a few bars of an old hymn.

William's grandmother had sung in the church choir, and he knew the words. He started humming with her, then began the words.

Slowly the man started humming bars even though he didn't add the words. William knew multiple studies had shown that music calmed people and that those with dementia responded well to songs they'd sung in their younger years.

William sang louder as he followed the group back to a room. The man shuffled slowly, and more than a few heads turned as the makeshift choir walked down the hall.

Improvisation was a skill every long-term ER professional learned.

"Why am I here?" The man sighed as he sat on the bed looking at his daughter. "And who are you?"

She pursed her lips, the pain of the final question heavy on her features. "I'm Etta."

"Etta." He grinned. "I like that name. I always wanted to name a daughter Etta. After Etta James. She sings like a goddess."

William only knew the name because his grandmother had been a fan. The singer had a beautiful voice. She'd also passed away more than a decade ago.

Etta patted his knee. "It's a great name. And you are here because you haven't had enough to drink. It makes remembering things hard."

"Any other symptoms?" Jessie asked as she stepped next to James.

Dementia was a terrible diagnosis. It robbed you of so much, but in later stages it became very difficult to determine when the body had other disease symptoms.

"He hasn't used the restroom much and there was some blood this morning in his diaper." Etta let out a sigh. Caregiving was just as draining as the diagnosis. Perhaps more so.

"I don't wear a diaper." James crossed his arms, then shifted as he noticed the adult diaper. "Wait."

"It's okay. It's fine." She put her hand on her head. "It's fine. It's fine." Etta sucked in a breath, her eyes widening as she looked at Jessie.

"Etta?"

William moved without thinking. He managed to get his arms under her before her head hit the ground.

James started screaming for Agnes.

Jessie pressed the call button and the medical team sprung into action. William hefted Etta onto a gurney, careful to keep her head and neck stable.

"You're with me," Georgia stated as she pointed to William. "I need to know what happened. Trauma 1. Let's go."

It was the right move. A doctor was needed with James, and Georgia needed to know exactly what had occurred before Etta collapsed. William moved quickly with Georgia, taking Etta to Trauma 1.

William looked over his shoulder to see Jessie trying to calm James. Lauren was already stepping in with her. The nurse and Jessie would manage James just fine.

But leaving Jessie hurt more than anything.

William leaned against the wall outside Etta's room. The woman had passed out from stress and exhaustion. And her blood pressure was high enough to warrant an overnight stay.

Even with everything going on, the only worry Etta had shown was for her father. She didn't have anyone else to take care of him…

Georgia had gone to see if there was any way to get James into respite services for a few nights. With any luck she'd find a way to give Etta a few days off. Though spending at least one of those days in the hospital wasn't exactly relaxing.

Georgia returned, a big grin on her face. "Jessie got him into respite over an hour ago. She cleared a whole week of medical emergency respite for Etta and talked to hospice to make sure that Etta has the resources to take advantage of respite care more regularly. That woman is amazing."

"She is," William agreed. Jessie probably had experience with respite care. If her parents hadn't taken advantage of it with her brother, she'd have seen other families use it.

But even if she hadn't, Jessie would have reached out to hospice for Etta. Thinking of others was what she did.

"How long you planning to be stupid about Jessie?" Georgia rolled her head, stretching out muscles long days in the ER left tight.

William wanted to reply that he didn't know what she was talking about, wanted to make the entirely false claim that he wasn't being stupid. But he'd been in triage for several shifts volunteering for what everyone knew was his least favorite position in the ER.

"I don't know."

"An honest answer." Georgia punched his arm. "I was already plotting out the reasons I knew you were being stupid when you denied it. You are stealing some of my fire here, William."

He shrugged. "Sorry, Georgia. But lying has never been my strong suit." His father had spoken so many lies, William wasn't sure the man knew the truth.

The only person William ever lied to was himself. And the

lie that he could make someone happy, despite the flaws buried deep inside him, was why Tess was no longer on this side of the mortal coil.

"Sometimes I wonder when you will actually see yourself." Georgia pushed off the wall. "Life is short, William." She gestured to the ER rooms, not saying what he knew deep down.

Tomorrow could be anyone's last day, whether they were prepared or not.

"Don't mess up your friendship with Jessie." Georgia looked at her watch. "Just enough time left for charting in my shift. A doctor's favorite thing." She rolled her eyes and headed for the alcove the docs used to chart.

Don't mess up your friendship.

He was letting the tension over the pregnancy and his need to be near her get in the way of the woman he cared about. Truly cared about.

He'd seen online videos with men complaining they'd been "friend zoned," which was a terrible term for being a bad friend. He'd never planned to fall into bed with Jessie. Yes, she was attractive. Yes, kissing her had felt like coming home. Sure, he found himself wondering what might have happened if he'd held her tightly that morning and asked her to give themselves a chance as a couple.

The risk was too great though. If it didn't work out—and none of his relationships had worked out—then he lost Jessie. Lost his best friend.

It was a price he couldn't pay. But if he was a bad friend, then he'd lose her anyway.

"Ugh." He pushed off the wall. He needed to find Jessie, but he also owed it to Lauren to go back to triage and finish up the shift he'd agreed to.

"You look pensive." Jessie grinned as she approached William. "Already planning what you're going to do after the shift?"

"Yeah." William looked at the clock on the wall. Lauren could handle triage for two more minutes. "Actually, I thought maybe we could grab dinner. You know, as friends."

"You don't have to say *as friends.* We agreed to that, William." Jessie bit her lip, looked toward the charting area, then nodded. "Sure. Dinner sounds..." she began and paused.

Was she contemplating if they could have a non-awkward dinner? Probably not. But small steps were the best path forward.

"Dinner sounds lovely. You choose the place." She nodded again, then headed toward the alcove where Georgia was charting.

An hour later he walked into the staff locker room and his heart dropped at the note taped to his locker. He didn't need to read it to know Jessie was bowing out.

He'd given her a hard time about the notes taped to his locker when they'd first started their friendship. He'd told her that texting was a thing. She'd made some sort of comment about not wanting to be a bother, that a note didn't make noise or come with the requirement of a read receipt. He'd laughed, asking her who'd told her not to make any noise.

It had taken years but at least he knew the answer now. Fat lot of good it did him.

Can't make it. Sorry. Raincheck.

Crumpling the note, he let out a sigh and leaned his head against the locker. Had he already irreparably damaged their friendship?

"You look like you're contemplating head-butting that locker. I don't personally recommend it." Georgia grabbed her bag and slung it over her shoulder. "If you see Jessie, tell her I hope she feels better."

"Feels better?" He reread the note. Nope, still the same basic something-came-up note.

"Yeah. She was charting, then turned a little green and rushed out."

The door to the locker room opened and Georgia turned her head.

"You look like you've been caught gossiping, Georgia." Eli grinned at his love, and William couldn't tamp down on the bite of jealousy their happiness raised.

But his ears buzzed as he waited for Georgia to keep talking. Had Jessie told her she was pregnant? If she had and asked her not to say anything, then Georgia would keep that to herself even if Jessie was nine months pregnant and clearly about to give birth.

"Not gossiping. Jessie isn't feeling well, and I worry she got the summer stomach bug that infected most of the pediatric wing last week. Admin doesn't want it to get out that more than half the nurses had to call in sick due to it. If the ER goes down…"

"It will run on half staff. You know that." Eli swung his arm around Georgia and she kissed his cheek.

"True. But with our luck, Dr. Mueller won't get it and he will slow everything down…or speed it up by sending patients home that should be admitted."

Georgia was still frustrated over a patient that had complained of chest pain a few weeks ago. Dr. Mueller had labeled the patient as a psych case. He'd said she'd been in so many times for the same thing and everything was always fine. "A frequent flier", he'd called her, which was a nasty term for someone seeking help.

"Let's not play worst-case scenario before we have to." Eli kissed the top of Georgia's head.

She looked at William as she wrapped her arm around Eli's waist. The pair were so perfect.

Happiness was the only emotion he should feel. Georgia had found her person. That was lovely.

But part of him craved the same thing. "I'll let Jessie know you are thinking of her. I'll grab some soup and swing by."

"Fine, but if you get that bug, don't expect soup drop-off from me." Eli winked.

"If he gets the bug, Jessie will drop off the soup." Georgia kissed Eli's cheek as they walked out of the locker room.

William wasn't sure if Jessie was experiencing pregnancy symptoms or the stomach bug. But either way, he was checking in on her.

Headed your way. Tell me what kind of soup you want.

He sent the text and grabbed his bag. His phone beeped and he let out a sigh.

I'm fine. Thanks, though.

He should have known better than to ask. Jessie didn't ask for anything for herself. Well, too bad—she was getting soup. Luckily, after years of friendship he knew she craved the bean-and-barley soup a local restaurant made. So, he was grabbing the soup and popping by.

Knock-knock.

Jessie closed her eyes, gripping the kitchen sink. Whoever was at her door was going to have to come back another time because if she moved at all she was likely to lose the tiny bit of liquid she had in her system.

Her peppermint tea was getting cold, but the few sips she'd

managed had done nothing to calm the roll of her stomach. If she found the individual who'd microwaved cod in the shared breakroom, she might deck them.

Knock!

Seriously. Whoever it was needed to get the hint.

A few seconds later, she heard the key in the lock and she let out a sigh. Apparently, William had not taken her seriously when she said she was fine.

I'm not fine.

The mental blast of truth was unneeded. The nausea pills she'd been prescribed weren't working—at least not completely.

"Jessie?" The concern in William's voice let her know she looked as bad as she felt. "This doesn't look fine."

His hands stroked her back as she tried to figure out if it was safe to move from the sink.

"Someone microwaved fish."

William's hands stopped for a moment before continuing their small circles. "I know aromas can cause issues during pregnancy, but this seems like something more."

It was. She knew that, but she wasn't ready to admit it. Not yet. She could power through. Jessie had sat through so many procedures. Her hip had ached for weeks following the donation she'd given Bran.

Her parents had told her to deal with it, that it wasn't like she had cancer. *It could always be worse* was the common refrain anytime she complained. Those were tough lessons but they were going to come in handy now.

"I'm going to be fine."

"I don't doubt that." William wrapped an arm around her shoulder. "But what if I moved in until the baby is here? I mean I am the baby's father—it makes sense that I should help out my best friend while she goes through this."

It was a great offer. One she should take. Except it wasn't

for her. He was here for the baby and her…as a friend. That should be enough.

But she wanted more. Craved it. Her heart wasn't strong enough to have him here every day. It just wasn't.

"No, thanks. I appreciate the offer, but the fun uncle doesn't play that role." Her soul nearly broke as she uttered that truth. He wasn't hers. She'd offered him the role of fun uncle and he'd accepted. Forcing him into something else wasn't fair.

Plus, she wanted him here for her. That was selfish. She should focus on what was good for her son or daughter. And she was prioritizing them, but for once it would be nice if someone prioritized her, wanted her—just for her.

"Fine." His voice was sharp, but he cleared his throat. "But I am staying tonight. Don't argue."

She nodded, turned away from the sink to see him holding up the cup of soup he'd brought.

"Bean and barley. Your favorite." He grinned, then frowned. "Want me to put it in the fridge for later?"

"Yeah. Not sure I can handle anything right this minute."

He put the soup away, then pulled her into his arms.

She drank in his scent, her body easing for the first time in days. William was her best friend, the person she needed. For a minute she contemplated telling him she wanted him here all the time. He should pack his bags that night, move in and never leave.

It was the depth of her desire that kept the request buried.

CHAPTER SIX

JESSIE RAN HER hand over her still-flat belly and mentally sent a note to the little one to please accept the ginger tea she was sipping and let her eat a little something.

She popped a few nuts into her mouth and sipped the lukewarm tea. One could not live off ginger tea, almonds and toast. But right now it was all she could tolerate.

"How are you?" Padma leaned against the locker next Jessie.

"Dealing." Jessie smiled. "My doctor has me on antinausea pills. They help. But this little one is bound and determined to only accept a few things." Even the bean-and-barley soup William had brought over a few days ago had been too much. And it was her favorite.

It felt wrong to complain about her pregnancy after so many years of wishing for children and thinking it would never happen. But this was beyond a rough start.

"It's okay to be frustrated." Padma looked at her buzzing pager. "I've got a delivery, but if you need anything, let me know."

As Padma walked out, William walked in. He put his stuff in the locker. The night he'd slept over, he'd gone back home before five the morning. Along with the note he left on the counter was a piece of corn bread that had come with the soup. She'd picked at it but her body had refused to accept it.

"You still in triage?" She knew there was a little snark to

the word, but he was still avoiding her. And it was driving her out of her mind.

Since he'd stayed over the other night, the distance between them had only seemed to grow. He'd suggested moving in and then pulled away when she'd said no. It hurt. She needed him but wasn't sure how to overcome the chasm they'd created between them.

"No." William bit his lip. "Any chance you want to get together tonight?"

She wanted to. She really did, but if they were just going to frustrate each other… "William…"

He crossed his arms. "You can say no, Jessie. It's fine. I just… I don't know how to go back to what we were."

"Maybe we don't." The words hurt. But they were the truth. "Everything's changed, and maybe we could have gone back, but…" She put her hand over where their child slept.

"But…?"

"But I don't think we can. I am having a baby. It's a lot and it changes things." She didn't know what else to say.

Her pager went off; someone else's emergency needed to be handled. And she hated how much she appreciated the reprieve.

Both of them took off, professionals ready to confront a crisis. They needed to figure out the next steps, needed to work on where they were going and how they were going to manage co-parenting. But that was a crisis for another time.

"Mother with severe burns on her arms, feet and neck. Grease fire. She's twenty weeks pregnant." Lauren listed off the condition as she pointed to room 17.

"Toddler with burns to the feet in room 18, and eight-year-old with burns on neck and hands in room 19."

Georgia darted into room 19. Dr. Serenity Bishop, an ER pediatrician, walked into room 18.

"Page Padma to let her know we have a pregnant woman

down here. That we are treating burn trauma first but she will need to be monitored by OB. Padma's on ER call today but in a delivery." Jessie gave the direction to a nurse at the desk, then pointed at William.

"You're with me." A few weeks ago she would not have had to point that out. He'd have simply chosen to work with her, if possible.

She walked into the room and made sure to keep her face impassive as she took in the second-degree burns on the woman's neck and third-degree burns on her feet. Tears were running down the woman's face and she looked past them.

"My boys. Where are my boys?" She moved and let out a cry.

"Your boys are in the rooms next to yours. They are being looked after by the best staff we have." Jessie went to the sink, quickly washing her hands. "I'm Dr. Davis and this my nurse, William."

"My boys first. Please. Noah was standing the grease on the floor. His feet are so burned and Lincoln was trying to put out the fire. His arms and face. Them…them first."

"They have the best staff treating them." She was reiterating what she'd already said, but in crisis sometimes you had to say things three, four or even five times before the patient's brain could register the words.

"Look at me." Jessie pointed to her nose as she kept her tone firm. "Your boys have great doctors and nurses looking after them. But you are my and William's priority."

William stepped next to her, offering a kind smile. She'd joked so many times that his smile lit up a room. He always laughed and said it was just his smirk. But it wasn't.

When he was relaxed, the smile was so open. But it was also the same when he was working with a patient. This was his calling, what he did so very well.

And she hated that the first time she was seeing that smile

in weeks was in a level-one trauma room while caring for a patient with third-degree burns on her feet.

"I'm William. What is your name?"

"Stephanie." She moved just a little and let out a screech.

"I know it's hard, but I need you to stay as still as possible." Jessie used a light to look at Stephanie's feet.

"I have never felt pain like this." Tears leaked down Stephanie's cheeks.

"The pain is actually a good sign. It means the nerves are still responding. You have third degree burns on your feet, which means we need to transfer you to the burn unit."

"No." Stephanie shook her head, tears streaming faster, but she didn't flinch—at least not much—as she sat up. "I can't go to the burn unit. I'm pregnant and the boys and I have so much that has to be done. I have to be at home."

A wedding band was on her finger but that didn't always mean a spouse was around…or supportive.

"Can the boys' father help?"

Stephanie let out a cold laugh. "Help is what he was supposed to be doing this morning. Getting the boys ready for nursery and school while I slept in for a few minutes. I just wanted him to feed them. But he left the bacon grease on the stove and the burner on low. Probably got a phone call he had to take for work."

She squeezed her eyes shut, tears leaking out the sides. "And now they are injured and in pain because I wanted to sleep in."

No. None of this was her fault. She should be able to rely on her partner.

"Sometimes I think maybe single-mom life would be the same as married-mom life." Stephanie let out a harsh sound as the minimal movement rubbed against the exposed nerves in her feet.

"Single moms have it rough. But it can be done."

I'm planning on doing it.

Aside from her doctor, only William, Padma and Georgia knew she was expecting. And saying it to a patient wasn't appropriate. But she saw William glance at her, noted the understanding in his gaze.

"Right now, though," Jessie said, keeping her voice level, "we need to clean the wounds. It will be very painful so I am going to get OB to clear you for anesthesia and have a general surgeon do it. You will be out of commission for weeks. I know—" She held up a hand to stop the argument she could already see brewing on Stephanie's face. "I know that is hard."

She avoided the look she saw pass William's gaze too. Asking for help was not something Jessie did well. Hell, it wasn't something she did at all. And she didn't have to look any further than telling William no when he'd offered to move in.

But Stephanie didn't have a choice.

"We will explain it to your husband when he gets here. I am sure the fire chief alerted him." It was standard protocol.

"But if I'm in surgery, who will explain?"

"I will," William commented before Jessie could say anything.

She looked at him. She couldn't read the expression on his face.

"Don't worry," William continued "When he gets here, I'll have a little chat and just make sure he knows what is happening."

She wasn't sure why the tone of *little chat* sent a bead of worry down her back, but there wasn't time to figure it out at the moment.

"Where are my wife and sons?" A tall man raced into the ER. Sweat was beaded on his forehead. He did not look like a man who didn't care enough to make sure his wife and children were safe before heading to the office.

William saw a few nurses cut their eyes toward him. The

reason for the accident had filtered quickly. The oldest son had said he tried to tell his dad the stove was still on. The youngest had talked about "Dada cooking."

"The boys are here, waiting for transfer to the pediatric wing. Your wife is in surgery."

The man sucked in a deep breath. Then another. Tears were streaming down his face. "I took that call. I'm always taking calls. Stephanie says I am so attached to my phone. But when I ask if she needs help, she says no."

He took another deep breath that William doubted was giving him much air.

"I know this hard. But I need you to take a deep breath. A real one. Look at me." William grabbed the man's hand and inhaled deeply.

It took a minute, but the man followed suit. Then he took another breath with William. The color began returning to his face. "My kids, my wife, my unborn daughter."

"Today is roughest day they've ever had. Tomorrow will not be good either." Sugarcoating the truth wouldn't change anything. The boys had severe burns. The physical scars would last a lifetime. The emotional ones would need just as much attention to make sure they didn't cause lifelong damage.

"But they are alive. Your wife will need you focused for the rest of this pregnancy." Jessie's voice was tight. Her face devoid of all color, but her spine was straight as she stepped next to William.

He'd been so focused on Stephanie's husband that William hadn't even heard her walk up.

"I've been working extra hours. The baby...the baby wasn't planned and the overtime... Steph said she was fine. Anytime I asked about something she just said it was all right..." His voice trailed off. "I grew up in poverty. I never wanted my family to struggle. And I ended up failing them anyway." He let out a ragged sigh and crossed his arms.

"You only fail if you walk away right now. If you don't change. This has happened. Now you move forward." Jessie nodded and pulled up the chart for the wife.

She turned it and showed the husband the images of his wife's feet. "I treated Stephanie. She has third-degree burns on her feet and second-degree burns on her hands and neck. She is in surgery for debridement right now. She will be in the maternity unit for at least a week. With the burns on her feet, she will need physical therapy and *lots* of help around the house."

"And the boys?" He was standing a little straighter. Once information was in hand, it was often easier for loved ones to calm down, when the fear of the unknown was replaced by the urgent need to focus on what came next.

"William can take you to their physicians." She looked at him. The color had not returned to her cheeks. If anything, she looked worse than she did when she'd walked up.

As soon as he was done with this task, he was going to find Jessie, check in with her. And he was not taking *fine* for an answer.

"It wasn't supposed to be like this." The man sighed as they started down the hallway that William knew felt long to patients' families. So many unknowns and uncertainties, tragedies and miracles traveled this corridor.

"What's your name?" William asked.

"Patrick." He stuffed his hands in his pockets. "I just want to be a good dad and husband. Make sure they had all the things I missed out on. I figured she'd tell me if something needed to change. But why did she need to tell me? I should have just seen it and acted. Instead of being a real partner, I caused chaos."

William didn't know what to say. Patrick spoke the truth. But he was also seeing himself in a new light, which was a growth path most never saw and fewer acted on.

Georgia stepped out of the room where Patrick's oldest son was resting before transfer to the pediatric wing.

William flagged her down. "This is Patrick, Lincoln's father. He's here for an update. I need to find..." He halted but he saw Georgia's small smile. She knew he needed to find Jessie.

"I've got it from here." She directed Patrick to a small bench right outside the room and took over.

William rushed down the hall.

"Hey!" Dr. Mueller's harsh voice echoed in the hall, and a few other nurses turned their heads.

William wanted to find Jessie, but Dr. Mueller was a bear when he was unhappy—which was the best state you could hope for. When he was displeased—or heaven forbid, irritated—the man became downright hateful.

"What can I do for you, Dr. Mueller?" He put a smile on his face, partly because it was the polite thing to do, but also because Dr. Mueller hated when people were nice to him. Maybe one day the prickly doc would see the world wasn't out to get him.

"You're with me. Since your bestie called out sick for the back half of her shift, my workload just doubled."

There were two other docs on the floor with him. Doubled was far from the truth, but that wasn't a point William wanted to argue.

"What's wrong with Jessie?" The question was the wrong one. If Dr. Mueller knew, and William doubted it, the man wouldn't share—mostly because someone else wanted to know.

"Aren't you two joined at the hip?"

They used to be. But that was not a conversation he planned to have with Dr. Mueller. Or anyone else.

"What do you need?"

"Stitches prepped in room 6 and look in on room 11. The woman is complaining of back pain, but I suspect she is drug seeking." Mueller made a few notes on his tablet and walked off before William could ask why he was jumping to the conclusion a patient was drug seeking. That kind of assessment could travel with a person who needed serious treatment.

And if they were drug seeking, they needed help too. Just a different kind. But Mueller wouldn't listen to that argument. William knew...because he and several of the nurses had tried to convince him.

Looking at the clock, he let out a sigh. Six hours remained on his shift. But as soon as it was over, he was going to Jessie's. And he wasn't going to listen to the *no thanks* or *fine*. He was going to make sure she had what she needed. He'd been her friend long enough to know she wouldn't ask for help. Rather than gently push or discuss it with her, he'd let his feelings get hurt and pushed her further away.

Jessie was his family, though maybe not in the traditional sense of the word. But showing up and helping out was his primary plan now.

CHAPTER SEVEN

JESSIE HEARD THE doorbell but there was no way she was getting off the floor of the bathroom. Everything she'd eaten for the last day seemed to have found its way out of her system. There shouldn't be anything left.

But she'd thought that two episodes ago.

Whoever was at her door would just have to come back another day. Or not at all.

"Jessie." William's voice carried up the stairs of her townhome. He never rang the bell. Only knocked and walked in, or used his key if the door was locked. It didn't make sense but her brain was too fried to do anything more than be happy he was here.

William. Her body relaxed just a little. William.

She started to call out to him, but another wave of nausea struck and she resumed the position she'd been all too comfortable with since someone microwaved fish in the breakroom—again.

If she figured out which person was doing it, she was going to throttle them. Georgia had pegged Dr. Mueller, but that was just because she and Dr. Mueller had gotten off on every wrong foot possible when Georgia arrived at Anchorage Memorial.

Jessie didn't know who it was. But she'd be on the lookout.

This time the smell had kicked off the worst hours she'd ever known. Making it home after getting sick at the hospital without another wave of nausea was a minor miracle that her body seemed inclined to make her pay for now.

"Jessie." His fingers were warm as they skimmed the nape of her neck, pulling her ponytail up and gathering all the loose strands.

"Since when do you use my doorbell?"

Had they really fallen that far? It wasn't a great greeting, particularly as her friend, the father of her child, held her hair for her. But it came out anyway.

"Not me. There was a door-to-door vacuum salesman standing on your stoop. I told him that you weren't interested. He insinuated that a lady of the house knows more about *these* types of appliances."

Jessie let out a laugh that made the sore muscles of her stomach clench. "He didn't."

"He did." William's voice was more serious than playful, but she appreciated the attempt at humor.

"It's the twenty-first century." Audacity at the stranger was easier than acknowledging that William was still holding her hair and looking over her with so much concern.

"That is what I told him. And that I was the one who did most of the housework as the stay-at-home partner."

He was far too confident in his phrasing to mean it as anything more than a joke, a kind gesture to get a pest out of the way. She'd spent the last several hours ill, and part of her still wished he meant something when he used the word *partner.*

"You ready for a shower, or would you prefer a bath?" William pointed to the nozzles.

"I want a bath, but I am not sure that is a good idea. Every time I think this is over..." She laid her head against the cabinet.

"That can't be comfortable." William reached for her and she was too exhausted to fight as he shifted her to lay her head on his knee.

This was far more comfortable. His fingers stroked her cheek in a gentle, soothing rhythm.

"That feels nice." Jessie closed her eyes, hoping in a few minutes she'd have the strength to stand up and take a shower.

"My mother always stroked my cheek when I was ill. Usually, I was lying in bed or on the couch watching movies or teen sitcoms, but it always made me feel better."

He never spoke of his family, never mentioned a mother. All of that was BA. Even after she'd unburdened herself the other day, he'd kept his before Anchorage time wrapped up.

She ached to know more. But she was too tired to push.

"It's nice." She'd already said that, but her exhaustion prevented her from coming up with anything else. Besides, the last thing Jessie wanted was to rush this moment away. Maybe he'd give her an answer as to why he never went home.

"Yeah. Mom was very good at the bedside when I was really little. I think she would have made an excellent nurse, if she'd chosen a different path." There was a wistfulness to his voice—one she recognized.

"When did you lose her?" Jessie kept her eyes closed. If he didn't respond, she'd drop it.

"I didn't. Not in the way you lost Bran at least. She is still here. She's in Kodiak, hosting garden parties, running my father's business parties. And looking the other way as he dives into every bed he can find besides hers. Grumbling but refusing to do anything to change her life."

The harsh words filled the room. What did one say to that? Her parents had seen her as an extra to the perfect family dream they'd created.

Two people in love with what they thought was a perfect child. Even after Bran's diagnosis, there'd never been any crack in their unit. They were a team. She couldn't fathom either of them cheating.

"When I found out about Will, I begged her to leave him. To choose a better life for herself."

For us.

He didn't say those words, but she heard them clearly.

"Who's Will?"

"My half brother. About three years younger than me. Looks just like my father. Which of course means he looks like my twin. Or he did until I decorated my skin with tattoos."

"I like the tats. They are so colorful. So you…" She let out a sigh as another wave of nausea struck. There was nothing left, but her stomach went through the motions nonetheless.

When she was done, she laid her head back on his knee and he started stroking her cheek again.

"Yeah. I like them too. The first one was out of spite. Who names their sons the same name? I guess it was so he didn't get us mixed up. It's why I refuse to go by anything other than my full name. Will gets the shortened name—I get the full one."

"Wow. My mother would have buried my father someplace no one ever found the body. Then acted the dedicated widow. Not a great mom to me but she loves my dad unconditionally."

"That would be a normal reaction." There was a wistfulness to his voice. Was he wondering if there was a universe where his mother had walked away, taking her son and dignity to make a new life for herself? What would his life look like if she'd made that choice?

It didn't matter because that wasn't what had happened. "She chose him over you?"

William's free hand tapped on the side of the tub. "*Chose* isn't quite the right word. She told me I was selfish. Told me that he provided for us. That his faults were what all the Harris men had, and she'd known it when she married him. Our relationship was never quite the same after that. And after—"

He paused, swallowing whatever words were on the edge of his tongue. "I finally saw that the foundation of my family was broken beyond repair. And it crumbled forever a few years later. And there was nothing solid to rebuild on."

There was more to that story. So much more, but silence hung in the room and neither of them seemed to know what to say next.

William reached over and started the shower. "Let's see if you can handle standing long enough to feel clean. I'll be just outside the door if you need me."

Just outside the door. So close…

William held Jessie while she slept. She was exhausted; her body was spent from the hours of illness. He'd put the soup he'd brought her in the fridge—next to the uneaten soup he'd brought the other day. Right now, she was surviving on thin broth and some water in small portions just to keep her from dehydration.

If this continued, they were going to need to take her to the ER where they worked. She'd told him Padma and Georgia knew about the pregnancy but if she needed fluids for dehydration, everyone would know.

He wasn't sure if Jessie was ready for that. But if she needed IV hydration, they were going, no matter the gossip that would bring. If she wouldn't ask for support herself, then he would take the task on.

His stomach rumbled loud enough he held his breath but Jessie didn't stir. He'd skipped dinner last night too. It didn't seem fair to eat while she was so miserable.

Her red hair was splayed across his chest. She'd gone to bed with it still wet and now it was wild.

Sleeping beauty.

His cheeks were hot with the memory of her asking him to hold her when she'd climbed into bed last night. The last time they'd been in this bed together was the reason she was now so sick. Holding her brought all the feelings, the emotions, the need raging back.

Not desire. Sure, he had that, but she was far too weak for that to be at the forefront of his mind. No, these feelings were far deeper than desire.

He snuggled closer, laying his hand over the still-flat portion of her belly where their child slept.

Last night she'd told him she needed comfort when she'd asked for him to hold her. She'd slipped into sleep so fast but he hadn't left. He'd been unable to bring himself to break the connection.

Comfort. He understood that need, craved it too. Was that why he'd spilled so much about his family last night?

He'd stroked her cheek out of habit. He hadn't spoken to his mother in years. He'd invited her to his college graduation, but she'd refused to come unless he invited his father too.

Frank Harris had cheated on her for their entire relationship. She felt that if she could overlook that, then he should be able to overlook the missed baseball games, band concerts, children with his mistresses, including a child who shared the same name as her son.

He hadn't really been around for Jessie since that hike. He'd seen her at the hospital, come over when she was ill, but he hadn't been truly present. Hell, part of him had been relieved when she'd told him she didn't need him to move in. At least then he wouldn't have to figure out how to control the feelings that came every time he was close to her.

That was his burden to bear. Right now, he was taking care of Jessie. Period.

His stomach let out the largest growl yet, and Jessie stirred.

"Your stomach growling makes me think you lied about eating before you got here."

The morning softened her features, but her cheekbones were more pronounced than they'd been a week ago. The circles under her eyes were lighter than yesterday, but even after a night of solid sleep, she still looked exhausted.

"How long has the nausea been this bad?"

"Nope. I asked a question first." Jessie bopped his nose, then rolled over like she was going to get out of bed. But she didn't sit up.

Was she still nauseous.? Or enjoying being close to him? It was too much to hope for after his actions this week.

"You didn't ask a question. You made an accusation." William winked as she made an obscene gesture. "Tsk-tsk. So feisty in the morning."

Her hand lay on his chest, burning through the cotton shirt he'd worn all night. "The nausea meds my OB put me on help, but scents can still result in…" She let out a sigh rather than rehash last night's events.

"Was it fish again?"

She scrunched her nose, the color blanching a bit. "Yes. Whoever it is better not let me catch them." Her thumb made tiny circles on his chest as she pinched her eyes closed.

He wasn't sure she was aware of the motions but his body was *very* aware of it. Before she could say anything else, he rolled out of bed. He needed to go home and get a few things so he could stay awhile, but first he wanted to see about getting some food into Jessie.

"You're right. I didn't eat. It felt wrong to put food in my body when my pregnant best friend is so sick. Skipping a meal isn't that big of a hardship." His stomach rumbled again., the traitorous organ yelling to the world that it needed sustenance.

"You can't keep skipping meals when I am ill. You'll miss too many." She groaned as she sat up. "Man, you never realize how tight your stomach muscles feel after tossing your cookies for hours."

"Do you think you need a larger dose of nausea meds?" He could call the OB for her right now, let them know she needed to change the dosage previously prescribed. Then he could pick up the prescription after going back to his place.

"Maybe, but I am trying to make do without, if possible."

"Why?"

Antinausea meds didn't hurt the baby. And not keeping food or water in the body was bad for fetal and maternal health. One of the reasons an osteoporosis diagnosis was more likely happen to women was because a baby would leech calcium from the mother's body when developing.

She looked at the floor, pink crawling up her neck. "It's embarrassing." She stood, took a deep breath, stretched to one side then the other while inhaling through her nose and exhaling through her mouth. Clearly, she already had a routine to keep the feelings from returning.

"What is embarrassing?" Nausea meds were dispensed to pregnant people all the time. It was one of the most common things ordered.

"The pills. They are large or at least they are to me. I… I… I didn't get sick as kid. Mostly because I wasn't allowed anywhere near germs." She laughed but there was no humor to it. "I didn't learn to swallow pills until I was teenager and I still hate it. I gag on them and then sometimes get sick. Which is the exact thing I am trying to avoid. It's a vicious cycle!"

She rolled her head from one side to the next. "I know that sounds ridiculous and embarrassing, and I mean, how dumb is it being a doctor who can't take big pills."

It wasn't embarrassing. It was simply another indictment of her family. Since Jessie had cut them out of her life, he didn't need to worry about running into them.

That was a shame because there were a few things he'd like to get off his chest. Though he doubted anything anyone said would change how her folks felt about the child they'd called a failure.

Their loss.

"All right. Well, why don't I go to the kitchen, get the ginger tea and some toast ready, unless you'd rather try to eat something else?" Bland foods were best after a night of illness, but as a nurse he also knew that when you craved something after illness it usually tasted better than anything else.

"Yeah. That works. Thanks." Jessie walked over to her dresser, then stopped and looked at him. "And thank you for staying last night. I just—" She looked at her dresser. "I just didn't want to be alone. Sorry."

He moved without thinking, wrapping his arms around her. She let out a small sob and he just held her while she released the emotions.

He'd hold her all day if necessary. Her body was going through a lot of changes. She'd needed help, but he'd taken her word for it that she was fine, even when all the evidence showed the opposite.

He'd done the same with Tess. He'd taken her word when she said she was fine…and ignored the final call she'd made late that last night. He'd planned to call her back when it wasn't 2:00 a.m. That was a mistake he couldn't take back.

But he was getting another chance with Jessie.

And he was taking it.

Food needed? Check. Hold the hair while she got sick? Check. Hold her while she slept? Check.

"Sorry." Sucking in a deep breath, she started to pull away.

Rather than let her go, he squeezed tighter. "Stop apologizing. You needed me. I am here. It is as simple as that."

He kissed the top of her head. His body froze as his lips connected to her head. It was platonic, a comfort kiss that didn't mean anything.

Lie.

"Thank you." Jessie ran her fingers over his wrists on her waist, then she stepped out of his embrace. "Toast and ginger tea. You will spoil me."

"You deserve it." He put his hands in his pockets. The pulse of need to pull her back into his embrace was pounding throughout his body. He needed to get downstairs to give himself a few minutes to recover.

CHAPTER EIGHT

SHE TOOK A SLOW, deep breath. She wasn't stalling. Not really. Her stomach was still uncomfortable. The nausea she'd felt for weeks had become her constant friend. Medicine kept a portion of it at bay, but it didn't stop it completely.

The slow breaths were recommended by Padma to calm her overactive system. It usually worked. Maybe it would've today, if she hadn't spent the night in William's arms.

She'd asked him to stay because she was desperate for a connection when she was feeling so under the weather. And he hadn't hesitated.

For the first time in weeks it felt like they were back on the same wavelength: two hearts that knew what the other needed. But the awkwardness remained.

Hell, when his lips brushed her forehead, she'd nearly lifted her head. Instead she'd forced herself to step out of his grip.

They were a family. All families looked different, but their child would know love. That was enough.

Last night he'd given her an insight into his family. She'd known it wouldn't be happy. A person didn't go no contact with their family for no reason. Still, the story was worse than she'd imagined.

Cheating and fathering children with mistresses was one thing.

Giving your children the same name? It was terrible, and icky. Who did such a thing?

She looked at her nightstand. The baby-name book she'd purchased on a whim at the used bookstore was on top of all her other books. Most people used the hundreds of online sites that made lists and charted popularity.

Names were important. She had one of the most common names for girls born her year. Apparently, her mother had asked a nurse what common names were when Jessie was born.

Jessica was the first name the nurse said. So she became Jessica. Jessie was the nickname she'd taken in college when there'd been more than a dozen Jessicas in one of her freshman classes.

The nurse hadn't lied. That was for sure.

Her child would have a name that meant something. But given William's history with names… She looked at the book and then marched over and picked it up.

At least this was a topic that didn't revolve around her nausea. She had no desire to discuss that any more than absolutely necessary.

She walked down the stairs, the spicy aroma of ginger wafting from her kitchen. William was already holding out a mug with steam rising from the top, and a water bottle was clasped in the other hand.

"Hot ginger tea, cool ginger-infused water? Which do you prefer while I make your toast?"

"Hot!" Jessie took the tea and stepped into the kitchen. "But I can make my toast."

"Nah." William waved away her offer. "You sit and tell me what you're reading."

"It's a baby-name book."

He almost seemed to miss a step as he moved toward her toaster. An impressive feat because it was less than six steps from where he was standing.

"I know you said you agreed to be the fun uncle, but I

thought…" She sipped the tea then started again. "I thought you might have some preferences."

"Not William." He offered her a thumbs-up before dropping two sourdough slices into her toaster. It was a fun gesture but she could see the hurt behind it.

"I figured, but I don't want to accidentally give our son or daughter a name you hate. Even if you don't want to play the role full-time."

William leaned against her counter, a look crossing his features that she couldn't identify.

"What if I wanted to change that descriptor?" His words were low, guttural. Like a calling from deep within his soul. One he wasn't sure he wanted to let out.

Heat rippled across her belly, the flame settling in her heart. Their child deserved William as their father. And he deserved that recognition.

If he wanted it.

"I want you involved. I want my child, our child, to know you. To love you. To be loved by you. But I also know this wasn't the plan."

"Plans change." The toaster popped and he turned to grab the toast. "Plans change."

The whispered repetition was clearly just for him.

He put the toast on a plate, grabbed butter, jam and silverware before joining her at the breakfast bar. "Not sure what you want on the toast. If anything."

"Thanks." She spread a light layer of butter and tore off a small piece. She ate it, hoping she'd keep it down.

She waited a moment to see if he'd bring up the change in title from fun uncle. Hope beat in her chest but the silence just stretched between them.

Swallowing the lump of bread in her throat, she picked up the tea. She couldn't sit here in silence. "Thank you for staying last night."

"About that." William turned, crossing his arms. This was his I've-made-a-decision stance.

She tore off another piece of toast but didn't bring it to her lips. Whatever William was about to say needed her full attention.

"I know you told me that you didn't need me moving in while you dealt with this, but you absolutely do." He held up hand, like he was expecting an argument. "If you get dehydrated, living alone—"

"I know. That's probably a good idea." She might wish there was another reason, but she really did need him.

"Don't interrupt on this, Jessie. I know you don't like asking for help but…" His voice caught. "Wait, did you agree with me?"

"I did." She looked at the toast she needed to eat but also couldn't herself bring to force down because of what she knew would come. She needed help. She should have accepted his offer before.

"All right." William nodded.

"So, names." She tapped the book. "I know it is early, and we don't know the sex, but are there any names, besides William, that are completely off the table?"

"Frank and Eleanor." William took a bite of his toast, and she was jealous of the thick layer of butter and jam.

"Not names I would choose anyway but good to know." Those were his father's and mother's names. He didn't have to explain for her to know it. In fairness, her mother's and father's names were off the table too.

"What names are you thinking?" He pointed at the book. "Anything in there popping out at you?"

"I haven't looked in it yet. I bought it on a whim, but there are a few names I've always enjoyed."

This wasn't how she'd planned to discuss naming children. In her mind growing up, she'd be married to—or at least living with—the father of her children. They'd be sitting on the couch, tossing out names and having fun and they'd be so in love.

Her throat burned with a thirst there was no way for her quench.

"Those names are…?" William gestured with his hand, urging her to stop the stalling.

"For a boy I've always liked the name Reese or Cole."

William nodded. "No complaints on those. I prefer Reese over Cole, but not by a ton. And if we have a girl?"

"Teressa—we could call her Tess. I—" The blood in William's face was gone. "William?"

"No." He cleared his throat. "No. Uh…" He looked at his watch, standing up and nearly knocking the chair over. "I need to…run home. Change clothes…grab some things for the long stay…"

William didn't typically have so many verbal pauses. But he seemed to be operating with part of his brain someplace else entirely.

"William? It's all right—the name Tess is out. Fair. I also like Eira. It means *snow.* Too on the nose for an Alaskan baby?"

She wanted him to laugh. She needed him to laugh, to come out of whatever fog the name Teressa had thrown over him.

He didn't seem to have heard her. He was wiping down her clean counters—like tea and toast created a huge mess.

"William."

"I can stay in the guest bedroom. Unless you need me in your…" Color rose up his cheeks but he didn't finish the statement. "I'm going to help out. I'm here for you and our baby. I'm here. So, clothes?" He patted his blue jeans and pulled out car keys. "Right. I am going to get clothes. And food. Cause I checked your stores, and I mean, come on, Jessie!"

"William!"

He was moving toward the front door, with her walking after him. “William.”

“I won’t be more than two hours. You text if you need anything. Anything.” He held his hand up and walked out.

“Damn.” Jessie pulled her phone out. Selecting Georgia’s number, she sent the question she hoped William’s friend knew the answer to.

Who is Teressa…or Tess?

She looked at the phone. Georgia always answered her quickly. She was probably dancing with joy that Jessie was finally asking about William’s past.

She saw the bubble pop up showing Georgia was typing. Then it disappeared. Minutes ticked by. Why wasn’t Georgia answering?

Finally, her phone dinged.

William’s former fiancée.

Fiancée?

A friend or a lover—those were expected. But fiancée? He’d sworn he’d never marry. It was something she’d learned early when he went out on a date with a woman who’d plotted out their whole lives. Granted, that was more than a bit much for a first date. But when William had told her he never planned to marry, she’d thrown a glass of water in his face and walked out.

Video of the incident had made the rounds on social media for a few weeks. Jessie would have appreciated the up-front conversation.

After all she’d been on her fair share of dates with men whose profiles said they were looking to settle down, only to be told they just wanted a hookup. There was nothing wrong with that, but the false advertising was unwelcome.

Another ping broke up her thoughts and she stared in horror at the link Georgia sent.

It was an obituary.

He left Kodiak the week after her funeral. He doesn't talk about her.

That would explain why he didn't want the name used. This was the real BA information. His family stuff was part of it. But this was the past he wanted buried.

She understood, but couldn't stop the ache in her chest. He'd always said he didn't want to marry. But that hadn't always been true. There'd been one person who'd made him think it possible. Why couldn't it be possible again?

Stop being selfish, Jessie.

He'd laid out his boundaries. Those were important.

Thanks.

She typed the single word to Georgia, who responded with a thumbs-up. Padma's emoji use was really rubbing off on Georgia.

William pulled up to Jessie's, almost two hours on the dot since he'd left. It wasn't enough time and too much time all at once. His bags were packed for a week. He had food for at least that long.

He could have been back an hour ago. If he'd just thrown a few things in his overnight bag and headed out to the store, he might have even returned in a short forty-five. But he'd stood in his bedroom for almost twenty minutes not doing anything.

He'd told Jessie he needed two hours to get ready because he thought that'd be enough time to mentally process the memories mention of Tessa's name conjured up. It wasn't sufficient time though.

Sure, hearing that Jessie was considering the name Teressa had shocked him. Shocked him to the core.

Tess never got the chance to name a baby. He didn't even know what names she might have liked. It was something he'd thought of over and over again at her funeral, and later anytime he got a notice that one of their mutual friends was reaching that milestone.

Today, though, for the first time, the pain and guilt that her name always brought up hadn't materialized. No. The emotion living in his chest was hope.

What did that mean?

He'd said he didn't want to be the fun uncle. Jessie hadn't asked him to elaborate. Which was kind, because at the time he hadn't exactly known that he wasn't sure what he was asking for.

I want it all.

William bit his lip as the truth racked through him. He wanted everything: Jessie, their child, the life he'd told Tess he never planned to have. It was the type of life she'd wanted so badly that she'd mourned its loss in drink the night after he ended their union.

Did that make him terrible? He hadn't wanted it then, but craved it now—with someone else.

His phone rang and even without Jessie's upbeat ringtone echoing in the car he would have known who was calling.

"Is there any chance you are calling because you want something from the store and are hoping I am still there?" He saw the curtain flutter in the front window. She'd been watching him for a few minutes at least, no doubt worrying about the reasons he was just sitting in the car.

"Do you want me to ask for something?"

Do you need more time?

The unasked question struck his heart. Jessie was giving him an out. The woman always worried about others and cared for others even when her body was literally refusing sustenance. She was worried about him when it should be the opposite.

"No. I'm on my way in."

"I'll come help carry groceries. Don't argue. I am pregnant, not incapable of carrying bags."

Jessie disconnected the call before he could say anything. She walked out the door, her gaze looking over him as she walked to the trunk of his SUV.

He grabbed the overnight bag, opened his door and went to meet her.

"Um..." She looked at all the bags in the back. "Did you buy the store out?"

William laughed, putting his arm around her shoulder. "*Your* cupboards are basically bare. When was your last grocery delivery?"

Jessie rolled her eyes but didn't dispute the fact. She grabbed the bags and headed inside.

He loaded up the rest, walking funny as he carried at least five bags on each arm.

Stepping into the kitchen, he laid the bags down and let out a grunt as the blood rushed back into his hands.

"More than one trip was an option." Jessie raised an eyebrow as she put the milk in the fridge. "Plus, it's summer, so stocking up isn't quite as important."

Anchorage was south of the Arctic Circle. Even though its average winter temperature was only a few degrees below freezing from November through March, supply lines coming from the lower forty-eight meant that options were slimmer in the winter months.

"It's a competition, Jessie. I know you and Bran didn't have standard childhoods, but didn't you ever see who could carry the most grocery bags? Or when you were at university, didn't you load up so you only had to do one trip up the dorm steps?"

Jessie shook her head, but he could see the pinch of laughter on her lips. She'd done it. She probably still did, but just didn't want to admit it right now.

Stepping over the groceries, he reached for her hand and pulled her to him. "Come on, I know you've done it…"

He pushed a stray hair out of her face, so aware that their bodies were touching. He'd reached for her without thinking and it felt so right.

Her emerald gaze held his, color flushing her delicate cheeks. "I *might* have done it a few times."

"I thought so." William squeezed her, then let her go. The groceries needed putting away. That was what he should be doing instead of holding her.

She grabbed a few things and stuffed them in a cabinet, then hopped up on the counter. "I know who Tess is. I texted Georgia. I'm sorry, William."

His mouth was dry. His tongue was frozen.

"I didn't realize that you'd once planned to marry. Losing her before your wedding—"

"There wasn't going to be a wedding. I called it off two weeks before but her parents were kind enough to put my name in her obituary since I was mourning her too." William pushed a hand through his hair. Her parents hadn't known about the call Tess had made to him. The one he hadn't answered. He hadn't willfully hidden it. Grief's fog had blinded him.

He'd released Tess because she'd wanted a life he hadn't planned to give her. That didn't mean it was easy, or that he didn't still love her. Part of him always would.

What would she think to see him now, having a child with his best friend? She'd likely be furious—or maybe she'd have smiled—at the change. Unfortunately there was no way to know.

Still, Jessie deserved to know the truth. Maybe then she'd understand why, even though his soul begged to reach out her, she should run far and fast.

Jessie blinked. Her mouth opened once, twice, as she clearly worked through that statement.

He leaned against the counter opposite her and crossed his arms. "I heard her talking the week before we were supposed to walk down the aisle. She wanted kids. Tess told me she didn't, but she was telling her maid of honor how she thought I'd change my mind in a few years. That I'd make the best dad."

"You will make the best dad. She was right about that." Jessie's tone brokered no objection, and he didn't have the strength to offer one right now.

"I guess we get to see." He looked to where their child grew in her belly.

He hadn't changed his mind, but life had offered a path and he was walking it.

"So you broke it off before the wedding."

"It wasn't fair to let her think I might change." Maybe he would have. But there were no guarantees.

Jessie crossed her ankles. "It wasn't fair that she wasn't honest either."

Maybe. That was a feeling he'd had when he'd first heard. When she passed…it had felt wrong to blame her for what happened.

"She didn't take it well. Of course."

"How did you take it?" Jessie tilted her head.

William opened his mouth but no words came out. No one had ever asked him that. He was the one that ended the engagement. Then she was gone. Her parents had been kind at the funeral but he was the outsider. That was a role he understood.

He'd not gone to the reception after they'd lowered her casket into the ground. That felt like imposing in a place that was no longer his.

"It broke me. I loved her. Part of me still does, and I hate… hate that she is no longer in this world." Relief followed those words. He'd never spoken of Tess. That was BA and fully off limits, but it felt good to acknowledge the grief he'd gone through. The hurt.

"The night Tess died, she went to the local dive bar…she drank too much. She called me, but I didn't answer. I was… I was…"

"Hurt? Frustrated? Angry? Sad?"

She listed the emotional pain he'd gone through. Each word stung a little as it was uttered.

"All of those. Every single one of them. I sent her to voicemail. She didn't leave one." William took a deep breath. "She got in the car and…"

Jessie hopped off the counter, wrapped her arms around him and just held him.

No one had done that after Tess's passing. Her parents hadn't blamed him but they'd offered no comfort. Her friends hadn't attempted to hide their condemning expressions when he showed up at the funeral.

"If I'd just answered the phone… I killed her."

"Excuse me!" Jessie pulled back.

"I—"

Her hand slapped over his mouth. "Nope. You are not taking the blame for someone else's decision. Absolutely not!"

"Jessie."

"Don't *Jessie* me. Uh-huh. She made the choice. Yes, she was hurt. She was right to be hurt—a relationship ending hurts. But getting behind the wheel when you are intoxicated is not the answer. *Ever.*"

"If I'd answered the phone."

"Things might be different." Jessie squeezed him tighter.

"They might not be. You don't know that she was asking for a ride. She might have been calling to tell you what a bastard she thought you were. Or maybe she was calling to tell you she loved you. Drunk dials are never pleasant to remember the next day."

William appreciated that Jessie was standing up for him against the past, but he knew the truth.

"Harris men hurt the women they love. It's our pattern." That he'd not planned on hurting Tess didn't change the facts.

Jessie took a step back but never dropped his hand. She placed it over her stomach. "Tess made a choice. A bad one. One I've seen far too often in the ER. But she was right. You will be an excellent father. She saw what everyone else sees in you—a caring man, with a heart big enough to take on the world, and a smile that calms the rockiest rooms."

"Careful, my head might get a little big." William sighed, trying to push the compliments off. He didn't mind when someone complimented his looks. He wasn't vain, but he knew he fit the standard Western beauty esthetics.

Looks were easy. They weren't really him—just the outside coating. Compliments on his character…those always came with the feeling of *if you really knew me.*

Jessie tilted her head, a few red flyaway hairs from her messy bun floating past her eyes. His hand was still pressed to her belly and he felt the urge to step away and to pull her close—warring factions in body and soul.

"Maybe you deserve a bit of a bigger head." Jessie's thumb ran over the back of his hand. Tiny sparks danced on his skin, then traveled straight to his heart.

"You aren't responsible for what happened to Tess." She waited.

After a minute, she pressed his hand to her belly, then lifted both her hands to place them on either side of his face. "You are not responsible. And you aren't cursed to repeat some patriarchal line." She stamped her foot and he let out a chuckle.

"I'm serious," She protested.

"I know." William pulled her to him. "I know you're serious and I appreciate it. I do."

"Appreciating is not believing." Jessie let out a little huff into his shoulder.

"Best friends for years and finally spilling all our truths, huh?" William leaned his head against hers. They'd spent hours, days, years together. Talking movies, books, politics, new medical science, dates that went wrong, anything and everything. Except the past.

"It was overdue for us to talk about the BA stuff." Jessie looked up at him.

"It was." His body was an electric wire as her full pink lips parted. Would they have ever brought it up if she hadn't gotten pregnant? He didn't know. But he was glad all of it was out in the open now.

The memory of how she tasted echoed in his brain. His heart screamed for one more indulgence. His fingers were laced around her back. He could draw her even closer, beg her for a chance at something more.

She'd whispered that he didn't want her when they were on their hike. She'd whispered that untruth into the world. But he wanted her. Every bit of her.

He just had to take the jump. Yes, it was a risk. But the reward was Jessie.

"I missed you." He squeezed her, and she lifted her head.

There was no thinking, only reacting. His lips brushed hers and she didn't pull away. Everything from the past two weeks seemed to vanish, but she didn't deepen the kiss.

It was over almost as quickly as it began. She looked at him but no words came from either of them.

Ask her to change the rules, William. Beg her to try this to give you a chance.

His brain screamed at him, but he couldn't give voice to the words.

"I missed you too." She patted his shoulder and walked off.

He hadn't found the words quickly enough…but maybe… just maybe the path they were on could lead somewhere new.

CHAPTER NINE

"THE TEEN IN room 7 is trying to impress his girlfriend by saying nothing feels bad. But he's got at least two broken ribs and needs stitches on his left calf." William rolled his eyes then winked at her as he passed the tablet chart her way.

She made sure their fingers didn't brush.

At the hospital it was easy to maintain the distance. Easy to keep the professional tone in check and remind herself that even though they were having a baby their friendship wasn't changing. At home…the place they lived together—unofficially—it was harder for her heart to stay in place.

Particularly following the kiss they'd shared the other day. She'd hoped he might say something when they parted. Hoped he might indicate he wanted more change than he was already offering. Part of her still hoped it might be possible.

"Men wanting to impress women is a tale as old as time." Jessie smiled as William nodded.

"And the results haven't changed in decades either." He wiggled his eyebrows, jest gleaming in his dark gaze.

"Decades?" Jessie shook her head. "I think this goes back much further than decades."

"Oh, men trying impress their love interest is one of the oldest stories in the book, but at least we no longer go to war for our love. Helen of Troy—"

"That's a myth. And even in the myth men started that because they couldn't control their emotions."

A look passed over William's features and she wanted to slap herself. The statement was true. Wars were started because humans craved something. Power. Land. Resources. And far too many were the result of powerful men not checking their own emotional issues.

But William still had this misguided belief that he was responsible for so many things that weren't his fault.

"Help me with the stitches?"

"I'll do the stitches." Dr. Mueller slapped his hand on the nurses' station. "You take the frequent flier in room 11. She told me she doesn't want me as her doctor of record. And she asked for you." He pointed at William, rolled his eyes and wandered off down the hall toward the room with the teen.

"I can't imagine why someone might not want him as their physician." The urge to stick her tongue out at the retreating Dr. Mueller was nearly overwhelming. If there weren't patients around, she'd probably do it. Every staff member would understand.

William looked at his tablet chart and started tapping his finger on the desk.

"Who is it?" Sometimes patients asked for specific staff, usually a doctor. And it was a difficult truth that some patients returned to the ER over and over again, whether because they had mental health complications, a chronic disease or just nowhere else to go.

"Molly Breckin. Heart issues. Or that's what she says is the issue. The EKG we ran last time was clear and Dr. Mueller sent her on her way. I tried to get Georgia involved but…" He pointed a thumb down the hall where Dr. Mueller had headed.

"He released her?"

William nodded. "In his defense—gosh I hate saying that—the tests were all clear."

"Panic attack?" A panic attack could mimic a heart attack. Many patients thought they were dying when a panic attack started. It was truly terrifying.

William looked at the chart. "I don't know. It felt… I don't know. It felt different than that. Like…"

He paused, but nothing more materialized.

"Like?"

"You're the doc, Jessie. I don't know. Maybe it was a panic attack but it just felt like maybe not. Nurse's intuition?" He threw up his hands.

She understood the frustration. Sometimes finding a diagnosis was hard. Sometimes it felt damn near impossible.

"Well, let's go see Molly."

He fell into step beside her. This was the friendship they'd had. The easiness. It felt selfish to want more.

"William, thanks for coming. Dr. Mueller was already saying I am just a mental basket case." Molly started talking as soon as they opened her door and William stepped in. "Maybe I am. But I swear the heart palpitations are real. They are."

Jessie looked at the monitor and she saw Molly's face fall as she watched the rhythm.

"The good news is that right now your heartbeat and rate are normal." She knew it wasn't the news Molly wanted, even though it was good. Great even.

Molly let out a sigh that was much closer to a sob. "It's not mental. It's not."

"Would it be so bad if it was?" Jessie held up a hand. "Not saying that it is. Just offering the option that mental health can be tricky. Anxiety, depression, panic attack disorder. Medication can relieve symptoms particularly if you have one or more of them—"

"Nope. Nope." Molly hopped off the bed and pulled off the leads and heart rate monitor.

William quickly shut off the buzzing alarms.

"Molly, I have other things I want to check." But the woman was already grabbing her stuff.

"No. I'm not crazy."

"I'm not saying you are." Jessie hated that word. *Crazy.* It was outdated and used far too often as an insult. "I want to check your heart. Please don't leave."

"Just let me sign the AMA and be gone. As you pointed out, I'm fine now."

AMA, or against medical advice, was a form the hospital required patients to sign when they were leaving before treatment started or concluded. As Molly was an adult, Jessie couldn't make her stay, but she didn't want her leaving like this either.

"Molly, I believe that you are feeling something in your chest. Either with your heart or something else. But I need you here to see it."

Molly hesitated, then looked to William.

"She's the best doc we have here. You should stay."

Molly started to sit. They would figure this out.

"Code Blue. Multiple gunshot wounds dropped in lobby. All trauma personnel report. Code Blue. Multiple GSWs—"

"Stay here, Molly. I *will* be back." She and William took off. Dr. Mueller joined them and several other nurses too.

"They dumped them. Car pulled up and pushed three young men out," Lauren stated as they pushed through the door to the waiting area.

The triage nurse was performing CPR on one of the boys. Dr. Mueller slid beside her. William and Lauren went to one and Jessie knelt by a young man who couldn't be more than twenty-two.

"I'm Dr. Davis."

The young man had no color in his cheeks. His hands were pressed against his belly—and coated in blood. Abdominal wounds were always bad. Gunshot wounds to the abdomen were many doctors' worst nightmare.

"I'm Mylo. Don't let me die. I have so much I haven't done. So much." The soft words were almost lost in the busy room.

She couldn't make any promises. "I need a transport cart. We are going to Trauma 2."

"Trauma 1," Dr. Mueller stated as he looked at his watch, called the time of death on his patient, then moved over to where William and Lauren were taking care of their patient.

"Dustin!" Her patient let out a strangled cry as he looked at the body. "No." He closed his eyes, a few tears leaked out, but he didn't reopen them.

"We need to move." He was losing blood too fast. "Now!" The trauma cart rolled up.

They laid a transport board next to him, she counted to three, rolled him and then held pressure on the wound while the staff lifted him onto the bed. Then they were all running together.

Racing the fates.

William rolled over and pulled Jessie into his arms. She was so warm. He buried his head in her hair, soaking in her scent.

Strawberries.

Usually his dreams weren't this good. Rather, they were teasers that whetted his appetite rather than sated it. William was not going to waste this subconscious gift.

He ran a hand down her back. Only in his dreams could he touch her. The cotton T-shirt his mind created was perfection. It was what Jessie wore, what he'd taken off her the night they'd spent together.

Sexy as hell. His subconscious luxuriated in what he didn't have.

But letting the dream go on for too long after he'd recognized it was a recipe for a cranky day. He held her for one more moment, then forced his eyes open.

He blinked when she didn't disappear. Her weight stayed in place on the soft mattress in her guest room.

William pressed his eyes closed, then opened them again. Then he repeated the process. His brain knew she was here, but his heart couldn't quite accept it yet.

"Jessie?"

She let out a soft groan, her T-shirt rising as she shifted against him. Dear God, she was really here.

"Jessie?" He stroked her cheek. Yesterday had been one of the low points anyone who worked in the ER was prepared for but never wanted.

They'd lost all three GSW patients. Jessie's patient passed just before they got him to surgery. William's made it to surgery, but not out. And when they were done, she'd found Molly had checked herself out AMA.

All in all, the shift had been one of the worst he'd worked.

"Sorry." Rose traveled across her cheeks. "I couldn't sleep and…"

"You're fine." William didn't mind finding her in his bed. Hell, he liked it a bit too much. "Nightmares?"

"Yeah." She laid her head against his shoulder.

They all got them. Some more often than others. No matter how well you compartmentalized your life, there were always patients that stayed with you. Patients you thought you could save—if there was just a way to go back in time.

The worst part of that was it was true. Not for every patient but for some. Occasionally there was a misdiagnosis that once you saw the answer it felt like you should always have seen it.

That wasn't true for these patients though.

"You did everything you could for him." If the car that had dropped them off had gotten there faster…if they'd called the emergency line as soon as the incident happened and been transported by ambulance… But even if that had happened, it was no guarantee.

"I know. I know that. But it doesn't change the sorrow nights like that cause." She blew out a breath and snuggled a little closer.

"Agreed."

"Mylo wanted me to promise to save him. Told me there was so much he had left to do."

It wasn't her first plea. His patient hadn't said much. No final pleas. No request to tell someone he loved them. Nothing.

Maybe he'd thought he was beating death. His thigh wound seemed like it was the least concerning, but the femoral artery had been nicked in three places.

"Regrets are the worst." He thought back to Elaine, the shingles patient with so much wrong. She'd been content, but she'd also lived a life. She was choosing her path.

Far too many people didn't get to choose. Or they waited too long to realize what was important.

"They are." Jessie took a deep breath. "You worry about regrets?"

All the time.

"Yes." William forced the word out. Most of his worries revolved around the woman in his arms. What if he screwed this up? What if they could be more? What if the Harris paternal curse followed him and she ended up hating him?

Did he deserve more if he'd broken things off with the women he'd loved because they'd wanted the life that seemed within his reach now?

"Me too." She raised her head, her jeweled gaze staring straight into his soul.

Before he could think of anything to say, she pressed her lips to his.

Don't be a dream.

Her hands lay on either side of his face as she deepened the kiss. Memory and desire overtook him.

All too soon she broke the connection.

She lay there, staring at him.

There were words that needed to be said, but he didn't want to lose this moment.

"William." She breathed his name and the world seemed to shudder. "William."

"Yesterday was a bad day." They'd fallen into bed after a bad day several weeks ago. Each had been seeking comfort from patients reminding them of their past, and they'd both found so much more than just comfort. If that was all that was happening now, he wasn't sure his heart could take it.

Jessie pursed her lips, then shook her head. "Yes. But that isn't what this is."

"Jessie."

She laid a hand across his lips, her gaze never dropping his. "I don't want to live with this regret. I need to know the answer."

"You haven't asked a question." His fingers continued stroking her back, like they had a mind of their own. He felt a desperate need to touch her for as long as she allowed it.

She raised an eyebrow. "Fine. I will spell it out. What if we gave this a try? A real try?"

"Real try?" William couldn't look away from her. Her red hair was splayed across his pillow.

His heart screamed. His soul seemed to dance. Only his brain had hesitations.

"Jessie." He breathed her name out, desperate warring factions begging for the final word within his body.

"It's okay to say you aren't interested." Jessie started to pull away.

His soul cried, and he pulled her back. "I'm interested. And terrified. Part of me is screaming to run. Another part wants to kiss my way down your body."

"Do I get to choose?" Jessie ran a hand over his hip, leaned forward, blanched, then darted out of bed.

He followed her into the bathroom and rubbed her back while she handled the morning sickness. After a few minutes, he started the shower and kissed the top of her head, then started down the stairs.

They'd gotten pretty good at keeping her morning sickness at bay, provided they followed the same schedule. Up by seven, ginger tea—hot—and piece of toast, then anti nausea meds.

After an hour she could have a little more breakfast. Small meals throughout the day made it easier. But they'd gotten distracted this morning.

Distracted…

He started the kettle and smiled as he looked around the kitchen. His coffeepot was now next to the kettle. His favorite mug sat next to it. The twelve-week ultrasound she'd had two days ago was stuck on the fridge, next to a picture of them hiking a couple of years ago.

In the weeks since he'd started staying here, he'd moved in more of his stuff. It was blending together.

He waited for the fear to build. The guilt that he was somehow getting what he didn't deserve. The worry that somehow, he'd mess this up like his father always had. But the only thing echoing through him was calmness.

CHAPTER TEN

WELP. THAT WAS not the way one wanted to start a relationship with the man you couldn't stop thinking about. Jessie threw on some clothes and went in search of William.

And the ginger tea.

He held up the mug as soon as she stepped into the kitchen, turned, pressed the bread down on the toaster and lifted his own cup. It was full of coffee. Black.

She made a face, and he tilted his head.

"Is the ginger tea not helping?"

"Oh. It's fine. I was just thinking about your coffee." She winked and took another sip of the tea. Its warmth traveled to her core.

"You want a cup of coffee?" William chuckled and playfully walked to the cupboard where she kept the mugs. "I'll pour you a cup right now."

"Pregnant people aren't supposed to drink coffee." Jessie stuck her tongue out.

"They can have a cup here and there. They are just supposed to limit their caffeine intake. Which you know, *Dr. Davis.*" He closed the cupboard and took a step toward her.

The world slowed as he looked at her. The first gaze was clearly assessing how she was feeling. The second… Heat pooled through her belly as his gaze traveled her body.

"You are so beautiful." William set his coffee cup on the counter and opened his arms.

She set her mug down and stepped into his embrace. "I have wet hair and you saw me at pretty much my lowest this morning after a poor attempt at seduction. Not exactly the definition of beauty."

William lifted her chin, shaking his head. "You're gorgeous, Jessie. Inside and out. Wet hair and sickness from our baby don't diminish that at all. And it was hardly a poor attempt."

His fingers grazed her hips but it was something else he'd said that sent warmth through her system.

Our baby.

Tears pooled in her gaze. It was the first time he'd referred to their child that way. She thought she'd been happy a minute ago. But that moment couldn't touch this one.

Bliss. Pure bliss.

"Jessie?"

"Our baby. You said *our* baby." She placed her hands on his cheeks and pulled him closer. "Our baby."

He moved one of the hands wrapped around her waist, laid it over her belly and grinned. Really grinned. "Our baby."

She kissed him then. He didn't move his hand. It stayed between them, over their growing child. Wrapping her arms around his neck, she gave in to the arousal, the aching desire she'd carefully leashed for weeks.

This was what she'd wanted. He was what she'd wanted. Needed.

Kissing him felt like coming home.

The toaster pinged and he pulled back.

She let out a tiny whimper.

William kissed her nose. "I want nothing more than to kiss you, pick you up and carry you upstairs and spend the entire day losing myself with you."

"Sounds like a great plan." Jessie raised her eyebrows and gestured toward the door.

He squeezed her hand, then moved toward the toaster. "You need to have something in your stomach." He quickly prepared her standard breakfast and passed it to her. "You know I'm right. You need to take care of you."

"For the baby." She let out a sigh. Padma and Georgia regularly checked in on her now. Padma had hinted more than once that she might want to consider reduced hours. Georgia, sweet Georgia, always seemed to have a granola bar or fruit strip that she just wasn't feeling and offered to Jessie. She was really taking a cue from her childhood friend William with that one.

Jessie appreciated the kind sentiments. "I'm doing what I need to for the little peanut. I've not gained any weight, but at least now I'm not actively losing it like I was in the first trimester. And most importantly, I haven't lost any. Which is my goal, according to my OB, given the morning sickness."

"Jessie—"

"No." She pressed on. It was sweet that everyone was looking after her, but unnecessary. "I'm getting enough rest. Stress...well, that depends on the shift and I can't exactly control the emergencies. I am a pro at taking care of myself for others."

"For others." William leaned on the counter. His gaze was boring into her. "I want you healthy for the peanut. Love the nickname by the way. But I also want you healthy for you. You don't just have to take care of yourself for others."

Jessie took a bite of the toast. Why did buttered toast taste so good even though she was eating it every day?

"I'm pregnant, William. I have to take care of myself for the baby." She tapped her head, making a silly face. "Duh!"

William grabbed the hand she'd used to hit her head. "What I mean is, I want you to take care of you. For you. Not because you are pregnant. Not because you owe someone something, not for any reason other than because you deserve to take care of yourself. I know that idea is foreign to you."

"No, it isn't." She finished the toast, keeping her gaze focused on anywhere but him. Her body had belonged to others when she was born. Now it needed nutrition and care to nourish her son or daughter.

William came around the counter and spun the high chair so she was facing him. He spread his legs, her knees between them, keeping the chair from spinning back. He placed his hands on the counter. His aftershave was invading her nostrils and making her lean a little closer.

If they weren't discussing breakfast, it would have been as hot as hell.

"You are worth everything. Just because you are you, Jessie." He didn't move. His dark gaze burned through her.

She lifted her chin. "You going to stare at me—or kiss me."

William dragged a hand along her bare thigh. His finger traced the bottom of the cotton shorts she was wearing. "There is no reason I can't do both." He shifted so now it was her legs open and him standing between them.

Dropping his head, he let his lips brush hers. The pass was so quick. She wanted more. His fingers slid to the inside of her thigh, slipping higher with each touch, but never going to where her body was starting to call him.

"William."

"My name on your lips is the hottest thing I've ever heard." William nibbled on her ear as his fingers wandered to the edge of her T-shirt.

His hand slipped under it and cupped her breast.

Her breath hitched as his finger found her nipple.

"No bra." His velvet voice caressed her. "Mmm."

She let her hand slip to the bulge in his pants. "I'm at home and comfortable. Why wear a bra?"

"Why indeed." William's thumb spun circles around her nipple as it rose in anticipation.

His mouth captured hers as she unhooked the button of his jeans and unzipped them with a frantic urgency she hadn't felt…hadn't felt since the last time they were together like this.

Slipping her hands down the front of his pants, she hummed as he let out a hungry moan.

"Jessie." He pulled her hand from his pants, kissed her fingers, his eyes blazing with hypnotic ecstasy. "If you keep touching me like that, I will not get to fulfill my fantasy."

"Fantasy?" She ran her hand up his shirt, before ripping it over his head.

The shirt dropped to the floor and before she could contemplate anything else she was in his arms. He kissed her as he carried her to the couch.

No one had ever carried her. She'd made fun of the moment in movies and television shows, calling it unrealistic and dangerous. Now that it was happening to her, she understood the appeal.

The couch was soft as he set her down and grabbed her T-shirt. "It's only fair. Raise your arms, Jessie."

She followed the command, arching a little as she sat before him topless. Shifting on the couch, she moaned. "I'm so turned on, William." Her body was drunk with urgency. She was heading into her second trimester…the extra blood flow to her lower region that she'd heard about while taking her turn in OB as an intern was just as nice as she'd heard women describe it.

She wanted him. Desperately. But he seemed in no hurry.

"Good." He kicked his pants off and knelt on the floor before her. He leisurely dropped kisses along her thighs. "No bra at home." His fingers moved to the edge of her cotton shorts, then slipped inside and gripped her bare buttock.

"No panties either." He slipped a finger into her and pressed his thumb to her mound.

Rocking against his touch, Jessie's body was close to fracturing. She panted as he slipped another finger into her.

"William." Every nerve was ablaze. "William."

He licked the inside of her thigh and she shattered.

She needed him. Now!

It was like he read her mind. In an instant he was on the couch, and she threw a leg over him, not bothering to remove the cotton shorts, just pulling them to the side as she slid down him.

Her body molded to his length. His strong hands gripped her hips.

"Jessie."

He was right. There was something sexy as hell about hearing your name from the lips of your lover when you were spellbound by them.

Leaning forward, she kissed him. Their bodies moved together through the storm of desire, the heady need building in her. This time when she crested into oblivion, he came with her.

"Ready?" Jessie gripped his hand as the nurse called her name.

This was their first OB appointment together.

"Yep." He was. He was. He was.

If he kept mentally repeating that to himself, it would be true.

The last week and half with her was the definition of perfection. They'd slid seamlessly into dating. They already knew so much about each other.

He held her every night. Kissed her every day. Life was brilliant.

And it was going to stay that way. He was not going to mess this up. He was by her side now. Always.

"Breathe, William."

He kissed her cheek. "I'm nervous. I shouldn't be." He'd

never expected to be here. Never expected to see a woman carrying his child. Part of him still felt so unworthy.

"But you are." Jessie kissed his cheek, mirroring the touch he'd just given her.

"Want to know a secret?" She laid her head on his shoulder as they followed the nurse to the room. "I'm nervous too."

They walked into the room and the nurse motioned for her to hop up onto the bed, then turned her attention to him. "Completely normal to be nervous about becoming a father. I promise."

"Thanks." He took a deep breath as Jessie lay back on the bed and lifted her shirt. She'd told him that this was likely to be a pretty boring appointment. She was being seen once a week because of the morning sickness.

William didn't care if these were just weight and check-in appointments. He wanted to be here for every moment.

"This gel will be cold." The nurse gave the warning a split second before dropping a large dollop on Jessie's lower abdomen.

He sat up a little straighter as the heartbeat doppler came out. They heard nothing for a second—the longest second of his life. Then the nurse shifted the doppler and the fast heart rate echoed in the room.

Their child.

"Heart rate is one-fifty-two. Nice and strong at almost fourteen weeks."

He swallowed as tears pressed against his eyes. "Nice and strong."

Jessie looked over at him, then reached out a hand.

He squeezed it, standing up because there was no way that was comfortable for her. He kissed the top of her head.

"All right, the doctor will be in with you shortly." The nurse smiled at them as she headed out.

"You okay?" Jessie beamed at him.

He was more okay than he'd ever been. This wasn't the life he'd planned. In fact, it was one he'd actively avoided, but right now, in this moment, with her, he couldn't imagine any other path.

"Yes."

"Hello." A knock accompanied the greeting, then the door was open. Dr. Keller, the OB, stepped into the room and pulled an ultrasound with her. "I heard Daddy was here and thought you two might like to see your little one today."

Jessie squeezed his hand. "Yes. Yes. Yes. I will always want to see them."

Dr. Keller winked. "Well, I am a little ahead of schedule today so I can squeeze it in. But that won't be the case every appointment."

"Of course." Jessie gazed at William. "We get to see the baby."

"The gel—"

"Is going to be cold. I know." She flinched just a bit as the gel hit her belly again. "I know that warming it provides an ideal environment for bacterial growth but still…"

Dr. Keller chuckled. "I know it's not the best but we can't risk the bacteria. It doesn't help that your body is more sensitive when you are pregnant."

That was a benefit he'd noticed. The briefest touch to her nipples made her moan—in the best way possible.

Dr. Keller ran the wand over Jessie's belly and paused as she found their baby. The little one was no bigger than a peach, but it looked like a baby now.

"They are sucking their thumb." The hand moved and Jessie giggled. "Or maybe they are just trying to figure out their face."

Dr. Keller took a few measurements. "You are a little over fourteen weeks. It's not uncommon to see them suck their thumb in utero around this time. They could also just be playing around."

She let them look at the baby for a moment longer, then turned her attention to Jessie. "How is the nausea?"

Jessie shrugged. "It's not any worse. I feel weird getting excited about that."

Dr. Keller made a few notes in Jessie's chart. "I know you were hoping it would go away completely, but no worse is a good sign. It means we have it under control. And it might still vanish. It happens for some women after they hit the second trimester."

She looked at her chart then back at Jessie. "You gained about half a pound. Which in the first trimester is fine. As you enter your second trimester, I'd like to see us get closer to gaining a pound a week. Two pounds would fine too. You were a little underweight when you got pregnant. The biggest thing is you can't lose weight."

As she said the words, the OB looked at William. He nodded. Put a little weight on Jessie. Done. Whatever she wanted and could tolerate, he'd get.

"And since Dad is here," she said as she grabbed the chart, "are there any known medical issues with your family?"

"I don't know."

"Right." Dr. Keller made a note, then looked at him. "Anyway, you could check. Ask a parent, a sibling, a grandparent?"

"William..." Jessie reached out a hand for him and he took it. She squeezed it twice and offered him a smile.

"I can reach out to my mom." He looked at Jessie. "I can't guarantee she will answer, there are some family dynamics at play."

"I understand." Dr. Keller nodded before turning her attention back to Jessie.

She'd no doubt heard it all. She didn't press. Not knowing

a parent's medical history didn't necessarily hurt a child, but knowing it made things easier.

He pulled out his cell and texted the number he had. It was only as he entered the number that he realized it was possible she'd gotten a different number. But there was no way to know without trying.

Can I have yours and Dad's medical history?

He hesitated for a moment. Did he tell her she was about to be a grandmother? After years of silence, did he even want her to know?

Eventually he just hit the send button. If she asked, he'd get into it. If not—that was an answer unto itself.

"Right, I will see you back next week for just a quick check to check if you are gaining any weight. At the twenty-week appointment we'll do the anatomy scan. Given your age, your insurance will cover an amniocentesis. I typically schedule it for week fifteen and sixteen. If you want some time—"

"I want it."

William's head popped up at the pain in Jessie's voice.

He reached his hand out, taking hers. "Sweetheart…" The endearment slipped from his mouth as he saw tears swimming in her eyes.

"I need to know. I need to know…" Her breath came in little bursts.

"I'll get it scheduled. And give you a few minutes." Dr. Keller stepped out.

William was out of his chair before the door fully shut.

"Sorry." She hiccupped and pushed a tear away. "This is so dumb."

"What is?" William pressed his lips to her forehead, holding her. She hadn't technically explained anything. That was all right, but he couldn't offer all the support if he didn't know what was going on.

"I had a dream—" She took a deep breath, but nothing followed.

"Many pregnant people report enhanced dream activity." William ran his hand down her back.

"I know." Jessie tensed, the flash of anger surprising him. "But this isn't having a litter of puppies or pregnant with a dozen kittens. This…this…this was Bran."

"You saw Bran in a dream?" He was her only sibling. She and Bran had been close, wouldn't seeing him make her happy?

The silence hung for another minute so he hugged her. "Did you tell him he was going to be an uncle?"

Another little sob. "He knew."

Two little words, said in a way that made him shiver. "And?"

"He asked if I was capable of saving this child when I'd let him die?" Another sob broke and he held her while she let the emotions loose.

"Bran wouldn't say that." Meeting the brother she loved so much wasn't possible, but from the things she'd told him, there was no way the boy who'd loved his sister when everyone else in the family saw her as spare parts would ever utter those words, dead or alive.

This was Jessie's fear: her worry that she wasn't good enough. That somehow she'd spent all the precious coins in a mythical karma bank.

"You don't know that. I failed him and—"

"Nope." William gripped her shoulders. "No." He grabbed her hand and placed it over her belly.

"You did not fail Bran. And you will not fail our son or daughter."

"What if…?" Fear danced in her eyes as she laid her other hand over the one he'd placed on her belly.

There were no guarantees in life. Pregnancy was a complicated process. She was past the time when most miscarriages happened, but that didn't mean other issues wouldn't arise.

They worked in healthcare, saw the devastation. But life was more than worst-case scenarios.

"If the amnio shows something, we will make the decision that is right for us and the baby. And if that is the case, it won't be your fault. You've never failed, Jessie. Not Bran. Not the baby. Not me."

She nodded. He wasn't sure she believed him but at least she didn't argue. Small wins were sometimes the biggest.

"We should vacate the room, let another patient in." She gripped his hand, slid off the bed and grabbed her small purse.

He followed, a knot of worry chasing at his heels. Would she ever feel like she wasn't responsible for everything that happened in her childhood?

CHAPTER ELEVEN

"YOU DON'T HAVE to keep checking your phone." Jessie wrapped her arms around his waist as he glared at his phone.

"Nothing." He looked through all the notifications, knowing there were none. Not that he needed to tell her. Jessie knew his mother hadn't responded. She knew that he'd sent a follow-up text, and another one. It shouldn't matter. He should have just left it at the one text. Taken the hint.

If it was for him, he would have just dropped it. But he was letting down Jessie.

And their unborn child.

She squeezed his waist and stepped back. "It's fine, William. It's not your fault."

It was like she was reading his mind.

"I know a lot of people don't know their family history, but it would be easy enough for her to answer. Or to tell me to back off. It's the silence…"

Why did that hurt so much more?

"You went no contact for a reason." She shrugged. "She can do the same. It sucks but we have so much more to focus on now."

He nodded, pulled up the message and decided to send one more. One more attempt. If his mother didn't respond he'd take the hint.

All the hints.

I'm not asking for me. My partner is having a baby, and we'd like to make sure we know everything. I won't ask again. Promise.

William hit Send and put the phone back in his locker. "I told her about the baby. Said my partner was having a baby and we needed to know."

"Partner?" Jessie tilted her head. "Not girlfriend?"

There was a twinkle in her eye that sent heat down his spine. They'd not discussed labels, but *girlfriend* didn't feel right. It felt too temporary.

Jessie wasn't temporary.

"Do you not like it?" If they weren't at the hospital, he'd wrap her into his arms, kiss her nose, then whisper sweet nothings in her ear as he let his fingers wander to all the places that made her arch into him.

She put a hand on her chin, playfully pretending to think about it. "Hmm…"

"I'll call you whatever you want me to, sweetheart."

"I like when you call me sweetheart."

Her grin lit up the small locker room.

They were at work; it should be easy to focus on other things. But all he could look at was her.

She was in scrubs, ones she couldn't tie as tight today. Her hair was pulled into a bun on top of her head. She was his lighthouse.

The rock he needed to guide him.

I love her.

Three little words echoed in his head. He loved her. He'd loved her for years. When that love had shifted from platonic friendship to this deep, abiding need, he didn't know.

"Jessie, your frequent flier is back. Same symptoms." Dr.

Mueller rolled his eyes as he threw a tablet chart into Jessie's hands.

William had been too focused on his revelation to realize that the annoying physician had stepped into the room.

"She is a patient, and her name is Molly. Stop referring to our patients by television stereotypes." Jessie took a deep breath and looked through the tablet notes.

"I will see to her now. William?"

"Right behind you." If this was television, he could stick his tongue out at the grumpy ER physician who should have chosen a different profession. The camera would slide in, and the audience would laugh at the moment of levity.

Unfortunately, the hospital human resources department wouldn't appreciate that kind of humor. And Dr. Ronny Mueller would definitely report it.

Georgia was right outside the room when they arrived.

"Georgia, I have a tough case," Jessie said.

"Molly Breckin. I know. William and I tried before but she left AMA. I am hoping maybe this time we will find something." She followed them into the small ER room.

Molly was sitting on the bed. She was hooked up to the EKG, and tears were falling down her face as she stared at the normal rhythm repeating over and over again on the monitor.

It was weird to hope for a diagnosis, but when patients were sure something was wrong, they were usually right. After all, the patient lived in their body.

"It's nice to see you again, Molly." Jessie moved to the bed, standing in front of the heart monitor.

"No, it's not. I shouldn't be here. Clearly." She waved toward the monitor Jessie was now blocking. "Maybe it is all in my head."

Georgia moved to the other side of the bed. "Molly, you have come in several times now—"

"Yep, the other doctor calls me a frequent flier."

"Dr. Mueller has outdated ideas," Georgia stated.

"Nice how you didn't even have to ask which doctor." Molly crossed her arms.

William let out a cough that didn't quite cover the chuckle.

Jessie gave him a look before turning her attention back to Molly. "I want to put in a consult with cardio."

Georgia nodded. "You need to see cardio."

"I have an appointment—in four months—with a cardiologist. Four months." Molly blew out a breath. "Four months. The earliest they could see me."

"What happened today?" Jessie's voice was calm, but he saw her look at the printout of Molly's heart rate.

"Same as always. Felt like my heart was in my throat. I was dizzy. I thought I might pass out."

"Did you?" Georgia had hated how Dr. Mueller treated Molly when Georgia was first back at Memorial. Molly had left AMA before Georgia could figure anything out.

Molly bit her lip but it didn't stop the small sob from breaking through. "No."

That was good. But it meant there was nothing she or Jessie could rule out.

"Right." Jessie made a few taps on the tablet chart she had. "I want to warn you that it can take a while for them to see you."

"Because there is nothing wrong with my stats." Molly said the words with a certainty experience with a chronic, undiagnosed condition brought. "I swear I'm not making this up."

"I believe you." Jessie looked at the chart. "I do. I promise. But I also want to give you a realistic expectation for your wait. But look at me."

Jessie waited but Molly didn't respond. "Molly, look at me." Was that the tone she'd use when their son or daughter wasn't paying attention? It was effective. Molly looked right at her.

"I am going to get you some answers. I am."

He saw Georgia's eyes widen and he bit the inside of his cheek to keep from responding. Molly had been in several times. There was no way Jessie could realistically make that promise.

And if she broke her promise, she'd punish herself, think that she'd failed.

"Fortunately," he said, needing to take the focus off that promise and put it on what they could control and see, "you are stable right now. *That* is a good thing." William knew it was frustrating, but in this line of work stability was the goal. And it could change so fast.

"William is right." Jessie picked up the printout of the EKG and the heart rate monitor. He could tell from her face that they were completely perfect. "It is important that you are stable. I know it seems like failure, but it's not."

"Right." Molly nodded. "So, I sit and wait and hope for another episode that makes me feel like I am dying. Got it." She brushed away a tear.

"I am going to find something, Molly. We will get this sorted."

There was that promise again. It was admirable how much she cared for her patients, but Jessie wasn't divine. It was possible she'd have to tell Molly there was no answer today.

"Ring the nurses' station if you need anything." William hated the resigned look on her face. "I mean it, Molly. If you need something, press this button." He held up the call button, pointing to the blue button.

She knew what it was, but he hoped by pointing it out, she'd know he meant it.

"Fine." A single-syllable word that he hated so much.

Jessie looked at him, he could see the list of possibilities running through her head. The hope for figuring this out for Molly…and the fear that she might fail.

It could be nearly anything…or nothing at all.

"I'll check back in when I can." Jessie nodded.

Georgia agreed to do the same and they all stepped out of the room.

Jessie leaned against the wall, taking a deep breath, her hands around her waist.

"You all right?" William was by her side in an instant. She'd had her normal breakfast this morning. Toast and tea. But she hadn't eaten the extra fruit or avocado the doctor recommended to try to help her put on a little weight. Her stomach just didn't want to handle those today.

"No." She took a deep breath.

"Do you need to go home?" Georgia asked the question before he could get it out.

"What?" Jessie pushed off the wall. "No. It's nothing to do with me. Molly keeps coming in. I believe that she is experiencing the symptoms but now she isn't trusting herself."

"It could be panic attacks and acute anxiety." Georgia rolled her head from one side to the other. "In all honesty that is the best-case scenario. Heart problems in your late twenties don't usually bode well for later-in-life care."

"Right." Jessie crossed her arms, then uncrossed them, before crossing them again. "Dr. Mueller failed her, and now I am. I can't give her anything more than a long wait."

William wasn't sure what to say. He had no insight on a diagnosis. All of Molly's vitals were perfect. Dr. Mueller had failed her, but Jessie and Georgia were doing their job. Sometimes there weren't answers.

Not often, but he'd seen it happen. But what he knew with certainty was that Jessie was going to do everything she could to make sure she figured out what was going on with Molly. Unfortunately, if she came up empty, she'd keep looking. She'd continue pushing herself, punishing herself if no answers materialized.

"What if you can't give her answers today?" Georgia asked the question on the tip of his tongue.

"We will. I have faith in us. We can do this." Jessie on a mission for her patient was a force to see. However, there were no guarantees—and she needed to take care of herself too.

"If any of us see Eli wandering around, we grab him and hustle him to this room. Agreed?" William looked to Georgia, then to Jessie.

Technically as a surgeon he wasn't likely to take the on-call request for Molly. But he was more likely to stop into the ER if he had a minute to see Georgia. William wanted a way to find an answer for Molly—and for Jessie.

"Agreed," they said in unison. Georgia offered a far more chipper expression than Jessie.

"Eli!" Jessie ignored the wave of nausea passing through her. She was dehydrated. There hadn't been much time between patients today, and her stomach had refused almost everything she'd put into it since the toast almost ten hours ago. Particularly after Dr. Mueller microwaved fish for his lunch. Again.

Georgia was nearly bouncing with vindication when she'd caught him warming up the cod.

Cod. Cod! It was basic microwave etiquette to not microwave seafood in a shared device. Not that Dr. Mueller understood etiquette.

At least the man had shown a tiny bit of shame when Georgia confronted him. According to Georgia, he'd blustered but color had invaded his cheeks when she pointed out that people had complained about the mystery fish warmer several times. So he knew. Maybe he'd start thinking of his colleagues occasionally.

And then his patients.

Though that was probably too much to hope for.

"Jessie." Eli put his hands in his pockets and rocked back on his heels. "I know you want me to stop in to see Molly."

So either Georgia or William had gotten to him first. Good. Hopefully that meant that he had at least some idea about what was going on.

"She's gone."

Those were not the words she wanted to hear. This wasn't happening. She'd promised Molly tests and a cardiology consult. She'd sworn to her she'd try to find something. William had given her that exasperated look of his, but he hadn't said anything.

"No. I stopped in about an hour ago." Molly had been waiting for nearly seven hours. It had been a long day and nothing in her vitals had changed. But she'd still been there.

A wave of dizziness threatened as Jessie forced herself to breathe in through her nose and then out. It was the end of her shift. She needed to get off her feet, get some fluids and some food. But this was important.

Eli cleared his throat and looked at his shoes. "I stopped in about twenty minutes ago. I guess there was some sort of confusion and a nurse asked why she didn't have discharge papers yet."

"Discharge papers?" Jessie was Molly's physician of record in the ER. She was the only one who could discharge her until shift change.

"Yeah." Eli shrugged. "There was a miscommunication regarding the patient in room 8."

"Polly Henderson? I put her papers in. She needed rehydration from the stomach bug that seems to keep going around." Polly could probably have gotten along fine at home with water and electrolyte drinks, but the ER treated tons of nonemergencies. It was what most of her shift was.

"Kit looked at the papers too fast, got Molly confused with Polly. Kit feels terrible."

"A mistake." Jessie clenched her fists, then released them. She'd find Kit and give her a boost. "It happens." But if it was going to happen, why couldn't it happen with a different patient?

ERs were chaotic at the best of times. She could see how patients with similar names in rooms right by each other could get mixed up.

"Molly thought Kit was trying to give her a subtle hint, no matter how much Kit and others told her they weren't. I got there about ten minutes after."

Jessie kicked the air, immediately regretting how the motion made stars dance in her eyes. After she was done with Eli, she was going to sit down for a few minutes. "That is three times she's left. That I know of."

"Yeah. It isn't that uncommon, Jessie. Run me through her symptoms."

Jessie repeated what Molly had told her and gave Eli all the details on the perfect vitals she'd seen.

"Same thing Georgia told me." Eli frowned.

"Is it ringing any bells?" She wasn't a cardiothoracic surgeon, but she'd done her rounds in cardio as an intern. She knew the answer before he gave her the soft smile.

"You don't have to let me down easy." Jessie took a deep breath, trying to push away the failure creeping in along her chest. There was no reason for her to be personally invested in this.

But Molly had looked so broken. So tired. So frustrated. To not have any answer to give her was heartbreaking.

"Panic attack makes more the most sense based on everything she describes."

He was right but it didn't feel good to Jessie. She'd been that scared person in the hospital suffering a panic attack. She'd thought she was having a heart attack about six months after Bran passed.

Part of her had even wished for it as a penance for failing her brother.

She'd been hooked up to all the same machines Molly had been, with the same outcome as her. Except the diagnosis had made her feel better. It had made sense. She was stressed as hell.

Her father had called her a baby, thanking her for wasting their time. It should have been a low point, but instead she'd felt better after finding out. Molly insisted something else was going on.

Maybe it was a panic attack. They were scary as hell. However, something about this case, about the frustration in Molly features when she'd mentioned panic and anxiety, made Jessie question the diagnosis that was sitting right in front of her.

It was like she was missing some important piece of the puzzle. Panic attacks were real though. They could mimic a heart issue so easily. Maybe—

"I know it sucks." Eli looked to his pager. "But it is a good thing that her heart is fine." He held the pager up. "I have to take this."

"Right." She blinked as more stars danced. "Eli?" She reached out a hand as darkness started chasing her.

She thought she heard her name, thought she felt hands wrapped around her as darkness closed in.

CHAPTER TWELVE

JESSIE TRIED TO ignore the beeping of her own monitors as she scanned Molly's records on the tablet chart she'd convinced one of the OB nurses to let her use while she waited for her discharge papers. She'd fainted yesterday and been admitted to OB…because of dehydration. She'd been administered IV fluids and IV antinausea meds and she was feeling better than she had since she'd got pregnant. She'd kept down dinner and her breakfast.

The only thing upsetting her right now was the fact that there was nothing in Molly's records indicating anything other than panic attacks.

Maybe that was what Molly was facing. It wasn't what Molly wanted to hear, but sometimes a physician's job was to give news a patient didn't want to hear. *Or accept.*

She scrolled through the first entry made in Molly's chart. It was basic information, along with a nurse's comment: "Patient says she feels better when upside down."

That was all it said. Upside down. What did that mean? Did it mean anything?

Jessie pulled a hand across her face. Nothing seemed to click.

"Great news!" William flung the hospital room door open and yawned. He'd curled up on the pull-out couch last night, refusing to go home to get some actual rest. The man hadn't slept well at all.

She pushed the tablet under the covers.

"I can confirm discharge papers are coming. With mild restrictions for until you can get in to see your OB next week." William slid into the chair by her bed.

He looked at her as if waiting for something. Finally, he took a deep breath. "You going to tell me why you have a tablet chart in here?"

Pointing to the bed where the chart was hidden under the blankets, William waited again.

"It's not a big deal." Jessie shrugged.

"That's why you hid it?" He crossed his arms, then uncrossed them. "Jessie, you fainted yesterday."

"Dehydration. It happens." Pregnancy changed just about everything in your body. "And with hyperemesis gravidarum, this might happen a few more times."

She was surprised she got the words out without them sounding shaky. Jessie was terrified by what had happened. The only reason she was able to work at all with hyperemesis gravidarum was because she didn't have much in her stomach very often.

At only fifteen weeks, there were still months of this pregnancy left and no guarantees the extreme morning sickness would dissipate. The longer she stayed sick, the more likely it was this would follow her the entire pregnancy.

"Jessie—"

His tired tone broke her.

"The baby is fine. Our baby is fine. I will make sure our child stays safe. If that means sucking ice cubes throughout the day, Popsicles and even those liquid IV packs we sometimes take on hikes, I can do it." She laid a hand over her belly.

"I won't let anything happen to my child." The little bean was unaware of the issues it was causing, but she held no grudge. And she would do whatever it took to make sure her child was healthy and happy.

"What about you?" William raised a brow.

Jessie pulled the tablet chart out from under the covers. There was no sense hiding it now. "I was looking at Molly's charts. All of them. There is an interesting note—"

"What about you?" William stood, took the tablet chart from her hands, setting it on the small table that held her meal trays.

"Hey."

"I will give it back when you answer my question. What about you, Jessie?"

"What about me?" She flung her hands up, wincing as the IV in her hand shifted slightly. "Forgot that was there."

"Only you could forget about an IV in your hand. Do you know how many patients complain about how much those hurt? And you forget it's there."

She looked at the IV. The nurse had done a lovely job placing it. Jessie had had enough IVs as a child to know the difference.

"Jessie…" William took a deep breath, sat back down in the chair and leaned forward. "We need to focus on you and your health."

"I won't put the baby at risk." She pointed to the monitors. "His or her heartbeat has been perfect this whole time. I just need to figure out this diagnosis."

"No. *You* don't. If Molly comes back, we can tackle it then. Or the cardiologist she is seeing in a few months can. This is not your responsibility."

Tears coated her eyes. *Stupid hormones.* He was right, but she felt like if she figured it out it would be a win for everyone.

"This isn't about the baby." William's hand reached for hers, careful to avoid touching her IV. "This is about you. You deserve to be taken care of."

"I know."

"Do you? Or are you trying to earn the health of our baby?"

"That is ridiculous." Jessie dropped his hand. "Since when is fighting for your patient such a crime? Something keeps bringing Molly back. So I am trying to get her healthy. I fight for my patients."

"And that is admirable. But right now, you need to fight for yourself. It is not selfish to do so." William didn't reach for her hand again.

She could reach for him, but she didn't.

They sat there for several minutes. Silence could be shockingly loud.

Her belly let out a loud grumble.

"Hungry?"

She nodded and William stood and grabbed the snacks the nurses had provided for her.

"While those intravenous nausea meds are working you should eat as much as you want." William put the whole basket on the bed.

Part of her wanted to mention that she'd heard the doctor this morning too. That instruction had been the biggest one: listen to your body. If it's hungry, you are in a window that will let you eat—probably.

She grabbed the pack of nuts and some raisins. If she kept these down, she'd attempt a turkey stick. Jessie ate a few nuts, shifting her eyes between the bed and William. It was weird to eat by herself in the quiet.

But she pushed through, for her child.

"So tell me what you found out about Molly."

Jessie grinned. "I think it's supraventricular tachycardia. Which also explains why her heart seems fine. Once the heart rate slows down there are no symptoms and it doesn't damage the heart long-term."

"SVT?" William didn't sound as impressed as she'd hoped.

"I mean it makes sense. Faster heartbeats, palpitation, breathing difficulties. But it can come and go and some patients don't even have symptoms. Plus the same complaints can indicate a panic attack."

And in a woman it was more likely that panic attack would be diagnosed. The medical community was starting to recognize their bias, but if Molly showed up after her heart rate calmed between travel time and waiting in the ER before she was hooked up—then it wasn't difficult to understand how it was missed.

"Of all the heart conditions she could have, that one is probably the best. And it's treatable with meds. All right, if she shows back up, we'll mention it to the doctors."

"If she shows back up, I'm her doctor." Molly trusted her. She was working this case.

William didn't try to hide his frustration, "Jessie, you need to focus on you. You are not responsible for—"

"I am." The words just popped out.

His dark gaze fell on her with a look she couldn't quite understand but it sent shivers down her spine.

"Why are you responsible?"

Jessie opened her mouth but no words came out.

William crossed his arms and leaned back in the chair, at least as much as the hospital chair would allow.

"I just am." It was a terrible response. Childish. But she couldn't put into words why she needed to figure this out. She just did.

Before William could say anything else a nurse walked in. "I have discharge papers!"

"Great!" Jessie let out a sigh. Saved by the interruption, but she could tell from William's posture that he still had concerns. Those were a problem for later though. Right now, she was breaking free.

* * *

His phone dinged and William reached for it. Jessie had texted him from their bedroom a few times since he'd told her he was running to the store. Each time was a request for some food she was craving.

It was like a switch had gone off yesterday—four days after she'd left the hospital for dehydration. Neither of them was getting their hopes up. Her OB had told them at her follow-up appointment yesterday that hyperemesis gravidarum could start to get better around this time in Jessie's pregnancy.

Or that she might start to have several days where she felt better. Then it would be back with a vengeance.

They were going to take the wins where they could. Jessie was thrilled to have a day or so where she could indulge in pregnancy cravings. When the cake and pickles she'd wanted last night hadn't resulted in any issues, she'd danced around the kitchen.

He'd bring home anything she wanted to try. Anything!

William's stomach dropped as he saw the text. It was not from Jessie. After weeks of radio silence, his mother had responded.

My family is fine health wise. No issues other than breast cancer and thyroid disease.

Cancer and thyroid disease. He wouldn't have labeled that "fine." Those were treatable, if caught early, but hardly nothing. Still, it was better to know.

Thank you.

He sent the response. He wanted her to know he appreciated it. Even if it had taken a while for him to hear anything.

As you know, your father's family is messed up. Your half brother is just like him. Currently going through his second divorce.

Heat rushed to his cheeks and he looked around the store, as if the dressing down was somehow directed at him. It wasn't.

It was a shame his half brother hadn't found his person. And divorce was always tough, but his mother might have been happier if she'd divorced his father rather than staying for some stubborn reason, never changing her opinion.

There was no need for him to respond. A divorce was sad sometimes. But most of the time it was because the relationship wasn't serving one or both partners. Ending that was a sign of strength.

Plus he didn't know the details. Maybe his half brother was the wronged party.

I thought you never planned to have kids. Isn't that the excuse you gave your ex-fiancée for ending it? Or did you just want to play the field like the rest of the men?

He had to give her credit. His mother could switch topics fast and with brutal effect. She was right. He'd told Tess he hadn't wanted children. At that point it wasn't a lie. Maybe it wasn't fair that he was getting the life Tess had wanted, but he couldn't change that.

Well, he wasn't like the men in his family. He was involved in his child's life. He loved Jessie—though there'd been no good time to tell her. Maybe he should bring home a cake with the words *I love you*.

She loved cake. But that didn't feel grand enough.

His phone dinged again and he rolled his eyes. There was

no need for his mother to keep responding. But it wasn't her and the text lightened his mood considerably.

Out of pickles. Yes. I ate them all. Yes. I would like more. Thanks.

There was also a picture of her holding up the empty jar, her fiery red hair spilling out of the bun. The constant circles under her eyes were better. Not gone, but he'd take a Jessie making demands any day.

He texted a quick thumbs-up and went to grab the pickles.

"Tell me you have pickles." Jessie was bouncing as she met him in the driveway.

"Got three jars. Will that be enough?" William laughed as he passed her the bag with the pickles.

Tonight was a fun night. Since she'd been hospitalized it felt like they were each walking on thin ice, each watching the cracks expand but never breaking through.

Right now, though, everything was happy. He was going to bask in the moment.

"I am eating as much as I want because if I wake up sick tomorrow, at least I will have had some good eating days." She grabbed another bag and practically hopped back up to the townhome.

One of the jars might be gone by the time he finished unloading everything.

Climbing the stairs he entered the kitchen, not surprised to see her sitting on the counter, a jar of pickles open next to her.

"I know it's cliché. Pregnant woman eats pickles, but these taste good." She bit into the pickle, closed her eyes and relaxed.

He mentally captured the picture.

She was happy. Not worried. Focused on what her body

was craving, not worrying about the hospital. Or things she couldn't change. Taking blame for things outside her control.

This was perfection.

"I got everything on your list. And a cake."

Jessie put a hand over her heart. "You are the best."

That was music to his ears.

"Well, I am glad you think so because I heard from my mother."

Jessie hopped off the counter, her arms wrapping around him.

"I still have things to put away. Things that are in my hands, sweetheart." He kissed the top of her head, but she only squeezed tighter.

"Don't care. Whatever hurtful thing she said, it wasn't true."

He kissed her forehead and sighed. "She gave me a partial medical history and said some horrid things too." He didn't want to bring up her reference to Tess. Or the insinuation that he was just like the men in his family. Tonight he wanted to eat too many pickles—assuming Jessie wanted to share.

"I'm sorry." Jessie looked up at him, her bright eyes flashing with anger—on his behalf.

He laid his hands over her barely-there baby bump. "I know. And since I plan to make it a point to be my father's opposite, it is a moot point. I will be there for our son or daughter, so I will be the one saying 'told you so.'"

Jessie pulled back just a bit. "Do you need to say 'told you so'?"

"Yeah." He chuckled. His mother was expecting him to fail. He'd done that before, when he'd lost Tess. Now he was getting the life she wanted—the life his mother didn't think him capable of.

"It will be nice to prove that despite looking like him, and acting like him when I was younger, that I'm not him. I will never disappoint our baby." Unlike his father, he was going to treasure the family he'd been unexpectedly gifted.

"You can't promise that, William." Jessie's hand cupped his cheek. "Disappointment happens."

Was she expecting him to fail? No. He pushed that errant thought away.

"I will never be like him. Unlike him I will be in my child's life." He wouldn't hurt the woman he loved. Wouldn't make the child he fathered wonder if he cared for them. The Harris line was changing.

"Right." Jessie nodded.

He kissed her nose, hating the pinch of worry he saw poking through her features. "Jessie?"

"Where is that cake? I feel like cake, with a side of pickles." She smiled, but the smile didn't quite reach her eyes.

CHAPTER THIRTEEN

JESSIE GRABBED A few nuts and darted into an empty bay, pulling the curtain so she had a few minutes of privacy. Exhaustion was wearing at her, but at least her nausea was holding off. She still had a wave or two of it, but it seemed like she was doing something right. The universe was finally siding with her. 'Bout time.

She ate a few nuts and took some small sips of water. Last night she'd eaten far too much cake and more pickles than she cared to remember. William had joked about it, laughing about if their baby would come out with an intense love or hatred of pickles.

Love. He'd said the word so many times last night. Her love for pickles. His love for the baby growing in her belly. Her love for cake. He'd wondered how all of it would affect their little peanut.

Everything was for their child. That should make her happy. She laid a hand over where their child slept and tried to calm the panic rising in her.

She loved William. She'd realized it last night. Loved him, not as a friend but as something so much deeper. He met a need that was anchored deep within her soul.

But what if the only reason this was happening was their child?

It is the only reason.

That thought refused to leave her. If she weren't pregnant, they would have found a way to stay friends, found a way through the awkwardness. It was the little bean that had brought them back together.

And that would have been enough. Except William was also here because of his father. Proving his father wrong by being there for their child.

He'd said so many times last night.

For their child.

Not for her.

What kind of a person did it make her, that she wanted both? She should be happy with the universe giving her one. She should be happy with the life she'd found. Maybe it wasn't perfect but it was so much more than she'd ever expected.

"Jessie looks better today." Georgia's words echoed through the bay curtain.

"Yeah. I actually got some food in her last night. A ton of pickles." William laughed.

"You look so happy."

Georgia's comment brought a smile to Jessie's face. She was overthinking this, looking for the universal catastrophe that always seemed to land on her doorstep. It was the payment for a life she could never get back.

William was happy. Everyone could see it.

"I am. My mother actually accused me of ending things with Tess because I wanted to play the field. Part of me really wants to send a picture to my parents to show them that I'm not my father. Jessie is my proof of that."

The nuts she'd just eaten threatened to rise back up. Proof. She was proof he was a good person. He shouldn't need proof of that...and he certainly shouldn't be thinking of her as proof.

"Your mother is pretty set in her thoughts." Georgia cleared her throat.

"Yep. The woman looks for the worst in every situation. I

swear she is hoping that Jessie one day reaches out to let her know I suck. But I won't give her the satisfaction."

Her heart was his. To her very core she loved him—and to him, she was a trophy. Something he could show off to make a point. Staying in her life meant his mother's viciousness was wrong. It meant the curse of his father's line was fiction, that somehow he wasn't forever cursed because the woman he loved had made a decision that resulted in her death.

He needed proof of something that he should know deep down.

Jessie had always been something besides just herself to others she loved. To her parents she was spare parts. To Bran she was the sister he'd loved but who he'd hoped was his savior. And to William—to William she was proof that he was a better man than he believed.

Why couldn't she just be a person people loved? She squeezed her eyes shut, grateful when she heard them walk away from the bay.

William would always be in their child's life. She didn't doubt that. It wasn't that he didn't want children; he just had reservations about his own ability to be a good father. If he'd realized before he'd broken up with Tess, they'd likely be celebrating a decade of marriage with a few munchkins running around by now.

It was good that he realized it now and knew he wasn't his dad. But she wasn't proof.

She was the mother of his child. She was the woman who loved him.

William had told her she needed to think of herself, needed to put herself first.

A tear raced down her cheek and she pushed it away. She still had four hours left on her shift. At least they'd taken different cars today. She could take longer to get home, gather her thoughts and figure out what her path was.

The universe had given her baby a father who would love it fiercely. That it hadn't granted her the same love…well, that was something she should have expected.

Jessie walked into the living room; arms crossed.

"You look like you are ready for battle." The last few hours of their shift had been off. It was like a tension that lived just under the happiness of his jokes about pickles and cake.

"You aren't your father." Jessie pinched her eyes closed like she was pushing back tears. "I need you to know that."

"I'm determined not to be. I mean—"

"No," Jessie interrupted. "I heard you talking to Georgia today. Heard you say that you were proving a point."

"Jessie." That wasn't what he'd meant. Not completely, anyway. It did prove a point, but it wasn't the only reason he was here.

"If the baby wasn't a factor, would this exist?" She waved a hand between them.

The question sent ice water through his veins. "Where is this coming from, Jessie?"

"Answer me. Please." A tear rolled down her cheek.

How was he supposed to know? Maybe. Maybe not. "You agreed we were better as friends afterward. I mean I'm glad we—"

"So no." Jessie scratched the side of her head.

"I don't know." It was the truth. They'd been so scared about messing up their friendship. But when he was with her it made sense.

"I want someone that chooses me." Jessie bit her lip. "Just me. No one ever has."

"That is not fair." William shook his head.

"I'm not a prop to prove that you aren't your father." Jessie stepped back as he moved toward her.

"Jessie. This isn't what this is. Why on earth are you pushing this? Are you punishing yourself?"

"What the hell is that supposed to mean?"

"Please." William crossed his arms, matching her posture. "You don't think you've earned this. You think you owe some karmic debt. Like you are so important to the universe your wishes alone could have kept Bran alive, and because you didn't, you deserve a lifetime of pain."

The color drained from her cheeks. He'd gone too far. God. He loved her. He loved her so much and rather than tell her that, rather than pull her close, walk her through this insecurity, he'd struck below the belt. So far below the belt.

After bragging that she was his proof that he was better than his father, he'd struck out at the woman he loved. William had taken the thing she was most ashamed of and thrown it in her face.

Once more he'd slung an arrow unintentionally toward the woman he loved. Unlike Tess, Jessie wouldn't drive intoxicated, but his actions had wounded her deeply.

"I'm sorry." The words were barely audible, but he could tell she heard them. "Jessie."

His heart urged him to step forward to hug her, to support her as she released the sobs he could see her swallowing down. But his brain refused to make his feet move.

He was a statue, hostage to the pain welling deep inside. He'd cut her deeply with words flung so easily from his mouth.

Jessie laid a hand over her belly and he saw her swallow another cry.

"I know you will be an excellent father, William. Our child is lucky to have you as their dad."

But.

The word hung in the silence's echoes.

Say something. Say something, you damn idiot. She is going to end this, and you are just standing here!

Another tear rolled down her cheek. Another piece of proof that he'd hurt her.

"I should go. Spend the night at my place."

"Maybe you should stay there." She hugged herself tightly, shrinking away from him. "We can co-parent, but…maybe we need a little distance for now. To recalibrate."

"Sure." William heard the word, but he wasn't sure how his mouth managed to push it out.

Jessie opened her mouth, but whatever she was about to say died on her lips. She stepped to the side as he passed, putting even more distance between them.

He didn't say anything. He'd hurt Jessie enough for one night. Hurt her enough for a lifetime.

CHAPTER FOURTEEN

"MOLLY'S BACK!" GEORGIA WAS nearly bouncing as she grabbed Jessie's hand. "Room 7. She is asking for you and—" Georgia paused, clearing her throat.

"And William." Jessie nodded. That made sense. William had listened to Molly from the first time he'd met her. He was a safe person in a medical minefield with no answers.

She was glad Molly had a few people she could request. She was glad she was one of them, glad William was one of them.

Even if seeing him nearly every day was killing her. They'd agreed to co-parent and she'd asked for space. He'd given it to her so willingly, as if he was letting go of some burden. He could be in their child's life, could be cordial with their mother. The fact that her heart broke every time she saw him wasn't his problem.

She'd wanted to be chosen for herself. The one time she'd asked for it—sort of—she hadn't gotten it. This was why she wasn't selfish. This was why nothing was for her.

Because nothing ever was. Hope only let you down.

"William is great at his job. I understand why Molly likes when he is her nurse." The words were true but the professional tone behind them cut.

Luckily Georgia didn't press.

"Let's go." Jessie didn't want to waste any time. Molly was

back, so she was racing to the room as quickly as she could. Molly was not leaving AMA this time.

"Take a deep breath for me," William was saying as she and Georgia stepped into the room.

There was no reason for her to look at him for more than a quick check. And she hated how thankful she was for that.

"I need to get upside down." Molly's heart rate was racing, which was not ideal, but at least they had it on record now. This was not a panic attack.

William looked at Georgia. "She keeps saying that."

Jessie tried not to let it hurt that he was keeping even his professional interactions with her limited. They were going to have to figure out how to work together and co-parent together.

"That was in your notes on your first visit, Molly." Jessie stepped in.

"Yeah, Dr. Mueller said it was ridiculous, but it helps." Molly closed her eyes.

Jessie didn't know how being upside down would help, but Molly lived in her body. "Will putting your head over the bed work or do we need to hold your legs up too?"

Georgia and William shifted their gaze to her, but neither said anything.

"If you hold my legs, it regulates everything faster."

"Let's do it then." William nodded to Jessie. "I'll take the right leg."

"I got the left," Georgia stated as she moved to the end of the bed.

"We are going to do this slowly, Molly, and I want to keep the leads attached to you so we can track what this does to your heart rate. If it doesn't work, we may need to shock your heart to get it back into a normal rhythm."

Molly swallowed as she slid to end of the bed. "It's never gone on this long. But at least you can see I'm not making it up."

Molly leaned her head over the end of the bed. William and Georgia grabbed a leg, and then they were holding her in a headstand.

The monitor beeps started to slow. Molly took a deep breath.

"Feel a little better?" Jessie knelt so she was close to Molly's face.

"I feel vindicated. And silly having a nurse and doctor holding my legs. But yes, also better."

"Georgia—" Eli's words cut off as he stepped into what had to be a unique scene.

"She says it helps," Georgia stated. "Glad you came so quick. The tape is over there." So while they were grabbing her, Georgia had also paged Eli.

Her falling in love with a cardiothoracic surgeon was a real win for the ER. And for Georgia, of course.

If only her own love life had had such a happily-ever-after.

Jessie swallowed the painful lump in her throat. This wasn't the time or the place for wallowing.

"Don't need it." Eli watched the monitor as Molly's heart rate stabilized. "Do you usually put yourself upside down like this to help?"

"Yes. I have been doing it for years. I thought it was normal but it's gotten worse. And I mentioned it to a friend who said that it was clear I needed to see a doctor. Then every doctor…" She paused, color flooding her cheeks even more than inversion was causing.

"Most doctors I saw thought it was panic attacks. I tried telling them about the upside-down thing. But it sounds so ridiculous." Molly closed her eyes but a few tears still leaked out.

"I think you can help her back up." Eli stood, waiting for Molly to get situated on the bed.

"So you know what is wrong?"

"We'll need to order some tests, but I think what you have supraventricular tachycardia. Commonly called SVT."

She saw William turn toward her. So she'd been right when she was in the hospital. It was weird that the satisfaction she'd expected failed to materialize. Nothing had made sense since he walked out of her townhome. So why should this?

"SVT." Molly wiped at the tears that kept flowing. "I'm fine. Sorry. I just am a little overwhelmed."

"Of course you are." Jessie stepped up. "This is overwhelming."

"Is it weird that part of me hoped I was having panic attacks? I know I fought you on it but..."

"The good news is that SVT is treatable. Why don't I walk you through what you can expect?" Eli offered.

Jessie looked at William and Georgia. There was no reason for her to be crowding the room too.

"I'll let Dr. Jacobsen explain this." She looked at Georgia, who nodded. She'd stay with Molly, and Jessie would move on to another patient.

Stepping outside the room, she looked around, waiting for the feeling of relief and the surge of adrenaline. This was what she was looking for: the win she'd ached for just a week or so ago.

"Nice job." William smiled as he stepped out of the room, but the look didn't reach his eyes. "You must feel very satisfied."

Jessie pursed her lips and shrugged. "I'm glad Molly knows what is going on. That is what is most important." She looked at her hip, grabbing her pager. It wasn't going off but she needed an excuse to be anywhere but here.

"I need to see to something. Um..." Her brain failed to come up with any excuse.

William didn't seem to mind though. He offered her another small smile and turned back to the nurses' station.

He forced himself to keep his eyes focused on the nurses' station. William was not going to look back at Jessie's retreating form, was not going to chase after her and call BS on the fake page.

She'd asked for time and space and like an idiot he'd granted it. Which was probably for the best. Without even trying, he'd cut her to the deepest part of her soul.

There was no way to explain away the choice either. He'd said it. He'd meant it. There was a part of him, a big part, that had wanted to throw Jessie and their child in his mother's face.

He'd wanted to show off that proof, as he'd called it.

A man truly in charge of himself, one looking for the good things, didn't think of the woman he loved that way, didn't see her as evidence he'd overcome *his* shortcomings.

He'd been right all along. Jessie was too good for him. That was all the proof he needed.

He was going to be in his child's life. He wasn't going to run. This was the point at which his father would have cut out. Well, he'd have cut out long ago, but when the going got really tough.

And he and Jessie? He'd make sure she was taken care of as much as possible. He would give her all the space she needed, be there in whatever capacity she wanted.

"Where's Jessie?" Georgia slid next to him as he leaned on the nurses' station.

"Not sure. She faked a page to get away from me." William blew out a breath; there was no point lying to Georgia. It was clear to anyone paying attention that he and Jessie were on the outs.

"Your honesty is always refreshing," Georgia said and cleared her throat. "You'll get through this."

"No." He looked down the hallway where she'd retreated. There was no sign of Jessie. This was his life now. The one he'd earned. Accepting that sucked, but it didn't change reality.

He wanted to change the conversation, move it to *anything* else. "How's Molly?"

"Relieved. Scared. Happy to know what is going on, terrified of what happens next." Georgia listed off the standard response to a chronic patient getting a diagnosis.

"I expected Jessie to be in the hallway celebrating. She told me a few days ago that if Molly came back, we needed to check for SVT. Some note she found in the original intake notes."

"A note she found while in the maternity ward, hooked up to fluids, working when she should have been recuperating. I swear she is trying to earn what is already hers."

The words flew with the hurt from his soul.

"I didn't mean that." William pulled a hand over his face. His mind felt like it went from pushing through slush to moments of rushed thoughts that refused to stay buried in the deepest recesses of his mind.

"I think you did. And I think you're right." Georgia pushed off the station. "She is trying to earn something. I don't know why and I don't need to. It's why she is such a workaholic—most people would have taken time off when they got such terrible morning sickness. Jessie..."

"Jessie powered through." William finished the sentence.

"She isn't the only one though." Georgia looked at him, her gaze soft as she ran a finger over the scar on her wrist. "You are trying to earn something too."

I don't deserve anything. I should have learned that with Tess.

He kept those words buried deep inside. Georgia would tell him he was wrong. She'd encourage him to see himself differently, offer him similar words to those he'd given her when she was struggling with Eli.

"I know Tess's death messed with you. That is understandable. But you didn't cause it. Whatever curse you think follows the men in your family is junk. There is no curse. It's just an excuse for their bad behavior. Which isn't yours."

"Thanks." William nodded. They were nice words. Kind

words. Words that should float into his soul and heal him. That was the way movies made it seem.

A best friend, or sidekick, reminded the hero why they were great. A big *aha* moment happened and the resolution quickly followed.

He looked down the hallway again, hoping for a glimpse of Jessie, some sign the universe agreed with Georgia. All he felt was the empty ache of reality seeping through.

He'd hurt the woman he loved, made her feel like she was some kind of trophy. A win for him for not sucking as much as the rest of the men in the family.

"You haven't messed up some universal karma, William. It's okay to look on the bright side every once in a while."

"I appreciate the pep talk, Georgia."

She rolled her eyes and stepped back. "Pep talks work. Whatever this was crashed and burned."

He offered her what he knew wasn't a convincing grin. "It will all be fine, Georgia."

"Not sure you believe that."

Lauren stepped in. "Man complaining of chest pains, Georgia. Can you see him now?"

"On my way." She gave William one more sympathetic look. "Your father runs from woman to woman. That isn't you. But your mother refuses to let herself be happy. Don't be like that."

She glanced at the clock. "I can't wait for this shift to be over."

Me either.

This should have been one the best days in the ER. A celebration. Even though Molly was going to have heart surgery and need to be monitored by a cardiologist for the rest of her life, they'd solved the puzzle.

Jessie had solved the puzzle. She should be bouncy and

happy, getting high fives from some of the staff and chatting about how she'd figured it out. This was her win.

Yet she was hiding away somewhere to avoid him.

That was another thing he'd stolen from the woman he loved. Another moment in time he couldn't give her back. Just like he couldn't give Tess back what she'd wanted.

The words stuck in his head but now it was Georgia's voice echoing in his mind. *Your mother...*

The truth struck him square in the face. Dear God. He'd been so worried about becoming his father, he'd never paid attention to the fact that he was terribly close to becoming his mother.

Rather than fight for the woman he loved, work through the issues that had arisen, he'd fallen back on the idea that this was his lot in life, that he'd somehow earned this. His mother refused to change her path, wallowing in what the universe had given her.

William pushed off the station. He needed to find Jessie. Maybe this wasn't the place, but he was changing his fortunes. He was not going to just sit back and accept.

Lauren stepped back into the ER. When it rained it poured in the ER. "I've got a little boy who jumped off the swing in his backyard. Landed against a pile of wood his dad was storing for winter. He's bleeding from a long cut on his forearm, but it's not gushing, and he's complaining of pain in his left foot."

"I got him." Helping the little one would keep his mind occupied until he found Jessie.

CHAPTER FIFTEEN

JESSIE PULLED UP to the townhome and pushed a tear away from her cheek. Her last patient of the day was a little one who'd gotten too excited on his swing set, jumped off and needed nearly twenty stitches in his arm and a wrap on his foot for the sprained ankle. The little guy was fine but seeing William with him had nearly broken her.

She'd watched him calm the little guy's fears, sitting next to him on the bed, opposite Mom. It reminded her of all the reasons she loved him. And he'd kept glancing at her. She'd catch him looking at her out of the corner of her eye and…

And her heart was broken beyond anything she knew how to repair. She'd left the second her shift was over. She'd wanted no chance of running into him in the locker room or sharing an elevator. She'd bolted.

Getting out of the car, she froze. There was a woman sitting on her porch. Not just any woman.

"Mom." Jessie blinked once, twice. She had to be dreaming. There was no way her mother was sitting on her porch in Anchorage, Alaska.

"Jessie." She stood, walked toward her, started to open her arms then closed them. "I…um… I…um…"

The single strip of gray on the right side of her mother's head that she remembered now had matching companions all over. In fact, the gray dominated the dark brown rather than the other way around.

There were more wrinkles too.

"What are you doing here? Is Dad all right?" She truly couldn't fathom why her mother would show up. "How did you even know where to find me?"

"I followed your career. I was in the stands at your med school graduation, then watched from afar on socials as you went through residency before coming here." She took a deep breath.

That was an answer to the second question, not to the first. Weird. Her parents had been inseparable.

"Wow, that sounds a little like I stalked you. And I guess I did. I just… I didn't know what to say or how to say it." She looked at Jessie, her eyes roaming over her features.

"Want to come inside?" Jessie grabbed her bag. "I just got off shift, so I am not exactly perky, but I can make some tea."

"I'd love that." She followed her in, not saying anything else as Jessie made the tea and set a mug in front of her.

Picking it up in her hands, her mom looked at her. "I started therapy a few years ago and it made me realize several things."

Jessie sipped her own tea. She was a big proponent of mental health and she was glad her mother had sought out help. But she wasn't going to interrupt or offer any sort of congratulations.

Maybe that was petty, but her parents had treated as little more than an extra set of parts for her brother.

"Your father and I divorced last year. We… Well, *he* refused to accept our role in some things that I can't get past."

Jessie felt her eyes widen and knew her mouth had fallen open. What was there to say about that?

"I owe you an apology. Actually, I owe you a lifetime of apologies. I don't expect you to accept them. I don't. But I wanted you to know that I know you weren't at fault for Bran's death. I said it over and over again when I was grieving. I was so focused on him, on losing him, that I never saw the wonder that was you." Her mom took a deep breath.

"I don't know what to say." Jessie set her mug down. Too many thoughts were running in her head.

"You don't have to say anything. I offer the apology with no expectations. I'm not asking to be in your life or to know you." Her mother's bottom lip quivered.

"You don't want to be in my life?" The question popped out. "I'm not saying I want you in my life. I…"

"Oh, honey. I would love to be in your life. I will take whatever relationship you want to give me." She let out a soft cry but didn't move around the counter. Didn't come toward her.

"Why did you come now?" Jessie crossed her arms. Is this where she found out that her mom was dying. Was this a deathbed sort of fix? A last-minute attempt to make things right?

Her mom pushed away some tears. "I was cleaning out your room. I left it just the way you had it. A memorial I guess, to the daughter I pushed away. But my therapist recommended going through it and I found this." She reached into her purse and pulled out a small green journal.

Her diary. Jessie had forgotten all about that. For years she'd kept daily records. She had several journals here that she wrote in occasionally but not like she had as a teen. In those years her diary had felt like her only safe space. She'd put all her hurt and pain into it.

Her mom opened to one of the back pages and Jessie knew what page it was: the day after Bran's funeral. The day her mother had told her it should have been her in the coffin.

"I should never have said that, Jessie."

"So you came to apologize for it." Jessie let out a sob. Even now, it wasn't really Jessie she was here for. Her mom needed to assuage a guilty conscience.

"No." Her mother flipped a few pages to words Jessie had forgotten she'd written.

> I failed Bran. I failed Bran. I shouldn't even be here. I failed him. There is no way I can ever make up for this.

"This page and the ones that follow are why I'm here. You are not to blame."

"I know." Jessie shook her head and tried to blink away the tears that refused to go. "I know."

She sucked in a deep breath and tried to say the words again. But all that came out was a sob.

Her mom was here. For her. And she was saying what William had said only a few days ago.

She bit her lip so hard she tasted blood, but she didn't let up. William.

He'd asked if she was punishing herself. He'd seen it, and rather than sinking into him, she'd pushed him away.

In her deepest heart, she hadn't thought she deserved him. She'd pushed him away, rather than fight for what she loved.

Her mother's arms wrapped around her, holding her tight as she sobbed.

She wasn't sure how long she stood there, consoled by someone she'd never expected to see again, but when all the emotions evaporated, all she wanted was William.

"I'm glad you came. I am…but…um… I need to go. I have to see someone. Um…" Jessie hugged her one more time. "You can stay if you want."

Her mother nodded and swallowed. "You have no idea how much I want that, honey. Go do whatever you need to. I'll be here. Or wherever you want."

Jessie put a hand over her belly. She wasn't sure what their relationship would be. There were years of trust to regain, but this first step meant the world.

"I'm pregnant. You're going to be a grandma." She hugged her mom one more time, then stepped away. She needed to find William. Right now.

William had tried to catch Jessie at the hospital, but she'd bolted as soon as the clock showed their shift was over. Usually she stayed to chart or to check in on patients. Honestly, he'd expected her to follow up with Molly.

Apparently, she had, but before the shift ended.

If she didn't want him around, she could say so. But he was at least trying. No more sitting back and accepting life. No more paying for things that weren't his fault.

Pulling up to the townhome, he saw her come out the front door. He put the car in Park and hopped out. Her eyes were puffy, her cheeks tearstained.

"Jessie?"

"William." She bolted for him, launching into his arms.

He held her, not sure what was causing this shift, not caring. "Jessie." She was warm and soft and he loved her.

"I love you." William squeezed her. "I shouldn't have thought of you as some sort of prize to show off. I've spent my life so worried about becoming my father—"

"You aren't your father." Jessie kissed his cheek as she pulled him even closer.

"I know." William leaned his forehead against hers. "But I did fall into the trap of negative thinking like my mom. I was so ready to just let you walk away from me without ever even trying. I was convinced the path I was on was the one I had to walk."

Jessie's hand rested on his cheek. "I love you too." She brushed her lips against his. "I should have told you that. Should have explained how your words made me feel, but the truth is that I didn't think I deserved you. Or happiness or anything else. Your accusation was right. I've spent my life punishing myself."

He hated that truth. Though he was glad she was seeing it now. "I know I never met your brother, but I cannot imagine that he would have wanted this for you. He would have wanted you to live, to love, to have everything."

She put her hand in his. "I know. I know that. I really, really do. He would have loved you, and our little one."

"You are my person, Jessie. The one who makes me whole. I should have said it the moment I realized it, but I love you. I don't ever want to be apart."

"So does that mean you aren't moving out of the town-home? That's good. Because I don't want you to be anywhere else either. I love you."

Then her lips were on his. He held her, never wanting to let go. This was his little slice of heaven. His family. His world.

When she finally broke the kiss, he looked up, shocked to see a woman standing in her doorway, hand over her heart.

"Um...you have company?"

"My mom showed up." Jessie let out a little giggle, then grabbed him as he started toward the older woman who'd made her daughter feel so unworthy.

"To apologize, with no expectations of a relationship. I guess, well, I don't really know what our relationship will be from here but I'm going to figure it out."

"And I will be right by your side as you do." William squeezed her hand.

"That is all I ever want."

He grinned. "That and pickles, right?"

"Right."

EPILOGUE

WILLIAM WAS ADJUSTING his tie and trying to pretend that he didn't see her rubbing her back.

"I'm fine."

"Uh-huh. I've heard that before." William raised an eyebrow but kept his focus on the tie—mostly. "Don't make me call your mother." He winked.

Jessie's mom had moved to Anchorage a few months ago. She and her mother had gone to therapy together. Their past relationship was over, and they were each focusing on being there for each other in the present. It wasn't a gift she'd expected but she was done questioning the universe's choices.

She stuck her tongue out at her fiancé. "I'm fine."

The contractions were still almost ten minutes apart. She likely had several hours before they needed to be at Anchorage Memorial. Another contraction struck and she saw William look at his watch.

"Nine minutes." Jessie breathed through the pain. "Nine minutes," she reiterated, more to herself than to her fiancé.

A knock sounded at the door and Georgia walked in. The cream wedding gown was covered in embroidered butterflies. She looked like she was meant to be walking in a fairy garden.

"I'm getting married!" Georgia blushed as she held up the bouquet. "Not sure what is more surprising, the fact that I'm finally committing or the fact that you are having a little girl."

She pointed to Jessie's belly as she walked over to William. "Less than an hour before you stand beside me as my man of honor."

"About that—"

"We can't wait to see you and Eli tie the knot." Jessie interrupted. She was not letting William mess up Georgia's big day. He was her man of honor, the only person standing up for Georgia. This was her big day.

Their little girl was just going to have to wait.

"And yes, we *can* believe you are getting married. Commitment-phobe no more!" Jessie clapped.

"How far apart are your contractions, Jessie?" Georgia looked at William, who nodded.

She stuck her tongue out. "Far enough not to matter to the bride!" Jessie crossed her arms, aware that the motion didn't have the same oomph when they rested on her inflated stomach.

"How far apart?" Georgia repeated.

"Nine minutes. And holding steady." She grinned, looked at the clock, mentally counted to twenty and took a deep breath as tightness spread across her abdomen.

When the contraction released, she took a small bow. "See, right on time. You are carrying blue hydrangea flowers. Do you have your something-borrowed?"

Touching her hair, Georgia turned just a little. "Padma lent me this comb. She's had it forever and swore it would work perfect for me."

Jessie took a step closer. Tiny emeralds dotted the comb above her low bun, creating a field of green on which two tiny diamond butterflies danced. "Padma is right."

"Text her and tell her to make sure everyone is in their seats." Georgia pointed at Jessie as she gave the instruction, then turned to William.

"Go tell Eli that my something-new is going to be here soon, and I am not letting Jessie miss the cake cutting. So we are pushing the ceremony up. Then get in your place."

"Georgia."

"Nope. I am the bride and what the bride says goes. Though I won't complain if you name that little one Georgia…ya know, since she is stealing the show."

Georgia said it in such a sing-songy voice that Jessie knew there were no real hard feelings.

"Or maybe you are already planning that—you know since you refused to tell any of us her name. Was it so others wouldn't be jealous? It's okay if they are a little jealous." Georgia winked as she linked arms with Jessie.

"Esme Bindi." Jessie sucked in a breath as the next contraction came on like a wave.

"Eight minutes. Looks like we are moving along. And that is a gorgeous name—though it is no Georgia."

"It means *loved butterfly*." Jessie said the words as her belly relaxed. "She's our new beginning."

"Aww, Jessie." Georgia took out the little kerchief she'd stuck in her bouquet. "I'm not supposed to cry until I'm walking down the aisle. But that is perfect."

Her phone dinged and she held it up. "Padma says we are good to go. That means I need to go get my seat."

"Try not to have your water break while I am taking my vows." Georgia laughed as she took her place to walk down the aisle.

"Of course not." Jessie winked, then moved to find her seat.

William caught her gaze as she sat in the front row.

He mouthed, *I love you*.

She ran a hand over her belly. *Love you too.*

* * * * *

COMING SOON!

We really hope you enjoyed reading this book. If you're looking for more romance be sure to head to the shops when new books are available on

Thursday 26th September

To see which titles are coming soon, please visit

millsandboon.co.uk/nextmonth

MILLS & BOON

FALLING FOR HER FORBIDDEN FLATMATE

Alison Roberts

'Grace?'

'My new housemate. The midwife who was at that last emergency C-section we did together.'

'Ah, yes…I remember her. Blonde. Cute. Seems quite shy.'

"Cute" wasn't quite the word Jock would have chosen to describe a woman who was not only gorgeous but intelligent and clever and…caring. "Shy" wasn't exactly appropriate, either. Grace was wary. And she had reason to be.

'Blonde and cute is way more your type than mine,' Dan said dryly. 'And, come to think of it, I did notice the way she was smiling at you when you were holding that baby. And you're living with her?' He gave Jock an incredulous glance. So how's *that* working out so far…?'

Oh, good grief…did Dan think he was incapable of keeping his hands off a gorgeous woman?

'She's my sister's best friend,' he said firmly. 'Which puts her completely off limits as far as I'm concerned.'

'Why?'

'It just does. It could end up messing with their friendship and my sister might never speak to me again.

It was Jenni who told her about the job going here and she made it clear that nothing was allowed to happen between us. So that's that.'

Continue reading
FALLING FOR HER FORBIDDEN FLATMATE
Alison Roberts

Available next month
millsandboon.co.uk

FOUR BRAND NEW STORIES FROM
MILLS & BOON MODERN

The same great stories you love,
a stylish new look!

OUT NOW

MILLS & BOON

Afterglow Books is a trend-led, trope-filled list of books with diverse, authentic and relatable characters, a wide array of voices and representations, plus real world trials and tribulations. Featuring all the tropes you could possibly want (think small-town settings, fake relationships, grumpy vs sunshine, enemies to lovers) and all with a generous dose of spice in every story.

@millsandboonuk
@millsandboonuk
afterglowbooks.co.uk
#AfterglowBooks

For all the latest book news, exclusive content and giveaways scan the QR code below to sign up to the Afterglow newsletter: